GETTING CLOSE

Carter stood behind Bailey, with his arms on the rail, enclosing her with his body. Right then, Bailey felt whole.

Carter pressed his lips against her cheek. "Let's go. I'll show you my place," he whispered huskily into her ear.

Bailey gripped the cement rail. Her mind was awhirl. She swallowed. The lion had invited her to his den. Now what? She blew out a breath. She just wasn't ready, even if it meant she'd have to drive home solo.

She put a hand to her hair. Maybe it hadn't been such a good idea to wear it down, wild and free. She reached inside her purse and pulled out the elastic band she always kept with her—just in case. With one quick motion, she scooped up her hair and slipped the band around it.

"I really need to get back to the room and do something with this hair," she said apologetically. "Before tonight's show."

Carter reached a hand up to the back of her head and snapped the hair band. Then he pressed his mouth firmly over hers and kept it there until she felt her knees go weak . . .

Books by Alexa Darin

GOOD WITH HIS HANDS

KISSES DON'T LIE

Published by Kensington Publishing Corporation

Alexa Darin

ZEBRA BOOKS
Kensington Publishing Corp.
www.kensingtonbooks.com

ZEBRA BOOKS are published by

Kensington Publishing Corp.
850 Third Avenue
New York, NY 10022

Please visit www.alexadarin.com

All Kensington titles, imprints, and distributed lines are available at special quantity discounts for bulk purchases for sales promotion, premiums, fund-raising, educational, or institutional use.

Special book excerpts or customized printings can also be created to fit specific needs. For details, write or phone the office of the Kensington Special Sales Manager: Attn.: Special Sales Department. Kensington Publishing Corp., 850 Third Avenue, New York, NY 10022. Phone: 1-800-221-2647.

Zebra and the Z logo Reg. U.S. Pat. & TM Off.

ISBN-13: 978-0-8217-8039-8
ISBN-10: 0-8217-8039-5

First Printing: October 2007
10 9 8 7 6 5 4 3 2 1

Printed in the United States of America

Chapter One

If you could sing, you wouldn't be out in this heat, trying to entice someone to drive off in that convertible, Bailey mused as she stared at a man outside her hotel window. He was standing in a small parking lot, next to a bright red car that had a RENT ME sign posted over its windshield, and he was wearing a white jumpsuit. And from what Bailey could see, he was cute, handsome even, down to every last black hair on his head. But Elvis wasn't a car rental agent. He was a singer, and a god among men.

One down. Forty-nine thousand, nine hundred ninety-nine to go.

She continued to watch the activity on Las Vegas Boulevard, where tourists moved in a steady stream down the sweltering sidewalk, many of whom, no doubt, had dreams of becoming the next big winner. Herself included. But it wasn't money she was after. It was a man. And not just any man.

Bailey Ventura was an Elvisaholic. She knew it. Her friends knew it. Her entire hometown of Coupeville, Washington, knew it. And, she wasn't interested in joining some twelve-step program that would help her snap out of it.

By the time she was three, Bailey couldn't count to ten, but she knew all the words to "Rock A Hula Baby"—

convinced it was really "Rock A Hula Bailey"—and could give an impressive performance, complete with hip shimmies, to a captive audience of teachers and pre-schoolers in her class.

By the age of ten, Bailey had seen every Elvis movie a dozen times and had decided that he was the only man she would ever love.

At twenty-five, Bailey still knew all the words to "Rock A Hula Baby," plus a hundred others, and she'd spent enough time listening to the King of Rock and Roll croon mournfully about doing things his way and lost love that she was convinced she was born to be his bride.

Unfortunately, the odds of that happening were worse than winning the megabucks lotto, because fate had dealt both her and the King a low blow: he was already serenading fair maidens in the biggest coliseum of all, beyond the pearly gates.

Not that a little detail like that was going to stop her. She had other options, which, admittedly, weren't as perfect as the real deal, but they were her only choices, and there were plenty of them. They were called Elvis tribute artists. Bailey had recently read that approximately fifty thousand lip-sneering, hip-swiveling, dark-haired impersonators walked this earth, and she was pretty sure at least one of them was meant to be hers . . . if only she could find him.

And if she couldn't find him in Las Vegas, Nevada, where the Elvis Impersonator World Championship Competition was being held, the right man for her just didn't exist.

Bailey sighed. Fate couldn't be that cruel, could it? It just wouldn't be fair.

The only woman who might love Elvis more than Bailey was her mother. She'd offered to come along as a chaperone. Bailey hadn't bothered telling her that, in her opinion, too much chaperoning was probably the cause of Elvis's failed marriage to Priscilla. It wouldn't have mattered. And anyway, Bailey suspected her mother's real motive in wanting to accompany her to Sin City was the chance that a miracle might happen and she'd catch a glimpse of the real deal, the man himself.

Olivia Ventura was one of the remaining two million—give or take a million—women who continued to believe Elvis Presley was still walking this earth and that he'd set up house somewhere in Kalamazoo, Michigan. "How else do you explain all those Elvis sightings?" Olivia would say. "That many people can't be crazy, or wrong."

Bailey's mom was sure that Elvis took pleasure in knowing others emulated him, and that he regularly attended events such as the one coming up day after tomorrow. According to Olivia, if there was anywhere one could go to get a glimpse of the King, it was Las Vegas.

God bless her. Probably they both needed a little therapy.

Bailey hated disappointing her mother, but she was on a mission, and besides, she'd already told her best friend, Liza, that she'd take *her*. For a couple of reasons: she had more sense than Bailey and would keep her out of trouble, *and* she didn't need any therapy.

"Do you really think you'll find a genuine guy among all those pretenders?" Liza had asked when Bailey picked up an Elvis Tribute Artist Guide from the check-in counter.

"A girl can dream," Bailey had answered with a wistful sigh.

But dreaming was all she ever did and it was time to either make those dreams come true, or settle for what she already had, which was basically a boy she'd known through high school—Mark Jefferson—who only wanted to be with her because she reminded him of Kate Beckinsale. Oh, she loved him—like a really, *really* good friend. The end.

"What are you going to do if you find this Elvis person?" Liza said from the bathroom doorway. She had a toothbrush in her hand and her hair was fluffed about her face. Her teeth were so white that when she smiled you half expected to see them sparkle like in one of those toothpaste ads. No doubt about it, Liza was beautiful, standing there all blond and covered in pink from head to toe, but Elvis wouldn't have liked her. He liked dark hair. Like Bailey's.

"Bring him home, of course," Bailey answered.

"And then what?"

"And then he and I will buy a bigger house, some-where other than Coupeville. We'll have children and live happily ever after. . . ."

Liza went back into the bathroom and dropped off her toothbrush. "I guess that's plausible . . . in a fantasy world. *Your* fantasy world."

"It's not such a fantasy. I'm not a bad catch."

"No." Liza shook her head. "In Coupeville, you're a goddess." She removed her clothes from her suitcase and placed them into small tidy stacks in the top dresser drawer. She also took two silk blouses and one dress over to the closet.

"What's that supposed to mean?" Bailey asked.

"Sweetie, do you think you're really going to get some man who's used to living around thousands of half-naked women to go home with you, where the typical attire is Birkenstocks and prairie skirts?"

"I don't wear prairie skirts." Bailey dug around in her bag and pulled out a light blue skirt that could hardly be worn on a prairie. "See?" she said, holding it up.

"Right," Liza said, touching a finger to her lips. "We'll see. How about you shimmy into that skirt and we go down to play some slots?"

Slots. Bailey shook her head. They were nothing more than the evil twin of cash machines. Money goes in; nothing ever comes out. She'd learned the hard way that she could actually save money if, instead, she went to a show or did some shopping.

Liza, on the other hand, didn't give up so easily. It was the only thing she wasn't sensible about. She'd lose a bundle and two months later, she'd be lamenting how she couldn't wait to go back and get her fingers on the cold, hard buttons of her favorite machines. "Even a blind hog finds an acorn sometime," she always said. Bailey figured if Liza ever tried pawning her clothes, she'd have to intervene, maybe even threaten her with gambler's rehab.

"Those machines aren't going anywhere." Bailey plopped herself down on one of the queen-sized beds and started flipping through the Tribute Artist guide. It contained photos and mini-bios of each competitor, and by the time Bailey got to the fifth page, she was dizzy. She put a hand to her forehead. Being so close to realizing her dream was making her blood pump through her veins double time. She had to pause, take a few deep breaths.

Johnny Thompson, Quent Flagg, Steve Sogura, Irv Cass, and *so* many others . . . How would she ever choose? Picking one over the other by looking at their pictures was like picking one M&M over another simply because she liked the color. No, she had to see them in person. Evaluate which of them could really walk the walk and talk the talk, not to mention do that funny little grin thing. But most of all, she had to find out who among them had truly captured Elvis's essence, and which of them, if any, could really sing the King's songs as though every word that passed over their lips came straight from their hearts.

Bailey tossed aside the guide with a sigh. Finding the total package in just one man would be like, well, winning a jackpot, and no picture or bio could answer those questions. Her heart skipped with reserved anticipation at the thought of having them all stand before her like some delectable smorgasbord.

She went back over to the window. The man in the

white jumpsuit was still out there. A couple of young women were chatting with him, and one of them reached out and touched the gemstones on his jumpsuit. Or maybe she just wanted to touch *him*. He did fill out the suit in all the right places, after all.

Bailey smiled. Maybe she'd even go down there and check him out—later. Right now, though, she had other things to do. Get settled. Unpack. Prepare herself for the adventure of her life.

She carefully lifted a black, shimmery dress from her suitcase. It was a Donna Karan knock-off that the shop clerk had said was guaranteed to make at least nine out of ten Elvis impersonators take a second, maybe even a third, look. But Bailey wanted at least one of them to do more than look. Some touching might even be nice.

She went over to the closet and, just as she suspected, she'd only been left one hanger. She didn't care; she only needed one. She hung the dress, and then took the rest of her clothes and dropped them all in a bundle into the second dresser drawer. There were far more important things to think about than folding her clothes into neat little piles.

In the bathroom were plenty of freebies. Soap, shampoo and conditioner, lotion . . . even mouthwash. Bailey gathered all but one bar of soap. Probably she'd never use them, but they were bought and paid for and she planned on taking them home and adding them to her stockpile. A girl had to be prepared for lean times.

Along with complimentaries, the Oasis was generous with space and detail. Her bed from home could easily fit inside the marble and glass shower enclosure. The stone floor was a rich brown color, with gold veins running through it, providing the perfect complement to the ornate gold fixtures that reached out of the wall like slender fingers on a beautiful woman. The towels were standard white, but even before touching them, Bailey could tell they were fluffy and soft and would feel like heaven against her skin.

"We're not going to spend all our time watching grown men swivel their hips around a stage, are we?" Liza asked. "I hope you've allotted a sufficient amount of time for slot play."

Bailey paused briefly from arranging her things on her side of the bathroom counter. "Is that all Vegas is to you? What about the shows? the restaurants? the shopping?"

"There's a twelve-screen cinema down the street from where I live, approximately one hundred restaurants within a five-mile radius, and Macy's is just a two-minute drive away. I think I've got it covered. Besides, we made a deal. You find a man who makes your pulse quiver and I play the machines."

"I guess that's not too much to ask, seeing as you'll only need a couple of hours before your money runs out."

"Oh, ye of little faith. It's exactly that kind of attitude that keeps you from being a winner."

"Really? Then what's your excuse?"

"I'll have you know I've won plenty."

"And lost even more," Bailey muttered under her breath.

Liza huffed and propped her hands on her hips, and Bailey knew she was about to get an earful about *this jackpot* and *that jackpot* and the time Liza practically *willed* a machine to stand up, do a jig, and spit out a free T-shirt.

"Okay." Bailey put up her hands in surrender. "We'll do the slot thing first. Then, after you've lost a week's pay, we'll scour the casinos for jumpsuits and leather. After all, I have to make the most of this opportunity. You never know when I'll have a chance like this again. I could be dead and buried—"

"For sure you'd be with Elvis then," Liza said.

Bailey slid her a look. "Don't let my mom hear you say that."

"Hey, I *know* . . . you could become a plastic surgeon and create your own Elvis."

Bailey's lips drew tight. "Uh, yeah, about that . . . I've kinda decided I don't want to be a doctor."

Liza raised an eyebrow. "Since when?"

"Since I realized it's not really what I want. I only agreed to go because it's what my Uncle Rex wanted. He says he promised my dad he'd see to it that I get an education, and since my Aunt Fiona is always worried about getting the Bubonic Plague or some other dreaded disease, I figured I might as well save my family some money and become a doctor." Bailey shrugged. "Seemed like the right choice at the time."

Liza shrugged. "You were a kid. What did you know?"

Bailey shrugged back. "What did I know?"

Liza laughed and slung her Kate Spade bag over one shoulder. "Okay." She flexed her fingers. "I am so ready. Let's go."

Bailey looked in the mirror at her own image and frowned. Her head had been smashed against the plane seat for two hours, and her hair resembled a rooster's comb. She put a hand in it and gave it a good toss. Now she looked like a cockatoo. Not an improvement.

"I need to start from scratch," she said, and Liza groaned. "Geez, go, get out of here." Bailey pushed her toward the door. "I'll meet you down in the casino. Just make sure you stick around the elevator area where I can find you. I'll be down in about an hour." Liza practically skipped out the door, waving a hand over her shoulder before Bailey could change her mind.

With her face washed clean, and her hair tucked into a band and piled high on her head, Bailey stepped into the shower. She turned the faucet handles, expecting great things, and wasn't disappointed. The water rained against her shoulders with a stiff pulse that helped ease all her tension away. It was the kind of pulse that could make a girl want to stay home on a Saturday night.

Of course, living in Coupeville made just about anything seem exciting. And that's why she had to get out, before she ended up like her mom: afraid to drive because she might run into a little traffic. To her mom, going for a drive meant running over to the store for that night's dinner. The farthest she ever strayed from home was an occasional outing over to Oak Harbor for a movie. And that was only if it was up for an Academy Award. But, then, she *had* wanted to come to Vegas. Bailey smiled. Of course, who wouldn't for a chance to see the King?

The one good thing Bailey could see about her mom refusing to drive was that she only had to fill up on gas once every month or two.

Bailey closed her eyes and took in a deep breath. With any luck at all, she'd soon be living somewhere where life happened. Though maybe not here in Las Vegas. With half-naked women running around everywhere, Mafia types around every corner, and enough sand to bury an entire city, Vegas was a little too much life. A nice place to visit, find a husband, see a show, but she didn't know if she could live here.

Visions of dark-haired men swiveled through Bailey's head as the fragrance of honey-scented soap filled the shower enclosure. Soon she was humming "Viva Las Vegas," and by the time she reached the chorus, she was squeaky clean and feeling so good, even the thought of losing a few bucks on the one-armed bandits couldn't dampen her spirits.

Bailey reached for a towel, but all she got was air. She squinted one eye open. She'd forgotten to hang it over the top of the door; it was waiting for her over on the shelf above the toilet.

She pushed the glass door.

It didn't budge.

Pushed harder.

It held tight.

Bailey looked at the door, examining it from top to bottom to see if there was some latch or secret button that needed pushing, but it was pretty straightforward as far as doors went. She grabbed the handle and jiggled it while giving it one more good shove.

Nothing.

With the warm water turned off, the efficiency of the hotel's air-conditioning system quickly became apparent. *Br-r-r.* Goose bumps jumped to attention on her arms and legs, and she wrapped her arms tightly about herself.

Getting colder by the minute, she considered scaling the glass wall, but that idea was quickly shot down when she imagined herself laid up in the hospital, bruised and broken with no way to meet the Elvis of her dreams.

Of course, she could turn the water back on, but then she wouldn't be able to hear if anyone were out in the hall whom she could call out to. Plus, though the warm water might help keep her warm, she didn't like the idea of standing for God knows how long in a rain shower. She'd had enough of that back in Washington.

"Help," Bailey yelled halfheartedly. After all, it wasn't like it was a real emergency, and, anyway, Liza would soon come looking for her and she'd be rescued. Bailey pondered that thought. Who was she kidding? Liza could play the slots for hours and think only a few minutes had passed.

Oh, God! She could be stuck in here all night.

"Help," she yelled again, this time with a little panic added for extra emphasis. "Help . . . someone . . . anyone?"

Great. Way to start a vacation, Bailey chided herself. She leaned against the cool tile, and her goose bumps grew until they were painful. It was karma. Probably she was being punished for not bringing her mother.

A minute later, she heard noises coming from the hall and she stopped her teeth from chattering to listen. Voices, non-English. A metal clanking sound. Room service? For the next room?

"He-e-el-l-lp," she shouted again. Another minute passed and the clanking sound started up again and then grew distant. Help was leaving. *"No.* Don't *leave."* Bailey pounded on the glass door until she thought it might break.

Finally, she settled back to watch some droplets of water run down the door and dissolve into a puddle on the stone floor. "How will I find my true love if I'm stuck in here?" she asked the puddle. It made its way over the stones and slipped down the drain without answering.

Another five minutes passed and her goose bumps had just about taken over her entire body. It made her think of her babies, Tucker and Maggie May, two beautiful yellow labs who, up till now, had filled the empty space in her life pretty well. What she wouldn't give to have a fur coat like theirs right now.

Bailey smiled. She'd given them a bath just before leaving, so that her Aunt Fiona wouldn't think they had germs, and make them stay outside. They'd curled into tight little balls to warm themselves and looked up at her with their big brown eyes and gave her one last pleading look not to go.

Bailey gave the floor an appraising look. It looked clean, but how many cases of athlete's foot had stood in that exact spot? She did a mental eye roll. Geez, Aunt Fiona's hypochondria was beginning to rub off on her. Maybe *that's* what was wrong with her. Maybe hating to drive was a family thing. God help all the Venturas if another developed her aunt's fear of, well, everything that might have germs.

Bailey tried to blow it off, but still, when she crouched and wrapped her arms around her knees, she made sure nothing vital touched the floor. Soon, her goose bumps began to retreat and she stopped shivering.

Tucker and Maggie May were smart dogs. Probably the smartest dogs that had ever lived.

Bailey rested her head against the wall and closed her eyes. Liza would be back.

Eventually.

"Ma'am?"

Bailey stirred and a perfectly good dream dissolved into thin air. She half expected to hear her mother tell her to wake up and get ready for school. Instead it was, "Ma'am?" again, and "Are you all right?"

That didn't make any sense. Bailey's forehead creased. Not only did she not live at home anymore, but she was also no longer in school, and unless her mother had caught a bad cold, the voice was far too deep.

Bailey grabbed for a blanket. Her fingers came up empty.

"Ma'am?" the voice said for the third time.

Such a nice voice. Soothing and calm. Sexy. Definitely not her mother's.

Bailey's eyes popped open.

Glass walls. Hard floor. Frigid air. And a tall man and a small woman were standing just outside the bathroom door, peering in at her—and her nakedness.

Chapter Two

Talk about a rude awakening.

That darn blanket . . . Where was it? Bailey grabbed for anything she could get her hands on, and she still came up empty-handed. She heard someone screech as her hands flew to cover her goodies, and it must have been her, since the other two people in the room were smiling.

"Who are you? And what are you doing in here?" she said, her voice rising in pitch with every word.

"You were calling for help," the man said, and the little woman next to him nodded vigorously. She muttered something in Spanish that made the man's lips curve upward.

Bailey screeched again. "I'm naked, for crying out loud. Can't you see that?"

"Clearly," the man said.

"What?" Bailey's voice squeaked up an octave.

"No, ma'am. I mean, sorry—ma'am."

Tall, dark-haired, and intimidating finally turned around, but Bailey could see the upward curve of his cheek and she knew he was still smiling. His sidekick muttered something more in Spanish. He muttered something back.

"Hand me a towel—*please,*" Bailey said.

The man grabbed a white terry towel from the rack over the toilet and tossed it over the top of the door to her.

"You can go now, Rosa," he told the little woman.

Rosa nodded and went on her way, talking to herself in Spanish all the way out the door. Bailey attempted translation, but high school Spanish was a long time ago, and she never paid attention in class, anyway. Probably she should've been more concerned about being left alone in her condition with a strange man, but there was something about him that made her feel totally safe. She supposed it could've been the badge on his lapel that read, HEAD OF SECURITY.

Bailey wrapped the towel around herself and tucked in one corner at the top of her left breast. After doing a little shimmy, she felt reasonably certain it'd hold for at least two minutes, long enough for security guy to free her from her glass prison.

"Okay," she said. "I'm decent."

The man turned back around. "Yes, ma'am." His gaze wandered up, then down, and finally settled somewhere in-between.

Bailey lifted her chin. *Take a good look, 'cause that's all you're going to get.* And now that she was covered, for the most part, it was her turn to take a better look at *him*.

He wore a dark tailored suit over a blue shimmery shirt that was open at his neck, revealing just enough chest hair to transport a message to certain parts of her body. Bailey bit her bottom lip and tried to ignore the message; her goose bumps were returning and she wasn't even cold anymore.

Security guy's lips were plump, inviting, made for kissing, and his mouth had a distinctive curve at one corner, which gave one the impression he might be smirking. At her. It made Bailey angry and dizzy, and she felt some unseen force clouding her mind with things that were better left unthought. Still, she was impressed with how those thoughts affected certain parts of her body.

His hair was thick, black, and dangerous looking, with thick sideburns to match.

Elvis had sideburns.

Perhaps Rosa should've stayed.

Bailey swallowed. "Didn't your mother teach you any manners?"

Security guy raised an eyebrow.

She flung out a hand. "You just stood there with Hazel, getting an eyeful. I could have you fired." Even as she made the threat, she knew that following through was only a remote possibility. If she did that she'd never again have the chance to gaze into security guy's big blue eyes.

"You could try," he said.

Bailey's heart flipped. She didn't know if it was from rage or from something else more primitive, but she narrowed her eyes at him, hating what she was thinking. If she didn't already have the kind of man in mind she intended to marry, she might consider giving a man like him a second or even a third look—against her better judgment, of course.

"Who *are* you anyway?" she said.

"Carter Davis," he said, nodding once. "Security. Rosa heard you calling for help and she paged me. What seems to be the problem?"

The elastic that held Bailey's hair snapped and locks of damp hair fell loosely over her shoulders and into one eye. Security guy's eyes lit up, and his mouth twitched in approval. Bailey blew the hair aside. She hitched up her chin. "Your shower is defective." She jiggled the handle. "I'm stuck."

Security guy stopped with the mouth twitch, and he walked over to the shower door. Bailey took a step back, pulling the towel tighter about herself. Having only a piece of material and a glass door between herself and a stranger was more than she'd bargained for so early in her vacation.

If security guy was uncomfortable, it didn't show. He was all business as he jiggled the handle. He gave it a hard push, just as she'd done, and something cracked, but the door didn't budge. He ran a hand up the door's length, pushing every couple of inches. Nothing. He finally walked around to one side and peered through. After taking a good long look, he came back around to the front.

"It's stuck," he said.

Bailey's mouth dropped open. *"Really?"*

"Really. I'll have to get a crew up here to take the door off its hinges—"

"A crew?" Bailey squirmed and she felt her towel slip an inch. She quickly hiked it back up. Being on display for this man was one thing, but an entire crew? "How about you just give it a little kick, or something?"

Security guy paused and gave her a powerful look and she squirmed a little more. She could almost feel him sucking any good sense she might have right out of her.

Finally, he took a step back. "Move aside," he told her in a forced manly voice, as though mocking her.

Bailey moved back against the shower wall as far as she could. She fumbled to hold the towel tight against her chest, while security guy lifted a foot and delivered one swift kick to the glass door.

It burst open. She was free.

Bailey suddenly felt a flush of warmth fill her cheeks. Now she didn't have even a pane of glass between her and Mr. Head of Security.

She brushed past Carter, moving quickly toward the bathroom door.

"You're welcome," he said. "Please. Don't hesitate to call me if there's anything else I can do for you, Miss . . ."

"Ventura," Bailey said. "And, thank you." She paused, giving him a tentative look.

"Glad to meet you," he said. He took one of her hands in his and lifted it to his lips.

Security guy's hand was soothing and warm, and his touch made her feel more than warm all over. The nerve. He couldn't even wait until she was dressed before he made his lame move. She pulled her hand free before it caught fire.

Carter followed her out of the bathroom, but he stopped at the entry to the main room, as though he were a perfect gentleman. Of course if he were a *perfect* gentleman, he wouldn't have looked—no, gawked—at her from head to toe while she was at her most vulnerable. Bailey motioned for him to turn around, and he did.

She pulled on her short blue skirt and a white tank top and then she gave him the okay to turn back around. His eyes focused on her chest momentarily and she crossed her arms, although she didn't know why. He'd already seen more of her skin than just about any other man on earth. And being a Las Vegas security man, he probably had all kinds of super powers that allowed him access to things the average person couldn't even imagine. Like built-in x-ray vision or some other equally disturbing talent. Heck, he probably had the entire shower episode on tape and was planning to sit down later tonight with a bowl of popcorn and a couple of friends to watch a replay of the entire event.

Amusement played at the corners of his mouth and Bailey felt her face turn pink again. In fact, he was probably reading her thoughts right that very minute.

She did her best to keep her thoughts in check, or at least G-rated, but it seemed security guy had special powers to control that, too. She took a long lazy look at him.

Carter Davis reminded her of her favorite pair of jeans. A little frayed around the edges, but solid and strong, and so undeniably sexy. He was certainly the kind of man she might consider having children with—under the right circumstances—and, being as he'd just seen her naked, they were already past that awkward first date stage.

Bailey fidgeted; Carter grinned some more.

Then he turned to leave.

Perhaps he'd sensed her discomfort, or maybe he really could read her mind and he didn't like the thoughts she was having about the two of them having children.

"Wait," she said. She didn't know why, but something crazy told her she wasn't quite finished with him. "Listen. I'm sure you're used to seeing all kinds of nakedness and stuff . . ."

Security guy turned. "You're not used to seeing yourself naked?"

"What? *No.*" Bailey shook her head. Either he was doing his best to annoy her or he was just an annoying person. In any case, she quickly changed her mind about thinking he might be the kind of man she'd want to father her children. "I was trying to say that I don't work in a place where weird stuff happens on a daily basis, and I don't walk into bathrooms where strange people are stuck naked in the shower."

"I get it. You're embarrassed."

Bailey's hands flew to her hips and she stuck out her chin. "I am not embarrassed. I have a perfectly nice body—"

"At last," he said, smiling warmly, "we agree."

She reconsidered the child thing once more. "Let's just forget this incident."

"It's forgotten," he said with a polite nod, and then he left.

Bailey watched him walk away. He had an athletic build and his black hair glistened all shimmery and touchable and was feathered back in a style reminiscent of, well, Elvis. For a quick moment, she imagined him in a white jumpsuit and a microphone in his hand, singing "Love Me Tender," but that idea quickly fizzled. Probably he couldn't sing a lick. Even so, it didn't stop her from keeping an eye on him all the way to the elevator.

He didn't even once look back before disappearing from her life.

When Bailey finally made it down to the casino, she found Liza feeding a Haywire slot machine near the elevator lobby. Bailey slipped into the chair next to her, but Liza didn't look up, or even question her as to why it took her more than two hours to join the party. And if Liza didn't ask, she wasn't about to tell.

"How're you doing?" Bailey asked. She started to rest her arms on the machine in front of her, but her nose wrinkled in disgust at all the smudges and smears on its front panel. Fingerprints, spilled drinks, bodily fluids. She wasn't touching it.

Liza shrugged. "You know, a few hundred here, a few hundred there. Nothing solid."

Bailey checked her watch. "I'm impressed. All this time and you still have money?"

"Listen, Missy, just because I lost one time"—Liza held up a finger—"that doesn't mean losing is my destiny."

"Uh-huh."

"'Uh-huh' is right. Me and these machines, we have a connection." Liza lost her last three credits and she swiveled her stool around. "See what you've done? Now we have to go to another casino." She grabbed Bailey's arm. "Maybe you'll get lucky and Slingo will take all my money and then we can devote the rest of our time here to finding your future husband."

"Wouldn't you rather conserve your money for later? How about we go work on our tans?"

Liza gave her a blank look.

"At the pool? Where people go to relax?"

"We don't need to lay by the pool to get a tan. This is Las Vegas. We'll get tan just by walking across the street. And I just got here, I hardly need to relax."

Bailey groaned. "But I do. I've had a hard morning." And traumatic. "I promise . . . if you'll go to the pool with me now, I'll spend the entire evening following you around to all your favorite slots," she added.

Liza grinned. "Now that's a deal I can't pass up."

Their trek to the elevator lobby was slow going. Even though they were only ten feet away, Liza managed to stop at three other slot machines before they made the ride back up to their room.

Bailey quickly changed into a lime-green bikini and slathered on a good shot glass full of SPF fifteen. She didn't know how long SPF fifteen was supposed to work, but she presumed it would at least be long enough to get her through one poolside drink and maybe even lunch. If sunscreen lotion makers would simply give some kind of timeframe on their labels, rather than a number that didn't mean squat to the general population, life would be so much easier.

Liza did the same, only she used SPF thirty, plus she added an extra-thick layer to her shoulders for freckle prevention. What she really needed was a swimsuit cover-up. Something large and bulky that hid what she had to offer, so that Bailey didn't feel like she was playing Sandra Dee in *Gidget*.

Liza's suit was small, Barbie doll size, and Bailey was pretty sure it wasn't meant to be touched by chlorine—ever. No question who was going to get all the poolside attention. Bailey said a silent prayer that there wouldn't be any Elvis impersonators out basking in the sun. With Liza's abundant show of skin, looking in *her* direction would be a mere accident.

Chapter Three

Carter rubbed a stain on the lapel of his suit. Wine. It could've been worse. The woman who'd done the honors had tried her best to soak him, but he'd managed to dodge getting splashed by most of the liquid from her glass.

Even though he'd been out of costume, she'd recognized him from the All-Star show, where he'd obviously done something to provoke the attack. Before she'd tossed her wine, she'd made an attempt to explain her motive, but drunks rarely made sense, and he'd told her he was in a hurry. From what he could gather, though, she was either angry about him not kissing her, or she was angry that he'd kissed her daughter instead.

Playing Elvis was risky business. But then, so, too, was security. He thought of the cute brunette in Room 1105 and smiled, barely aware of his manager's voice droning on in the background.

Bailey Ventura. She'd checked in with a friend just that morning, and they were due to check out the morning after the competition. She was a little younger than the typical Elvis fan, but then it wasn't unheard of to have fans as young as five or six attend his shows.

Maybe he'd be lucky enough to see Miss Ventura in the audience.

"Do you even care?" Marty Dicks said.

The cute brunette's image dissolved. "Sure I care," Carter said. He didn't have a clue what his manager had been saying, but more than likely it had something to do with women. "What do you want me to do about it?"

"Knock that shit off."

Carter grinned. "You ever have a horde of women throwing themselves at you?"

"That's not my problem. Anyway, I'm not so sure they're gonna let you in the show this year. That little incident last year with that gal in her hotel room is still too fresh in everyone's mind, especially the people who had to clean up after you."

Carter went into his Elvis persona. "Ah, we was just having a little fun," he said.

"Fun?" Marty snorted. "It might've been called fun if the two of you had stopped at spraying each other with whipped cream. Or, even if you'd stopped after filling the tub with that white shit. But, *nooo*, you two had to jump in, get yourselves all creamed up, and then have the sorry sense not to keep it in your room. Housekeeping had to spend the next week getting that crap out of the carpet, painting the walls . . . that stuff is toxic. What the hell were you thinking?"

"Like I said, we was just havin' some good ol' fun. You should try it sometime." Carter gave Marty a boyish sneer.

Marty held up a hand. "Save your act for the women. On second thought, don't. You don't need any more woman trouble." He reached inside his desk, pulled out an envelope, and tossed it over in front of Carter. "These people here are funny about that kind of fun. If you really were 'the man,' they'd probably laugh and tell you to go ahead, have a good time."

Carter picked up the envelope and took a look inside. "What's this?"

"Royalties from that there video, *All the King's Men*." Marty ran a hand through wispy strands of hair on his near-bald head and got up. His distended belly jiggled as he walked over to the door. "Take my advice. Forget about the competition this year. All the spots are filled, and even if one of the other guys drops out, it's doubtful The Palace will let you inside their doors. Tough break. Maybe next year," Marty said. "I gotta go. I've got another potential client waiting."

Carter swore he could almost see the dollar signs rolling like slot reels in Marty's eyes as he walked out the door.

The door clicked closed, and Carter stared out the window into a sky so blue with heat he could see it sweltering off the rooftop below. Next year? He huffed. Not if he had anything to say about it. If Marty was right, and the competition was full, his only hope would be to take someone else's place. Carter considered everyone he knew who had made it in. They'd all worked hard to capture one of the coveted spots, so unless one of them were to suddenly get sick, the odds of him getting in were worse than playing the roulette wheel. Hell, even illness being his ticket into the competition was unlikely. Most of the guys he knew would go on even if they were having severe chest pains.

Carter blew out a heavy breath. The only way he could see it happening was if he could convince one of them that splitting the pot was better than getting no pot at all. No problem. According to his fans and even most of his competitors, he was sure to be in the running for first place this year.

Carter stuffed the envelope into the inside breast pocket of his suit. Hell, if he could get one of them to step aside, he'd gladly give them all the prize money. All he wanted was to just once take that first place title.

He looked down at his lapel. Rubbing the stain had only made it worse. He'd spent an obscene amount on the suit, and now it had a dark blotch right in plain view. Too bad he hadn't been wearing his jumpsuit with the red, white, and blue gemstones. The bright colors would've helped hide the spot.

The green beach loungers were comfy enough to make a person fall asleep, but all Bailey had done since she lay down was think about security guy. God knew why she couldn't get that man off her mind. He was arrogant, and so . . . maddening; he hadn't deserved to see her naked.

Two hours passed. Liza had been generous with her slot winnings, paying for a piña colada and a turkey sandwich for each of them. She even offered to buy Bailey a second drink, something less fruity, more alcohol, but Bailey suspected the idea was for her to get liquored up enough that she wouldn't complain if they played slots the rest of the day and all through the night. Oh, she might've promised Liza they could play slots all evening, but getting intoxicated wasn't part of the deal. Besides, she had to keep her wits about her in case they happened upon any dark-haired men who sported a prominent lip curl.

Another twenty minutes passed. Carter's face had tortured Bailey long enough. She needed to find something else to occupy her mind. She sat up. "I've had enough sun," she said abruptly and she tucked her book into her bag. She took a quick glance around to make sure she wasn't leaving anything behind, then she slipped her pink-painted toes into her sandals and stood. "Let's go—now."

Liza barely kept up, but Bailey had to give her credit for not giving in to the *ding, ding, ding* of temptation.

She and Liza got on the elevator and Bailey pushed the number eleven. The doors closed, and the car hummed upward. It opened on the seventh floor and they waited. After a moment, when no one entered, Liza stuck out her head. A man was at the ice machine filling a bucket.

"It's an omen," she said, pulling her head back in. "Look." She pointed to the number seven. *"Lucky* seven. We should get off here."

Bailey poked out her head. The man was still filling his ice bucket. "And what, ask that man if we can join his party? I don't think we're dressed appropriately."

"I have a feeling," Liza explained. The doors started to close and she pushed HOLD.

Bailey shook her head. "You'd be wasting your time. I'm sure there are no slot machines on this floor."

"Ha, ha."

The elevator jumped, then dropped a few inches and Bailey and Liza held onto each other and waited for a long minute. No sound, no more movement, nothing but some soft music by James Taylor, the beating of their hearts, and a few gasping breaths. Bailey looked at the control panel. All the numbers were dark.

Stuck again. Twice in one day. It wasn't a *sign.* It was an omen. And maybe not a good one. Bailey shivered. She considered pushing HELP but quickly decided against it. What if who showed up to rescue them was security guy? How could she face him again? So soon after he'd seen her nude? Maybe if it'd been a day or two, when the image of her nude body was dim in his mind . . . Although it'd take more than a day or two to make those blue pools of intrigue he used for eyes grow dim in *her* mind.

"Well?" Liza looked at her expectantly. "Are we just going to stand here? Or are we going to call for help?" She reached for the control panel.

Bailey swatted at her hand. "Help is for people who are in some kind of distress."

Liza looked at her. "I *am* in distress. Every minute we're detained is one more minute I won't have to play the machines or, in your case, another minute you won't have the opportunity to search for your true love." Liza fluttered her eyelashes.

Bailey considered seeing security guy so soon after their little shower episode. No, she couldn't take the chance he'd be the one to rescue her again. "Let's just get out here," she said, pushing DOOR OPEN.

The man at the ice machine was gone. They stepped out onto a white marble floor and crossed over to the other side to try another elevator car. Every button was dark, but Bailey pushed them anyway—just in case. They watched and waited for a long minute, but the indicator lights remained dark.

"We can take the stairs," Liza offered. She nodded at a red EXIT sign above a door. "How bad could it be going up four floors? All those stairs should be good for at least one day's worth of calories."

Bailey couldn't argue with that. She and Liza went through the door and began their traverse up. They passed a door that was painted with the number eight . . . then nine . . . until Bailey stopped suddenly and plastered herself against the wall.

Liza raised an eyebrow. "Who are you supposed to be? Secret Squirrel?"

"Sh-h." Bailey put a finger to her lips. She pulled Liza back against the wall and pointed upward. "Do you hear that?"

They held their breath and listened. Voices. Men. One floor up.

Bailey took a quiet shallow breath. "I saw an episode on the Travel Channel that said meeting someone in a stairwell in a strange place is something to be avoided.

Especially in Las Vegas," she whispered. She poked her head around the corner and tried to get a look at the men who owned the voices, but her view was obstructed by the gray stair railing. Two quiet steps up and she felt a squeal rise in her throat. There were indeed two men—and one of them had on a white jumpsuit.

But it was the other man, the one who had his back to her and was wearing a dark suit, who made her heart do a little backflip. His voice was deep and sultry and so reminiscent of Elvis's that it gave her palpitations. The only thing that kept her from running up and introducing herself was good manners. The men were obviously having a private conversation, and didn't want to be bothered, or they wouldn't be standing in a stairwell.

Bailey listened for a moment, trying to decide if she and Liza should wait it out, or if they should turn around and quietly head back down the stairs. It wasn't her intention to eavesdrop, but the men weren't exactly speaking in hushed tones, and from what she could gather, they were attempting to work out some kind of deal concerning the upcoming Elvis competition. If she and Liza had stumbled onto some kind of shady contest-fixing deal in the works, they might very well be in danger. Bailey shuddered at the thought.

"Marty said they weren't letting you in the show this year," the man in the jumpsuit said to the other man.

Bailey's forehead wrinkled. His voice wasn't anything like she'd expected. Certainly nothing like Elvis's. Though when she thought about it, it did make sense. A tribute artist couldn't possibly remain in character 24/7. If he did, he might have some identity issues or possibly even some deep-seated psychological problems.

"Like I said, you think about it," the man in the dark suit told the man in white.

Bailey's toes tingled at the sound of his voice. If only

he'd turn around . . . She glanced at his backside. Though that was a pretty good view, too.

A humming started up behind the wall. The elevators were back in service.

Liza tugged at her sleeve and pointed at the door with the nine painted on it. "Let's get out of here," she whispered.

Bailey sighed to herself. She took one last look at the back of the man in the suit, and reluctantly tiptoed after Liza.

When they were safely back in their room, she leaned against the wall and let out a real sigh. First the shower incident and then this. Another lost opportunity. "Imagine that, an Elvis impersonator, almost close enough to touch."

"Yeah. Imagine that," Liza said. She pushed hair back from her forehead and blew out a breath. She pressed a hand to her forehead. "My God, I'm all flushed from just breathing the same air."

Bailey rolled her eyes. "Very funny."

Liza let Bailey shower first, but before Bailey stepped inside the glass enclosure, she tested the door a couple of times. It opened and closed without any hint of trouble.

Oh, well.

In no time, the women were ready to hit the casinos. They'd each slipped into a flouncy short skirt and a brightly colored tank top, and looked as though they could be sisters, except for their choice of lipstick, and the way they wore their hair. Liza wore a hot pink frost that shimmered and sparkled when the light hit her lips, and Bailey wore a coral matte cream. Liza wore her hair down and Bailey's was pulled up into its usual ponytail.

"Take me to the nearest Slingo," Bailey said.

Liza slid her a smile. "Now that's the right attitude."

During Liza's quest for the perfect machine, they stopped at the Elton John store, where Bailey purchased a gray camisole with the words NAUGHTY LITTLE GIRL printed in bright red lettering across the front. It could've said anything—she simply liked the color.

They made their way through the casino until they finally came to a carousel that made Bailey come to a dead stop. A shiny new Thunderbird convertible sat gleaming under the casino lights, three feet up from the floor on a pedestal. And it was red—nearly the same red as on her new camisole. Bailey stared up at it for a long minute. If she'd ever been given a sign, this was it. *She* was supposed to win that car.

"Let's play," she said and sat down.

Liza followed suit, quickly pulling some cash out of her purse and muttering something about not wanting to stand in the way of progress.

Bailey glanced around before she put in her money. Only four other people were playing. A man sat on one side of her, looking as though he could use a break. His eyes were glazed over and he was pushing the Max Credit button without blinking. Could be he was taking a break, but Bailey suspected he was the victim of too much free alcohol, as evidenced by the three glasses that sat empty before him. Even if he won, it'd take him a while to regain enough consciousness to realize what had happened. The other three people were on the other side of the car, so they wouldn't be a distraction.

Bailey moved an ashtray, bulging with butts, over to the machine next to hers. She knew she was supposed to have some sort of *feeling*, but having that smelly thing sitting in front of her only made her feel nauseous. Liza was two seats down.

A woman draped in a honey-colored sheet and wearing twigs in her hair offered her a drink, but she declined and asked for water instead. She slipped a crisp five into her machine's hungry mouth and gave Liza a quick glance. Liza's machine had already gobbled up its first ten and she was directing some obscenity at it. She ordered a White Russian from the woman in the sheet.

Bailey studied her machine's legend before pushing any buttons. At fifty cents a push, she'd have ten pushes on the Max Credit button. Ten chances to win the sexy little two-seater. No problem. She'd only been playing Washington state's lotto for the last five years and had never won a penny. She was overdue.

Her entire five dollars was gone in under a minute. At that rate, she'd be out of money by bedtime.

She reconsidered ordering a drink. Losing might go down easier if her blood cells were medicated. Liza put another twenty into her machine and quickly lost it. Alcohol wasn't helping her.

Bailey slipped in a ten. This time, before pushing any buttons, she closed her eyes and envisioned all three reels landing on *Wild Card*. What she got was two black sevens and a skinny blue bar. In other words, nothing. She pushed and envisioned, pushed and envisioned, and kept right on pushing and envisioning until she was down to only eight credits.

It was time to get serious.

She grabbed Liza's glass and took a long drink, and then one long, deep breath. Focusing harder than when she took her finals in her last biology class, she jammed her index finger into Max Credit.

Liza swore at her machine and scooted over to the chair beside Bailey, who didn't mind, so long as Liza kept her swearing to a low roar. "These machines are cold, and I'm not so sure anyone really ever wins these cars anyway," she said as the reels on Bailey's machine spun.

Bailey stared straight ahead. The first reel clicked into place, *Wild Card*, followed by the second, *Wild Card*, and finally the third, *WILD CARD!* The next thing she knew someone was gripping her arm and every sound in the casino had hushed.

Wild Card, Wild Card, Wild Card!

Don't move, Bailey told herself. *Don't move, don't breathe, don't do anything.* Her heart thumped wildly as she stared at the machine's display window. Each reel rested precariously on the payline, and she didn't dare do anything that might make them start to roll again.

Blink, blink, blink, fireworks lit up inside her brain. Or it could've been the little white light blinking on the top of her machine. She couldn't be sure.

Her fingers were sore from gripping the front of her machine, and she didn't give a second thought to all the smudges and smears.

Then it hit her. Something wasn't right. Where was the confetti? The marching band? Liza had won five thousand dollars once, and all kinds of things happened. Lights, music, whistles . . . an entire friggin' orchestra!

Bailey stared hard at the three Wild Card symbols and waited. No bells, no whistles. And certainly no confetti. Her gaze was drawn to the notice on the front of the machine, and only then did it occur to her that it might actually mean something.

In case of machine malfunction, there will be no payout.

Her heart thudded. She was going to be sick.

Chapter Four

"We got us a winner," Zack Gray called out as he stared at the monitor fixed on carousel four. "Lucky bird. Let's take another look." He rolled the film back to watch the replay.

Carter Davis looked over in time to see the three Wild Cards roll to a stop on the front of a shapely brunette's machine. Lucky bird indeed. She'd just won herself a new car.

The brunette stared straight ahead at her machine for a quiet minute—not unusual for such a win—and then she swiveled around in her chair. A knot twisted in Carter's gut.

"I'll be damned," he muttered. His damsel in distress. He had Zack rewind the tape again, even though he knew the result would be the same.

Bailey Ventura pushed the Max Credit button without so much as a six-credit win when she suddenly stopped. For what? To pray? That, too, was not such an unusual thing to see a guest do just before using up their last few credits.

Bingo! A clear win. Nothing suspicious. His brunette was now the proud owner of a brand-new, torch red

Thunderbird, plus a nice little progressive jackpot of four thousand dollars, which would help ease the tax bite.

Carter continued watching. Bailey looked up at the blinking light on top of her machine and a woman, who Carter assumed was her traveling companion, sat next to her with her mouth hanging open. Both women looked confused.

Carter frowned. Where the hell was the bell? Possible malfunction? Say it ain't true. It was far easier to give away the car than to try to explain to a guest that they hadn't really won.

"What's the problem with that bell?" Carter asked.

Zack did a quick scan on the machine. "Relax, boss. It's just broken."

"Well, get it fixed—yesterday."

"I'm on it," Zack said.

Bailey glanced around. Another common reaction for big winners. They were never quite sure they'd really won, and many would reserve their screaming and jumping around until someone actually confirmed it for them.

Carter smiled. Today, he'd be that someone.

He went into his office and grabbed his suit coat, slipping it on as he walked out of the control room. He stuck his head inside a small office that sat just off the main room. "Bruce, Mike, let's go. Winner at carousel four. Ford Thunderbird." Two men stood and grabbed their suit coats. They followed Carter to the elevator.

The men stood quietly, arms folded across their chests, facing a large mirror. Carter stifled a chuckle. They looked like a group of Mafia men on their way to a hit.

As soon as the elevator doors slid open, a noxious cloud of cigarette smoke hit them. Carter wanted to hold his breath. No matter how many fans, filters, or deodorizers the hotel used, the odor infiltrated everything and being inside a casino for as few as five minutes was enough to make a person stink.

Carter led the way through the casino, cutting though crowds of people, and then there she was. His brunette. She looked lost, still not sure what was happening. He was just the man to save her. His chest muscles tightened— in a good way.

Despite the absence of a ringing bell, a small crowd had begun to gather around in response to her machine's blinking light. People loved a winner. And, contrary to popular belief, casino personnel loved presenting guests with their winnings. It was just plain good for business.

"What have you done?" Liza said with a sputter. Her mouth gaped open like a fish out of water. "Have you won a *car?*"

Bailey nodded, then she shook her head, and she finally ended with a shrug. "I'm not sure."

"My God." Liza slipped off her chair and stared at the display window. Seconds later, she was bouncing around like she was on a pogo stick. "You've won a car!" She looked up at the T-Bird and pointed. "That car!"

Bailey's stomach twisted and turned. If Liza said it, it had to be true. And she wasn't sure, but she had the feeling that she, too, should be doing some leaping about, but instead, she was using all her energy to keep from throwing up.

"Wait—" Liza said, and she stopped bouncing. "I'm not so sure . . ." She looked up at the machine's blinking light. "There's no bell. Where's the bell?" She looked at Bailey with fear in her eyes.

"How should I know?" Bailey said. "*You* should know. You're the one who has experience at winning. Did I win or not?"

Liza slid a look at the Machine Malfunction Notice,

and the expression on her face made Bailey's stomach drop. Her little red car was slipping away before she'd even had a chance to sit in it. Even some of the onlookers began to shake their heads and walk away, and Bailey heard one woman mutter, "Poor girl," and another, "How awful."

She'd been duped. Just like Charlie Brown with the football. Well, she shouldn't have been surprised. It wasn't the first time. She was just six years old when a boy named Tommy Wiggins was all she could think about. He'd told her he'd give her a lick of his ice cream cone if she could guess what hand he was holding it in behind his back, but no matter how many times she tried, he'd switch hands and she'd fail. It never occurred to her that the boy she was in love with would cheat. It wasn't even the ice cream she was after. It was Tommy's germs. She wanted to lick where he'd licked.

The friend she was with that day—who just happened to be Liza—had stood there and giggled at her silliness. She sure didn't want to hear Liza giggle right now.

Why? Why did she have to be the one they chose to make an example of with their dumb Machine Malfunction Notice? *Why? Why her?* Just as Bailey felt herself begin to dissolve into complete despair, Liza tapped her on the shoulder. And she wasn't giggling.

"The bell may not be working, but I think you really did win that car. Look," she said, nodding over Bailey's shoulder.

Bailey swiveled around. Three men in suits were headed toward them. They had power in their walks and determination on their faces. No hint of a smile. A sheet-attired woman, carrying a bucket with a bottle sticking out its top, followed closely behind them.

Bailey swallowed. She glanced around nervously. All eyes were on her. God help her. She'd unknowingly done something against some Vegas code of ethics and she was either going to jail, or worse, would soon be a new lump in the sandy Nevada desert. She had a momentary vision of vultures circling high in the hot sky, and her mouth dried up, her pulse fluttered. If only she could faint, it would all be over by the time she came to.

Breathe, she told herself. *Get some oxygen to your brain.* Bailey quickly analyzed the situation and came up with three pretty good responses for when the men in suits questioned her: she could pretend she didn't have a clue what they were talking about, she could bat her eyelashes at the leader and hope he showed her mercy for being young and stupid, or she could stand up for her rights and demand that they honor her win.

Bailey steeled herself and squared her shoulders. She'd won that car fair and square, and she'd be damned if they'd take it away before she even had the chance to put the key in the ignition. She was ready to argue her point.

She gazed right into the eyes of the leader and her mind went on hiatus. All fear about being buried in the desert disappeared. She *wanted* to be buried. In fact, she had an incredible urge to go running and screaming from the casino.

Security guy was the leader.

They wouldn't have to kill her. She was going to die from embarrassment. Of all people, why did they have to send down the same man who'd seen her naked before they were even properly introduced?

"Congratulations," Carter said to her in a most official sounding voice as he came to a stop in front of her.

He was so close she could smell the remnants of a breathmint, all sweet and fiery as though he was expecting to be kissed. Bailey supposed that wasn't so farfetched. People probably did all kinds of crazy things when they won something as big as a car. Not her, though. He'd already gotten all the reward he was getting from her.

"Looks like you've won yourself a car." He held out his hand to her, giving no indication he remembered her—or her naked body.

Bailey forced a smile. "Yes. Can you believe it?" was the only response she could come up with. *Duh*. She gave herself a mental head slap. Of course he could believe it. He probably gave away a car every day. Just like he probably saw women in every stage of undress every day.

"I'm Liza. Bailey's best friend," Liza said, sticking out her hand.

Carter shook it and gave her a warm smile, then he turned his attention back to Bailey.

The woman in the sheet set down the bucket of ice and champagne. She handed Bailey and Liza each a glass, and then filled them with bubbly. Bailey took a large swallow for bravery, and then she set her glass down. She wanted this moment to remain clear in her memory.

"I know it's fast, but we have some options for you to consider," Carter said.

"Oh?" Bailey did her best to sound nonchalant.

He laughed politely. "You're in shock."

Really? That was an understatement. He continued talking, but Bailey's head was elsewhere, back in her room, in the shower. Could it be that he really didn't remember her? After seeing her *naked?* She gave herself a mental assessment. Nice legs, perky breasts—not that she gave a hoot if *he* thought so—but, how could she be that forgettable?

Another mental slap. He was a man.

Well, fine. If he wanted to pretend he didn't know who she was, that was fine with her.

Bailey watched his even white teeth as he spoke. His brooding eyes, his perfectly coiffed black hair that looked even more dangerous than when she'd first met him. She certainly remembered *him*.

"So, Miss Ventura, what would you prefer?" Carter asked.

"Prefer?" Bailey swallowed, and Carter took notice of the slender curve of her neck, perhaps the only part of her body he hadn't already committed to memory. He resisted laughing. She hadn't heard a word he'd said to her in the last five minutes.

"As I was saying, you can take the car—in which case you'll have to pay income tax—or you could take forty thousand dollars cash."

"Cash?" Liza said with a gasp.

Carter nodded. "Or, we could give you a voucher to purchase another car once you return home," he explained.

Bailey stared at him blankly. She was numb. He recognized the signs. Wide eyes full of wonder, the inability to talk coherently, let alone think about filling her purse with forty thousand in cash. Who could blame her? Of course, he could do her a favor and pinch her just to let her know she wasn't dreaming. That'd wake her up. Hell, thoughts like that had parts of *him* waking up.

His brunette chewed her lip in a cute sort of way and her wide eyes narrowed as though she suspected he wanted something in return. Which he might—later.

"I'll take the car," she said quickly.

Carter laughed and held up a hand. "Don't worry, I won't take back the offer, if you'd like to think about it for a minute. Like I said, you'll be responsible for paying the income tax," he said.

"Income tax can be a bitch," Liza said to Bailey. "You should think about it." She gestured up at the car. "It's not going anywhere."

Bailey gazed all starry-eyed up at the T-Bird. Carter had seen that same look on her face at least one other time, when she'd been looking at *him*. She raised up on her toes to try to see the car's interior, but it was up too high, and she was just a little thing, maybe five foot three.

If she asked politely, he'd gladly tell her that it had soft black leather seats, with red inserts that were just waiting for her to sink her lovely behind into. He'd also tell her that he wouldn't mind taking her and her lovely behind out for a spin, so she could feel the open road on her face, before making her decision. Then he'd have yet another opportunity to see her.

"I'll give you a few minutes by yourself. In the meantime, if you have them with you, I'll need your driver's license and a Social Security card."

She grinned up at him smugly and her eyes sparkled as she dug through her bag. She finally came up with a handful of business cards that she shuffled through until she found her i.d. Her face beamed like she was handing over a report card full of straight As, as she handed them to him.

The left side of Carter's mouth notched up. He held her gaze for a few powerful seconds, until her face turned a pretty shade of pink. "My people here will get a picture of you and I'll be right back," he said. He felt daggers in his back as he walked away, and he smiled through the pain.

It wasn't just security guy's hair that made him dangerous. He had a way about him. Bailey glanced over at Liza. Evidently, she thought so, too. She hadn't taken her eyes off him and, at the moment, looked as though she might be running obscene possibilities through her mind. Bailey gave her a good jab.

Liza rubbed her side. *"Hey."*

After one of Carter's men took her picture, she and Liza stayed put and waited for Carter's return. Liza used the time wisely by continuing to celebrate with the bottle of champagne. She didn't bother playing any of the slot machines, claiming that the odds of someone else hitting the jackpot on the same carousel so soon after Bailey's win were astronomical. Bailey thought the odds of her ever winning the car in the first place were pretty astronomical.

Just as Liza poured the last of the champagne into her glass, Carter returned with Bailey's license and Social Security card. Liza's consumption of nearly a full bottle of champagne had given her a glow and she had a gleam in her eye that Bailey recognized as man hunger. Bailey considered giving her another jab. No way was she letting her friend feed on security guy. He was hers—not that she wanted him. But he was at least worth some consideration. After all, in just over six hours, he'd given her a forty-thousand-dollar car, seen her naked, and filled her mind with impossible thoughts.

They were halfway to bliss.

The only one who didn't seem to be aware was security guy. He left them standing there with only a promise to get back to her in a day or so for her answer about the car.

Bailey told herself she didn't care. She'd show him. She'd go and win another jackpot and let some other hunky man in a suit make her day.

Riding the high of the biggest win of her life, Bailey had renewed confidence in playing the slots. She eyed a row of megabucks machines and decided that three dollars per push for a chance to add four million to her bank account no longer seemed like such an absurd idea. Ten minutes later, her purse was two hundred dollars heavier and Liza was whining in protest at how unfair it was for Bailey to hog all the good machines.

Bailey knew just the cure. Comfort food. And all the

comfort food they could ever want lay straight ahead at the Oasis food court. Plus, it would be time well spent if it saved Liza from feeding the slots the last of her money.

They both ordered fish and chips with extra tartar sauce for Bailey. By the time they finished, Bailey was ready to win another hundred or two. Heck, make that a thousand or two—the amount was wide open. Plus, the slots provided a valuable service; they kept her mind off security guy. Somehow watching those little reels spin over and over had a way of filling the mind with something that could be compared to "white noise." Maybe that's why so many people resembled mindless robots after they'd been sitting in front of a machine for a while.

Bailey slipped a twenty into a Triple Double Diamond and it quickly became ninety. Damn security guy anyway. Giving her all that money. If he'd stopped at ogling her in the shower, it probably wouldn't have taken more than a week or two to get him out of her system. But presenting her with a brand-new car and four thousand dollars cash? Well, that would brand him into her memory for at least as long as she kept it—or however long it took her to spend forty thousand cash, whichever she decided to take. In any case, the four thousand was going to keep both her and Liza busy at the slots.

By the time midnight rolled around, Liza was completely discouraged and didn't want to play anymore. She claimed Bailey had stolen her mojo by winning the car, and that the odds of either of them winning another large jackpot during this trip were zip to zero. Not that they weren't anyway, Bailey wanted to remind her. But she didn't.

Instead, she let Liza lead her down the Strip so that she could try her luck at several other casinos. They stopped in Bellagio, where Liza played Wheel of Fortune and quickly lost fifty dollars. Then they went into the Paris hotel and she lost another twenty on a Zodiac machine.

Bailey put in a five and racked up a quick hundred credits, which only added to Liza's misery.

Bailey had never seen Las Vegas past midnight. It was exciting and scary all at the same time. Family hour was over, and the crowd that was out now was younger and hungrier looking. Bailey convinced Liza they should stay inside the casinos as much as possible.

After losing steadily for another hour, Liza started eyeing the nickel machines. Afraid her friend might be broken, Bailey convinced her to hang in there and they continued down to the MGM Grand.

That's when Liza's losing streak finally came to an end. She immediately won three hundred dollars on a Little Green Men machine and another hundred on a Double Wild Cherry. Bailey figured the gods were being so generous because of all the money they'd deposited at that casino in the past. With so much good fortune being thrown her way, she thought it might even spill over into her search for those elusive men in jumpsuits or leather, or even a GI uniform.

Bailey kept her eyes wide open, but she was getting discouraged. Except for the impersonator in the stairwell, the only man she'd seen who could rival Elvis in plain old sex appeal was her very own overly confident, frustratingly handsome security guy.

Where were they? Was this or wasn't this Las Vegas, home of more Elvis impersonators than any other place in the world? At this point, she'd have been happy to get another glimpse of security guy and his snarling lip. She sighed at the thought, and her imagination quickly moved in amorous directions. She'd dressed him in black leather several times over the last five hours and had never once been disappointed. Heck, even if he couldn't sing, he could lip sync and women would be so busy watching him gyrate that they wouldn't notice.

Bailey cashed out of a Sinatra machine fifty dollars

richer and was just about to give up her quest to find anyone or anything resembling Elvis when she heard the sound she'd traveled more than a thousand miles to hear. Her head snapped around to find its source and she held her breath, listening.

"It's him," she whispered, closing her eyes and sucking in some air. She held the back of a chair to steady herself. "Don't you hear him?"

"I sure do," Liza said, her eyes gleaming. She started to walk away, and headed toward a bank of empty Elvis machines that were lined up against the far wall. "Jail House Rock" was blaring out the front of one.

Bailey frowned. That wasn't what she'd heard. And it certainly hadn't come from some scratchy machine recording. "Wait," she shouted after Liza, but Liza didn't stop. Bailey ran to catch up. If she allowed Liza to sit, they could be at those machines for hours—maybe even days. They were some of the most sought after machines in Vegas, and people didn't give them up easily once they found a good one.

The Elvis machine went quiet before they reached it, and then Bailey heard the singing again. A voice ringing sweet and clear through the casino settled comfortably around her like a warm summer breeze.

"This way," she said, pulling Liza after her in the opposite direction.

A minute later, they were in a big open area just below MGM's Studio 54, staring up at a large stage.

Bailey's mouth went dry.

Chapter Five

Elvis had entered the building.

Two dozen of them, in fact. They were lined up at the back of the stage, each awaiting their turn to step forward and work the room into a frenzy. Black leather . . . gold lamé . . . jumpsuits in a variety of colors and patterns . . . It was an invasion of dark-haired, hip-swiveling hunks of burning flesh, hot enough to dry up every wetland in the state of Washington.

Bailey stared in open-mouthed awe, and she had a strange urge to start ripping out her hair.

Liza nudged her. "You okay?"

"Uh-huh," Bailey managed without drooling. She thought that spinning around and singing something from *The Sound of Music* would be appropriate, but her knees were like Jell-O. "Oh, Liza, aren't they beautiful?"

Liza nodded once. "They're gods." She looked at her watch. "Okay, let's get the show on the road. Pick one. My luck has turned and I don't want to waste another minute."

Bailey frowned. "This is far too important a task to just pick one. I've got to watch them, hear them sing . . ."

"I know, I know . . . you've got to examine their scruffy sideburns to see who's faking it."

"That's right," Bailey said, not taking her gaze from the stage for one second. One of the men moved forward. Quent Flagg. God bless America. He was dressed in a GI uniform and his hair was piled high in early Elvis fashion. The audience screamed their approval. No surprise there. His outfit hugged his tall, fit frame in all the right places, giving women plenty to scream about. Scream they did, becoming louder with each note, and by the time Quent was halfway through "GI Blues," even Liza had stopped fretting about lost time on the slots.

"I *like* him," she said. "You know how I enjoy a man in a uniform."

Bailey knew, all right. Liza made that fact known each and every time she came to visit her on Whidbey Island. Liza *liked* the men at Whidbey Island's Naval Base so much that Bailey was beginning to suspect they might be the only reason she ever showed up on her doorstep.

"That's Quent Flagg," Bailey told Liza. "I like him, too."

"Okay, so grab him, get his number, whatever, and let's go." Liza nudged Bailey toward the stage, but Bailey planted her feet firmly in place.

"I can't make a snap judgment. This is serious business."

Liza gave her a look. "You're here to marry a man just because he wears a jumpsuit. How serious can it be?"

Quent took his place back in line and another man rushed forward with a series of martial arts kicks and enough squats and thrusts to constitute an entire week of workouts. His voice was strong and he moved around the stage provocatively inside a tight, blue jumpsuit. Bailey's breath caught in her throat as her chest rose and fell with mighty heaves. He definitely had the power. Woman power.

"Steve Sogura," she whispered, her voice all breathy like she was running out of air.

Steve started with "Kentucky Rain," holding the audience captive with his smooth, soulful voice. The only one who didn't seem impressed was Liza. Liza had taken an emery board out of her bag and was working some rough spots out of a nail that had taken a beating on the slots.

Bailey frowned. "He's from back home, you know."

Liza kept filing. "Does he have on a uniform?"

After Steve finished "Kentucky Rain," he fell to his knees in a mournful wail that made every woman in the place want to fall to *her* knees. "Hurt" was one of Steve's strongest performances, and if any song could make a woman hurt for a man, that was it. He even made Liza forget about her chipped nail.

Bailey swallowed. Her throat was the only part of her body she could move. Steve was sure to be a contender for first place in the competition. And if he won by singing "Hurt," then he deserved it.

When Steve finished the song, Liza's head swung around and she gave Bailey a raised eyebrow. "If you don't like that one, there's something wrong with you."

"He's taken," Bailey said on a sigh.

Liza propped her hands on her hips. "If you already know everything about these men, why can't you just pick one?" She checked her watch. "We only have two more days, nine hours, and fifteen minutes remaining. My thumb is going into spasms without something to push."

"Suck on it," Bailey told her. She might know these men—God knows she'd seen enough videos of them, had even seen several of them perform live—but choosing a husband wasn't the same as choosing an outfit to wear. Finding one to share lasting happiness with was a delicate operation and as good as Steve Sogura was, he was indeed taken. Her hunt had to focus elsewhere.

Bailey continued looking each man over, pausing long enough to either check him off her list of possibles, or put him on her short list. Married . . . too old . . . just plain wrong. Even after working her way through half of them, her short list remained virtually empty. Her gaze went from one end of the stage to the other, and it all became one big blur. While nothing compared to seeing them in person—larger than life—picking wasn't going to be as easy as she'd thought.

Discouragement settled in the pit of her stomach. Maybe she was being too picky and this was all just a silly dream. Maybe no living man would ever be able to fill Elvis Presley's jumpsuit. Not that anyone could. But if she could even find one in the vicinity . . . one who could remove just one of her shoes with a single kiss . . . And he didn't really need to *look* like Elvis . . . well, maybe a little. But please, God, let him at least have some of Elvis's charisma, to have the ability to command attention when he walked into a room. And, of course, let them share that all-encompassing chemistry. It had to be overpowering and overwhelming. In a word, she had to be overrun with emotions when he looked at her, touched her . . . kissed her. Her heart had to sing loud enough to burst. Was that too much to ask for? She didn't think so. Not when she intended to spend the rest of her life with him.

With a sigh, Bailey checked another impersonator off her list, but she perked up when a man she wasn't familiar with stepped forward.

What was this? A newcomer? Bailey tried to recall if she'd ever heard the voice, or the look, but he was definitely an unknown—to her anyway. He'd probably been one of those men who'd been happy going through life being himself, when finally, the prodding of his friends or family got him to take that first step. In Bailey's opinion, if a man reached adulthood before ever considering this impersonator business, it was simply a novel idea that wouldn't last. To be a serious Elvis tribute artist, a man had to have it in his blood from a very early age.

Bailey studied the stranger. A little reckless looking and full of self confidence, he had her complete attention as he moved over to the edge of the stage and gazed directly into her eyes. He began singing "Kiss Me Quick," a snappy tune that only a third of the audience seemed to know.

Bailey felt a jolt pass through her, and she had to make a conscious effort not to scream or pass out. It took several attempts for her to get out the words "It can't be . . ." Then she squeezed her eyes shut and muttered something else unintelligible, and Liza handed her a water bottle. Bailey took a large swallow and shook her head, hoping to rattle things into clarity.

A sign. It had to be. First he'd saved her from the shower, then he'd given her a car, and now this . . . What *was* this? A bad *joke*?

Maybe she was hallucinating.

She let one eye slip open, then the other.

Nope. There he was, still there, singing and smiling at her.

Oh, God. She was delirious. The fish she'd eaten had been bad. Bailey suddenly felt sick to her stomach. She had to sit down.

She stumbled over to a chair in front of a slot machine. She drank the rest of what was in Liza's water bottle, and put her head between her hands. She was seeing things. That had to be it. After she got her pulse to settle down, she looked back up at the stage.

Gone. Security guy was gone.

No! He couldn't be *gone.*

Bailey swung her head from side to side, looking up and down the entire length of the stage. No sign of him. Her chest hurt like she'd been kicked and the longer she searched for him, the more it hurt.

"Are you okay?" Liza asked. "Do you need a doctor or something?"

"Did you see him?" Bailey asked, her voice bordering on panic.

"Who?" Liza looked around.

"*Elvis*, for God's sake."

"Take your pick," Liza said, gesturing toward the stage.

"Not *them*." Bailey tossed a hand at the line of men. "*Him*. The one who just finished singing."

Liza nodded. "Honey, everyone saw him." She grabbed Bailey. "Wait. Don't tell me you've found your man. Hallelujah! Does this mean our work is done? That we can spend the rest of our time here playing slots?"

"Yes. *No*." Bailey shook her head. "Where did he go?"

"I don't know. After he finished serenading you, he just kinda, *poof*"—Liza tossed her hands up—"disappeared." She shrugged and looked around. "We could go back stage and try to find him—"

"*No*. God no."

"Okay . . . so he's not the one." Liza looked up at the stage. "So how about this one?"

Bailey looked up in time to see Jesse Aaron, another giant in the business, blitz forward. Fans couldn't get enough of him. And for good reason. His voice, all deep and sultry, saturated the audience like melted chocolate, cloaking every woman within hearing range. Liza licked her lips. Poor girl, Jesse wasn't available for her consumption.

"Married," Bailey said.

Liza scowled. "Are you sure? What about divorce? It happens, y'know."

"Married."

Liza pouted briefly. "What about the one before him? I swear your eyeballs nearly popped out of your head when he looked at you."

"So you really did see him?" Bailey asked.

"Everyone did, and come to think of it," Liza said, looking thoughtful, "he looked kinda familiar. Pretty good, huh? I'm getting so I can tell them apart."

"Yeah. Pretty good." Bailey took another look at the stage, and was raked with frustration. She didn't know what kind of game security guy was playing, but she didn't like it one little bit.

"What's his name?"

Bailey gave Liza a nervous look. "Who?"

Liza narrowed her eyes suspiciously. "What do you mean 'who?' *Him.*"

"I'm not sure." And that was the God's honest truth. At that moment, Bailey couldn't even remember her *own* name.

"You sure looked at him like you knew him."

"Well, I don't." Bailey grabbed Liza by the arm and led her through the screaming crowd. "Let's go play some slots," she said, hoping to steer Liza's interest elsewhere.

They returned to Oasis where Liza's winning streak continued, and by two A.M., she'd managed to win back everything she'd lost and was satisfied to finally call it a day.

"You go ahead," Bailey said. "I want to take another look at my new car."

"So you've decided to take it? You do realize it won't fit in the cargo compartment on the airplane?"

"Of course. I'll drive it home," Bailey said. She immediately had the sensation of sweat beading up on her neck.

"Yeah. Okay, that I'd like to see."

"We could take turns driving. How hard could it be? We could get a map . . ." The more Bailey thought about it the queasier she felt. God, she *was* turning into her mother.

She and Liza parted at the elevator and Bailey took a sharp turn around a corner. She saw stars just before everything went dark. When the lights came back on, she was staring into the most perfect pair of blue eyes, and they were attached to a vision in white.

Chapter Six

"Elvis?" Bailey whispered. She reached out and touched a lock of dark hair.

"Ah, close enough, honey," the vision said. He had both his arms around her and his heart beat solidly against her chest.

"How?" She squeezed her eyes shut for a few seconds, expecting him to disappear just as he had earlier, but he didn't. His arms were still firmly around her when she looked again.

"Fate," he said with a grin.

Fate? Bailey's head suddenly cleared. *"You."* She pushed off him and stepped back, out of touching range. Her eyes narrowed as she looked him up and down. "Is this supposed to be funny? Why are you dressed like that? Are you and my friend Liza in cahoots?"

"Ah, yeah," Carter said. He grinned and took her by the arm, pulling her gently to one side, out of the path of foot traffic. "You're not making any sense. We should find somewhere for you to sit down. You might have a concussion."

"You haven't answered me. Why are you dressed like that?"

Carter spread both hands. "What you see is what you get." And then he smiled a perfect crooked smile.

Bailey lifted her chin. "I don't know about that. Yesterday you claimed you were head of security . . . now you're doing some wannabe Elvis thing—and poorly, I might add."

Carter laughed. "By the way you were watching me tonight, I'd say my performance was perfect."

Bailey frowned and crossed her arms. "That shows how much you know." Carter grinned and she knew why. "So you've seen me naked. That certainly doesn't mean you *know* me."

He grinned some more. "Why don't you just admit it, you liked what you heard."

Bailey found his grin annoying, but at the same time, it made her insides feel all mushy and gushy, and she wanted him to keep on doing whatever it was he was doing. He was probably used to that reaction from women, though, and she certainly wasn't about to let him think that she, too, had fallen victim to his charms—even if it was true. "Maybe you can sing—a little," she said.

"That's a start. Now, let's go somewhere and we'll talk." Security guy took her hand and led her across an acre of casino floor to a place called Pure. Pure play, as far as Bailey could see. She wondered what he had in mind bringing her here. He'd said he was taking her somewhere where they could talk, but the music was so loud, she didn't see how that would happen.

They squeezed through a small area at the back of the club that was packed with young people who all looked like they belonged on the front of *GQ* and *Vogue*, until they came to a staircase. A large man in a dark suit stood at the bottom, arms folded in front of him. He smiled as they approached. Carter leaned in to him, said something that Bailey couldn't hear, and the man smiled again and slapped Carter on the back, before unhooking the rope to allow them access to the stairs.

Carter led her up the stairs, still holding her hand tight, and Bailey was beginning to think she *did* have a concussion, letting a strange man take her up a dark staircase. Either that or she was having a very interesting dream, which she hoped wouldn't end until she at least got to see what was at the top.

The sky opened above them, and a warm breeze whipped through Bailey's hair. She felt free, on top of the world. She could see the entire Strip in all its glory. Blinking colored lights, giant screens flashing the hottest acts in Vegas, and hordes of people moving down each side of the Boulevard.

She took in a deep breath of smoke-free air. She could almost feel the toxins being expelled from her lungs.

"You okay?" Carter asked in a loud voice. He pushed a lock of her hair gently from her face.

And to think she'd been worried.

Bailey nodded and he led her over to a table near the rail that had a RESERVED sign on it. It was separated from all the other tables by plenty of space and tall tropical plants, and it had an almost intimate feel—if it hadn't been for the volume of the music, that is.

"So you were expected here tonight?" Bailey said. She nodded at the RESERVED sign.

They sat and Carter scooted his chair close to hers so they could hear each other without having to shout.

"You could say that," Carter said.

The summer sky, candlelight flickering gently in the breeze, a table set away from prying eyes . . . This was a place a man brought a woman for a night of seduction. Just who had he intended to bring here tonight? she wondered. Certainly not her. He couldn't possibly have known they'd run into each other. Literally.

Unless he'd planned it.

Bailey swallowed. What if he *had?* A quick shiver skittered up her back. She was sitting at a table in a strange place with a strange man who'd seen her naked. What was she thinking?

Carter allowed his leg to rest gently against hers. Her heart thumped. She looked at him and tried to glean as much information as possible about him from his face. He wasn't giving anything away. But neither was she. She'd lied to him. He wasn't just *okay.* As an Elvis impersonator, he was perfect with a capital "E." So perfect, in fact, that it'd be very easy to forget about his alter ego, security guy.

Security guy bordered on scary, in a cozy, seductive sort of way. She suspected that he was the half who had the super powers, the ones he used to gain power over women. Obviously he'd used them on her and that was how he'd gotten her to come to this place with him.

Carter smiled gently, and Bailey turned her attention back to the bright lights on the Strip. It was probably best to keep her private thoughts to a minimum, in case he really did come equipped with super powers, such as mind reading.

Carter ordered her a martini without asking her preference and she sipped it to be polite. It'd been several hours since she'd eaten and she didn't want the alcohol to make a beeline for her brain.

"What can I do for you, honey?"

What *couldn't* he do for her? "For starters, you can answer a question."

"You have the general idea. I work security during the day; at night I work the stage."

"Not *that* question."

Carter raised an eyebrow.

"Why did you pretend not to know me when I won the car?"

The left side of Carter's mouth curved boyishly. "What happens in Vegas stays in Vegas, baby."

Bailey did a quick recall of their shower episode together. A few more sips of her martini and her brain might only function at half capacity, but right now, she was 90 percent sure that nothing had "happened" between them. "Excuse me?"

"You were embarrassed. I was trying to protect your honor. If I had acknowledged knowing you, it might've gotten even more embarrassing. You might've had to explain to your friend that we'd already met. Someone might've questioned your winning the car. I was sparing you any more discomfort."

"I was not—I have nothing to be embarrassed about." Bailey stared at a wet spot on the table. It was safer than looking at his blue eyes. His thigh rubbed against hers and her insides tumbled.

Carter's cell phone rang and he excused himself to answer it in private. Bailey gave a relieved sigh. She'd dreamed of a moment like this, and, now, here she was having a drink with the only man who'd ever made her feel like throwing up, and she didn't even have anything nice or witty to say.

Some of her Aunt Fiona's words of wisdom came to mind. "If a man makes you sick enough to puke, it must be real love."

Love? How ridiculous. She and Carter had just met. Bailey glanced over to where he was standing with his back to her. A gust of wind ruffled his hair, and God how she wanted to rush over, put her hands in it, smooth it back into place. She stifled a laugh. It was only the alcohol making her think such things. Security guy might have some very becoming qualities, but he also confused and infuriated her.

Nevertheless, her leg was getting lonely and she hoped that when he returned to the table, he'd let his thigh snuggle up to hers again. Although with his thigh pressed against hers, their legs just might get so hot, they'd ignite.

Bailey giggled. It had to be the alcohol. Why else would she be feeling like this? Whatever *this* was. She suspected it was pure lust. No doubt her Aunt Fiona would have even more words of wisdom. Like, "If he makes you want to strip and do it doggy style, it's lust. If he makes you want to throw away your birth control pills, it's love."

She took a large swallow of her martini. Security guy would make beautiful children.

Bailey sputtered at the thought. Good God, what was wrong with her? The last thing she needed was a man who made her gasp with fear. What she *needed* was a man who made her gasp from his kiss. She pushed aside her martini glass, and scooted her chair over, a safe distance away from Carter's.

Martinis were evil drinks. One little glass and she was a mess. Her libido was on full throttle, and she couldn't feel her legs. She knew she still had a lot of questions for security guy, but none of them were near the surface of her brain where she could gain access. One thing was clear, though. She and Carter had started out all wrong and if she wanted to find out if they shared a connection that went deeper than pleasures of the flesh, she had to try and make it right.

When Carter returned to the table, Bailey smiled and held out a hand. "Can we start over? I'm Bailey Ventura." *And I've been waiting to meet you my entire life.*

A smile lifted the corners of Carter's mouth and it reached clear to his eyes. He gathered her hand into his and Bailey's heart melted. "Happy to meet you, ma'am."

Ma'am. The boy at the grocery store called her ma'am and she always wanted to tell him she wasn't a ma'am. Not yet anyway. Maybe when she was fifty or sixty . . . but not yet. Still, having security guy call her "ma'am" made her feel all comfy inside, like warm apple pie.

"How long have you wanted to be Elvis?" she asked.

Carter laughed. "Ah," he said with a shrug. "I don't know that any of us want to *be* Elvis. All that fame and fortune . . . It'd be pretty hard to take. I've always been told I resemble him. I guess it was just a natural choice, living here in Vegas."

Bailey looked closely at his hair. Although a person could get a good dye job, she could tell his was naturally dark and that his sideburns were real, but the lip curl . . . that was something he'd definitely practiced to perfection.

"My parents listened to Elvis's music nearly every day," Carter continued. "When I first started singing, I did it simply to bug them, but after a while, the words began to sink in, mean something. Pretty soon, my parents were begging me to perform for them and all their friends. Even offered to pay me." Carter shrugged. "By then I was hooked. They didn't have to ask, or pay. I worked harder at learning Elvis's music than I did on my schoolwork."

Bailey smiled. Carter's security guy persona had completely disappeared and before her sat a man who was humble, yet confident. Boyish, yet sexy. A pretty darn good imitation of the King. Sometimes when she saw an Elvis impersonator who had no chance of living up to the King's image—if he shared no resemblance, or if he couldn't sing, or if he was doing it just to be funny— it made her angry in a sad sort of way.

Carter was not one of those impersonators. He was one that Elvis would surely give his stamp of approval, and that earned him big bonus points with her.

"So your plan to torture your parents backfired," Bailey said.

Carter grinned. "You could say it turned out to be a win-win situation."

That was for sure. Win-win-win, in fact. "Are you singing in the competition tomorrow night?"

He nodded. "Will you be there? The competition is stiff this year. I could use an extra fan in my corner." His leg still rested snugly against hers.

Bailey's heart did a little flip. "I don't think you'll need any help at all," she said. In her mind, he'd already won. Of course, it could've just been the alcohol running through her system, or that he smelled as good as he looked, but as far as she was concerned there were only a few others who might be capable of outsinging the man who was sitting next to her.

Quent Flagg for one. He'd be tough, especially now that he was a little older. Irv Cass was a dream, but he'd already had his share of big wins; perhaps he'd move over this time. Then there was Steve Sogura. With a voice so rich and pure, he was sure to be a huge threat. He'd already won the World Championship once and she figured he'd like to make it twice. He knew how to charm the audience, too, making sure to hand out plenty of sweat-soaked scarves. The women didn't care. They loved him sweat and all.

Bailey studied Carter's face. A man like him had to have at least one flaw. Something that would bug her enough to make her stop thinking the kind of thoughts that would only get her into trouble.

"If I don't win this year, I guess I'll stick with my day job." Carter's gaze moved around the room. "Security isn't so bad. As it is, I almost didn't make it into the show. I had to make a deal with a friend. I'll be singing in his place."

Deal? Bailey remembered the men in the stairwell. *They* were making a deal. Carter kept talking, and the more he talked, the more she was sure he'd been one of those men.

"I think your chances of winning are great. And so must your friend or he wouldn't have agreed to let you take his place."

They locked eyes and Bailey felt like he was trying to scan her brain. She stared back daring him to break through to her deepest thoughts. It was too much. She soon weakened and had to look away in order to regroup.

"You seem to think you know a lot about me," he finally said, a wave of seriousness squelching the twinkle in his eyes.

"Me and my friend were using the stairs yesterday, on account of the elevator going dead, and I think I saw you talking to someone."

Carter made a distinctive move to draw his thigh away from hers. "You were eavesdropping?"

Bailey felt like she was being accused of some kind of wrongdoing. If it was that big a deal that she'd overheard him, *he* was probably the wrongdoer. She lifted her chin. "Not intentionally. You weren't exactly whispering."

"You didn't make yourself known. Perhaps when you hear two people having a private conversation in a stairwell, you should go the other way. Folks have been killed for less in Las Vegas."

Chapter Seven

Bailey's mouth hung open for a long beat. "Are you threatening me?"

Carter resisted smiling. He'd learned a long time ago not to rile a woman any further when she was in the throes of indignation. "Relax. I'm simply giving you some good advice."

Bailey stood and Carter saw her press her fingertips to the table to steady herself. She wasn't used to drinking. He took a good look at her. He'd examined her driver's license when she'd won the car, and she was old enough, but with that pixie nose and those innocent wide eyes, she could easily pass for a minor. He doubted she'd ever had a martini in her life.

"I can help you to your room," he offered.

Her eyes smoldered like a slow burning fire and he knew what her answer was before she did. Of course, he'd done this on purpose. Gotten her drunk, so that she'd be vulnerable to his charms. Not such a bad idea, and although he'd been guilty of that very thing a time or two, this wasn't one of them.

"I don't need any help," Bailey said, pronouncing her words carefully. "And I'm certainly not going anywhere else with you. No telling where I'd end up." She waved an arm through the air and tipped to one side. Carter reached out to steady her, but she avoided his touch and reluctantly sat back down. "I'd like you to leave now, if you don't mind," she continued. "Anyway, my friend will be joining me in the casino soon."

"Right. Look, why don't you just let me help you to your room?" Carter stood and held out a hand, but she didn't take it. Smart woman. No telling where skin-to-skin contact between them might lead. Still, he wasn't about to leave her there alone, where someone could come along and take advantage of her.

He leaned toward her. "Swallow your pride," he said quietly, "and you'll never have to talk to me again." She looked at his hand like it was covered with open sores and then she picked up his glass and emptied it. Good for her. If she had to endure the death march with him to her room, she was darn well going to make it as painless as possible. He was liking her more every minute.

Bailey took his arm and Carter sucked in a breath when she pressed her lithe body against his for support. She did the careful walk thing in her high heels. He was impressed. He'd seen women have trouble keep their balance when they *hadn't* had too much to drink, and he couldn't imagine having to walk in those things while perched on his toes.

"Tell me, honey, what's your game, other than slots?" He smiled at his own question. Although it wasn't his intention—he just wanted to find something to talk about to steer his mind in some other direction than how nice her body felt next to his—it sounded like some lame pick-up line, but Bailey didn't seem to notice.

"I don't really gamble. My friend, Liza . . . she's the one who likes to play. She has an agreement with the slot machines. She puts in her money and some multiplication thing happens and the machine spits out even more."

"She ever win a car?"

Bailey did a little girly hiccup and she put a hand to her mouth with a giggle. "Nope. So, I guess that makes up for all the money I've lost."

"And then some, I'm sure," Carter said. He felt his body temperature and other things rise with every step they took. God, her body felt good next to his. The only cure for this pain would be a cool jet of water gushing fast and furious over the top of his head.

They got on the elevator and Bailey swayed to her left as the car began to move. Carter squeezed her body tight against his. He pushed the eleventh floor button and the doors hummed shut. She nestled comfortably into him and began to absentmindedly finger the jewels on his jumpsuit. Carter scolded himself for his thoughts. The words to "Devil in Disguise" ran through his mind, only this time the devil wasn't a woman.

No doubt about it, playing Elvis gave him a lot of power. Maybe too much. It was as if he had a secret weapon that forced women to do his bidding, whether they wanted to or not.

They made it to the fourth floor and her hand still rested on his chest. His heart thumped wildly. *Breathe in, breathe out, in, out.* She had a secret weapon, too, and she didn't even know it.

Bailey smiled up at him. "You okay?"

Carter nodded once without looking at her. "Perfect."

A man and a woman got in on the fifth floor and Bailey pointed a finger upward and said, "Beaming up." The couple grinned and stood over to one side.

Carter caught Bailey's reflection in the mirror that covered one wall of the elevator. Her hair was pulled up into a thick ponytail, making her look fresh and clean, more like a schoolgirl than a full-fledged woman, but the rest of her body betrayed that image. She had on a short skirt that shimmied when she walked, accentuating the full curve of her hips, and her legs . . . Could they be any longer? Her lips curved gently at the corners, in a perpetual smile—even when she was angry—that thoroughly enchanted him and made his stomach lurch. He could already tell, this gal was going to be a problem.

Carter looked at his own reflection. He wasn't sure *he* even liked what he saw—what could a nice girl like Bailey want with a guy like him? He'd seen a certain look in her eyes when he'd looked down at her from the stage and sang to her, one that he'd seen plenty of times—each and every time he looked down into an audience of women— but the way Bailey had looked back was different. It was as though she'd finally found something she'd lost.

He wanted to believe it was more than the fact that he looked, dressed, and sang like the King, but that might be too much to hope for seeing as she'd already made it clear she wasn't fond of his other half. No, she wasn't one of those nice girls who had the bad boy syndrome, a girl who'd gotten bored and was looking for a way, or a man, to temporarily spice up her life. And it was too damn bad. His lip curled slightly. He knew that role, and he played it very well.

Carter led Bailey down the hall to her room and waited while she stood there looking up at him like she expected something. Normally that *something* was a kiss, or more, but he didn't think *she* even knew what she wanted at that very moment. Clearly, they were both confused.

"Room key?" he finally prompted her.

His brunette came back from fantasy island or wherever it was that women went to when they had that starry look in their eyes. She rummaged around inside her bag for a minute and then stopped.

"Why'd you pick me out of that crowd and sing to me?"

Because you make me crazy with your little ponytail and your cute little mouth that any man would want to kiss. Not to mention, I've seen what's hiding beneath those clothes. "We have a history," he whispered in her ear. Her body was warm next to his, like burning embers, and she smelled good, even through the casino smoke—spicy, floral, powerful. He could only wonder how her mouth would taste. But that would have to wait for another time, when they were somewhere more private. Oasis had eyes everywhere and they frowned on dalliances with the winners of jackpots.

Bailey relaxed against him as though standing had become a chore, and her silky hair rested softly against his cheek. He felt himself grow hard and he knew he had to do something, now, before things got out of hand. He took her bag from her and she didn't object when he rummaged around inside it for her room key. He'd had a lot of experience escorting women back to their rooms, and helping them inside. It came with the job.

Bailey gazed up at Carter's face, his lips in particular. They were so close she could almost taste them. She felt a flush of color fill her cheeks, and a rush of something else filled all her private places. What was *wrong* with her? One moment she couldn't stand this man, and now . . . well, it had to be the alcohol, because right now her knees were weak from thinking about kissing him.

Something her Aunt Fiona had once told her came to mind. "A woman can tell a lot of things by a man's kiss. If his kiss doesn't make you want to go all the way to the end zone for a touchdown, move on."

Bailey wasn't going anywhere until she found out.

Carter smiled as though he could hear her thoughts. He leaned toward her and she felt another rush of some-thing that might even be described as fear, but it quickly changed to something more primitive.

Bailey closed her eyes, puckered her lips, balanced on her toes, and waited. And waited. The seconds ticked off, each one feeling like a minute, and she seriously consid-ered grabbing his rhinestone-studded collar and pulling him to her, but that would be too drastic a move. Elvis hadn't liked women who were overly forward.

Wait. What did she care what the real Elvis liked? This was security guy.

"Well?" Bailey said, opening her eyes. Carter raised an eyebrow. "Will you or won't you be kissing me?" Carter grinned and she fluttered her eyelids closed and tilted her lips upward once more.

Soft lips brushed over hers, with the barest of contact, and Bailey gasped when she felt her nipples contract. The hallway began to spin round and round and round, and she didn't think it was alcohol-related. Her eyes slipped open and she looked into the face of desire, or lust, or something equally inviting.

Carter's mouth continued moving along her cheek, making certain body parts hum, and just as it was getting real good, he suddenly stepped back.

Bailey whimpered as Carter took a deep breath. "Time to say goodnight."

Slam. Like hitting a brick wall. *Goodnight?* That didn't feel like "goodnight." That felt more like "Won't you invite me in for a drink?'" Or maybe, "I could sure use a cup of your complimentary coffee."

Bailey considered her options and had just about come to a decision when she heard the floor creak behind the door. Her womanly intuition sensed an ear pressed against it. Liza's ear. A few seconds later, the door opened a crack and a pair of green eyes peered out.

"I thought I heard heavy breathing out here," Liza said. Her eyes fixed on Carter.

"Uh, I'm a little busy out here," Bailey told her.

"I can see that. I'm just making sure everything is okay. This is Vegas after all."

Bailey did a mental eye roll. Liza lived in Seattle— downtown. It'd take a lot more than heavy breathing coming from the hallway to give her cause for concern.

Carter chuckled. "Bailey's safe. I was just seeing her back to the room." He nodded politely and told them both "goodnight."

Neither woman turned away until the elevator was humming downward.

"I almost had an orgasm just looking at him," Liza said.

"Uh-huh," Bailey muttered and pushed the door closed. She gave Liza a quick recap of the last two hours, leaving out the part when Carter made his subtle threat about people who eavesdropped.

Bailey quickly performed her get-ready-for-bed routine and was soon snuggled under the covers. After messing with the AC that morning, she'd finally gained some control over the temperature, and now the room was a perfect seventy-two. No pajamas for her; all she needed to wear to bed was a smile.

She lay in the dark with her skin tingling from Carter's touch. Not that there'd been anything sexual in the way he'd held her while he assisted her to her room, but he had kissed her when they arrived at the door. Sort of.

She smiled. It might have only been a simple whisper of a kiss, but it was enough to let her know it was going to be good when it *did* happen. Now she understood why women proclaimed they'd never again wash after being kissed by Elvis.

The soft steady rhythm of Liza's snoring and the faint buzz from the ice machine outside their room had her yawning in just a few minutes. And then she slept.

By morning, her body had purged all the effects of the evil martinis, but the whites of her eyes were having a hard time returning to normal. Bailey squinted into the mirror.

"That's why God made eyedrops," Liza said from the doorway. "Think of all the people who'd be out of work if no one ever tied one on. You're doing your part." She twisted off the plastic end of a Refresh ampule and handed it to Bailey.

Bailey tilted her head back and aimed. Five squeezes later, she'd managed to get one drop into her right eye. She positioned her face below her raised hand and tried for the left, but nothing came out. The ampule was dry.

"Under ordinary circumstances, one of these will last through three mornings." Liza twisted the top off another. "I only brought three, so you might want to make this one go further. Especially if you plan on going out and getting blottoed with hunk o' love again."

"I didn't *plan* on what happened last night. Like I told you, I just kind of ran into him and we ended up having drinks. Martinis. Take my word for it, they're evil."

Bailey held the ampule above her head and rolled her eyes back. After only three tries, she managed to get in one drop. She used a Kleenex to wipe the excess liquid from her face and handed the ampule back to Liza, and Liza demonstrated her proficiency by squeezing a drop with accurate precision into each eye.

"Show-off," Bailey said.

Someone knocked, and they both looked in the direction of the door, but neither one of them moved to answer it. If it was housekeeping, they'd just use their key and let themselves in. Another heavy pound got their attention.

"You expecting anybody? Room service perhaps?" Liza asked, her voice filled with the hope of a hungry woman.

Bailey opened the door and a man stood before her, hands clasped in front of him like he was her own personal butler.

A girl could dream.

"Mr. Davis requests the pleasure of your company." The man checked his watch. "Half an hour. His office. I'll wait out here." He stepped back from the door.

Bailey tried to recall anything from the night before

that might have sounded like a breakfast invitation. Nothing came to mind. "Uh . . ."

"Uh, nothing. Don't even think about it," Liza broke in. "Let's not forget yesterday. You were supposed to meet me and I didn't see you for nearly two hours."

And here she'd thought Liza hadn't even noticed her absence. Go figure.

The man smiled, his eyes glinting with knowing amusement, and Bailey felt her face fill with color. She *knew* it. Security guy *did* have a tape of the shower incident and he'd shared it with the entire hotel staff. She crossed her arms over her fully clothed chest. "I have plans this morning. Tell Mr. Davis perhaps we'll run into each other later."

The man gave her a chilly look. Probably it wasn't wise to refuse a request from a man wearing a funeral suit.

"You sure, Miss?"

Maybe. No. Bailey raised a finger to her mouth, where she could still feel Carter's lips. She wouldn't mind investigating his Elvis impersonator abilities further, but Liza was her best friend and she wasn't going to desert her again. Yet.

"Absolutely."

Chapter Eight

Carter sat in a black leather chair in front of a half-dozen monitors, all with different views from inside the casino flashing across their screens. The floor was abuzz, but nevertheless boring. Nothing eventful going on that would keep him entertained, or awake. His head bobbed and then jerked back up. He ran a hand roughly through his hair, scrubbing it back and forth, and his gaze caught the monitor that covered carousel four, where the red T-Bird sat. He visualized Bailey behind its wheel, her hair flowing in the hot desert breeze. That is, if she decided to take it.

The money or the car? What would a gal like her do? Forty thousand dollars was a lot of money for a young woman to pass up. Hell, it was a lot of money for anyone to pass up, but the car, sitting there under the glow of the casino lights, was something that would last a lot longer than some crumpled bills that'd be gone after a few spending sprees. Plus, there was the story of how she came to own it. He smiled, wondering if any part of the telling of that story would include him.

The story alone was reason enough to keep the car. With the odds of winning a car on the slots being approximately one in ninety million, his brunette had pulled off somewhat of a miracle. But, of course, this was

Las Vegas, land where miracles happened and dreams were fulfilled, on a daily basis.

If *he* had any say, she would indeed take the car, and that meant he'd need to have the detail crew drive it off the floor and get it all cleaned up before some other lucky soul came along and won it. Not such an absurd idea, considering that carousel four was the winningest carousel in any Las Vegas casino.

Then he'd have to explain that they could have a car just like it—maybe in a different color—but not that particular one. People were funny about things like that. Never mind that they'd just won something worth fifty grand; they wanted what sat right there in front of them.

Carter went over to a cherry wood credenza and poured his third cup of coffee for the morning. He returned to his chair and propped a foot on the window sill, spent a long minute thinking about the way Bailey's hair smelled, the way her skin felt. He shook his head. Speaking of dreams . . . Then he chuckled, remembering the way she'd puckered her lips waiting for him to kiss her. God, how he'd wanted to oblige, but the instant he'd touched her lips and felt her heart beating against his chest, something had told him to back off.

Under normal circumstances, if *she'd* been normal, he'd have taken that beating heart and played with it for a while before giving it back. But for reasons he couldn't figure, he didn't want her to become just another notch in his rhinestone studded belt. But it damn sure didn't mean he'd back off next time.

Carter shook his head and chided himself. "You're either getting soft or you're losing your mind."

He leaned back in his chair and clasped his hands behind his head. Women and Elvis. What magic had that man possessed that made women want to give themselves, without question, to him? Hell, even the Queen mother would have raised her silk gown and allowed

Elvis to touch her untouchable foot. If only that magic could be captured and manufactured—that's when men would truly rule the world.

The sound of footsteps in the doorway brought a smile to his lips, and he swiveled his chair around. "Good morning, Ms.—"

But it wasn't Bailey. It was Mike Shur from the control room.

"Sorry, Boss. She wouldn't come. Something about already having plans. She said she'd see you later—maybe."

Carter raised an eyebrow. "Maybe?"

Mike shrugged and walked away.

Maybe? Sure she'd acted offended when he'd scolded her about eavesdropping, but he thought they'd gotten past that. She was probably embarrassed. She'd had a drink, probably thought she'd acted improper. He replayed the previous evening over in his mind. Yeah, she was just embarrassed.

Carter looked back over at the T-Bird on the monitor and smiled. Well, she couldn't avoid him forever.

He finished his cup of coffee, filed a couple of expense reports, and was contemplating shutting the privacy screens so he could kick back in his chair for a few minutes, when a shape filled the doorway.

"A good day for living, don't you think?" a voice said.

The voice belonged to a man in his early fifties. He was smiling, but it was more like a dog baring his overabundant teeth.

Carter felt his own lip curl into a snarl. He wouldn't mind relieving the man of a few of those teeth.

Frank Zoopa. Powerful, wealthy, smarmy casino owner. The man was an insult to Las Vegas gaming, always had his hand in questionable deals that were just legal enough to slide past the Gaming Commission. He had no reason to pay Carter a visit, other than to piss him off. That was okay. Zoopa was pissed off, too. And if Carter had his way, Zoopa would stay pissed off. He'd never own Carter the way he'd owned Carter's parents.

The left side of Zoopa's suit bulged slightly, and the odds were pretty good it wasn't a Clive Cussler novel he had inside there.

Carter sat forward in his chair. "Frank." He slid a hand under his desk top and pushed a button, releasing the lock on the middle drawer—just for insurance, and to put them on even ground. The click was barely audible, but he thought he saw his visitor blink. "What brings you out of your lair?"

"I'm lookin' for Twinkie," Zoopa said. He sank into the chair opposite Carter's desk.

"Haven't seen her," Carter said. "She doesn't work here." His molars ground until he thought they'd break.

Zoopa grinned. "I'm having an intimate get-together tonight—a little party—and I'd like Twinkie to work it."

Carter scoffed. "Work it? What exactly does that mean?"

"C'mon, Carter. You know how it is. I need her to serve drinks, keep some Whales happy." Frank paused and then changed the subject. "How're things goin' over here? How's your little act?"

The question was merely a dig, Zoopa didn't care about anyone but himself, but Carter wasn't about to give him the satisfaction of knowing he'd hit a sore spot. Besides, Frank knew everything that was going on, even before whomever it concerned knew.

"I'll tell Twinkie you're looking for her," Carter said.

Zoopa grunted in acknowledgment. "About tonight . . . why don't you join us? It'll be interesting. You might even enjoy yourself."

An intimate get-together at Zoopa's? That could mean anything from a small dinner party to a gathering of two hundred or more. Indeed, it might be interesting, but never enjoyable. Still, it was always smart to know what certain people were up to, so long as he kept them at arm's length. The muscles in Carter's jaw tightened. "I'll be there."

"And you'll talk to Twinkie?"

"If I see her."

"Good, good. My house. Eight P.M. Dress for success."

Dressing for success meant only one thing. Zoopa had big plans and he intended to spill them to a bunch of important people.

"I always do," Carter said.

Zoopa glanced at the white jumpsuit draped over the back of a chair over in the corner. "Yeah," he said and turned. "Don't forget to talk to Twinkie."

"I got it," Carter told him, irritation edging into his voice. He didn't have attention deficit disorder, for crissakes.

He shifted uncomfortably in his chair, watching Zoopa leave the glass control cage. His office had heated up about ten degrees the instant Zoopa appeared, and Carter tugged at his collar to loosen his tie. The only place in the casino where the air-conditioning was lacking and it had to be *his* office. If they didn't fix it soon, he'd be sticking to his chair like a wad of gum. He rolled up his shirt sleeves, and dialed Twinkie's number. Seven rings later, he hung up.

"Damn it, Twinkie. Why can't you have an answering machine like the rest of the world?"

Carter tried to remember the last time he'd seen her. It was close to a week ago, over at the MGM. She was working, carrying a tray of drinks, and he was at one of the blackjack tables with a winning hand.

She'd looked frazzled, and they hadn't talked. It was best to leave her alone when she was frazzled, and anyway, she'd known he was there if she needed him. He'd figured she'd probably had one drunk too many groping at her in the short skirt and revealing top that served as her work uniform, and was just plain fed up. Poor schmucks. A guy could lose a hand—or worse.

A frown creased Carter's brow. If she was so busy at work that she hadn't had time to keep in touch, that was fine, but still, it was unusual for an entire week to go by without them having some kind of contact. He pondered another possibility. That one wasn't fine.

Carter blew out a breath and tried to reset his frame of mind. Twinkie was a big girl. She had a right to live her life the way she saw fit. He thought about that for another minute. *The hell she did.* The way she lived her life was no good, and he was going to see to it that it changed—the sooner the better.

Bailey talked to herself the entire ride up in the elevator to Carter's office, just as she'd talked to herself all during breakfast and for the last hour while Liza played the slots, and she still hadn't been able to decide if she wanted the car or the money. And of course, that's why Carter wanted to see her. What other reason could there be?

As the car moved upward, she waffled back and forth with her decision. To be able to go out to her driveway every morning and see that beautiful car would be like having a dream that she never woke up from. But the money, well, it was enough to get her out of debt and then some.

Bailey put a finger to her lips, pondering her choices. Money . . . car . . . voucher . . . Then she pondered the night before with Carter. *Stop it!* she told herself. She shook security guy's image from her head. She couldn't let the sound of a man's voice influence her choice. What about his lips brushing across her lips? Could she let that influence her?

Bailey sighed. Maybe.

The elevator doors opened, and she stepped out onto

a cloud of carpet. Thick and plush, it surrounded her feet and curled around her toes and she was tempted to kick off her shoes. Last night, she might have. But then, last night, she might have done a lot of things.

Her footsteps were silent as she moved down the hallway. She came to a big room, enclosed by walls of glass, and it made her think of her first encounter with Carter. That was reason enough to turn and run the other way.

Too late. A man inside the glass room saw her, the same man who'd come to her room that morning. He nodded her in with a smile, and then directed her with another nod to Carter's door, which was open a crack.

She peeked inside. Carter looked disheveled. He had on a suit, but he'd taken off his suit coat and his shirt sleeves were rolled up. His tie—red, for power—hung loose about his neck, like he'd already had a rough day. She recalled Carter's warning about eavesdropping getting people killed, and a chill swept across the back of her neck. She certainly didn't want to be accused of that again.

Bailey pushed open the door, but Carter didn't look her way. His attention was focused on a cluster of monitors that took up one side of his office. She took a quick glance around his office, and was surprised to see that it was clean and orderly.

Bailey glanced over at the monitors and saw that her car was on one of them. Even in black and white, it was stunning. And it was hers! *Wow.* She still couldn't believe it.

She cleared her throat. "You sent for me?"

Carter swiveled his chair around and greeted her with a big smile. He got up and came over to her and Bailey breathed in the scent of his morning shower. Dial soap, with aloe. Same as she used. He dipped his head to kiss her cheek and her legs went all spongy. If he went any further, started nibbling on her neck maybe, she didn't know what she'd do.

He didn't. Instead, he reached up and pulled her hair band from her hair.

Bailey could feel her bottom lip tremble.

"Coffee?" he offered. "It'll warm you up, though I don't know how you could be cold in here." He reached up and pulled his tie from around his neck and tossed it onto his desk. Then he unbuttoned the two top buttons of his shirt.

A soft breath escaped Bailey's lips. "Yes, I will. I do," she whispered.

"Pardon?"

Bailey blinked. Hard. "Coffee. I need coffee."

"One sugar or two?"

How about a dozen? Kisses, that is. Bailey put a hand to her forehead. "Maybe something cold might be better."

Carter raised an eyebrow. "You okay?"

"You kept me up so late." She gave him an accusatory look. "Got me intoxicated." *Almost had your way with me.* Bailey propped her hands on her hips and did a pretty good job of feigning indignation.

The corners of Carter's mouth twitched. "Guess I should be ashamed of myself. Let me see if I've got anything cold in here." He stepped away from her and walked over to a small refrigerator. "You really aren't supposed to be in here, you know," he said, pulling out a single-serving orange juice, "without an escort anyway. I only make special exceptions." He smiled and chuckled lightly as he handed the juice to her.

He was toying with her. Bailey looked up and fluttered her lashes just once. "I was careful to make sure I wasn't followed."

"You refused to come up here with Mike," Carter said, nodding toward the man outside the window. "How did you know where to find me?"

Bailey shrugged. "You're security guy. I went through the door marked Security."

"And no one stopped you?"

She shook her head. "I know enough to wait until the coast is clear."

Carter laughed. His eyes twinkled with amusement. He took a seat behind his desk and studied her. Of course, she had a different scenario running through her mind. He'd have held out a hand to her, called her over . . .

"Come on over here, honey." The left side of Carter's lip curled into a boyish grin.

His sudden change to Elvis mode threw Bailey into a tailspin. How could she resist an invitation like that? She set her orange juice on the corner of his desk and sashayed toward him. When she got within reach, he grabbed her by the waist and pulled her onto his lap.

She started to gasp, but his mouth was on hers before she could get it out. Oh, God, there it was. That tingly sensation, and it was headed straight for her goodies. She did her best to ignore it, but by the time Carter finished with her lips, every part of her was screaming, "I'm yours."

"Oh, my," Bailey whispered, mentally fanning herself. "Something wrong?"

They eyed each other for a minute, until finally, she tore her gaze free from his. She mentally slipped off his lap. "I need to go." She didn't know where she was "going" to, but she knew it had to be out of security guy's office. Being near him made clear thinking nearly impossible.

It'd been far too easy, them meeting her first day in town, him being so handsome, so talented—so dangerous. Did she really want to settle for the first Elvis impersonator who came along? Moreover, did she want to become involved with a man who made her pulse race from something that closely resembled fear?

Carter stood and reached for her. Placing one hand

firmly on the small of her back, he pulled her close and squeezed her so tight, she squeaked. He traced a finger along her neck. "Leaving so soon? You just got here. Wouldn't you like to finish your juice?"

Gulp.

Bailey nodded her head, and then shook it.

Carter released her and leaned back against the edge of his desk. "Is that a *maybe?*"

Bailey was helpless. He was using some kind of super security guy power to manipulate her brain. Her imagination was running amok, thinking about all the other powers he might have. She felt her gaze being drawn to his chest, to his waist, to his . . . Bailey heard a whimper. Hers.

"I *really* need to go," she said on a breath. She spun around and rushed out of Carter's office. She didn't take another breath until she was safely on the elevator, leaning up against the wall for support.

She had to do something to take her mind off security guy. Anything. Play the slots, go shopping, take a cold shower. *No.* No shower.

She quickly found Liza, and a half hour later, they were poolside working on their tans. Everything was fine—soft music overhead, no kids running around, enough breeze to keep her comfortable—then *he* showed up.

There *he* was, over on the other side of the pool talking to one of the poolside cocktail waitresses. Bailey groaned and closed her eyes. She did her best to ignore the sound of his voice and, eventually, he went away.

After a couple of hours, she and Liza went inside and got cleaned up, then they went back down to the casino where they settled into a couple of chairs for a long session at a pair of Double Double Diamond machines. Ten credits in, Bailey heard a *ding, ding, ding* sound. She looked over and saw a blinking white light, and a few minutes later, Carter arrived to congratulate the winner.

This was not going to work. If she was going to make

the right decision as far as the car was concerned, she needed to forget about that man. *Right.* The only way she saw that happening was if she went somewhere where she could be sure not to run into him. Away from the Strip would be good, where the air was clear, where the toxins from cigarettes didn't clog her brain, where he wasn't around every corner.

"I need to take a break," Bailey told Liza.

Liza looked at her watch. "It's early. How could you already need a break?"

"I need to get out of town. Let's take a drive out to Lake Las Vegas."

Liza gave her a hard look.

"Don't worry. They've got slot machines out there."

"Yes, I know. I've been there. They've also got slot machines right here. Like this one, for instance. In case you haven't noticed, I'm up five hundred forty-two credits."

Bailey glanced over at the jackpot winner. Carter was still there. The jackpot winner handed him something. His i.d., she supposed.

"I think you need something more than a drive in the desert," Liza said. She glanced in Carter's direction and he looked their way and smiled. "Why are you trying to avoid him? Isn't he the reason you're here?"

"He scares me," Bailey said, biting her lip.

"And you're scaring *me.* For God's sake, girl, go get him. Either that, or cross him off your list."

"All right. I'll go without you," Bailey said, sliding off her chair.

Liza tossed her head back and laughed.

"What?"

"Sit down. You and I both know you're not going anywhere. Not without a driver." Liza pushed Max Credit and got three blue bars, another sixty credits.

"I can drive myself."

Liza looked at her and gave her a "c'mon" look. "I think the water here is getting to you. We're not in Coupeville."

"You think I can't drive myself?"

"Nope." Liza pushed the Max Credit button again. Another thirty credits.

Bailey's lips drew into a thin line. She glanced over at Carter. He saw her and gave her a quiet nod. "We'll just see about that."

Liza didn't even look up when she walked away. She was just going to let her go off into the desert alone. By herself. Well, she'd show her. She could drive if she really wanted to. Bailey felt a moment of anxiety, and she looked over her shoulder. Liza still had her eyes focused on the reels in a determined effort to win a jackpot.

"Fine," Bailey muttered. She steeled herself, and kept walking, all the way to the front desk, where they gave her a map and pointed out the black line that connected the Strip to Lake Las Vegas. A whole lot of sand filled the space between the two. If she allowed her imagination to run wild, she could almost see the hundreds of unmarked graves that lay beneath all that sand. If something happened and she never made it back, Liza would only have herself to blame.

She made a quick trip up to the room and tossed some things into her handbag that she thought might be important for a girl to have on hand while driving alone in the desert—two bottles of water, a tube of SPF lipgloss, and some blister pads for her feet, in case she ran out of gas and had to do some walking.

A much bigger purse would have been appropriate, too. Something that would hold a large gun, but the best she could come up with was a couple rolls of quarters that would pack a small wallop should she need to use her purse as a weapon against desert creatures.

Chapter Nine

Carter finished his shift, then went over to the MGM to look for Twinkie. He didn't know if Zoopa had found her yet, and he didn't care, since he planned to advise her not to do Zoopa's party, anyway.

She wasn't on the floor, and one of the other cocktail waitresses told him she hadn't been at work for a couple of days. He supposed he should feel good that she wasn't just avoiding *him,* but he didn't. He was mad as hell, and she'd be lucky if he didn't wring her skinny neck when he did find her.

He got on the elevator and pushed eight. The MGM provided a room to some of its valued employees who had been there for at least a year, so that they could just go up to bed when they got off work late at night. Carter hoped that was where he'd find Twinkie, but if she wasn't at work, it was also unlikely she was in her room.

The elevator made one stop, and three young men who were typical first-timers in Las Vegas stepped inside. Taking a much educated guess, Carter figured they were in town on a bachelor's excursion, and it was clear that one of them had already had a real good time. They got off on the same floor as Carter, and Carter walked behind them as the young drunk's buddies helped him down the hall.

Most likely they were just depositing him into their room before they headed out for some more *fun*. Good friends, good times.

Carter stopped outside Twinkie's door and paused, listening. No light showed under the door and he couldn't hear anything inside. He knocked anyway. She didn't answer.

"Damn female," Carter said under his breath, giving her door one last pound.

He looked at his watch. Zoopa's party was at eight and it was almost six. He had enough time to make one more stop. Twinkie had another place she occasionally called home. A place where she holed up when life got the better of her. Carter let out a heavy breath. Like she was the only one who got tired. Hell, he was tired right now. He'd like to take a few days off, sit in front of his new, big screen TV and catch up on some episodes of *Charlie's Angels,* or some other show that didn't require any thinking.

Vegas had a way of doing that to a person. It came with the territory. Why the hell Twinkie always felt like she had to take a leave of absence was beyond him. And why she couldn't even answer her phone was a mystery he'd never figure out—and was probably better off not trying. Odds were, too, if he showed up at her door, she wouldn't answer it. It was all Twinkie's world and nothing could get through to her when she wanted to recharge. Carter suspected she had some kind of disorder, like major PMS, or maybe even something more serious, but whenever he said anything to her, she always laughed him off and told him to basically go screw himself.

That was fine. But to leave work and simply not show up for a few days, without explanation, was not the way to handle too many gropers and drunks. A thousand women stood in line waiting for her job and if she wanted to keep it, she'd better suck it up. The drunks were never going to change, and it would be a cold day in hell before the casinos would stop serving alcohol.

Carter took the elevator down to the garage and got into a silver Porsche. He stuck the key into the ignition. "Twinkie Martinson," he said as the car's engine purred to life. "What are you doin', girl?"

He motored out of the garage and turned left onto Las Vegas Boulevard. Forty minutes later he pulled into the driveway of a small, brown stucco house. The grass had turned to dust long ago, but on the front stoop sat a potted cactus that was thriving in the hot Nevada sun, adding the only touch of color to the otherwise drab yard.

The only thing that distinguished Twinkie's house from the other houses on the block was the hot pink curtains over the windows. That was Twinkie. Hot and flashy. And it usually brought her nothing but trouble.

Carter looked both ways, up and down the street, before leaving the comfort of his air-conditioned car. A black Jag—perhaps a rental—was parked alongside the curb. Other than that, the street was bare. Not even a stray dog, which wasn't so unusual in this heat. Every creature in Vegas sought shelter by nine A.M. on a day like today.

Carter opened his car door and was hit with a blast so hot and thick he could see it swirling in the atmosphere. It made him feel like if he moved too fast, he might spontaneously combust.

The neighborhood was quiet. The day still. Like a prelude to something unimaginable. It made the hair stand up on the back of his neck. He frowned and shook off the feeling. His ears were simply too accustomed to hearing the noise and commotion inside the casinos.

Carter moved quickly over the baking asphalt to the front door, but even so, the soles of his shoes felt like they were sticky with hot tar. He pulled a key out of his pocket and used it to get inside.

"Hey. You home?" he called out. His question was met with the same dead silence he'd encountered outside. Carter felt all his shoulder muscles tense. Unease rested heavy on his chest, and his hand automatically reached up to feel for the bulk of his .44.

He dropped the key onto a small table at the end of a tan sofa, and stepped into the kitchen. A glass sat on the counter, and it still had ice in the bottom. He picked it up and smelled it. Bourbon. The good stuff. And judging by the degree of ice melt, the drinker hadn't gone far.

Carter glanced out the kitchen window that overlooked Twinkie's small backyard. Most of the view was obstructed by sheets and clothing hanging from a line. The window was open a few inches, allowing the sweet flowery fragrance of fabric softener to waft in. It reminded him of a time not so long ago, when he and his ex-wife had rolled in sheets that were perfumed with a similar scent.

A noise behind Carter made him spin around, his gun drawn.

He immediately felt foolish as he stared down at an orange tabby rolling around like a fat powder puff at his feet on the linoleum. Romeo. The cat had a wad of paper between his front paws and was kicking at it playfully with his hind feet. "Damn cat," he said affectionately, reaching down to scratch the cat's belly. Romeo immediately turned his attention away from the wad of paper, and instead focused on Carter's hand. In an instant, the cat's fangs were sunk into Carter's flesh.

"*Hey*," Carter yelled, snatching his hand away. "Damn cat."

He started to slip his gun back into its holster, but he heard sounds coming from the back of the house. Moving quietly down the hall, Carter paused just before each open door and took a quick look inside. He finally reached the door at the end of the hall—the only one that was closed—and he didn't have to wait for long before he heard a woman's voice.

Twinkie's.

Carter smiled and brought his foot up, slamming the door open with a loud crash.

A woman's shriek filled the small house, and if the neighbors had any sense, they were calling the police at that very moment. When the shrieking stopped, the only sound that remained was that of the splintered door swinging gently by its frame.

"*Damn*," a man with too much body fat said from the doorway of the adjoining bathroom. He had a bottle of Listerine in one hand, and was reaching for a gun on the nightstand with the other. All he had on was a towel, but it was probably more than his bed partner had on. Carter didn't even want to speculate. She had a sheet drawn up tight around her chest, covering most of her, and a tousled mound of blond hair hung down around her shoulders, covering what remained.

Carter smiled. "How's it going, Twinkie?"

A large breath escaped the blonde's lips, and she glared wild-eyed at Carter. The overweight man decided he didn't need his gun, and he moved back into the bathroom, leaving the door open.

"Son of a bitch, Carter!" Twinkie said. "You'll give me gray hair. Look what you did to my door! For future reference, there's no lock on it." She waggled a finger at the door. "You could've simply turned the knob."

The man took a swig of mouthwash, swished it around for a few seconds, and then swallowed it.

Carter gave him a narrow look. "That might've ruined the element of surprise. Why the hell didn't you answer the phone when I called? Or, how about a few minutes ago, when I yelled to see if anyone was home?"

Twinkie nodded toward the man. "He suggested otherwise."

Anger swelled in Carter. He considered plugging the man, but he at least had *some* sense, unlike the woman in the bed. "You going to introduce us?"

"No. You can't just come in here whenever you like and get all up in my business."

"You gave me a key," Carter said. "I figure that's an open invitation. We need to talk." Then he turned to the man. "Put on some clothes and get the hell out of here."

Twinkie drew her knees to her chest and reached over to the nightstand for a cigarette. The man lit one for her and started to get into the bed.

Carter stared at him for a long second. Maybe plugging the guy wasn't such a bad idea, after all. "You're not seriously thinking about climbing into bed with her, right in front of me, are you?"

The man paused, and he and Carter did a manly stare-down, until the man finally withdrew his leg from the bed. He disappeared into the bathroom and shut the door without a word.

Twinkie rolled her eyes. "Thanks, Carter. Now who's going to fix my door? Turn around," she said and did a twirly thing with her hand. Carter looked away while she slipped into a shimmery blue robe.

"How about Zoopa? It's my guess he's got something to do with you being here with that guy."

Twinkie shrugged, and took a long drag from her cigarette. "It's my job to entertain an occasional Whale."

The man came out of the bathroom. "Frank's going to hear about this," he said, looking from Carter to Twinkie.

Carter glared at the man. "You have one minute to get your fat ass the hell outta here."

As soon as they heard the front door slam, Twinkie laughed. "What the hell is wrong with you? You know Frank is going to blow a blood vessel, don't you?" She chuckled. "Not that I give a rat's ass."

"You weren't really going to sleep with that guy, were you?"

"No. I was going to give him a massage. You haven't spent one day with me in the last month. How are you going to come here and tell me what to do?"

Carter gave her a long look. "I have a job. Two if you count me playing Elvis. I can't watch you every minute. Why can't you make things easier on both of us and behave yourself?"

Twinkie scoffed. "Look who's talking." Her face softened and she brushed her hand gently along his chin. "You'll make a wonderful dad some day. God help that child if she's a girl."

"God help *me*," Carter said. "Anyway, that's a road I'll probably never travel, seeing as I don't plan on ever getting married again."

"Life is complicated. Things happen."

Carter and Twinkie were both quiet. He finally gave a nod, not necessarily one of agreement.

"Drink?" Twinkie asked. She stubbed out her cigarette and went to the kitchen. Carter followed.

"I'm good." He forgot his frustration with Twinkie for a minute as he thought about the previous evening with Bailey. "I had a few too many last night, and I imagine I'll have enough at Zoopa's party."

"So that's why you're all dressed up," Twinkie said. "I thought maybe you were going to a funeral. There's word going around you're not going to be allowed in the competition this year." Twinkie shook her head and made a *tsk, tsk* sound. "What a shame. All those poor women who'll come to see you in that jumpsuit, and to hear you sing . . . why, it'll break their little old hearts." She leaned against the counter and took a long drink of scotch.

"I've taken care of that little problem," Carter said, one side of his mouth notching up.

"Obviously. That's why you have the time to come here and knock down my bedroom door."

Carter huffed. "It's better than knocking you down."

Twinkie took a drag off her new, freshly lit cigarette and shrugged. "You don't know everything."

"I know that SOB wants you to work his party tonight."

Twinkie nodded. "I got the invite. So if all you wanted was to come here and harass me, you can save it. I need to get going."

Carter stared at her thoughtfully. "If you let me, I'll get you out of Zoopa's hold. Give me some time and everything'll work out fine."

Twinkie's eyes narrowed. "What do you think you're gonna do? Pull your little gun on him and tell him to get out of Vegas?"

"First, my gun isn't little. . . ." Carter didn't bother responding any further. At this point, it wouldn't matter what he said. On a day when the mercury rose past a hundred, Zoopa could tell her it was snowing, and she'd hold out a hand to catch a snowflake.

She ran a hand through her hair and Carter swore he was looking at a woman twice her age. Twenty-five years old and she wore enough life on her face for a fifty-year-old woman. It made him sad for her.

"Why don't you forget about tonight? Get out of here, just a day or two. Go over to my place. Hell, make it a mini vacation. I'll tell Zoopa you're sick."

"You know I can't do that, Carter."

"You can do anything you want."

"Ha! You got a stash of money layin' around so we can get out of town when Zoopa gets pissed and sics his dogs on us?" Twinkie wrapped an arm around his waist and walked him over to the door. "I could use a couple of days off, though." She blinked her clear, blue eyes innocently. "Maybe we'll talk later, after tonight's party, about me getting away from all this."

Carter smiled, but he wasn't buying it. He'd have to be a fool to think she'd give up that easy. She was a woman, after all.

Bailey eventually made it off the Strip and headed north on I-15 toward Lake Las Vegas. So far, so good. Her heartbeat was steady, she didn't have sweat rolling down her back, she could breathe. She was even enjoying the scenery.

Although she loved the green that blanketed Washington state, she marveled at the beauty of Nevada's brown hills. Nature, she decided, was beautiful no matter the color.

A little more than a half hour out of town, she passed a couple of large housing developments, and curiosity made her turn off at an area called Calico Ridge. The homes were a far cry from the image she'd had in her mind of desert living. Rather than small stucco hovels, the homes were large, their architectural design stunningly detailed, with sharp edges that rose high into the sky, only to soften into gentle curves and arches. The yards consisted of carefully planned rock gardens, and vegetation such as cacti, bird of paradise, jasmine. Anything that could withstand the heat grew in abundance.

Bailey let out a wistful breath. Her mom and Aunt Fiona would be envious of yards like these, where flowering plants could grow during the winter months, without getting drowned by daily rain showers.

She continued motoring through the neighborhood, keeping her eyes out for any FOR SALE signs, curious about how much it'd cost to live in all this warmth and sun. There were none. Evidently, everyone in Calico Ridge was perfectly happy. Or maybe the development was still too new for any residential turnover. Everything certainly looked brand-new, right down to the perfect little winding sidewalks that lined the streets. That's one thing she wished Coupeville had. It'd be nice to have something other than the shoulder of the road to walk her dogs on, especially at night.

The setting sun glowed orange, filling the sky with a heat-filled hue that reached up to meld with the coming darkness. A breeze kicked up, bringing with it a moment of relief from the heat. She'd have been happy to pull up a chair and sit there until dark—which was quickly approaching—but being out in the desert alone during the day was challenge enough.

The *dark?* What could she have been thinking? Driving at night wasn't something she'd planned on. She shivered at the thought of driving back to the hotel in pitch black.

Bailey got back on the highway. With dark closing in, the landscape had turned from brown to near black, and the rich brown hills were now just dark silhouettes against the sky. She scolded herself for letting unpleasant thoughts creep to the front of her mind. "That's it," she said. "No more watching scary movies within a month of going on vacation." At least not ones where people got chased on some deserted stretch of road, or got stranded in the middle of nowhere. Movies like *Identity* and *Joy Ride* might be fun to watch while curled up on the sofa in the arms of a big, strong man, but right now, she wished she'd never seen them.

No matter how she tried to steer her mind elsewhere—to fuzzy little kittens running through a meadow of clover, or her two dogs chasing tennis balls—the only images she was able to conjure up were ones that nightmares were made of.

Bailey glanced in her rearview mirror. No other cars in sight—for miles. No sense worrying about a ticket if she was the only one out here. She stepped on the gas pedal, trying to keep up with the approaching darkness.

The car responded well—for a minute—but just as it reached the fifty-mile-per-hour mark, it coughed and sputtered, and began to slow down. Bailey glanced at the speedometer. Forty . . . thirty . . . twenty . . .

"What?" she shouted, and she stomped harder on the gas pedal. More sputtering. She'd evidently rented a car that was coming down with a cold. What were the odds? Probably not as long as her winning a car, yet she'd somehow managed to do *that*.

A little red light blinked on in the dash—the temperature gauge—informing her the car was hot. *Duh.* Bailey suddenly remembered something her Uncle Rex had once told her about pulling over immediately if any red lights ever came on. Certainly, he hadn't meant if she was out in the desert. *Alone.*

Bailey pushed on the gas pedal, weighing her options: keep on driving and claim she hadn't noticed anything when the rental car agency questioned her about the car's demise, or pull over and hope highway bandits weren't cruising this particular part of the Nevada highway. The car made her decision for her by emitting one long sputter, and then a cough, as its engine died. She kept her foot off the brake and let the car roll as far as possible off to the side of the road. Probably if she let it sit and cool a while, she'd be able to get it started again and then she could at least drive it to the next populated area.

Bailey looked out over the terrain. What she could see of it, anyway. With no lights anywhere, black was the only thing in front of her. Miles and miles of thick black. She bit her lip. The next populated area could be hours away.

In a momentary lapse of good sense, she considered getting out and walking. But as she cracked open the door, she heard a strange sound, and an involuntary arm jerk pulled it back closed. If night marauders didn't get her, the lizards, snakes, and God knew what other creatures that dwelled in the desert would. Better to stay in the car and wait.

Night quickly closed in, surrounding her in a cold blanket of fear. Bailey punched the door lock button. If there was one thing she'd learned from watching those scary movies, it was to *always* lock the doors. For some reason, the young actors in those movies always forgot, and things never turned out well for them. Foolish kids.

A shadow moved through the sky, and Bailey shrank back against her seat. Far too big to be an owl or a bird—probably closer to the size of a Boeing 747—it had to be some kind of terrifying raptor creature. Her teeth were on the verge of chattering as she pictured its talons tearing the doors off her small rental car and reaching inside to get her. It'd fly off over the desert with her in its grasp, taking her to its nest of fledglings who were awaiting their next meal.

A mournful cry filled the night and Bailey closed her eyes to pray for help, or at the very least, a quick end to her suffering, should it come to that.

A moment later, something tapped on the car window. Bailey's stomach leaped into her throat. She squeezed her eyes tight. Then another tap. *God help her.* Did she dare chance staring into the eyes of some horrifying creature that meant to eat her? She felt herself begin to hyperventilate, but that was quite all right. Soon her head would feel light, then euphoria would set in, and she'd be able to withstand whatever came next, no matter how painful.

One more tap on the window made her grimace, but she finally squinted through one eye.

Chapter Ten

Hallelujah!

Carter Davis, her hero, was standing right outside the car. He was smirking and she didn't even care. He motioned for her to roll down the window.

"Car problems?" he asked. "Or, are you lost? Out of gas maybe?" He leaned into the window and peered at the fuel gauge.

Bailey took a deep breath. He still smelled of Dial, but with an added touch of aftershave. She couldn't help smiling. He was just what she needed to chase away all thoughts of being devoured by some desert carnivore.

The only thing on her mind now was how close his face was to hers, and how all it'd take for their lips to touch would be for her to lean a couple of inches to her left. Bailey felt Carter's unseen force pulling her closer, and her lips parted.

So . . . very . . . close . . .

Carter pulled his head back from the window.

"You've got plenty of gas, and I see you have a map." He glanced at the passenger seat. "Must be car problems, which I have to tell you, I'm no good at fixing." He stepped back from the car and looked it over from bumper to bumper, scratching his head. "That's a shame. It'll take a while to get a tow out here."

"A while?" Bailey's eyes grew wide. She couldn't spend *a while* out in the desert—in the *dark*. Her lower lip trembled.

"Ah, honey." Carter's voice was tender as he cupped her chin. "Don't worry. You can come with me. I'll have someone pick up your car."

Go? With him? Bailey could breathe again, though the thought of going anywhere with Carter made her heart pound. She took a good look at him. And where exactly was he going? Even in the dark, she could see that he was dressed for a special evening out. Expensive suit, white shirt that glowed luminous in the moonlight, gold cuff-links with the initials *CD* engraved on them.

Bailey looked down at her own clothing. Gap, through and through. "I seem to be slightly underdressed," she said.

Carter grinned. "I can help you there, too. We'll stop down the road and pick you up a dress. On me, of course."

Bailey's mouth went dry. When Robert Redford purchased a dress for Demi Moore, he expected a lot more in return than just a simple "thank you." Still, it took only a few seconds for her to decide she was better off going with Carter—wherever that might be—than to sit out here in the dark all alone.

They locked up the rental, and Carter drove her to a swanky upscale shop in Lake Las Vegas, where he picked out a sexy black number that made Bailey feel worldly and sophisticated. She walked out of the dressing room and stood in front of a full-length mirror, turning this way and that, to get the full effect. Evidently, Carter wanted to get the full effect, too, because he walked up behind her, slipped an arm around her and held her gently, while he reached up with his free hand and snapped her ponytail holder. As her hair fell in waves about her shoulders, she heard his intake of breath.

Bailey closed her eyes. This was all wrong. She'd left the Strip to get away from him, to clear her head. How was she supposed to think and make any kind of decision when he kept appearing and . . . and touching her?

"This is a night for wearing your hair down," he said against her cheek. His breath was warm and it made her feel something lovely and painful that went all the way through her. Like she'd been shot by Cupid's arrow straight through to her soul, her entire body shuddered, and she let out a moan. Forget *Elvis*. Security guy had her securely in his grasp, and she couldn't think of anywhere else she'd rather be.

Bailey rode beside Carter quietly. It took several minutes for her heart to settle down, and when it did, they were parked in front of a house as big as a hotel. Others were arriving in limos and cars that looked like they cost as much, or more, than a college education, and Bailey half expected to see a red carpet rolled out.

The women had on gowns such as she'd only seen in magazines. Next to them, she looked, well, amazing, but who wouldn't in Vera Wang? Still, she couldn't expect to just stand around all night, looking good. Eventually she'd have to open her mouth. Then what? What could she possibly talk about with people who lived larger than life? The stock market? How their husbands had been caught boffing the maid? It'd only take a few minutes for them to see through her Vera Wang facade and know that she didn't belong.

What she wouldn't give right now for one of those evil martinis.

Luckily for her, Carter had his mind-reading powers turned on, because he grabbed one of her hands and tucked it into the crook of his elbow. "Relax," he whispered. "I'll protect you." And then he grabbed a champagne flute from a passing tray and shoved it into her hand.

Protect her? That's not really what she needed to hear right then. How about, "Relax, I won't leave your side," or "Relax, you're the most beautiful woman here and you'll do fine." Now, not only did she fear looking like an outsider, but she also had to wonder what, or who, could be inside that she might need protection from.

She had only one choice: take a deep breath and hold on tight. And Bailey did just that. She held her head high as Carter led her down half a dozen steps and into a large room. An honest to goodness ballroom.

A couple dozen chandeliers hung from the ceiling, each of them dripping with crystals that scattered prisms of color over all the walls and into every corner of the room. Windows, like dark pools of water, surrounded them on all sides and the lights reflected in them reminded Bailey of fireflies dancing in the night. A shiny, black grand piano—the largest she'd ever seen—filled one corner of the huge room, and a woman in an elegant black and white gown sat before it, playing something soft and lovely.

An ice sculpture of a large waterfall sat atop a round marble base in the middle of the room. It glistened, slowly melting, giving the effect that the water was indeed moving. Bailey marveled that it could hold its own against the Las Vegas heat, but she soon saw that its secret was a large elegant fan directly overhead that bathed it with just enough cool air to allow for minimum melt.

Bailey took it all in, turning her head from side to side.

This was Carter's world, and it was daunting.

She took a quick sip of champagne, and felt a ribbon of warmth flow all the way into her extremities. She hadn't eaten since breakfast, and was thankful when

Carter steered her over to one wall, where long tables sat laid out, ready to feed an army.

A few minutes later, she had a small plate filled with crab cakes, pieces of raw vegetable, and some little unidentifiable squares of meat stuck on a toothpick. Even after eating a couple, she couldn't figure out their source, but they were tasty and she helped herself to a couple more.

Carter placed some things on his plate, but he barely touched them. He seemed happy with just keeping the both of them supplied with champagne. Bailey intended to avoid doing a replay of the previous evening and she emptied at least half of each glass he gave her into a nearby potted plant. Even so, her brain was soon feeling fuzzy around the edges, and she had the urge to spin around the floor like some ballroom dancer, except her date had such a sour look on his face that she didn't dare.

Carter hadn't stopped frowning since they'd arrived. His Elvis side had been tucked away, where Bailey couldn't even get a glimpse of him.

"Relax. I'll protect you," she whispered in his ear, pressing her body close to his. Something hard jabbed into her chest, and a cold chill scurried through her. No way was something that big a ballpoint pen.

Reality check. She wasn't in Coupeville anymore, where the most dangerous thing a man brought with him on a date was an expired condom. This was Las Vegas, land of just about anything imaginable, and this wasn't the man she'd seen on stage imitating Elvis the night before. Security guy was out in full force.

Perhaps she'd have been better off staying out in the desert with the rental car.

She grabbed a fresh glass off a passing tray.

Half an hour later, Bailey completely forgot about guns and threats of violence, and so too it seemed, had Carter. His interest now lay on a woman who was serving drinks to a group of loud men. Bailey could hardly blame him. The woman had been blessed with the three B's. Beautiful, blond, and most important, bountiful. So bountiful, in fact, that if she turned without warning, a person standing too close might get an eye poked out. She was a piece of art, and if she had brains to boot, well, she had it all.

Bailey took a self-conscious glance down at her own chest and wondered if anyone on the planet would consider it bountiful. Highly doubtful.

"A friend?" she asked Carter, squeezing his arm, just in case he needed to be reminded of her presence.

Carter gave her a blank look.

"Over there." Bailey nodded in Miss Bountiful's direction.

"Something like that," he grumbled.

The waitress finished serving her tray of drinks, then she turned toward them with a wide, warm smile and headed in their direction. Carter smiled, too, but judging by the creases in his forehead, Bailey didn't sense any romantic link between them. Someone from his past whom he would rather forget, perhaps?

A girl could wish.

"What's a beautiful blonde like you doing in a place like this?" Carter said to Miss B when she stopped in front of them. His voice bordered on cold, but he continued forcing a smile. The blonde's smile was anything but forced, however, and, in fact, she seemed to be taking delight in Carter's irritation.

"Why, Carter, you make me blush," she said. She glanced over at Bailey, holding her smile. "Who's your friend?"

Carter managed a dry laugh. "This is Bailey Ventura. Bailey, Twinkie Martinson."

Bailey caught herself before she laughed. *Twinkie?* Who on earth would name their child *Twinkie?* Though how fitting for a bountiful Las Vegas blonde. And with a name like that, maybe she didn't have all three B's, after all. Bailey grinned and stuck out her hand. "Glad to meet you."

Twinkie's eyes gleamed with genuine interest and she held Bailey's hand longer than was necessary. "*Very* happy to meet you, too."

Bailey shuffled her feet. Maybe the blonde played for their own team. Twinkie gave her hand back and then she whispered something into Carter's ear that must have been very funny because he erupted into laughter. Real laughter. Rich and deep, it filled the air, and others—mostly women—stopped in the middle of their conversations to give him an appraising glance.

Great. Carter and the waitress had some happy little secret that they weren't going to share. Bailey took a good, long look at the both of them. She tried hard to hate Twinkie, but it was impossible—the woman was engaging and her smile infectious—so she tried to put her hate on Carter. That, too, was futile. As frustrating as he was, he'd gotten under her skin, and it was going to take a whole lot of naughty little secrets to get him out.

Then Carter threw her a new curve. He whispered something into Twinkie's ear and she whispered something back and laughed. In a flash, his eyes turned cold and he grabbed one of Twinkie's arms, making her flesh bulge. Her smile turned into a grimace and Bailey shifted on her feet, wondering if she should give them some privacy.

"I hope you know what you're doing," Carter said.

"I'm a big girl, Carter. I guess I can take care of myself."

"I'm not so sure anymore. You're playing with the devil."

"No need to warn me." Twinkie laid a slender hand on Carter's chest. She stepped back and gave him a smile that was just as fake as his had been a few minutes earlier.

"Somebody's got to warn you," Carter said.

"That's not your job." She leaned in and kissed his cheek. "I've got work to do." She slowly, but firmly, eased her arm free and walked away, going back to serving guests like nothing had happened.

When Carter finished glaring at Twinkie's back, he mumbled some explanation for their exchange, something about some trouble he was helping her with, and that she was being a typical woman who wouldn't listen to good advice. Bailey only hoped the trouble Carter was speaking of wasn't the kind involving guns and torture and a lot of blood.

Bailey gave the room a nervous once-over. From her limited exposure to the criminal element, she surmised that at least 75 percent of the guests were probably packing a gun or some other form of deadly weapon. The other 25 percent were what might be called innocent bystanders when things went awry.

Ice zipped up her spine. She wasn't one of the gun toters.

"Ladies and gentlemen," a voice rang out, and the room hushed. "As all of you know, I'm Frank Zoopa, and I'll be your host for the evening." A few polite chuckles filled the air.

Frank Zoopa was not a tall man, but he was impressive and he seemed to command attention simply by being. He had a fairly good tan that made the grey at his temples and his numerous white teeth stand out. His flashy suit shimmered when he moved, and he was with a woman who had on a necklace that could probably buy Bailey's entire home town.

Bailey suddenly felt naked. She put a hand up to her throat, grasping a tiny cross that had stones in it that were so small they might or might not be diamond chips.

Zoopa and the woman walked over to a small table that was draped in a piece of white, satiny fabric, and a group of half a dozen men moved into place behind the table. After careful scrutiny, Bailey guessed that a full 100 percent in that group were carrying weapons—maybe even two. She swallowed a lump of fear and stood straighter. After all, she had her own security guy right by her side. And he'd promised to protect her.

"Who are they?" she asked Carter, trying to keep her voice from squeaking.

"Zoopa calls them associates. I call them yes-men." Carter straightened his tie and grabbed another glass of champagne from a passing tray. "Now comes the fun part," he said, and they moved closer to the group.

Bailey kept a firm grip on his arm.

"I know all of you are wondering what tonight is all about," Zoopa continued.

Carter's face was an unmistakable mask of contempt. A deep vein of hatred obviously existed between the two men, and that led Bailey to only one question: why had he brought her to a party hosted by a man he so clearly hated?

Zoopa stepped closer to the table and gave the material a tug. It slipped away and landed in a silent, soft heap on the floor. What remained on the table was a complex architectural model that had everyone "oohing" and "aahing," and even Bailey "oohed" once or twice, which garnered a look of admonishment from Carter.

"This, my friends, is The Majestic, the next billion-dollar adult fantasy hotel to be born to Las Vegas Boulevard. Four thousand rooms, six pools, twenty restaurants, two theaters, three thousand slot machines, thirty boutiques, two wedding chapels, and a world-class museum. And it'll all be open to the public just over a year from now.

"The opening of this hotel means thousands of jobs, and an experience for tourists the likes of which they won't soon forget." Zoopa's face beamed like a man whose wife had just given birth to triplets.

A little more "oohing" and "aahing" and the guests

moved in for a closer look, but Carter gripped Bailey's hand tightly, holding her back. Men shook Zoopa's hand, did the backslapping thing, and gave him their congratulations. They circled the display and talked among themselves, their faces showing true interest in the new billion-dollar baby, but the sour look on Carter's face said he'd like nothing more than to shove that model right down Zoopa's happy throat. It didn't take a genius to figure out that the danger zone was anywhere between the two of them.

"What do you think?" Zoopa asked, suddenly turning to Carter.

"It'll be a hit," Carter said. "No doubt about it. If the yearly increase in visitors holds at its current 3 percent, you'll be able to expect over a million new fish to swim in your pond every year. A hotel of such magnitude is sure to thrive."

Carter was doing his best to be diplomatic, but his blood was boiling like magma under his skin and his jaw was clenching so hard he thought his teeth would break. One little push was all it would take and he'd be all over Zoopa. Hell, forget a push, he'd take a nudge.

Zoopa reached into his breast pocket for a couple of cigars, revealing, in the process, a very large gun. Carter felt Bailey stiffen at his side and he gave her arm a reassuring squeeze. She smiled and did a very good job of pretending that she was unaware of the anger that fused the air between him and Zoopa. Poor girl. She was out of her element, with nowhere to run. He made a mental note to make this up to her later.

Zoopa grinned smugly and handed one of the cigars to Carter. "Let's say, it's a boy."

The nudge was coming, Carter could feel it. He glanced around the room. Frank's men had their eyes on them. "I didn't know you had your sights set so high," he said to Zoopa.

"The higher the better." Frank turned to Bailey and his face brightened. "Don't you think, Ms. Ventura?" His eyes glowed a hazel-yellow color, unblinking, just like a desert lizard's.

Carter hadn't introduced Bailey to Zoopa, but he wasn't surprised that Zoopa knew her by name. This *was* Las Vegas. Whatever happened here might stay here, but if a man like Zoopa wanted to know something about a person, he'd know it—from the moment their plane hit the tarmac.

"Mmm. Yes. I suppose." Bailey nodded. She averted her eyes from the lizard and gave Carter a nervous glance.

Smart girl. Twinkie could learn from her.

Carter and Zoopa made small talk for a few minutes, until they were both tired of being polite, then Zoopa made an obscene comment about Twinkie in Carter's ear, followed by a raspy chuckle.

That was the nudge Carter needed. His free hand curled into a fist at his side.

"Chiseler!" A loud shout broke through the steady buzz of voices and music.

The piano music stopped mid-melody, and all heads turned in the direction of an open doorway, where a man with a round belly, and legs that seemed too short for his body, stood. His face was red and his eyes pierced the air with an invisible arrow that led straight over to Frank Zoopa.

Carter placed a hand on Bailey's back and guided her away from Zoopa, over to the side of the room, toward the food tables. Situations like this had a way of escalating. Should that happen, he wanted her out of the way.

The round man quickly closed the distance between himself and Zoopa, and Zoopa's men took their cue to move in closer to their boss.

"Mr. Azuri, what seems to be the problem?" Frank rested a hand on the man's shoulder. Mr. Azuri shrugged it away. Venom filled his eyes and a thick wad of spittle formed at the corners of his mouth.

"You know what is the problem," Azuri said. He pointed a finger into Zoopa's face and Zoopa just stared at him with those cold lizard eyes. "Don't think you'll get away with so much as your life if—"

"Don't you worry, Mr. Azuri, we'll talk later. As you can see, I'm having a private party at the moment." Zoopa turned away and began talking to another guest. He hadn't given any discernable orders to his men, but two of them approached Azuri, one on each side, and they ushered him away—through a different door than he'd arrived.

Bailey nervously chewed her lip. "This is a real Las Vegas party, huh?" she said, and Carter gave her a reassuring smile.

"Yeah, a real Vegas party." He took her hand and started walking. He'd seen enough. And so had Bailey. Putting her in a situation that could very well end in a bad way would probably not be her idea of a fun date.

Bailey stopped abruptly. "Wait." She pulled her hand free from his.

"Not now, honey."

"Not *now?*" Bailey frowned. "What about that man? Where are they taking him?"

"It's not any of our business. Time to go."

"So, I'm just supposed to go along with whatever you decide, follow you anywhere? No matter what?"

Carter looked at her and pondered her question. Only one right answer that he could see. "That's the gist of it, yeah."

Bailey crossed her arms and stood firm. "Not this girl. I'm not one of your groupies. Just because you do a pretty good impression of the King doesn't mean I've lost my mind over you. Where did those men in funeral suits take that little man? For all you know, the world has seen the last of him."

Carter stifled a laugh and gave her a long look. Things could get complicated with this woman. He looked over at the door and gave a sigh of resignation. "Okay, honey. I'll check later and make sure Mr. Azuri is okay."

"Later could be too late."

Carter shook his head. "It won't be too late. You think Zoopa's going to *off* some guy right after that little display of affection? Trust me, Azuri is fine." He glanced around. The party was in full swing—people had already gone back to laughing and dancing, just as though nothing had happened. "Look, do any of those people seem concerned? This is Vegas. Shit happens here, honey. Get used to it."

Carter's demeanor softened—slightly. He brushed a lock of hair back from her face and let his hand linger on her cheek. "Come with me. And don't argue." He led her over to a pair of French doors on the other side of the room, opposite from where Mr. Azuri had taken his departure.

Fresh air. Jasmine-scented. Bailey took a deep breath and immediately felt more relaxed. All thoughts of guns and violence and the little fat man dissolved and blew away on a warm breeze. She and Carter stood at the side of a fifty-foot pool. Its surface shimmered and rippled under the moonlight, and blue lights inset into the surrounding stone lent a soft, soothing glow around the pool's perimeter. At one end, water plunged into it from a man-made waterfall that stood a good thirty feet high. A small cabana sat at the other end, with a magenta bougainvillaea growing up one side and over the top, swathing it in vivid color.

The mansion's roof line also glowed softly with blue

lights that were discreetly hidden under its arches, and heavy vines hung down the side of the house, blossoming with red trumpet-shaped flowers.

The effect was magical. She'd entered a different world. Maybe even a dream.

She gazed up at Carter. A tuft of his hair frolicked in the warm breeze, inviting her to reach up, brush it from his face. If this *were* a dream, she hoped she hadn't set her alarm for anytime soon.

Palm tree fronds danced in the breeze and Bailey closed her eyes, let herself get lost in the sound of the falling water. Carter slid his arms around her waist, making her jump. But she didn't resist. He dipped his head and took her earlobe gently between his teeth.

The night, the stars, the moon . . . the man with his teeth on her ear . . . she was floating and everything around her was swaying. Good God, she was about to swoon.

Chapter Eleven

Swoon.

Bailey giggled to herself. A funny word, swoon.

To become enraptured . . . to float . . . a state of ecstasy. Yes, that was a perfect description of how she was feeling right then. She sighed, enjoying the comfort of Carter's arms. So this was what all those old movies her mom and aunt loved so much were all about. This was one of those forever-after moments.

Carter kissed the side of her neck, and her knees went all rubbery. If he were to let go of her right now, she just might fall into the swimming pool.

His mouth moved back to her ear, sending a jolt to her goodies. "You ever do it in the nude?" he whispered.

Bailey froze, stopped breathing. In the *nude*? Was there any other way? Her brain might be scrambled from being in his arms, but she certainly knew how two people *did it*. Although she definitely could see how a woman might be so filled with passion that she'd fall into the sheets without taking the time to remove all her clothes. Not that she had ever been lucky enough to experience anything that intense. In fact, there had only been one other man she'd been intimate with, and it had been an experience entirely worth forgetting.

"I'm, um, not sure what you mean." Bailey licked her lips nervously as her heart fluttered about inside her chest. Carter nuzzled her ear some more and she sucked in a deep breath. With his cheek warm next to hers, she was rendered powerless. He could do whatever he pleased.

And whatever he pleased took her breath away. He turned her around and squeezed her to his chest. "I think you know exactly what I mean," he said. His tongue touched her lips, and she parted them to allow him full access. He explored her mouth for a long minute, and then he stopped and looked into her eyes.

"Well?" he said, still holding her firmly to him.

"Well?" Bailey squeaked.

"Let's do it. Right here. Right now."

Bailey sputtered. Boy, talk about moving in for the kill. How could any normal, red-blooded female say no to a man who'd just kissed the breath out of her? Vital parts of her anatomy had been awakened, as had his, from what she could feel, and her only shot at resisting was to put a little space between them.

Bailey gently pushed away from him. "Carter," she said, mentally fanning herself, "you kinda catch a girl by surprise."

He quickly closed the gap she'd put between them, ran a hand up her back, into her hair, gently taking a handful in his fist. "C'mon, live a little," he said, and then he kissed her again.

Bailey whimpered. She felt herself weakening.

The French doors suddenly burst open and a man and woman stumbled out of the house in a fit of laughter. As soon as they saw Carter and Bailey, the man nodded an apology and quickly ushered the woman back inside.

Saved. Bailey glanced upward with a silent "thank you."

Carter tried to continue where he'd left off, but, too late, the spell he'd put her under had been broken. She placed her hands against his chest in firm resolve.

"Whoa. Wait a minute. In case you've forgotten, there are a couple hundred people in there." She waggled a hand toward the house. "And Murphy's Law tells me that if we do this, several, maybe even dozens, will probably come out and witness our . . . you know . . ."

"Ah . . ." Carter said, sounding a lot like a young Elvis. And it didn't help matters when the left side of his mouth raised a notch in that sexy Elvis kind of way. Oh, yes, that look, the one she'd first taken for a sneer of self-satisfaction, when he'd rescued her from the shower. Now she knew better. His sneer was really just one of his many weapons of seduction.

"Don't do that." Bailey shook her head and put her hands over her ears. "Don't talk to me in that voice. And don't look at me like that."

Carter pulled her hands down and pushed them behind her back, holding them firmly in place. Seductive . . . savage . . . strangely stirring. She loved it.

"If anyone comes out, they can join us," Carter said, his voice low and husky.

Lord help her, she'd never wanted a man so bad, and maybe what he was suggesting was the norm for folks in Sin City, but she was Bailey Ventura, small town girl, obviously with some very naive big city dreams.

She wrestled her hands free and planted them on her hips. "Carter Davis, I am not that kind of girl. I don't *ménage à trois* or participate in any other group activities that are meant to be one-on-one."

Carter's laughter filled the night, and every insect and creature within hearing range ceased chirping, clicking, and cooing. "Honey, that pool will hold fifty people. If it was meant to be one-on-one, it'd be a hot tub."

"Pool?" Bailey glanced down at the aquamarine-colored water. She bit her lip. "I thought . . ." She did a mental slap to her forehead. "Swim?"

Carter's eyes crinkled at the corners and his lips

quivered. "You thought I was asking you to have sex? Right out here? Right now?"

"Of course not," Bailey said, shaking her head. Then she nodded. "Maybe."

"*Swim,* baby. Not sex. Let's go for a *swim.*" He nodded toward the pool.

"But, I don't—"

Carter put a finger to her lips. "I'm sure there's an entire wardrobe of suits right over there, inside that cabana. And if not"—Carter slipped the strap of her dress off one shoulder and ran a finger under her bra strap—"this here pretty undergarment will do just fine."

Gulp.

Then he kissed her—tenderly. His lips were warm and delicious and they molded to hers like her favorite lip balm. Boy, was she a goner.

Carter nuzzled her hair and spoke softly. "Baby, I'd never think of making you do something you don't want. I won't even make you dangle your feet in the water, until it's what we both want."

Security guy was a powerful man indeed.

"Liar," Bailey responded in a quiet whisper. He had to know that she had no will of her own when he was holding her and doing those things to her with his lips. She gazed into the sky as he held her. A million stars twinkled brilliantly against the night's canvas, but one in particular stood out and she closed her eyes to make a wish. The very idea that it might come true made her tremble.

When she opened her eyes, Carter was looking at her.

"You okay? Cold?" he asked with genuine concern, and he took off his suit coat. He draped it across her shoulders and then took one of her hands in his, enveloping it with warmth. Bailey knew then, she never wanted him to let go.

* * *

Uh-oh. She had that look. Bailey Ventura was thinking things she shouldn't. Next thing, she'd probably ask him if he could see this relationship ever going anywhere. His answer: not likely. But he had a question, too. Was it him she wanted, or was it really the King she wanted a piece of and he just happened to fit the suit?

God knows, Elvis had possessed a powerful weapon. He'd had the ability to convince thousands—no, millions—of women he was a god, and any man who could sing like him, or who clothed themselves as he did, had a little piece of that weapon.

Bailey didn't come across as being one of those women, but it was still hard to tell what was really going on behind her big brown eyes.

"Have you decided? Shall we swim?" Carter slid the strap of her dress off her shoulder again.

Bailey grabbed it and pulled it back up. "No. I don't think I'll be stripping and dipping with you. Not tonight anyway."

Intriguing. It wasn't often that a woman turned him down, and not ever when he played the Elvis card. He smiled and took her by the hand.

"Okay. Then how about a walk? The grounds here are beautiful, even in the dark."

They strolled along a stone path that was lit by soft lights. The air was heavy with the smell of jasmine and damp earth from earlier sprinkler activity. Insects hushed as he and Bailey approached their section of the world, and then started up again as soon as all danger was past. Tropical plants hung over the walk, making the path barely visible, but it didn't matter. Carter knew his way along this path very well. He could've walked it blindfolded. As a teen, he'd shared this path with many a girl, causing many a gray hair to sprout on his mother's head.

He and Bailey made their way through the shadows, and after a few minutes, the sound of plunging water dissolved into the background noises, along with the laughter coming from inside the house. Only the soft click of Bailey's heels joined in with nature's chorus now.

As they walked, Carter thought about the model Zoopa had revealed of his new casino. He had, no doubt, used his own desert oasis as the inspiration for his new hotel.

Carter felt his back muscles tense. It wasn't right that a man like Zoopa should live in the house his parents had worked so hard to build. Until his dying breath, he'd do whatever it took to get Twinkie away from that bastard.

Memories of hearing his parents arguing late one night flooded into Carter's mind. He'd awakened to a crash, something hitting the floor in his parents' bedroom, and then he'd heard his mother cry out, "He might get my house, but he won't get everything in it."

Carter knew she'd just smashed one of her "treasures," as she called them. He also knew that when morning came, she'd regret having broken it.

It was at those moments that he hated his dad for getting so in debt that it put the security of their home in jeopardy, and made his mom cry.

Months before, the house had been filled with laughter and excitement at what the future held. Carter had never seen his dad so happy. He'd somehow managed to forge a deal that would allow him to become part owner of a soon-to-be-built luxury resort and casino. He'd said it was a sure way to make the future bright and secure for all of them.

From conversations Carter had overheard between his parents, he knew the deal had involved some kind of balloon payment that had to be made by a certain date in order for the deal to be completed. Unfortunately, the ability to make that payment hinged on the new casino opening on time, so that there would be plenty of cash flow.

For reasons that were unknown at the time, there were numerous delays in the onset of construction and, all the while, the balloon payment's due date drew nearer and nearer.

Without the casino up and running, there was just no way his dad could make that payment. The roof was caving in on his family. That is, until Zoopa swooped in and offered a helping hand.

It'd seemed a miracle, at first, but it'd turned out to be the worst deal his dad ever made. Problems surrounding the start of construction continued to pop up and, ultimately, the deal Carter's dad made with Zoopa went south, too. The end result was that Zoopa took ownership of their house, along with his dad's share of the new casino.

It was a shady deal all the way around, one that Carter never fully understood until he got older. Working at the casinos, a person heard things and, eventually, he heard enough to know that most of the construction delays had been the result of favors owed to Zoopa. Rushing in and "saving the day" when someone was in financial trouble— even though it was he who caused the trouble—was how Zoopa had acquired much of his wealth. Along with his shady gaming practices, of course.

Finally, Carter and Bailey reached the end of the stone path and they stopped. A gust of chilly air blew over them and Bailey crossed her arms over her chest, rubbing them against the cold. Carter gathered her close. This might be something he could learn to enjoy again—but only if he was a fool.

Bailey relished the warmth Carter provided. She envisioned them together, back in Washington, on a cold winter's day, white flakes falling around them, while they threw snowballs for her dogs. She wouldn't mind seeing how Carter would protect her from that kind of chill.

She gazed up at him. He had a faraway look in his eyes, and all traces of the arrogant security guy she'd first met were gone; the man she was with now was someone different. Vulnerable, somehow. She snuggled deeper into his arms, and tried to return some of the warmth and comfort he'd given her.

After a minute of quiet, Carter tipped up her head and he pressed his mouth to hers, letting his lips linger for several seconds, as though wanting to send her some kind of message.

Message clearly received. All the way to her most private places. And though she desired him in the most urgent way, she needed to guard the tenderness of her feelings. She had to proceed with caution, to be sure this was more than just pure lust that was driving her—though she had no doubt that lust played a big part in Carter's feelings. He was a man, after all.

Bailey sighed to herself. The place she wanted in his life was not one of just another doe-eyed fan. "It's time I get back to the hotel," she said, but she secretly hoped he'd try to talk her out of going back to her room.

He didn't.

But he did leave her with one last very unforgettable kiss.

Bailey paused just inside her door, leaning against it, savoring the end of their evening. All their chemistry. All her heart pounding. It was amazing she'd been able to stop herself from doing something crazy.

Luckily, Liza was already asleep or she'd have been bombarded with questions that she had no clue how to answer.

Not so many hours later, the sun peeked through the save-me-from-hangover-hell drapes. It was morning.

"The day" had finally arrived. Tonight she'd see, and hear, more than a dozen Elvis impersonators trying to convince an audience of hundreds that they should be crowned the ultimate Elvis tribute artist.

Bailey needed no convincing. Not about his singing, anyway. She was 100 percent sure Carter could sing the jumpsuit off any of the other competitors. Still, she was only 95 percent sure she'd found her man. The last 5 percent still needled her. Conflicting advice from her mom and her aunt had her rattled and overthinking things. "Don't settle for less than what you really want," her mom had drilled into her for the last twenty-five years. "Take a chance; live a little," was her Aunt Fiona's motto. *Live a little?* That's what Carter had said to her last night.

Bailey sat up, drawing her knees to her chest. Her stomach growled. Food. A good breakfast and her brain would function better. She looked over at the lump in the next bed. "You awake?" she said to the lump. She wasn't sure, but she thought she saw the lump move. Good enough.

Bailey got up and tugged open the drapes.

The lump didn't stir.

But it did make a nasally, whining noise.

Bailey waited for half a minute. Nothing else happened, so she started rapping her fingertips on the table top. Nada. The tune "I Got Lucky" bubbled from her lips, and by the time she reached the song's second chorus, the lump gave a violent kick and an eye peered out over the top of the bedspread.

"What the hell's wrong with you?" the eye said to her.

"Would you look at that," Bailey sang out, waving a hand at the window. "It's a beautiful day."

The eye ducked back under the covers. "I'm not looking at anything until you close those drapes."

"But it's time to get up. The birds are singing."

"I don't hear any birds."

"Imagine." Bailey grabbed some shorts and a tank top from the dresser.

This time two eyes peered out from under the covers. "Again I ask, what the hell is wrong with you?"

"It's an exciting day. I'm excited. Aren't you excited?"

"Thrilled. Does your exuberance mean you and hunk o' love went to third base?"

Bailey continued with her song and headed to the bathroom.

"You must be in love," Liza shouted after her.

Bailey giggled. Love. Indeed. She was floating.

She looked into the mirror and dropped, with a thud, back to earth. After a long minute of contemplating the virtues of plastic surgery, she went to work.

An entire ampule of Refresh in each eye had them looking brand-new, some Neutrogena moisturizer brought back her skin's youthful glow, and an extra layer of mascara had her looking all wide-eyed and perky. She stepped back and admired her work. Not perfect, but what did she expect after a full night of smooching and only a few hours of sleep?

Now for the hard part: her hair.

She'd gone to bed with it wet, and now it floated about her shoulders in wild curls like it was immune to gravity. Bailey put her fingers to her head and tossed the strands about. A female warrior stared back at her from the mirror. A spear in her hand would have been more appropriate than a brush, but it was nothing that a ponytail holder couldn't cure.

Bailey started to gather her thick tresses in one hand, but she paused as she remembered how Carter had broken the one she wore last night. She took another look at her warrior self. Today was a good day to wear it loose. It'd save Carter the effort later. Though she did rather enjoy the way he grabbed her and pulled it free.

Heck, Bailey thought, *why not go all the way?* She squirted a large dab of Dove gel into her hand, then rubbed her palms together and smoothed the gel through her hair, making sure it was evenly distributed before going at it with the blow dryer. After a final tousle, she stepped back from the mirror for an appraising look.

Scary.

And now it was time for something even scarier. She had a decision to make.

Car? Or money? As far as she was concerned, there was only one right answer to that question: car.

Bailey picked up the card of the casino host she'd been assigned after winning the T-Bird. She flipped open her cell phone and punched in Jennifer Torch's number. Ms. Torch was delighted that Bailey had decided to take the car, and she told Bailey that it would be ready for pickup the following morning.

Bailey slapped the phone shut and smiled. It was a done deal. She'd really and truly won that zippy little car. Geez, if this turned out to be just a dream, she'd be so disappointed. She was ready to slip into the car's soft, leather seats, toss all the onlookers a beauty contestant wave, and hit the open road.

A quick calculation told her that it would take about two days to get home, which meant she and Liza would get home a day later than they'd planned. No problem— except that Liza had just started a new job. Maybe she should have talked to her first. What if Liza couldn't take the time to drive back with her? Yikes! Then what?

The voucher. That's what. She could take it to purchase a car back home. She frowned. It wouldn't be the same. And, sure, she could take the cash. Having that much money would make for a very nice shopping spree, but after it was spent, what then? Without that cute little car sitting in her driveway, it'd be as if it never really happened.

That settled it. She *had* to take the car.

"Good God, you look like Phyllis Diller on steroids," Liza said from the doorway. She grabbed the Dove gel off the counter. "Give me that before you hurt yourself. I told you to let down your hair and live a little, not make a complete leap from reality."

Bailey looked in the mirror. Warrior woman stared back. "Too much? Should I wear my usual ponytail?"

"No." Liza went over to the toilet closet and sat. She didn't bother closing the door. "Just don't ever wear your hair like that around the Jefferson twins. Mark, in particular. You had your chance with him; it's my turn."

"Oh, don't worry. He's all yours," Bailey said.

"By the way, there's someone knocking at our door," Liza said with a yawn. "I suspect it's for you."

Bailey opened the door, and her insides went all squishy when she saw Carter standing there wearing the latest security guy stud wear, sans the sunglasses. His eyes took in her hair. He didn't say a word, but his mouth twitched in approval.

"I wasn't expecting you." Bailey resisted the urge to pat her hair into place, and anyway, it would have been futile. Every strand had run amok and that's the way it was going to stay until she washed it. "Did we have a date?" It was entirely possible she'd forgotten about any plans they'd made, after the spell he'd put her under last night.

"God, I sincerely hope so," Carter said, still eyeing her hair. And then he kissed her like he was starving.

When he finished kissing her, Bailey stepped back for some air. A kiss like that was one way to get her motor running so early in the morning. "Liza and I have plans for breakfast," Bailey told him with much reluctance.

"What about lunch? I have some business to take care of over at the MGM, then we can meet . . . say around noon?" He didn't wait for an answer. Instead, he kissed her once more, softly, filling her with a promise of things to come. With one last lingering look at her hair, he smiled and left.

Well, that settled it. Every last ponytail holder she owned was going into the trash.

She and Liza spent a perfect morning, first ordering room service, then lounging by the pool until it was time for Bailey to go meet Carter. Liza went along with her over to the MGM, and since they still had a few minutes to kill, they stopped at the Rainforest Cafe for a smoothie.

"I've decided to take the car," Bailey said. She sucked a strawful of cold, frothy liquid into her mouth. "And I'm just a little apprehensive about driving it all the way home by myself." It was a blatant hint, but that's what friends are for.

Liza looked at her for a long time. "How long are you going to do this?"

Bailey raised an eyebrow in question.

Liza placed a hand over Bailey's. "How long are you going to make me drive us everywhere?"

Bailey's eyebrow notched higher. "I don't make you drive *everywhere*."

"Look, you're afraid to drive," Liza said. "There. I said it. Now it's your turn to say it."

Bailey's chin raised. "Fine. I admit I'm a little *concerned* about being behind the wheel of a car, but I'm not *afraid*. And anyway, what do you expect? I live in a town that's filled with nothing but old people who can barely see over the tops of their steering wheels. Why do you think I want to get out of there so bad? So I can be normal again. Like you."

"There's help for people like you. Hypnotism, acupuncture, whatever . . ."

"Does that mean you won't help me drive the car home?"

"You know I can't." Liza shook her head. "My new job awaits me. You'll just have to arrange to have it shipped."

Bailey waved a hand. "That's the silliest thing I've ever heard. It's a car. It's got wheels that'll get it from here to there."

Liza shrugged. "That's the best I can come up with. Sorry."

They sat quietly, sucking smoothie through their straws, until suddenly, Liza's eyes grew wide.

Bailey followed her gaze, and she sputtered pink stuff out her straw when she saw Carter. With Miss Bountiful. Together. And neither one of them looked happy. He was guiding her through the casino like a parent who'd just caught his child doing something wrong, and she was pouting like she knew what was coming.

"Wow," Liza said. "He looks intense. Who's the blonde he's manhandling?"

Bailey frowned. She felt a new line being permanently etched into her forehead. She was in no mood to get into a discussion about Carter and Miss Bountiful. "I have to use the bathroom," she said, and excused herself, quickly heading in the direction of the closest ladies' room, which also happened to be in the same direction Carter and Twinkie were headed.

Bailey weaved and maneuvered her way through rows of machines, keeping them in sight, until at one point, Twinkie yanked her arm free and they stopped. Bailey slid into a seat at a Double Wild Cherry slot machine and dug a dollar out of her pocket. She shoved it into the machine, feeling somewhat spylike, but what else could she do? No way was she going to toss her heart out to a man who didn't deserve it.

Bailey sneaked a glance around the machine. Carter had on his mad face and he was glaring at Twinkie like he wasn't quite sure what to do with her.

"We agreed you'd stay over at my place for the next couple of days," Carter said to Twinkie.

Twinkie struggled against Carter's grip. "I lied," she said.

"Tell you what," he said to Twinkie. "We're going up to your room and you're going to pack a few things."

"You're a pig," Twinkie said, giving Carter a death glare. "You can't make me go with you. That's called kidnapping."

"Prove it," Carter said. "Somebody's got to get you on the right track. You obviously don't know what's good for you."

"And you obviously don't know what's good for you, either. Frank's not gonna be happy about this."

"Don't worry, babycakes, it'll be over soon. One way or another," Carter said and he pulled her along.

Over? Soon? Who *was* Carter Davis? Bailey wondered if she should call the police or the FBI or some other equally powerful agency. After about two seconds' thought, she decided against it. No reason to get caught up in something she knew nothing about. She'd seen *The Untouchables* a couple of times and she knew the police couldn't really protect people who got in the way. Besides, what if the situation between Carter and Twinkie was something completely innocent? Then she'd look like a silly, hysterical female and she really hated it when that happened.

Boy, she sure hoped Miss Bountiful was right when she'd said she could take care of herself.

They rounded a corner, and Bailey followed, catching up just in time to see them get on the elevator.

They got off on the eleventh floor.

Lucky eleven.

Maybe not so lucky for Twinkie.

Bailey's heart pumped wildly. She was afraid and confused all at the same time, just like when she'd first laid eyes on Carter. What kind of man was she falling in love with, anyway?

Chapter Twelve

Carter and Twinkie approached Twinkie's hotel room and Carter stopped short. The door was open a crack. He unholstered his .44 and put out an arm to prevent her from going any farther. He gave her a head gesture to stand back against the wall. The door creaked as he nudged his way inside. The drapes were closed, but enough light came in from the hallway for Carter to make out shapes and forms in the main room. Nothing ominous. Whoever had come to call was already gone, but they'd left a very powerful calling card. Sweet and noxious, the scent of roses filled the room.

Carter breathed into the crook of his arm and flipped on the light switch. Two dozen vases or more sat on every available space. "Jesus. You becoming a florist?"

Twinkie followed him inside. Her eyes instantly lit up, and she clapped her hands together, rolling her eyes heavenward.

Carter wanted to puke. He swiped at his eyes.

"What's wrong? You don't like anything that smells better than you?" Twinkie teased. She flitted about from vase to vase, bending and sniffing, giggling as she breathed in the spicy scent.

"You hardly need to stick your nose in them to get a

whiff," Carter said. He walked over to Twinkie's bedroom door, pushing it open just to make sure they were alone. Clean. A small envelope on her dresser caught his eye and he picked it up, turning it over in his hand. No writing on it, not even a name. He started to open it.

Twinkie snatched it from him. "Thank you," she said. "I think that's meant for me."

"It's not addressed."

"I live here. It's in my room."

"I didn't miss your birthday or something, did I?" He stood over her shoulder as she read the card. *Thanks for a job well done . . . and for one helluva good time. Frank.*

The smell . . . the card . . . maybe he *would* puke.

Twinkie returned the card to its envelope and dropped it back onto the dresser.

"When did you run out of self-respect?" Carter asked.

"I beg your pardon?" Twinkie stood straighter. "It's not any of your business what I do, or who I do it with."

God, she could be a brat. Carter seriously considered turning her over his knee and giving her a good paddling, but what good would it do? She'd just pout, tell him to go to hell, and refuse to talk to him for the next three weeks. Zoopa would love it.

"What're you doin' with that guy?" he asked.

"Is that why you forced me to come up here with you? To ask me that, for the hundredth time?" Twinkie rolled her eyes skyward and shook her head. "I could've given you an answer down in the casino." Twinkie propped her hands on her hips. "And guess what, the answer is still, 'it's none of your business.'"

"Nice try. You know damn well why I brought you up here. So we could talk—in private—so there'd be no chance anyone could link you to the Azuri diamond thing."

"There is no Azuri diamond thing. The fat little man

lost it. Case closed," Twinkie said with a quick tilt of her head and a smug smile.

Carter gave her a sideways glance. "It's a hell of a way for you to live your life, Twinkie. You can do better than Frank Zoopa."

"Yeah, at least I'm living, Carter. The only way I know how. Face it, you entered this picture show way too late."

Twinkie's words hurt, and he hated it, but they were true. While he'd been off playing Elvis, Zoopa had been her lifeline. He'd been there to pick her up when she was down, and odds were, she was never going to walk away from him.

At least not until circumstances afforded her a chance at another life. Not until someone handed her that chance.

And since he was the only one of them with any sense, that job fell to him. Impersonating the King was fun, kept him feeling young, but his serious side had finally taken over and he'd come to realize Twinkie needed his help—whether she liked it or not.

"You need to let me be," Twinkie continued. "Just because you don't feel the need to be close to other human beings, doesn't mean I don't."

"You're exaggerating a little, aren't you? Calling Zoopa human?" Twinkie opened her mouth to say more, but Carter held up a hand. He was in no mood to hear her defend that SOB. "Let's not get into it again. Not now." He ran a frustrated hand through his hair. "And I do have people in my life," he said.

"Yeah, I know. Women. And from what I hear, lots of them." Twinkie's frown softened and she smiled gently. "What about finding that special someone, Carter? Someone to spend your free time with? Like that woman—what was her name, Bailey?—you brought to Frank's party last night?"

Carter shrugged. "She's okay."

"Okay?" Twinkie laughed lightly. She picked up a pack of cigarettes from the dresser. "She was lovely. Just your type, I'll bet, or you wouldn't have taken her out back, to the garden. To your *special* place." She giggled.

Carter grinned. She knew him too well. He lit her cigarette and she stood there quietly for a moment, studying him. He knew exactly what she was thinking: he'd finally met his match. Could be, he supposed, but so what? The cute brunette would be leaving his world in another day or two and that would be the end of them.

Carter shook his head. "She is lovely, I suppose, in a cute kind of way, but she's more into the Elvis side of me. Before she knew I could sing, she wasn't the least bit interested. I can't be Elvis 24/7."

"Jesus, Carter. Don't tell me you really believe that. Of course she likes it when you sing, but this guy standing right here in front of me . . ." Twinkie touched a finger to his chest. "This guy is enough to make a good girl go bad. Or even a bad girl go good."

Carter laughed. "It'd never work. I already took that chance once and it was a disaster. No more adoring fans for me. If I ever take another shot at love, it's going to be with a woman who doesn't want me because of some act."

"Not every woman wants you just because you move like you have a hot tamale in your pants."

Carter laughed and curled his lip. "Why, thank you very much."

Bailey's heart ached. The lump in her throat was so big it threatened to choke her. No matter how she tried telling herself she didn't care that the man she'd fantasized about was up in some hotel room with another woman, she did care, and it hurt, and she was having a heck of a time keeping her tears in check.

Shit.

Well, what did she expect? A man like him, living in a place like Las Vegas, land of countless naked dancers and a couple thousand half-naked cocktail waitresses, of course he was going to be involved with at least one of them. And with a voice that could melt ice, it was a sure bet, about a million other women were at his disposal at any time of the day or night.

Including her. If only they had more time.

As Bailey made her way through the casino, back to the table, she prepared herself for the advice that Liza was sure to offer. Like, "pick a new one at tonight's competition," which was exactly what Bailey knew she should do. But how? She was out of time. She'd spent every spare minute with Carter. And except for his dark side— and, of course, the fact that he carried a gun—Carter was perfect for her. She couldn't explain it, but whenever she was near him, she felt like she'd just won a million on the slots. She reached a hand up to her neck and touched the spot where his lips had so recently been pressed against her skin.

Her head hurt. She could almost feel her brain swelling from going back and forth between security guy and *Elvis*.

Bailey got back to the table and slid onto the bench seat without a word. She grabbed her glass and sucked melted smoothie into her mouth.

Liza stared at her. "Are you okay?"

Hardly. Couldn't Liza see she was in distress? "I'm fine," Bailey said.

Liza stared at her some more. "You see your lover with another woman—excuse me, potential lover—and then you head off to the bathroom, and when you come back you have nothing to say, except that you're fine? Wow. You must really think I'm a dumb blonde."

"Mmm, hmm." Bailey nodded and finished the last of her smoothie.

"Hey! I take offense at that," Liza said with a faux pout.

Bailey shook her head. "No, *no*. Sorry, I didn't mean that. I'm just . . . confused."

"Me, too. Only I don't know why," Liza said. "The answer seems simple to me, though. Dump him." She slammed her hands on the table top. "*Just dump him*, and pick a new one. Like him." Liza nodded at a man in a white jumpsuit.

Steve Sogura, tribute artist who could warm a frigid woman in ten seconds flat, passed their booth. He gave them a crooked grin and kept on walking. Liza stared after him. "God knows he's got . . . I don't know . . . something—"

"I told you, he's taken," Bailey said, gazing at Steve's backside.

"So's the other one, far as I could see."

"That was just business." Bailey thought if she repeated it to herself enough times, she might really start to believe it.

"Looks like he needs a vacation from that kind of business," Liza said.

Suddenly Bailey felt like *she* needed a vacation. She needed to put the top down on that hot little car and let the open road carry her away. She sat quiet for a minute.

"That's it!" Bailey said.

Liza raised a questioning eyebrow.

"Don't you see? A vacation. I can ask Carter to drive home with me. Everyone likes a little vacation." Bailey threw her hands up in the air. "I don't know why I didn't think of it before."

"You'd actually let a strange man drive you a thousand miles?"

"He's not so strange."

Liza gave her a look. "He's a grown man and he wears a jumpsuit with rhinestones."

"That doesn't make him strange."

Liza gave her another look.

Bailey shrugged. "He's an Elvis tribute artist. It's his job to wear a jumpsuit. And then when I won that car, he was the one who came down to congratulate me. It's a sign, don't you think?"

"It was meant to be." Liza rolled her eyes.

Bailey drew in a deep breath and let it back out with a sigh. "There was one other little incident . . . he's *seen* me."

Liza narrowed her eyes. "What exactly do you mean, he's seen you?"

"I *mean* he's already seen the goodies."

Liza's eyes twinkled with mischief. She made a *tsk, tsk* sound. "And here I thought . . ."

Bailey shook her head. "You thought right. We haven't. It was purely accidental."

"That's original."

"It was our first day here. You'd gone down to the casino and I stayed behind in the room to freshen up."

Liza's mouth twitched with contained laughter. "Let me guess. You ordered room service?"

It was Bailey's turn to roll her eyes. "*No.* Maybe you haven't noticed, but the shower in our room is defective. I got stuck in there, and when I called for help, it was Carter who came to my rescue. Don't you see?" She spread her hands. "It's a sign."

"Call the preacher," Liza said. "My gal's getting married."

"Not so fast. As my friend, it's your responsibility to make sure I don't do anything stupid."

Liza laughed. "Somehow, I don't think that's an issue anymore."

"Am I wrong to want true love? And can you blame me? Don't you think Carter is, well, perfect for me?"

Liza had a faraway look in her eyes. After a long pondering moment, she spoke. "Considering your family, you're right. He'll fit right in. Not to mention he's quite a tantalizing tidbit. But, sweetie, I'm just not sure you'll be able to convince a man like Carter to come and settle down in a small town like Coupeville. He's got ties here. One, in particular." She waved a hand in the direction Carter and Twinkie had headed.

"What should I do?"

"Forget the car. Take the money and run—to the high limit slot room. That's my advice and I'm sticking to it."

Bailey groaned.

Liza patted her cheek softly. "It's okay. There's still tonight. I have a good feeling . . . you'll find your man. Now, what do you say we go hit the slots?"

"You go ahead. I'm going to stay here, wait a few minutes more. Like I said, that woman Carter was with is just a friend. Probably it was just a simple little disagreement they were having."

"Okay, but in my opinion, friends don't have simple little disagreements like that."

"It's complicated. You don't understand."

"It always is. And no I don't. Don't wait long," Liza said, softly. "I'll be right over there, if you need me." She pointed to a row of Elvis slots.

A couple of minutes went by and Bailey's brow drew into a worried frown. What if Carter didn't remember their lunch date? What if he was having lunch with Miss Bountiful? In her room? Bailey made a futile attempt to wipe the image of what the two of them might be doing— in addition to having lunch—from her mind, and the longer she thought about it, the more she worried she might be driving her new car home alone.

Yikes!

Well, fine, if Carter didn't want to keep his lunch date with her, she'd show him. She'd go to the competition, give him a piece of her mind, and, then she'd let some other Elvis wannabe woo her with his swiveling hips and his luscious lips.

Bailey sighed. Who was she kidding? The only man she wanted singing in her ear was Carter. And his were the only lips she ever wanted to kiss again. In a perfect world, he'd come home with her, meet her family, fall so deeply in love with her that he'd be proposing and talking about building a perfect little family, complete with ebony-haired children, before they even had sex.

After that, they'd have a fairy-tale life. Instead of bedtime stories, he'd serenade their children to sleep each night with a snappy little Elvis tune, and then they'd retire for the evening and he'd whisper in her ear how much he loved her and their life together.

Unfortunately, that dream was so far from reality she wanted to cry. The only sure thing that lay ahead of her right now was more than a thousand miles of cold, hard pavement. Bailey sucked air from the bottom of her glass and pondered spending two days alone on the open highway. It wouldn't be so bad. Only half of it would be at night.

Now she really wanted to cry.

Her mouth went dry, like a cup of sand had just been dumped into it. Hadn't she recently read an article about crazed highway killers in the Nevada desert? Her bottom lip quivered. How ever was she going to get her new car home? As far as she could see, she could either drive home alone and risk becoming one more lump in the Las Vegas desert, or she could forget about the car and, instead, take the cash.

Bailey sighed. Life wasn't supposed to be this hard. If she had to go through all fifty thousand Elvis impersonators and get thrown for an emotional loop each time, it would make an old woman of her. Now she wasn't even in the mood to go tell Carter off at tonight's show.

Maybe it was time to let go of this silly dream. Bailey rested her head back against the bench seat and closed her eyes. When she opened them, Carter was standing next to the table, giving her a warm smile.

"Rough morning on the slots?" he asked.

Bailey's heart leaped. He looked disheveled, with a shock of unruly hair hanging down over his forehead, and she didn't even care how it had gotten there. He was here, with her, and Miss Bountiful was nowhere in sight.

They had a quiet lunch. Carter was distracted, and Bailey supposed it had something to do with his *business* with Twinkie, who she didn't even want to think about right now.

Over the course of their meal, Carter's mood improved and he seemed to return to his old self . . . whoever that was. As far as Bailey could see, he had at least three sides, and she needed to get to know each of them better before saying the big "I do."

She and Carter shared a sinfully chocolate desert, and then they walked along Las Vegas Boulevard, until they came to the Bellagio hotel.

A small body of water lay before them, placid like a country lake, and Bailey imagined herself and Carter, back in Coupeville, rowing around in a small boat on a warm summer day. She'd be wearing a flirty white summer dress with a wide-brimmed sun hat, and Carter would be looking all dashing and sexy in one of his security guy suits. Of course, the sun would quickly become too hot for all those clothes and they'd both have to strip down to the bare essentials. Essentially nothing. Bailey did a quiet sigh.

Carter stood behind her, with his arms on the rail, enclosing her with his body. Right then, Bailey felt whole. Carter filled her all the way up.

People passed behind them, their voices melding with the sounds of motoring vehicles, but all Bailey heard was the murmur of her heart, telling her he was "the one."

After a few minutes, the placid surface of the water

began to bubble, and Josh Groban's voice filled the air with "So She Dances." A moment later a thousand fountains of water rose up from the man-made lake and blossomed into a lovely water dance. In Bailey's opinion, Josh Groban had the voice of an angel, second only to Elvis, but unlike Elvis, he'd continue to bless the world with new music for years.

Tourists moved quickly, filling in all empty rail space to watch the geysers spout upward. By the time Mr. Groban hit the second verse, Carter had his lips pressed against her cheek.

"Let's go. I'll show you my place," he whispered huskily into her ear.

She gripped the cement rail. Her mind was awhirl. She swallowed. The lion had invited her to his den. Now what? She blew out a breath. She just wasn't ready, even if it meant she'd have to drive home solo.

She put a hand to her hair. Maybe it hadn't been such a good idea to wear it down, wild and free. She reached inside her purse and pulled out the elastic band she always kept with her—just in case. With one quick motion, she scooped up her hair and slipped the band around it.

"I really need to get back to the room and do something with this," she said apologetically, "before tonight's show."

Carter reached a hand up to the back of her head and snapped the hair band. Her hair cascaded down and floated about her shoulders.

Bailey ran her tongue across her lips, wetting them, but they quickly dried in the Las Vegas heat. Carter didn't wait for her to wet them again. He pressed his mouth firmly over hers and kept it there until she felt her knees go weak. The Bellagio's fountains provided just enough breeze to keep her conscious but, still, she had to grip the rail to keep from sliding all the way down to the pavement.

"Put your arms around me," Carter told her in an even tone.

An elderly woman standing nearby smiled at and gave Bailey a look of envy.

Bailey let go of the rail and she wrapped her arms around him, but her brain was wrapped elsewhere—around the fact that her ability to resist him was quickly crumbling. If she'd had any questions what his intentions were, they were answered when he pressed his body to hers.

In a rush of anger, mostly at herself for letting his charm and sultry brute force get to her, Bailey pushed away from him—just a couple of inches, so that her brain could function.

Think. She pressed fingers to both sides of her temples. *You can't continue holding this man at bay by batting your eyelashes and acting like you don't know what he wants.* Bailey's mind scrambled for a solution. Anything . . . something that would shock Carter into backing off.

She looked up into his eyes. They were heavy with his seductive energy.

She was a goner.

Taking a mental look skyward, she blurted out the first thing that popped into her head.

"I'm a virgin."

The elderly woman standing nearby looked startled and Bailey didn't blame her, because even *she* was startled.

Where the heck had that come from?

Carter loosened his grip. He gave her a long stare, until finally, his eyes crinkled at the corners and his mouth spread into a full smile.

Bailey bit her lip. That wasn't the reaction she'd expected. Or hoped for. He was amused, pleased even. Geez, what had she done?

Chapter Thirteen

Everything changed with that one sentence. Carter reverted to calling her "ma'am." No more "baby" or "honey." His touch became hesitant, careful, as though he wanted to be sure not to overstep his bounds.

Now what? Bailey hadn't planned on telling him she was a virgin—which she wasn't—but something had taken over her brain and it had just popped out. She couldn't help it. A woman could only take so much passionate duress. Her willpower had just about been used up, and the situation had called for drastic measures.

Over the next hour, the only kisses she received were friendly pecks on the cheek. Carter was sweet, a perfect gentleman, and Bailey didn't like it one little bit. Not only did she miss his amorous advances, but it made her uneasy that his behavior was based on a lie, and lies were never a good thing for a blossoming relationship.

Finally, with the afternoon behind them, Bailey was glad for the reprieve. When she got back to her room, Liza was sitting on the bed counting a wad of cash.

"Good day on the slots?" Bailey said without much enthusiasm.

"Spectacular." Liza slapped the bundle down onto the table. "Six hundred dollars spectacular."

Bailey dropped her purse on the bed and went to the bathroom to see what damage Carter's hands had done to her hair before she'd scared him off. A minute later, Liza appeared in the doorway, and she started drumming her fingers on the doorjamb. Bailey continued fussing with her hair.

"You and *faux* Elvis had a good time, huh? Your hair sure looks like *it* had a good time."

Bailey leaned into the mirror and plucked a gray strand from her head. Probably a lot more would show up in the next couple of weeks as punishment for lying to Carter.

"Did you guys do it?"

Bailey plucked another hair, and rubbed her head where it'd been. "That's private, but no. Not even close." And probably they never would.

Liza stepped into the small room. "Just checking . . . I mean, since he's already had a preview."

Bailey did an eye roll. "I told you, the shower door is defective." She pulled on the door handle to demonstrate. It swung open without a hitch. "Okay, *was* defective."

"Uh-huh." Liza grabbed a tube of hot pink lipstick from the counter and swiped it over her mouth. She rolled her lips together and then blotted them lightly with a Kleenex.

Bailey pulled up her hair, twisted it around her fingers, and fastened it with a clip. No doubt about it, the just-out-of-bed look was sexier, but what was the point now? As far as Carter was concerned, she was off-limits.

She went to the closet and pulled the purple dress that she'd brought to wear to the competition from the hanger. She slipped it over her head. "Zip, please," she beckoned to Liza, sucking in her already flat stomach.

She turned her head from side to side. Purple was a perfect complement to her dark hair and, together, she and Carter would make a most attractive couple. Bailey tousled her now-loose hair a bit more and misted it with spray to keep it that way.

Liza slid her a grin. "What's this?" She picked up two of Bailey's broken hair bands.

Bailey smiled. "Carter has a problem with tidy hair." She pulled another broken band out of her pocket and dropped it on the counter with the others.

"You *did* do it," Liza said with a squeal. "A man doesn't just break your hair band for no reason. He does it to tangle his fingers in your hair while in the throes of passion."

"My hair being down doesn't mean we *did* it," Bailey said.

"Okay. How close did you come to *not* doing it?"

"Not even. I told you, Carter's a gentleman."

"Oh. I see. He's boring."

"He's not boring. It's just that building a real relationship is serious business and I want everything to be just right before we do *it*."

"I'd say you're off to a good start," Liza said. "You've managed to get through the adolescent years with him already. He's peeked at you in the shower, pulled your ponytail, and next, I suppose he'll be giving you his i.d. bracelet."

Bailey did a mental eye roll. *Really.* An i.d. bracelet? Make that a ring.

At eight o'clock sharp, Bailey and Liza walked into the Imperial Palace showroom, where tables and chairs were set up to accommodate just over eight hundred people. Bailey gave their tickets to one of the ushers and they were directed to a table right at the front of the stage. Elegant red drapery that hung from ceiling to floor was pulled closed, but there remained a gap wide enough for Bailey to see people backstage rushing about. Elvis tribute artists. It was a beautiful sight.

Bailey kept her gaze glued to the gap in the curtain,

hoping to catch a glimpse of Carter. Her heart did a half flip when she finally spotted him. He had on black leather pants, a dark blue shirt, and a black jacket. His hair was all black and shimmery and his sideburns were trimmed to perfection. She sighed. *He* was perfection.

Bailey kept her gaze fixed on Carter, hardly even taking notice when Quent Flagg and Steve Sogura walked past until, finally, he looked her way. He gave her a head gesture to join him up on stage.

Bailey jumped up. She didn't need to be told twice.

"Where are you going?" Liza yelled after her.

Bailey waved a hand over her shoulder.

"Kiss me," Carter said to her when she reached him.

Bailey sighed to herself. Now that was more like it. She'd been wondering for the last two hours whether she'd ever feel his arms around her or his lips on hers again.

He pulled her to him, crushing her against his chest, and kissed her until she gasped.

"Wow," she said, waving a hand in front of her face to cool herself. Tingles, toe curls, that swirly feeling in the pit of her stomach that made her want to run for the nearest bathroom. It was all there, all that silly stuff that let a girl know she was falling for a man, just like her Aunt Fiona said it would be.

"Hey, the show hasn't even started yet. Wait until you see *me* sing," an *Elvis* voice said behind her. She turned to look. Irv Cass, World Champion, sidled up to her and Carter and he gave Carter a friendly slap on the back. "Didn't know you'd made it into the show tonight," he said, without taking his eyes off Bailey.

"I got that rookie Stapleton to give up his spot," Carter told Irv. "Convinced him I stood a better chance of winning. He'll get his share."

"Yeah, but you're gonna have to beat me first," Irv said with a laugh, eyes still on Bailey. "Who's your friend?"

"This is Bailey. She's here for a few days, won a car. You know . . . the usual Vegas stuff."

"No kidding? Won a car? Now that's something you don't see every day." Irv squeezed Bailey's arm gently. "Don't let this guy fool you," he said, poking a finger at Carter. "There's only one Elvis here."

Carter laughed. "That would be me," he said.

"Guess the lady will have to see for herself." Irv touched Bailey's cheek. "Keep your eyes on me, honey," he said and walked away without looking back.

"Ah, you're not falling for that act, are you?" Carter asked, giving Bailey a crooked grin.

"No." Bailey shook her head. "Well, maybe," she teased. "He is very good."

Carter's forehead wrinkled into a frown.

"Don't you worry. You're the one they all have to beat," she assured him. She left the stage and returned to her seat. She took a quick peek at the program and saw that Irv Cass was closing the show with "My Way," a sure crowd pleaser. That could be trouble. Still, Carter remained her firm choice as winner. And she was pretty sure it wasn't just because she was falling in love with him.

At ten minutes past showtime, the audience began to get restless. Finally, a lanky man who walked as though his legs were controlled by strings came out onto the stage. He had big eyes and wore big glasses that were probably the reason his eyes looked so big.

He squinted into the audience. "Good evening, ladies and gentlemen."

Screams filled the room and Bailey wasn't able to hear much more of what he had to say. It really didn't matter. All she wanted, all any of the women wanted, was for the show to start.

First up was Doug Church. He gave a better than average performance with his rendition of "Suspicious Minds." Women in the audience squirmed and squealed their delight. Bailey clapped lightly; she was reserving her energy for Carter, in case the judges based part of their decision on audience response.

Several others performed, including Robert Washington, John Loos, and Brandon Bennett. Then, finally, it was Carter's turn to swivel his stuff.

The MC announced him through a torrent of screams, and he breezed out onto the stage into a blaze of lights. He opened with "Devil in Disguise" and somehow Bailey got the feeling he was singing it especially for her benefit. He'd probably used his security-guy-mind-reading powers and already knew what a liar she was.

By the time he reached the first chorus, women were pulling at their own hair, and by the second, their chests were heaving. *God, please don't let any of them have a heart attack,* Bailey prayed.

By mid-song, sweat was trickling down Carter's forehead and into his eyes. He pulled a blue silk scarf from around his neck and swiped it across his face, then held it out over the audience, where two women fought for position. One of them finally conceded as the other yanked it from his hand.

Carter went directly into "I Can't Help Falling In Love," and Bailey heard some heavy pounding. Her heart.

He paused after the first verse to grab a handful of colorful scarves and placed them around his neck. The screaming rose in volume until his voice could barely be heard. Carter wiped one of the colorful pieces of silk over his forehead and tossed it out to a hundred raised hands. It was like sharks in a feeding tank. One would think Carter really *was* the King. Even some of the men were involved in all the excitement.

Three seats down from Bailey a cute blonde, mid-twenties, sat swaying gently to the music. She had stars in her eyes and probably something indecent on her mind—just like every other woman in the theater. Bailey had thoughts of killing her right then and there, or at least taking her out back and beating the lust out of her.

A moment later a piece of pink silk floated from Carter's hand, and right into the cute blonde's grubby little perfectly manicured fingers. If Bailey had been just one seat closer, she could have snatched it away. Who knew what plans the woman had for that scarf?

Carter smiled and the woman gave him a look that made Bailey see red—or green. She was all too familiar with that look and so, too, it seemed was Carter. No doubt, he saw some version of it every day of his life. He reached down and touched the blonde's hair and it was amazing that the woman was able to keep from sliding off her chair.

All the women in the first three rows stretched out their arms, straining for a piece of Carter's flesh, wanting to give him a piece of theirs in return.

Bailey had never considered herself the jealous type, but she was pretty sure that if she looked in a mirror right now she'd see green slime oozing from her pores. She had to keep reminding herself that these women only wanted him for his body, whereas she wanted him to sing her to sleep every night for the rest of her life.

A pair of panties sailed over Bailey's head and landed at Carter's feet. Brazen hussies the whole lot of them. She looked over at Liza just as she sling-shotted her own piece of lace toward the stage.

An elbow to the ribs was the only cure for that behavior.

"Hey," Liza said, rubbing where bone had connected with flesh. "I'm just doing what's expected."

Carter glanced down at Bailey and gave her a quick grin before backing up the runway to the main stage. She was glad for the acknowledgment, but even more glad that he'd retreated. She was in no mood to get in a fist fight with two hundred women.

Without pause, the music picked up and Carter began

singing "Burning Love." Bailey looked up at him and he stared right into her eyes. Burning was right. All the way to her soul. The way he was looking at her, coupled with the way she felt, she was pretty sure he wasn't going to let the virgin thing hold him back much longer. And neither was she.

Carter went down to his knees and slid over to the edge. He pulled a lavender scarf from around his neck and let the soft fluff of material tease Bailey's cheek. She reached for it, but just as her fingers touched it, he pulled it back. She felt her heart pounding in her ears. Once more he dangled the scarf in front of her, and this time he didn't pull it away. She held it to her nose and breathed in his scent.

Bailey glanced over and gave the blonde who'd received the last scarf a smug look. The blonde glared back.

Carter saw the exchange and he grinned at Bailey. A spotlight beamed over the two of them and a hush fell over the audience. He put another scarf to his lips, then leaned down and gently wrapped it around Bailey's neck. He pulled her to him and their lips met. He let them linger for a very long pause, until finally, he smoothed a hand over her cheek and backed away, leaving Bailey with her head tilted up and her mouth still puckered.

Liza grabbed hold of her and pulled her back into her seat. "You two keep that up and there'll be a lynching. Yours. You think these women want to see you kissin' on that man while they're creamin' their seats?"

Bailey glanced over her shoulder. Women were screaming and it wasn't with lust for Carter. The screams were focused at her. Every woman in the place wanted to beat her to a bloody pulp.

"Let Carter do his job," Liza said. "You'll get yours later."

Eventually, the screaming died down, but each time Bailey glanced in any direction other than the stage, she

received venomous looks. She didn't care. She'd die in
Carter's arms and be happy about it.

Carter approached the edge of the stage again and
the woman sitting on Bailey's left, who looked old
enough to be Carter's mother, moaned up at him. He
reached a hand down to her and she reached up just as
another pair of panties and a black lacy bra whizzed by.
At that moment, Bailey understood her mother's un-
yielding belief that the King still lived. He was in their
hearts and there he would always stay.

It was touching. And unnerving. The air held a charge
and Bailey had the feeling that at any minute one of
these women could snap and do something crazy.

The older woman continued her frantic wave at Carter.
Hunger burned in her eyes—she wanted more. A whole
lot more. Forget the polite touch or a piece of material
soaked with his sweat, she wanted living, breathing flesh.

Ever mindful of his obligation to please those who
made it possible for him to do what he loved, Carter
kneeled and gave her a light peck on the cheek.

He quickly backed off, but the woman was spry. *Eeek.*
Her eyes filled with a crazy gleam, and she was all over
him like a starving dog on a bone. Carter tried pulling
away, but the woman was a human octopus, and he was
firmly in her tentacles.

Bailey continued to watch the struggle between man
and beast, and to her horror the frenzy was beginning to
spread. The audience began stomping and clapping and
rooting the woman on.

Carter gave Bailey an imploring look, but what the
hell was she supposed to do against a roomful of rabid
women? Anything. That's what. Whatever it took to save
her man.

Bailey grabbed the woman's arm and gave it a good
yank. It held firm. She grabbed the woman around the
waist and tugged with both hands, putting all her weight

into pulling the woman back, away from Carter. Finally, the woman's grasp slipped a bit and with a determined breath, Bailey gave one final pull. The woman let go of Carter's hand and, together, she and Bailey both fell back in a heap onto Bailey's chair.

Liza looked over at them. "Boy, if you thought your hair was wild before, you should see it now."

Bailey shoved the woman over to her own seat. "You could have helped."

Liza raised an eyebrow. "Are you kidding? You're lucky Carter escaped with both his arms intact. I have to bowl next Wednesday night."

Bailey did her best to pat her hair back into place. She looked up at Carter and he gave her a smile, mouthing the word "sorry"; then he retreated backstage.

The audience screamed his name, demanding an encore, but all they got was the lanky man with the big eyes. Bailey supposed he was announcing the next performer, but the screaming was so loud she couldn't hear a word he said. He pumped his hands up and down in an effort to try and quiet everyone, but that only enticed the audience into a booing frenzy. A small green object sailed past Bailey and it hit the MC square in the forehead.

It was a grape. Someone had come prepared. Two more grapes sailed past and only one of them hit its mark. The MC made his exit and the screaming continued without pause for what seemed like ten minutes. Probably it was really only one or two, but to Bailey's eardrums, it was at least ten.

"I didn't know you'd chosen the hottest thing in Vegas as your date," Liza said. Her voice was hoarse after doing her part in the screaming frenzy.

"Me neither. Geez."

"I hope you realize that if you take that man home, your mom will be just like these women and you'll have to fight *her* off, too."

Bailey saw Carter back behind the curtain, leaning against a wall to catch his breath. If the volume of the audience's response to his performance was any indication of who would win this competition, he had no worries.

Steve Sogura passed by Carter and said something and Bailey supposed it was kudos on a job well done. Carter gave him a nod of thanks. Finally, the hysteria was rolling down to a simmer and the MC bravely poked his head out once more. When no one booed, his gaze darted around the showroom for a minute, and then he stepped from behind the curtain to announce Irv Cass.

Irv Cass was a legend and Bailey was thrilled to be in the same auditorium with him. Maybe not as thrilled as she was to be with Carter, but still.

Irv was more than ready to perform. He whisked out onto the stage with both arms raised high, cape spread. He paraded around the stage, turning this way and that, giving every audience member the opportunity to see his gem-studded attire. His entrance promised an extraordinary performance and he didn't disappoint. "If I Can Dream" brought sniffles and even a tear or two, and Bailey felt the genuine anguish in his lyrics. He ended with "My Way," another solid, winning performance. Carter was in trouble.

Irv bowed as several pairs of panties sailed overhead. He caught one pair in his fist and held them high like they were a trophy. The screaming increased to eardrum-buster level.

Bailey chewed her lip. She looked up on the stage at all the pairs of panties and lacy bras. If the judges took into consideration how much underwear was thrown during each artist's performance, she knew Carter had Irv beat when it came to bras. Panties were a wash. Together, there was enough lingerie on stage to open a small shop.

Underwear aside, based on screams, there was no clearer winner than Carter.

What it would really come down to was luck, but with Irv's two heartfelt performances, he had the clear edge.

After several minutes, the MC finally appeared, looking more than a little nervous as he started to read the results.

"It's my pleasure to once more crown"—his eyes skirted around the audience, no doubt on the lookout for flying fruit—"Irv Cass as World Champion. Steve Sogura comes in at number two . . ."

Bailey held her breath and crossed all her fingers and both her legs and she even said a quick prayer. *Third place, third place, third place. Dear Lord, please.*

"And coming in a close third is . . . Carter Davis."

Bailey breathed.

Chapter Fourteen

Bailey wanted to meet those judges to check to see if any of them wore hearing aids, and had them turned off during Carter's performance. How could he not have won? He'd almost started a riot, for God's sake. The longer she sat there and thought about it, the more her anger boiled inside her. Just as it surely boiled inside Carter. But a few minutes later, when all the performers returned to the stage, she looked into Carter's face and all she saw was contentment. His gaze met hers and he smiled down at her. If there was any disappointment behind his eyes, he wasn't about to let it show.

After a final bow, he disappeared with the others behind the curtain. Another few minutes passed and he reappeared. He'd changed his clothes, but was still dressed in black. He'd replaced the leather with a lighter fabric that shimmered loosely over his muscular frame.

Liza didn't waste any time making herself scarce, saying how she'd enjoyed meeting him and that she hoped to see him again soon.

Carter took Bailey's hand without a word. He led her out of the showroom, past dozens of women who had stayed behind to see if they could get lucky for a night with one of the performers. Several envious looks were shot at Bailey as they walked by, and she wondered if Carter knew any of them, or had ever used his special powers on them.

Better not to even think about such things.

They made their way through the casino to an open lounge that was semi-quiet for a Saturday night, and sat on stools at one end of the bar. Carter ordered a bourbon on the rocks.

"Tough break," the bartender said to Carter, pouring his drink with a heavy hand.

Bad news traveled fast.

"Sorry you didn't win," Bailey piped in. She laid a hand over his, covering his ring that was a replica of Elvis's TCB ring.

Carter shrugged. "Third place is nothing to be ashamed of." He took a long drink.

"No, it's not. But the judges need to clean their ears. Every woman left that theater without her undergarments, in large part because of you."

Carter looked at her like he could see through her clothes. "Even you?"

Bailey felt her face warm. "No," she said quietly. "I thought I should save something for you to look forward to, seeing as you've already seen what's under my panties and bra."

Carter gave her a once-over. "So I have." He signaled the bartender for another bourbon.

"If you'd like I could go back to the theater with you; we could beat the crap out of those judges. You really were the winner. Just ask any of your adoring fans. Most of them were ready to have your baby."

Carter laughed. "Sometimes you don't know what'll please the judges," he said. "Maybe they were offended by all those undergarments. Political correctness and all." He pushed his glass away, snagged a hand through his hair.

"Maybe I need a break. A vacation. Somewhere quiet. Away from all this." He gestured wide with his hand.

Bingo! "I know somewhere quiet," she said. *Like the night of the living dead.* "The casino is having my car washed and detailed. They told me it would be ready tomorrow morning. I'll be leaving around nine A.M., if you'd like to go for a long drive with me."

"Before you head home?"

"Not *before*. *When*."

Carter had left his Elvis persona back at the Imperial Showroom. Right now, it was security guy's eyes who looked back at her. Bailey shifted in her chair. He studied her for a long time and she began to finger the corner of her napkin.

Had she made a mistake? Would he think her too forward? The last thing she wanted was for him to think she was just like all the others. Women who were willing to do anything for a chance to be with him.

"Where's home?"

A million butterflies took flight inside Bailey's stomach. Could it really be possible that he'd actually consider going home with her? "Coupeville," she said, trying to keep her voice from squeaking with excitement.

"Coupe what?"

"Ville. It's a small waterfront community in Washington state. And it's very quiet."

"Ah, that's a pretty long drive, honey." *Elvis* was back. "You sure you wouldn't like to just drive on up to the dam, or how about over to the Grand Canyon? Either one of those drives will break your car in."

Bailey's heart thumped all the way into her throat. This was no time to be shy, not if she was going to convince this man to travel more than a thousand miles with her. "Home. With me. It'll be worth it," she said, dropping her voice seductively and looking up at him through thick lashes.

Carter grinned. His blue eyes darkened with curiosity. "What about your friend? How will she get home?"

"She's got wings."

Carter raised an eyebrow.

"She's flying home in the morning."

"Ah, I don't know. If my men don't give me proper notice when they'll be gone, I get after them. I wouldn't want to set a bad example."

Bailey's thumping heart threatened to come to a thudding stop. So close, yet so far. She shook her head. "No. You don't understand. I mean, you wouldn't want to let a helpless female drive all the way home by herself, would you? What if I were to get hijacked by marauding bandits?"

Carter's mouth twitched into a smile. "Sounds scary. I haven't heard of that happening in a while. I have a feeling, though, that you're far from being a helpless female."

Only when she was near him, and that's what scared her. He made her feel out of control. "Maybe I'd just like the company." Bailey felt all hope sinking. Still, she wasn't one to beg. She glanced at her watch. If she had to drive home alone, she was going to need a lot of rest so that she could keep her eyes open every lonely mile. She slipped off her stool. "I guess this is good-bye then." She stuck out her hand. No sense in torturing herself any further by dragging out their parting.

Carter stared at her hard, and then he grabbed her. "You're not getting away that easy."

Okay, so maybe they'd end things with a kiss. She wetted her lips, and Carter pressed his mouth to hers. His tongue searched around for a while, and then he finally let her go, just before her legs gave out. Okay, so maybe she didn't need *that* much sleep. It *was* Saturday night. Sin City was alive and kicking and so was her libido.

"I told Liza I might be tied up for a while, that I might not get back to the room until late."

Carter grinned.

"Will I?"

His eyes gleamed. "Ah, I don't know, honey. How tied up would you like to be?"

"Very."

"Then you've come to the right man." He held out his hand. "Come with me."

They spent the next hour strolling Las Vegas Boulevard, stopped to watch the fountain show at Bellagio, and then wandered into an open air nightspot, where Carter pulled her into his arms and held her there while they danced to something slow. His body was pressed to hers, his lips nuzzled her hair, his gun was once again jammed against her chest. It was perfect. What more could a girl want?

A lot more. And she knew the reason she wasn't getting it. She'd lied and this was her punishment.

They left the nightspot, and Bailey argued with herself all the way down the Strip. Should she just come clean, tell Carter that there'd been another, but that he was *practically* her first? It wasn't that she hadn't *wanted* to feel his hands roaming around her body. She just wanted to be cautious, make sure he was *the one*. Was that so wrong? My God, if she played warm the tootsies with every guy who thought he could sing like Elvis, she wouldn't have any time left over for, well, *life*.

They continued walking until Bailey's feet ached. She'd probably walked farther in the last twenty-four hours than she usually did in an entire week back home, and she was still no closer to her goal. But, hey, at least she had a new car. And a few really good memories.

Bailey sighed to herself. The thought of becoming nothing more than a distant memory to Carter was too depressing. She had to give Carter something to remember her by.

"Let's go to your place," Bailey said, stopping short.

Carter looked at his watch. "Now? It's one A.M."

"Right now." She grabbed Carter around his neck and pulled him to her, putting everything she had into her kiss. Years and years of pent-up waiting was a powerful thing, and she knew it was good because she could feel Carter's response telling her it was.

He looked at her long and hard, like he might be mulling over how far it was to the nearest bed. Of course, before things went too far, they'd need to have a talk about her virgin status. Surprises were not a good thing in the heat of the moment.

"I don't know, honey. You're leaving town . . . I don't think . . ."

Bailey put a finger to his lips. "Don't think. Let's just do." Maybe they didn't need to talk about her virgin status. Maybe he wouldn't even know. Carter ran a hand up her back in a way that made her nipples harden.

Oh yeah, he'd know.

He kissed her forehead tenderly, letting his lips linger longer than was necessary. Then he slipped from her arms. "Sorry, honey. I don't want to be responsible for you not getting enough sleep for your drive."

Bailey felt like the wind had been knocked out of her. Not that she went around offering her body to men, but to be turned down when everything about it seemed so right, geez, she might as well be a virgin.

Carter walked her to her room and they stood face-to-face, her with her back to the wall; him just out of reach, figuratively *and* literally.

It was quiet, except for the occasional hum of the elevator, starting and stopping and depositing people on their respective floors. Bailey didn't know what else she could say. She'd done her best and it wasn't enough. Carter obviously didn't care for her the same as she cared for him.

That thought made her feel hollow. Like her heart had

been sucked empty. Could this truly be the last time she'd ever see him? He leaned close as though he could sense her emptiness. His breath was warm on her hair, and his heartbeat was strong against her chest. They stood like that for a long time and then he finally broke away.

She stifled a soft cry that lay ready on her lips. This man could very well be the love of her life. How could he say good-bye? Tears welled in Bailey's eyes and she turned her head away so he wouldn't see.

In the back of her mind, she heard her mother's wise words. "The truth always wins."

Damn.

"I'd better go," Carter said with a warm smile.

Bailey gazed longingly up at him. *Before you leave, couldn't you just throw me down right here in the hallway and have your way with me?* Carter's crooked grin turned into a full smile. Bailey blushed. He was using his super-security-guy-mind-reading powers on her.

"Goodnight," he said. He took one of her hands and brought it to his mouth, kissing it gently before turning away. He walked to the elevator and stopped. "What time?"

"Time?" Bailey looked at her watch.

He shook his head. "What time do we leave?"

Carter found Bailey's T-Bird in the Oasis detail center. They hadn't started working on it yet, but it would only take a couple of hours to wash it and give it a good buffing. By morning, it'd be glowing. Hell, even with layer upon layer of smoke resin, it glowed.

Many a guest had stopped and stared at this car, just as he was now, wishing it was theirs, but he had other wishes. It still wasn't too late to back out, and God knew he should but he knew he wouldn't. It would have been nice to think he was going home with Bailey simply because she wanted him to, but that would be a lie. Maybe not completely, but darn near.

Carter stepped up to the car. He looked in the window. Black interior, with red accents. Cute, in a sassy kind of way. Fitting for the woman who'd won it. He chuckled. Fitting for a *virgin*. She might not be the type to jump in the sack with every date, but a virgin? A woman with hair like that? A body like hers? No way. He could be wrong, but he wasn't. Still, if that's what she wanted him to believe, he'd go along with it. For a while.

Carter smiled. So many of the women he encountered would do just about anything to slip between the sheets with him, especially when he was doing the King thing. Not Bailey. She wanted him, that much he was sure of, yet she'd done everything she could to stop him from going too far. It was refreshing—and baffling.

He checked the car's passenger door. It was locked. He went around to the driver's side and tried that door. It swung open and he slid into the soft leather seat. Not a lot of headroom. It'd be a tight ride to wherever Bailey was taking him, but he'd manage.

Seeing some lucky winner drive off with a prize like this was just plain good for business. Half the onlookers would have a new confidence that they, too, could win and they'd rush inside to stuff the machines with their hard-earned money. Hell, anything could happen in Vegas.

Carter relaxed his head back against the rest, closing his eyes for a long minute. Finally, he reached into his breast pocket and pulled out a small black cloth bag. No need to look inside—he'd already done that back at Zoopa's—but he did give it a good squeeze, feeling the hard object against his palm.

"Call it payback, Frank," he said. Carter stretched his arm back behind the seat and dropped it into the hinge assembly area where the soft top was neatly folded down into the car.

"Hey," a voice said.

Carter jumped, hitting his head on the roof of the car. He looked up and saw Mike, from the control room, staring down at him. "Jesus. You want to give an old man a heart attack?" He rubbed his scalp. "What're you doing down here anyway? Shouldn't you be up in the casino harassing our guests?"

Mike laughed. "I think that's your job. I got a call from your gal. She wanted me to have you come down and make sure her car would be ready to go." He shrugged. "I couldn't find you, so I told her I'd do it myself, seeing as she was the boss's lady."

Carter gave him a look. "I don't have a lady, and for your health, I hope you didn't really say that to her."

Mike shrugged again.

"SOB," Carter mumbled and got out of the car. He circled it, giving it a good once-over. "It's too bad they're going to quit making these. Seems like they just got started. Guess they're not practical, being two-seaters."

"Hard to carry a family," Mike said.

"Isn't it time you head back upstairs?"

Mike laughed. "I'm gone. Say hi to your lucky gal for me." And he left.

Yeah. Lucky. Carter had a sudden twinge of guilt for involving Bailey in his mess. It'd be easy enough to follow through with Azuri, give him back his diamond, but that wouldn't be the end of it. Frank would only find a way to get the diamond back. If, on the other hand, the Azuri diamond went missing for a while, Azuri could claim the loss and Frank would be out of luck. Carter let out a long breath, shoving aside his guilt for the time being.

In a perfect world, Zoopa would be in jail, Twinkie would be free, and he and his little brunette *virgin* would see each other as often as time and travel allowed.

* * *

After only a few hours' sleep, give or take two to account for Liza's snoring, Bailey woke up to a knock at the door. Her head felt like it weighed a hundred pounds, but she managed to raise it from the pillow. Liza was still wearing her skimpy black robe, and a dark-haired man pushing a cart followed her to the center of the room. He gave Bailey a polite "good morning," then handed Liza something to sign before he disappeared.

"What's that?" Bailey mumbled.

"Food." Liza waved something that smelled like bacon in front of Bailey's face.

"It's too early for food," Bailey groaned into her pillow.

Liza sipped something frothy and wet that looked suspiciously like orange juice. She stabbed a piece of melon and popped it into her mouth and made *m-m-m* sounds while she chewed.

Bailey lay there for a few seconds taking in the smells, and then it hit her. If Liza was already up, she was late. Bailey sprang to a sitting position. "Why didn't you wake me? I'm supposed to pick up my car this morning."

Liza swallowed her melon. "I don't know . . . maybe because I wasn't informed of your schedule."

Bailey scrambled out of bed and took a warm muffin from under a tin lid. She grabbed some comfortable clothes—a skirt and a tank top—to wear on the drive home, and then she went to the bathroom to assess the damage.

Not bad. A little gel, a little mascara, some heavy lipstick and she was ready to go. She'd called the control center last night, a while after Carter had left, to make sure what time her car would be ready, but what she'd really wanted was to hear his voice once more before going to sleep. When he wasn't there, she'd used the car as her excuse for calling, and Mike had promised he'd personally check on it.

Bailey packed in record time and then bid Liza

farewell. Liza wished her a safe drive home, saying she'd pray for her, but this time, Bailey wasn't worried about being out in the desert. She had her very own security guy. And he carried a big gun.

Bailey hurried through the casino, weaving around and through a group of men in cowboy hats, almost knocking one of them to the ground. She was supposed to meet Carter at Guest Services at nine A.M., and she was on the verge of being late.

Carter was there waiting for her. He looked none the worse for his lack of sleep. No big surprise there. Probably his super powers enabled him to skip sleeping entirely. His black hair glistened under the lights and he was dressed, as usual, in all black. Shirt, pants, shoes . . . perfect.

Carter pulled her over in front of the Wheel of Fortune machines, and they sat and waited until a woman in a flashy red business suit walked over to them and handed Bailey a piece of paper. The title to her new car, and, right there, under Legal Owner, was her name, Bailey Ventura. Free and clear, the T-Bird was all hers. No five-year waiting period before she got the pink slip.

Bailey stared at the paper, and she began to get a strange sensation. Like something wonderful was about to happen, and there was no stopping it. She was giddy. It was finally hitting her that she'd won a car. The joy she should have felt when the reels on that slot machine landed on jackpot was finally bubbling to the surface. She leaped up, threw her arms in the air, and twirled around in a full circle.

Both Carter and the woman in red laughed, watching her in her delight.

Bailey didn't care. She didn't care if she made a crazy fool of herself. She'd won herself a brand-new car.

The woman in red asked Bailey and Carter to follow her outside to the front of the building, and they were instructed to wait at the curb while someone brought the car around.

They stood in the warm morning sun. Bailey was happy to soak up as much of it as possible before they left for Washington, where it was not unusual for several weeks to pass without even a hint of sun or warmth. So many times, she'd wished she lived somewhere else, but right now, the weather didn't matter one little bit. Carter was going home with her, and she had a feeling things were going to heat right up.

The anticipation was killing her, but finally, there it was. Her brand-new torch red Thunderbird. She watched it circle up from the garage and roll to a stop right in front of them. Washed and waxed, it was the most beautiful car in Nevada. Maybe even Washington.

The driver handed Bailey the keys and she just stood there. What now? Did she just get in? Drive away? Just like that? No signing anything?

Carter took hold of her arm and steered her to the passenger's side. He opened the car door and whispered in her ear to give the newly formed crowd a little wave. She did and then he nudged her into the seat.

"I'll drive until we get out of this traffic," he told her.

Bailey gave him a blank look. She'd heard him, but it was as though she were dreaming. She'd go along with whatever he said. The only thing she was aware of at that moment, other than Carter's voice, was the smell of stale cigarette smoke. Her beautiful new car stunk like a smoke-filled casino.

Carter grinned. "Buckle up, honey. It's gonna be a long ride."

Bailey did as she was told, and then she drew in a breath of clean air out the window. A long ride was right. Twelve hundred miles long. Maybe if they drove with the windows down all day, the stink would be gone by the time they reached Washington.

Carter drove slowly, snaking his way through congested Las Vegas Boulevard, and a half hour later, their stop-and-go progress turned into smooth movement. They'd reached the open highway.

Surrounded by brown hills and miles of road, Bailey relaxed into her seat. Carter seemed in complete control, driving a steady sixty miles per hour, keeping his eyes on the road. She blew out a long breath. This wasn't going to be so bad, after all. She glanced at her watch. She didn't have to worry for another thirty-six hours or so. That's when Carter would meet her family.

Oh boy.

Chapter Fifteen

Since winning a car hadn't been on the itinerary, Bailey hadn't made any hotel reservations for the trip home. But even if she had to drive straight through without stopping for sleep it would be worth it to have Carter sitting next to her. Probably if they did stop, she wouldn't be able to sleep anyway.

Her excitement wasn't long-lived. Once they escaped the city, and the open road lay before them, Carter pulled over and Bailey got that annoying queasy feeling in her gut that she always got when faced with the chore of driving. Surely, he didn't already need to be relieved.

"I think you should drive now," he said.

Bailey looked at her watch. They'd only been on the road for forty-five minutes. She gave him a curious look.

"Traffic is light, the weather is agreeable. It's a good time to get familiar with your new car."

Bailey glanced around. Traffic was nonexistent, the weather was perfect, and she was having a perfectly good time waiting to get to know her new car. There'd be plenty of time to do that when she got back home. "Do you *need* a break?"

"Honey, if I *needed* something, I wouldn't ask." Carter

got out of the car and walked around to her side. He opened the door and waited.

Bailey didn't make a move to get out. Instead, she looked up at him with doe eyes. That tactic had certainly worked on a few of the officers back home. "Don't you think it's a little soon to trust me behind the wheel? I mean, we only just met three days ago."

"I'm very well aware of when we met." His eyes gleamed dark. "I think I know you well enough for just about anything."

Bailey stayed put. Although she'd never stipulated who would do the driving, she just assumed him being the man and all, that he'd want to do the manly thing and drive. A real gentleman would insist on doing *all* the driving. She glanced around at their surroundings. Rush hour was probably an SUV with a family of four, a bus full of tourists, and a convertible packed with testosterone-infused boys on their way to becoming men. And her guess was rush hour wasn't going to hit anytime soon.

"C'mon. Let's make some time." Carter dangled the keys in front of her.

Bailey took them, and went around to the driver's seat. "Buckle up," she said, sliding Carter a nervous look. He grinned, ready for whatever came. Fine, then. She could do this. She took a quick inventory of the car's dash, located the important things, like the air-conditioning button and the controls for the stereo. If she could have put the top down, everything would've been perfect, but Carter had said that they'd only bake under the sun, and not only that, but they'd have nowhere to store the hard top. The trunk had just enough room for their bags, and the shelf behind the front seats was crammed full of things she'd purchased in Vegas.

Bailey pulled away from the shoulder, and she soon had the T-Bird cruising at a comfortable sixty miles per hour. Carter found a station on the stereo that played classic rock, then closed his eyes and settled back into the seat. Bailey glanced around the dash some more. Heated seats, air bags, buttons she wouldn't understand until she'd read the owner's manual. Her new car had it all, including one gorgeous man sitting next to her. Carter shifted in his seat to get comfortable. She hoped not too comfortable. If traffic picked up, she intended to hand the keys back to him. She looked in the rearview mirror. Nothing. Up ahead the same. She had a feeling she'd be driving a while.

They made a few necessary stops over the next couple of hours, for gas and some bottles of water, and some brownies that the clerk said were baked fresh that morning. At one stop, when they returned to the car, a large black man with a bald head that glistened under the hot sun was standing next to it.

"Man, that is a clean-ass Thunderbird," he said. His lips stretched wide to expose a row of perfect white teeth as he gazed at the car.

Bailey told him she'd won it in Vegas and his lips stretched even wider. He high-fived her, and she and Carter got back on the road.

Next stop was for lunch at a small roadside café, where a dozen motorcycles and three big rigs were parked out front. Desert charm. Bailey ordered a plate of fried jumbo shrimp and was surprised that they were the best she'd ever had, doubly surprising considering they were a fair distance from shrimping waters.

A few more hours down the road, she and Carter rolled into a small town that lay tucked into a hillside dotted with ordnance storage bunkers. The bunkers were a stirring reminder that the US had enemies they needed to always be ready to defend themselves against.

They pulled into a gas station slash convenience store, and the clerk, a woman in her mid-fifties, ran outside before they could even get out of the car. She gushed over the T-Bird like she'd never seen such a car, and when Bailey told her how she'd won it, the woman invited them to spend the night. She wanted to call all her friends to come over and see the car that someone had actually won on a slot machine.

"We'd love to" was on the tip of Bailey's tongue. She'd driven more in the last several hours than she usually drove in three months, but Carter quickly squelched the idea, saying he wanted to cover a lot more ground before they stopped for the night. After filling up on gas and buying a few more snacks, they were on their way.

As dark settled over the landscape, and fatigue caught up with both of them, Carter finally gave the okay for them to look for a place to stop and rest.

Bailey took the next exit and they found a vacancy sign at one motel, although if there hadn't been someone inside the office, she'd have passed it by. It had a large piece of plywood over its front window and the light fixture swung gently by its electrical cord over the door.

They walked inside and a woman at the counter greeted them. She had a cigarette hanging from one corner of her mouth, and she was wearing a bathrobe. There was a door just behind her and Bailey imagined a cot was probably set up on the other side of it where the woman could go to lie down when things got slower. If that was possible.

An inch of ash fell from the woman's cigarette onto the counter. She wiped it to the floor and then stretched her neck to peer around them at the T-Bird. When they asked about the vacant room, she told them they should probably go look at it before deciding whether or not they really wanted to stay the night.

Not a good sign.

Bailey thought they should keep driving, but Carter

didn't seem put off. Probably he was too tired from his eight-hour stint as passenger.

The woman pointed in the direction of a one-story building that sat across four lanes of a not-so-busy road. They could have walked the distance in two minutes, but it was dark and the place was strange and it felt better knowing she and Carter had a quick getaway, if it became necessary.

They quickly located room twelve. It adjoined room eleven and from the looks of room eleven, they wouldn't have to worry about the neighbors making noise. Its windows were also boarded up and the light bulb over the entry was lying shattered on the cement porch.

Room twelve's light was intact, but was not on, and Carter fumbled with the key. Bailey stood close behind him, shivering, although it was a good seventy degrees out.

The seconds ticked off and she began to fidget. Her skin felt all prickly on the back of her neck as she glanced around in the darkness. She *really* had to stop watching those horror flicks. The longer Carter took with the key, the more her imagination worked her over. She remembered several scenes from movies where the victims were desperate to get away, but for some reason, they couldn't get the key into the car door lock.

They died.

She considered suggesting Carter kick in the door, the same as he had the shower door, but the thought of spending even a minute behind bars in that town was worse than standing out there surrounded by dark shadows.

Bailey fought the urge to jump back into the car and lock its doors. The only thing stopping her was that she'd have to leave Carter's side and make a go of it twenty feet alone in the dark.

Finally, the room door squeaked open—nearly a foot. Carter nudged it. It moved another inch. He reached his hand inside and located a light switch. Light flooded the room. Bailey peered over his shoulder, only to be sickened by what she saw.

A bed that was covered with a puke-orange bedspread was blocking their entry.

Carter put his shoulder to the door and pushed. The bed moved six inches, enough for them to squeeze through.

She and Carter stared at the bed. Never mind the horrible color, it was probably crawling with thirty years worth of dead skin cells, and its center dipped nearly to the floor.

So much for romance.

And it was a pretty sure bet the hotel didn't offer daily maid service.

Carter looked around the room as though he might actually be considering spending the night.

"I'll keep driving. You can sleep," Bailey said.

Carter grinned. "Scared?"

"You bet, and I'm not afraid to admit it."

"You don't want to spend the night with me?"

Things did, after all, tend to look better in the dark. Bailey took another look at the orange bedspread. A brownish stain, the size of a basketball, was right in the center. She gagged.

Carter laughed. "Don't worry. I won't torture you," he said and Bailey smiled. "Yet," he added with a dark gleam in his eyes.

Ha! Little did he know, he'd already been torturing her for three full days.

"Just let me use the bathroom and then we'll get out of here. You can wait outside if that'll make you feel better."

Bailey looked over her shoulder. It was still dark, and there were still those ominous bushes waiting for some unsuspecting victim. "I'll stay," she said.

She and Carter moved as one toward the kitchenette. The bed hadn't been the worst of it. The room came equipped with some other equally distasteful furniture. An aqua-colored vinyl lump that used to be something akin to an ottoman sat on one side of the bed. Its sole purpose: to hide a large hole in the wall.

There was no dresser, which didn't matter one iota because no way would anyone in their right mind allow any of their clothing to come into contact with anything in that room.

The kitchenette had a refrigerator that was the color of a gray Seattle morning. Strange color for a refrigerator, Bailey thought, until upon closer inspection, she saw that the gray was simply a layer of grime. Peeking inside was not an option.

She stared at a closed door off the kitchenette. The bathroom. And darned if she didn't have to go, too. The thought of what might be lurking behind door number two made drops of sweat run down her back. She gave Carter a look and he gave her one back.

He was a good man.

He understood her plight.

"Stand back," he said, taking a step forward like he wasn't afraid. "I'll go first."

Her hero.

Carter kneed the door open and stuck his head inside. She was impressed. Most guys would have placed the flat of their hand on the door and given it a good shove.

To her relief, nothing creepy slithered forth. Not even any odious odors.

Carter opened the door wider so that she could see inside and determine for herself whether or not she *really* had to go. It was a fairly normal looking bathroom, compared to the rest of the room. Even the toilet seat lid was down. She stared at it. Once again, Carter understood. Without pause, he exposed the contents of the bowl. Bailey quickly turned her head. She didn't want to be traumatized. If Carter gave the okay, she'd sit—sort of.

"Coast is clear," Carter said. "Clean, in fact."

"You wouldn't lie to a girl, would you?" Bailey asked.

"Not about something as important as this, honey."

Carter had used his Elvis voice, so she knew it must be true. She squinted through one eye. Indeed, the toilet was clean. Still, she quickly reached into her bag and pulled out a couple packets of finger wipes she'd gotten from one of the casinos. She handed one to Carter, and he unfolded it and wiped the rim.

"Good enough?" He stepped away and left her to do her business. Less than thirty seconds later, she was out of there, setting a new female record for shortest time spent in a bathroom.

After leaving the room from hell, she and Carter went back across the street and the woman gave them an understanding look as she took back the key.

Once they were back on the highway, Carter used his cell phone to call ahead to some of the hotels in Reno to check for vacancies. No such luck. The Annual Rifle Convention had everyone booked up solid. Bailey had mixed emotions about the possibility that they wouldn't find a place to stay. The good thing about it was that she'd still have a while before she had to face her lie. She shrugged off her weariness and got her second wind.

Except for the stars, the sky was black, and they covered miles of open road with only an occasional set of car lights to light the night. Bailey glanced over at Carter now and then to see if he was awake. She thought so, but his eyes had that glazed-over look like he'd been staring at the road divider line for too long.

Just having Carter next to her—all that sexual energy and all—helped her to stay awake, but after a few more hours, she was fighting a losing battle with sleep. Her head dipped a couple of times, and then Carter came to her rescue. He began singing "It's Now or Never," in such a way that she felt it was directed entirely at her.

Oh boy.

No doubt about it. She'd make it through the night now. She glanced down at the speedometer. Her pace of sixty miles per hour had crept up to seventy plus, closing the gap between Nevada and Washington in good time.

Bailey checked her rearview mirror every now and then, just to break the monotony, and she was surprised to suddenly see two white dots coming up fast behind them. She glanced down at the speedometer again. Eighty-five. Great. That's all she needed. A ticket. She eased up on the gas pedal, rather than using the brake to slow down. If it was a cop, she didn't need to alert him that she was hitting the brake.

The speedometer dipped back down to sixty, and the car behind quickly gained on them. When it was still a good seventy-five feet back, it crossed into the other lane to pass them.

"Keep a safe distance back after they get around us," Carter told her in an even tone. He had his eyes fixed on the side mirror.

Bailey tapped her brakes after the car passed, slowing to a comfortable fifty. "Crazy driver," she shouted. Out of the corner of her eye, she saw Carter reach under his shirt, and a little bit of fear hummed through her.

The other car's tail lights disappeared around a bend and Bailey reduced her speed even more, to forty. Carter pulled out a big gun.

"Oh God," Bailey said. Her heart thumped hard in her chest.

Carter rested a hand on her arm. "Relax." His voice was soothing and made her almost believe she *could* relax, until they went around the bend.

Tail lights. Straight ahead, in the middle of the road.

Bailey braked hard. She threw up a hand in front of Carter's chest as her body vaulted into the shoulder harness, and one of his hands reached instinctively for the car's dash. The other continued holding his gun.

"You okay?" he asked when they came to a stop.

Bailey looked at him with her mouth open. "What's wrong with that driver?"

Carter checked his gun and Bailey's mouth went dry. She didn't know anything about guns, but she did know Carter's wasn't the same kind that John Wayne used in all those westerns. It had some kind of cartridge that he took out and then clicked back into place.

"What are you doing?" Her voice squeaked up a notch. "You're not going to *shoot* him?"

Carter gave her a look.

"Well, how do I know? I barely know you, remember?"

"Relax. We'll get to Mooville alive."

"That's Coupeville. What did I do to piss him off?"

The driver of the other car took his time getting out and Bailey felt ice run through her veins. She was going to be sick.

Breathe, she told herself. She tried looking at Carter's gun as insurance, like when she went walking at night and brought her dogs along for protection.

It didn't help.

"Oh God," she whimpered. She was breathing deep, beginning to see stars. She didn't know how this game was played—and she didn't want to know—but Carter and the driver of the other car seemed to have all the rules down pat. All she could do was wait and watch.

The driver of the black sedan got out and Carter slipped his gun back under his shirt. "We've got company," he said.

Bailey took three large breaths and then she did what she thought any normal girl in her situation might do. She dug inside her purse and pulled out her cell phone. "I'm calling the police," she announced, straining to see the numbers on the dial.

"Put that away," Carter told her.

"You put your gun away."

"You want me to shoot him?" Carter asked calmly.

They looked at each other for a long couple of seconds.

"No, I don't want you to shoot him." *Maybe.* "Only if I can't get some help on the line." Bailey felt the face of the phone and counted the buttons until she located the nine.

"Help for what? This guy hasn't done anything yet." Carter grabbed the phone from Bailey and tossed it over the seat.

Bailey jerked her head around, but the phone had disappeared into the crevice behind the front seat. "He could be a crazed highway killer. At the very least, he needs to be reported."

"And what will you tell them? That you're out on the highway to nowhere, about fifty miles from somewhere. Yeah, they'll get here in time to save us."

Bailey's hands were shaking, and panic was building in her chest. She was from Coupeville, for crying out loud. Things like this didn't happen in Coupeville.

The lunatic driver from the other car walked toward them, and Carter relaxed into his seat, seemingly unconcerned.

"Oh God," Bailey whispered again. "Let this be a nightmare and let me wake up before I get killed." Her focus went from Carter to the big bald man who was almost at her window. Her heart was beating so hard it hurt. Maybe he liked her car. Maybe he just wanted to carjack them. *Please, God, let Carter be packing two big guns,* Bailey silently prayed.

"Roll down the window," Carter told Bailey.

"What? No!" Bailey shook her head vigorously.

"This is not a good time to be stubborn. Roll it down." Bailey touched the button on the side of the door, but no matter how she tried, her fingers wouldn't work. Carter got tired of waiting. He reached across her and pushed it himself, holding down the button until the window was open all the way.

"Davis." The bald man at the window leaned down and nodded. His partner stood back, staying close to the sedan. He seemed uninterested in what was going on between his friend and Carter. In fact, he looked around like he was bored with the whole thing.

"What's up?" Carter asked.

"Where you headed?"

"The lady won this car a few days ago. We're taking it out for a little drive."

The man gave Bailey a look. A good one. His eyes roamed over her body like he was caressing her. It gave her the creeps, but it was better than being dead. He looked familiar, and she racked her brain for where they might have crossed paths. After a minute, it came to her. He was one of the men who'd escorted that man Azuri out of the ballroom at Frank Zoopa's house.

"Ma'am," he said to her with a nod.

Bailey didn't offer him a greeting. Her tongue was stuck to the roof of her mouth.

"How about you get out and let's talk," he said to Carter.

Oh God, oh God, oh God. She felt dizzy.

Chapter Sixteen

Carter unbuckled his seat belt and got out. He walked with the man a few feet away from the car and they talked in low voices. Bailey kept an eye on them in the rearview mirror as best she could, but the T-Bird had a huge blind spot, so she had only a partial view through one of the small portholes.

The men's voices grew in volume, until, suddenly, baldy grabbed Carter and pushed him up against the car. Bailey jumped in her seat. She put a hand to her mouth and glanced around for something she might use as a weapon. No stray guns lying around. Not that she'd know how to use one anyway.

The man frisked Carter and found his gun. He tossed its cartridge, rendering it useless, and handed it back to Carter. When he was done searching for God knows what, they spoke for a minute, and then Bailey saw the man move around to her side of the car. *Oh God, no.* Icy fingers raked up her spine. She'd never been frisked, not even by someone she liked.

"Get out," baldy said to her. "Ma'am," he added as an afterthought.

His adding "ma'am" didn't make it more polite, nor did it make Bailey feel any better. She swung her legs out of the car and stood, giving a tug to the hem of her skirt. She didn't know what he was looking for, but certainly he could see that nothing much could possibly be hidden beneath the small piece of fabric covering her legs. She glanced over at Carter for reassurance. He gave her a warm smile.

Bailey kept her gaze focused on Carter while the man ran rough hands up her legs. Up, up went his hand, all the way, and she began to get a sick feeling in the pit of her stomach.

"Careful," Carter said, his voice a low rumble.

Bailey had heard Carter use that tone of voice once before, when he'd been manhandling Miss Bountiful, and it'd scared her, but this time his growl was welcome. The sick feeling ebbed and she relaxed as much as a woman who had a strange man's hands on her could.

The man stopped short of violating her, but still, just having his hands running over her bare skin made her want to run to Carter and have his tender arms close tight around her. She endured the rest of the search, over her back, under her hair, a swipe across her chest and a quick peek down her front, and then he gave her a gentle push over toward Carter.

"Just doing my job," the man said to Carter.

"Be done with it then," Carter told him in an even tone.

The men gave each other a look of mutual respect, which Bailey didn't understand at all, considering one was a bad guy and the other a . . . a sort of bad guy—but only half of him. In any case, she sensed that the man probably did not intend them any real harm.

The man slipped into the driver's side of the T-Bird. He checked the middle console, the glove box, under the seats, and every inch of the small shelf space behind the seats.

Finally, he got out of the car, seemingly satisfied that

whatever it was he was searching for, wasn't there. He nodded at the trunk. "Open it."

Carter took the keys from Bailey and pushed the trunk icon. The man pulled out their luggage, went through Carter's things, then started on Bailey's. His grim mouth turned into a smile when he came across a pair of black lace panties.

Bailey felt her face flush warm. Carter's body stiffened next to her. He may have already gotten a good glimpse of her, but he had yet to see any of her private collection of Victoria's Secret undergarments.

"Have a nice drive," the man said when he finished perusing her things. He gave Bailey a wide grin.

She held Carter's arm until the two men drove away and then she pushed a large breath from her lungs. "What did they want?"

"A diamond."

"Whose diamond?"

Carter steered Bailey to the passenger's side and let her in, then got into the driver's seat. "The Azuri diamond is missing. Zoopa thinks I've got it."

"You?" Bailey slid Carter a look. She'd only known him for a few days, long enough to think she might be falling in love, but she didn't think she could already be so blinded by her emotions that she'd become involved with a jewel thief.

"You okay?" Carter asked. He brushed a hand through her hair and cupped her face in his hand.

Bailey nodded. Carter's hand was warm against her skin, and it was all the reassurance she needed. Frank Zoopa had lost his mind.

They drove on for what seemed like a million more endless miles, until finally, around two A.M., she no longer cared if she and Carter had to share a bed, a bathtub, or even a room like the one they'd left back in the town with no name. She needed some sleep. Susanville was the next exit, and to her relief, Carter took it.

They found a Holiday Inn with one room available—and one bed—but Bailey was already half asleep and Carter wasn't far behind. He let her shower first, and by the time he'd finished, she was deep into dreamland.

Two minutes later, or so it seemed, someone gave her a gentle shake and a voice said, "Time to go."

Bailey strained to see who the voice belonged to, but the face looking down at her was a blur. She rubbed her eyes and tried again.

"*Carter.* What are you doing here?"

Carter waggled his eyebrows. "We spent the night together. Was it good for you?"

Bailey sprang to a sitting position, holding the sheet tight against her chest. She glanced around the room. Neon green blinked at her from the nightstand clock. Six A.M. Four hours had passed since she last looked at that clock, hardly enough time to qualify as them spending the night together.

She glanced over at the other side of the bed. It was only slightly mussed, but enough to tell someone—Carter—had been in it. Her brow furrowed as she tried to remember anything that might have happened in the last four hours. She looked up at Carter and he touched her cheek lightly.

"Don't worry. You're still pure."

Relief slid through Bailey. She slouched back against her pillow. "Why did you wake me up?"

"Time to go."

Bailey didn't move. She had only enough energy to lie there and gaze at the most perfect smile . . . imagine how it would have felt if they had . . .

Carter must've had his security-guy powers turned on because he shook his head and said, "Later." He kissed her lightly on the cheek. "Much later."

Eighteen hours later, Bailey and Carter cruised past the WELCOME TO COUPEVILLE sign, and Bailey rolled her window down to take a deep breath of sea air. The small waterfront community had never looked, or smelled, so good. She directed Carter through town and had him turn left onto Front Street. They drove a few blocks more and then pulled into the driveway of a small blue and white cottage that overlooked Penn Cove. Penn Cove was famous for its mussels, and Bailey had never even tried them. *Yuck.*

Bailey's cottage had once been a rental property for tourists, which her mom had purchased when the owner died. She'd cleaned it up, given it a fresh coat of paint, and handed it off to Bailey when she'd graduated from high school. Living just a few blocks from her mom's house, Bailey sometimes felt like she was still living at home.

She and Carter got out of the T-Bird and Bailey saw her neighbor, a weatherworn retired seaman who had a penchant for collecting old guns, peering at them out his living room window. His real name, as far as she knew, was Henry Winston, aka old man Winston.

Old man Winston cracked open his door, and checked them out as he gathered two days' worth of newspapers from his front porch. He scowled and turned to go back inside and Bailey heard him mutter something about "damn kids and their fast cars nowadays." Pretty much that's what he said every time any of Bailey's friends pulled up in front of the cottage. Since old man Winston was on the dark side of eighty, nearly everyone was a kid to him, even her mother.

"Nice old character, huh?" Carter said with a laugh.

"Mr. Winston? He's a classic," Bailey said. "Don't you worry about him. He's no bother." She considered telling Carter to duck if he ever saw the end of a rifle poke through the curtains, but heck, coming from Las Vegas, Carter had plenty of experience with guns and criminals and such. Who was she to tell him how to avoid getting a backside full of lead from an old man?

The phone rang as soon as they stepped inside the cottage. It was Bailey's mother.

"I just talked to Liza. She said you'd be home today and that if you weren't, I should call the FBI."

"Hello to you, too, Mom. As you can hear, I'm home. No need to call anyone." Bailey heard her mother sigh with relief.

"I was a wee bit concerned when she told me you were driving yourself home, but then she said you had a friend helping you. I can't wait to see that car. Maybe we could go for a drive. A long one. Your auntie has been driving me crazy and I could use an outing away from her. She's been reading those cards from that game and she's convinced she's got Yellow Fever. Says a mosquito landed on her a couple of days ago and that it'd gotten its fill of her blood before she could smack it. She's in her room right now resting. Wants me to call Green Gardens Funeral Home to make sure her plot is still available."

"Did you tell her that Yellow Fever isn't endemic?"

"It's not?"

"No, it's . . ." Bailey started to explain, but decided it was far too much information for her mother. "It doesn't matter. Just tell Aunt Fiona I'll be over to see her before she expires. How're my babies?"

"Your babies are spoiled rotten brats. I don't know how you can get a moment's peace. They demand more attention than your aunt."

Bailey smiled. "Give them a kiss for me and tell them Mommy's home." She hung up and turned around to find Carter giving her a look. "What?" she said.

"I didn't know you were a mother."

"Yes . . ." Bailey moved close to Carter and looked up at him innocently. "Does it matter?" she asked.

Carter gazed down at her with tenderness and confusion. "I thought . . ."

Bailey giggled. "My babies are two eighty-pound yellow labs. Maggie May and Tucker."

Carter pulled her to him, put a finger under her chin, tipping up her face. "I'll bet you're a wonderful mother."

His look was inviting, but before Bailey accepted an invitation to that party, they had to get over a couple of hurdles: her family for one, her lie for another. Getting the thumbs-up from her mom wouldn't be a problem since she'd take one look at Carter and fall in love. But her aunt and uncle . . . no telling what might happen there.

"Let's go. I'll show you around town, we'll get some lunch, and then we'll go over to my mom's. She's eager to see the car." *Which she'll completely forget about as soon as she lays eyes on you.* Bailey smiled.

"We could have lunch here." Carter squeezed her. He pressed his lips firmly to hers in that take-charge way she was growing to love about him. It looked like things were back to normal.

How tempting it was to let his kiss lead them down the hall to her room, but she had a feeling if that happened, they might not make it out of the cottage all night. Bailey pulled herself from his arms. What they both needed was a good dose of fresh air and a real meal. The crisp sea air would provide the air, and Bailey had the perfect place to take Carter for lunch.

She pulled him out the door, and he squinted into the sunlight. He pulled a pair of sunglasses from his shirt pocket that went perfectly with his shiny black hair. In fact, he looked like he'd just stepped off a movie screen. She'd be lucky to keep him to herself for more than one day.

They walked down Front Street, until they came to a staircase that descended down the side of an old weathered building. Knead & Feed was Bailey's favorite lunch spot, and it also happened to be where she worked.

Secretly, of course. She'd had to bribe all the locals with homemade marionberry pies, so that they wouldn't tell her family.

The small eatery seated only twenty-five, and on weekends it was always full. People from all over the state came on weekends for their share of the homemade soups and pies that were offered, and Bailey was the proud baker of most of those pies. Her secret was in the berries that she picked fresh right there in town along the waterfront.

Bailey spotted a table over in the far corner. She led Carter past the sign at the counter that said PLEASE WAIT TO BE SEATED, and they sat at a small, square lacquered table. Because she was an employee, the rules didn't apply to her.

Their table overlooked Penn Cove Bay, where they could look out and see all the way to the bottom of the water at an underwater garden of rocks covered with barnacles, hundreds of starfish, and acres of sea kelp. A breeze whipped through the small window, bringing with it the smell of salt water, and a dozen seagulls glided effortlessly in the blue sky.

Today's choice of flower, a single red carnation, sat on one corner of the table in a cheap glass vase.

Bailey stared out for a long minute pondering the last few days. They were but a blur. Winning a car . . . meeting Carter . . . falling into something that she was almost ready to call love . . .

Macy Drew approached their table with an order tablet. She eyed Carter over the top of her glasses, and muttered, "Well, well."

Bailey ordered for both herself and Carter, choosing turkey breast sandwiches with cranberry cream cheese spread, and two bowls of shrimp bisque soup. Conversation between them stopped after Carter took his first bite and she took that as a sign that his first dining experience in Coupeville had received two thumbs-up.

They topped off their meal with a piece of homemade marionberry pie—not one of hers, of course, but nearly as good—and a cup of fresh brewed coffee. Not a mocha, not a latte, not a cappuccino, just good home-brewed stuff, with real cream and sugar.

When Carter finished, he dropped his napkin on his plate and leaned against the back of his small wooden chair. "That was the best lunch I've had in months," he said.

Bailey smiled. She was glad for the few minutes they had to themselves. This time was probably the only quiet time they'd have together. Once word got out a star had arrived in town, they'd be lucky to have five minutes of peace. And from the way the women in the kitchen kept whispering and peering at Carter from the doorway, that five minutes was just about up. Even a few of the patrons were already giving them curious looks.

Carter didn't seem to notice, but of course he was used to the attention. His face was smooth, frown-free. He seemed relaxed, but looks, especially on him, were deceiving. He was a complicated man and there was no telling what things really blew through his mind. She remembered Liza's warning about a man such as Carter not being satisfied to live in a small community like Coupeville. That was okay. She wasn't either. But was she ready for as big a change as moving to Las Vegas?

Coupeville wasn't a fancy city, but it did have some things that made visiting well worth one's time. Clean sea air, nearly non-existent crime, and a slower pace that could possibly cure high blood pressure, maybe even a host of other ailments. Unless, of course, you happened to be like her Aunt Fiona. Bailey didn't know if anything could cure a constant state of hypochondria like hers. God bless her.

As nice as all the serenity was, though, Bailey could think of a few things that would make living in the small community more enjoyable. A Starbucks for one. Entertainment for another. In any form. With no theater, no mall, and not even a bowling alley, teenagers got their kicks any way they could, and they usually ended up doing mostly innocent coming-of-age things, like stealing kisses under the dock along the waterfront, or raiding their parents' liquor cabinet and getting wasted. Or, if they were old enough to drive and were lucky enough to have access to a car, they'd spend their weekend nights in Oak Harbor, where the closest movie theater was located. Even so, some Coupeville teens were so bored, they couldn't help but get into trouble.

Like Mark Jefferson. He hadn't really been a *bad* teen, but he *was* considered the evil twin between him and his brother, Brian. And he also happened to be the boy who'd deflowered her.

They'd taken a moonlit stroll up near Deception Pass with a bottle of peach schnapps and, after tossing back half the bottle, he'd managed to convince her that his boys would burst wide open if he didn't release some of their pent-up squigglies.

Bailey didn't really care about Mark's squigglies, but it was Halloween night, he'd dressed like Elvis, and he'd promised to serenade her with the Elvis classic "Stuck on You." She'd have followed him anywhere.

As it turned out, not only couldn't Mark sing like Elvis, but he didn't even know the words to the song. That night, Bailey promised herself to be more selective when it came to men who claimed they could sing like the King.

And no more peach schnapps. Ever.

Besides Penn Cove mussels, Coupeville had one other small claim to fame. A cute movie, starring Sandra Bullock and Nicole Kidman, had been filmed in the tiny waterfront community. Bailey had been lucky enough to get Ms. Bullock's autograph and she still kept it tucked safely away in the back of one of her drawers.

Penn Cove and a Hollywood movie. At least it was something.

The minutes ticked off. She and Carter sat in silence. The sound of salt water slapping against the wood pilings outside the window had a relaxing rhythm, but Bailey was full of anxiety. In a few minutes, she'd introduce Carter to her family and he'd either run or he'd smile. She prayed for the latter.

A few minutes later, they rolled up to the curb at her mother's house, and the screen door burst open. Two large yellow dogs charged toward them and Bailey braced herself for contact with the larger of the two. Tucker, the male, heaved his body against her and then fell submissively to the ground at her feet. He laid on his back, flicking his tongue in and out, wearing a big doggy smile, while Maggie May stumbled all over the top of his head. He fluttered his eyes to keep them from getting poked out.

Bailey spent the next five minutes cooing her love to both of them, and then it was time for them to meet Carter.

"These are my babies," Bailey announced proudly.

Until now, Tucker had been so caught up in his doggy happiness that he'd only given Carter a glance, but now, as Carter reached out to him, he leaped to his feet and growled a warning. Then he scrambled backward up the front steps to peer at the stranger from a safe distance.

Maggie May wiggled over to Carter, her rump zigzagging from side to side so furiously that her back legs nearly left the ground. After performing her welcoming dance for a long minute, she raced up the steps and into the house. Bailey and Carter followed, and found her up on the back of the sofa, where she continued her dance, all the while making funny warbling sounds in her throat.

"It's an identity problem," Bailey said, gently helping Maggie back down to the floor. "She spent the first eight weeks of her life with a litter of adventurous kittens. I think it traumatized her."

Carter spent another minute with Maggie, and he

even got Tucker to stand still so that he could pet him. Big bonus points. Bailey smiled her approval. If her dogs didn't like someone, that someone didn't last long in her house.

"Mom?" Bailey called out. A moment later a fiftyish woman, going on forty, appeared at the top of the stairs with a finger pressed to her lips. Aunt Fiona must have been asleep. Bailey could only imagine what had gone on while she'd been away.

Her mom looked tired, but one glance at Carter and she put a hand to her chest with a gasp. After a moment's pause, she glided gracefully down the stairs and stopped in front of them.

"I could give you a couple of Maggie May's tranquilizers if you need a rest," Bailey offered.

Olivia shook her head without taking her eyes off Carter. "I can handle your aunt. I'm not ready to give her dog pills. It's inhumane."

"Exactly," Bailey told her. "Aunt Fiona outweighs Maggie by at least twenty pounds. It wouldn't have as heavy an effect on her as it does on the dog."

Olivia slid Bailey a quick look, and then immediately turned her attention back to Carter. "Hello," she said, stretching out a hand. "I'm Bailey's mom, Olivia."

Carter knew exactly what to do with that hand. As his lips met her skin, Olivia sucked in a breath and her eyelashes fluttered in such a way that Bailey wondered if they had any smelling salts in the house—just in case.

"You must be Elvis," Olivia said in a breathy whisper.

Bailey rolled her eyes. "This is Carter Davis, Mom. He's an Elvis *tribute artist.*"

Carter gave Olivia his best crooked smile. "Nice to meet you, ma'am."

"Oh, my," Olivia said. She patted her hair and smoothed her sweater.

"*Tribute artist,* Mom."

"Yes. I heard you the first time," Olivia said. "But you don't mind being called Elvis, do you?" she asked Carter. "After all, Elvis *is* the King and to impersonate him is the highest of compliments." Olivia reached up a hand, but stopped herself before touching Carter's hair. "The resemblance is remarkable."

"So how were things while I was away?" Bailey thought she should nip this in the bud. Whatever *this* was. From the way her mom was breathing all hard and fast, and how her face had gotten all flushed and pink, Bailey wasn't so sure she'd nipped *it* in time.

"Ah, thank you, ma'am," Carter said, using his Elvis voice.

Bailey nudged him in the ribs. "Don't encourage her. You'll be in for more than you bargained for." She stepped between her mother and Carter and took an arm in each of hers. She steered her mother to the loveseat, then she and Carter sat on the sofa. Best to keep the two of them a safe distance apart until she was sure that her mother accepted that Carter wasn't the real deal.

"I take it Aunt Fiona is napping," Bailey said.

Bailey's Aunt Fiona and Uncle Rex lived in the two-story colonial with her mother. Even though Fiona was her mom's sister, she and Rex were more like grandparents than aunt and uncle. They were twenty years older than her mother—at least—and with her real grandparents gone, they'd taken over and done the job very well.

Her mother put a hand to each side of her face and shook her head. "Thank God. We just convinced her she wasn't dying from Yellow Fever and then your cousin comes over and gets her to play that game again and so now she thinks she's got some other blasted disease. Worse yet, she's convinced she got it from Maggie May."

They all looked over at the eighty-pound lab. Maggie May was spread-eagle on the floor, looking very ladylike.

"She's the sweetest dog. I don't care what your aunt

says, you can't get a disease just because she eats other dogs' poo. Your aunt saw it happen. Then Maggie licked her . . . Well, you can only imagine."

Bailey prayed this was a dream. She hadn't really left Las Vegas yet, had she? She gave Carter a quick look, expecting to see disgust. He was smiling.

But this was only the first course.

"I've got ringworm," came a shout from the top of the stairs.

Bailey took a deep breath. And here was course two.

Olivia's eyes rolled back in her head. "Maggie's tranquilizers are looking better and better," she whispered. "It's not ringworm, it's that scar she has on her left thigh." She waved a hand. "Though even if it was ringworm, I don't know why it'd stop her from being able to come down those stairs. I better go help her. Next house, we're getting a rambler."

Olivia went to help Fiona, and Bailey and Carter sat there looking at each other in silence. Bailey wasn't sure she should even try explaining her family to him. Perhaps she should have started when they'd first pulled away from the curb of the Oasis back in Las Vegas.

"She isn't really my aunt," Bailey said. "By blood. I was adopted." She glanced up at her mom and aunt as they came down the stairs. "But don't tell them. My parents died when I was young. These people took me in. They think I don't know," she whispered.

Carter nodded and kept a straight face. He was a good man.

Olivia and Fiona reached the bottom of the stairs and Fiona eyed Carter for a long minute before finally walking over to him. They stood face-to-face as she examined every inch of his face and hair.

"Are you a punk?" she asked.

Bailey's mouth dropped open, but Carter only smiled and took one of Fiona's hands in his.

"No, ma'am. I'm a friend of Bailey's," he said, raising her hand to his mouth and kissing it, just as he had Olivia's.

Not only was he a good man, he was a *smart* man.

Fiona looked him up and then all the way down. "Black pants. Black jacket. Black hair. You look like a punk to me."

Punk rocker. Now Bailey got it. "Auntie, he's not a punk rocker. He sings Elvis Presley songs. He's what you call an Elvis tribute artist. His name is Carter."

Fiona's scowl warmed into a wide smile and she showed a mouthful of even, albeit age-yellowed, teeth. "Sing me a song," she said.

"Now, Auntie." Bailey put a hand on Fiona's arm and she gave Carter an apologetic glance. He'd been a good sport up to now, but fatigue lined the skin around his eyes and she was pretty sure the last thing he wanted to do right then was sing. "Carter and I have been driving for nearly two days. Maybe he'll sing later."

"I might not be here later," Fiona said.

"Oh? Are you and Uncle Rex going out tonight? Playing bingo?" Bailey gave her mom a quick look.

Olivia shook her head and mouthed, "Don't ask."

"Bingo?" Fiona shook her head and her mouth curved down. "I don't think I'll ever be able to play bingo again. The Centers for Disease Control and Prevention will need to quarantine this house soon." Fiona looked over at Bailey's mother. "Didn't your mom tell you? I have but a few hours left on this sweet earth."

"Now, Auntie, what gave you such an idea?"

"That game your cousin Freddie brought over. I've got actinomycosis. I've got the symptoms. Once you get the symptoms, it's just a matter of time."

"Well," Bailey said, tapping a finger to the side of her head. "I happen to know the cure for that. It's a little known secret, but I'm happy to let you in on it."

Fiona eyed her suspiciously. "You wouldn't be foolin' me, would you? I'm not afraid to die. At my age, you gotta expect it." Fiona's eyes misted up. "I just hate leavin' poor Rex behind. How will he ever get along without me?"

A lump formed in Bailey's throat. Indeed, how would any of them get along without her? "We'd take care of him just fine, but like I said, I've got the cure for your condition." Bailey looked at her mother, giving her a sly smile. "Come with me." She took Fiona's arm and led her to the kitchen.

Olivia followed close behind, keeping an eye on every move Bailey made. Probably her mother thought she intended to slip Fiona one of Maggie May's tranquilizers, but she had another cure up her sleeve. Peach-flavored tea. She filled a mug from the ready-hot water spout and dropped a tea bag inside. She let it steep for a minute, added a squirt of honey, and then set it on the table in front of her aunt.

"Here," Bailey said. "Drink this and you'll be cured."

Fiona put her nose to the mug. "Smells like cat piss."

Maybe she'd slip her some of Maggie's meds after all. "It's peach, your favorite. Now, drink up," Bailey ordered with what remained of her official doctor's voice.

Fiona picked up the mug of hot tea, smelled it once more, then took a sip. She licked her lips and then took a couple more sips. After she'd downed at least a third of the cup, Bailey felt Fiona's forehead and pronounced her cured. Her mother smiled gratefully as Bailey led Fiona back up the stairs to finish her nap.

When Bailey and her mother joined Carter in the living room, he, too, had decided it was nap time. Bailey pulled the chenille throw from the back of the sofa and gently laid it over him. He didn't move a muscle.

With both Fiona and Carter in dreamland, Bailey and her mom took the opportunity to pop over to the store to pick up some dinner items. What could happen with both of them asleep?

Chapter Seventeen

When they returned home, Aunt Fiona was sitting at the kitchen table filling out some form she'd cut out of a magazine.

"Whatcha got there, Auntie?" Bailey asked.

Fiona's face shone proudly as she held up the Wilhelmina 40+ Model Search Official Entry Form. "All I need is a current photo. I have one from when my picture was in the paper for growing the best local dahlias five years ago. Do you think that will do?"

Bailey nodded. "I think that would be perfect."

Fiona's face beamed as she continued filling out the form.

Bailey poked her head into the other room and Carter was no longer on the sofa. "Would you happen to know where my friend went?"

Fiona waved a hand toward the door. "Your Uncle Rex came home. Asked him if he'd like to go for a walk. I think he wanted to take him down to the Hall and show him off. It's not every day that Elvis comes to town, you know." Fiona reached over and grabbed the latest Victoria's Secret catalogue. "I think your mom ought to order something from in here. She might get lucky with that man."

Olivia's eyes lit up and she reached for the magazine.

Bailey grabbed it away. "I don't think Mom needs to buy lingerie to impress *that* man. He's *my* friend." Bailey turned to her mother. "We better go rescue Carter. I'm sure he didn't realize what he was getting into with Uncle Rex."

They took Olivia's car, a 1974 yellow Nova. It had original paint, no radio, new tires, and a backseat. A real sweet ride, according to the Jefferson twins, who owned and operated the only auto repair shop in town. They'd been eyeing it for some time, talking about how if it were their car, they'd do this and that, and how if Olivia wanted, they could trick it out for her at cost. She told them she liked it just fine the way it was, but that if she ever did decide to sell it and buy something new, she'd give them first crack at it. That was unlikely since she didn't like learning anything new, nor did she like to drive anywhere farther than Coupeville's city limits. Bailey considered that her own aversion to driving could be genetic.

Bailey and her mom came upon Uncle Rex and Carter a half mile away from the Hall. Carter had sweat running down the side of his face, the same as when he performed, and Bailey guessed he might appreciate some water.

Olivia slowed the car and Bailey held a bottle of Evian out the window. "Something to wet your whistle?"

Carter's eyes filled with gratitude, much like Maggie May's when she was about to be fed.

"Rex, where are you taking this boy?" Olivia asked.

Rex looked both ways up and down North Main Street and then shrugged. "He was all laid out on the sofa. I asked Fiona who he was. She said he was a punk, and I didn't like the way she was staring at him when I came in the door, so I figured the safest thing to do would be to take him to the city limits and let him hitch a ride out of town." He stuffed a craggy hand into his pocket, pulled out a handkerchief, and wiped sweat from his forehead. He offered it to Carter, but Carter declined with a wave of his hand.

"Well, you should be ashamed of yourself taking this poor boy out walking in this heat with him wearing those *hot* clothes."

All three of them looked at Olivia. It was indeed hot out—by Washington's standards anyway—and Bailey would've been touched by her mother's concern over Carter's comfort, but her emphasis on the word "hot" had her concerned that her mom might be entering the beginning stages of a mid-life crisis.

"He told me he's from Las Vegas," Rex said. "You can fry a damn egg on the sidewalk in Las Vegas." He waved a hand at the women and kept walking.

Carter looked back and forth between Rex and the women like he wasn't sure if he should do the macho thing and follow Rex, or if he should do the smart thing and get in the car.

Smart won out.

As dangerous as it might be, Bailey got out of the car and let Carter slide in between her and her mother.

"Will you be home for dinner?" Olivia called after Rex. Rex didn't turn around. "I guess that means no. Lord, sometimes I don't know how Fiona puts up with him."

"Love," Bailey said. "She's in love."

Olivia pursed her lips together and made a *hmmf* sound.

Yep. Dinner should prove interesting.

Bailey half considered sparing Carter the experience, but decided it'd be better to let him jump right in and see what he'd be getting himself into were he to join her family.

While Bailey and her mom went to work preparing dinner, Carter waited in the living room with Aunt Fiona. With all his experience handling women, Bailey was reasonably certain he could handle thirty minutes of old lady sitting. She'd calculated that was how long it would take to chop the onions for the meat loaf and get the salad tossed. Aunt Fiona could be a handful, though—anything more than thirty minutes and she'd have to leave her mom to do the rest.

Twenty minutes later, Bailey finished with the onions and had begun rinsing the lettuce, when the kitchen door swung open. It was Fiona. Her face was white and pasty, and she looked as though she might faint. Carter stood directly behind her, his face a mask of bewilderment and apology.

"What happened?" Bailey asked, not sure she really wanted to hear the answer.

Carter held out his hands. "I don't know. We were playing a game and she suddenly clutched her chest. Her eyes rolled skyward and she started gasping for air like someone who'd just lost their life savings on the roulette wheel."

"What game?" Olivia asked, her voice raising a notch.

"Some game in a yellow box. She read a card—"

Olivia glanced skyward. "Sweet Jesus."

Fiona's eyes were big and she was making a strange gurgling sound.

Bailey turned to Carter. "Go get the card."

Carter ran back into the living room and he returned with a card that said "How to Recognize Heart Failure."

"Lord," Olivia said, putting a hand to her chest.

Fiona stopped gurgling long enough to look down at her ankles. "Are they swollen? They look swollen to me." She grabbed Bailey's arm for support and Bailey walked her over to the table. Fiona sat and took several deep breaths with her head hanging between her knees. "Look at me. Just crossing the kitchen and I'm out of breath. I used to be able to walk for miles with your Uncle Rex."

Bailey read the card again. If she'd thought her aunt

was really experiencing heart failure, she'd be the first one to dial 911, but she'd been through this enough times now that she'd been "desensitized."

"Look," Bailey said, pointing to the list of symptoms on the card. "You don't have bluing under your fingernails." She looked down at her aunt's ankles. "And, I swear, any woman would be proud to have ankles like yours."

Fiona sucked in some air. "Really?" she said, daintily sticking out one leg, turning it this way and that.

"Really."

"And you're short of breath because you're old," Olivia offered.

Fiona slid her a look. "Is this your *professional* opinion?" she asked, looking straight at Bailey.

Bailey nodded vigorously. One thing she did know about was heart failure. She'd gotten high marks during her studies in that section of the human body. She hugged her aunt and rubbed her back gently, feeling the bones through Fiona's house dress. Age wasn't pretty or fun and Bailey felt a twinge of guilt for quitting school. Most assuredly, there'd come a day when her aunt would really need her and odds were she wouldn't be much help.

"Here," Bailey said, handing the heart failure card back to Carter. "Put this away. And never EVER let her talk you into playing that game again. It's hazardous to everyone's health."

Carter disappeared into the living room just as the back door opened.

"Look what the dogs dragged in," Fiona said, scuttling over to give Rex a hug.

Olivia mumbled something about needing to chop more lettuce and she went to the refrigerator.

Rex gave Bailey a kiss on the cheek. "Welcome home, little girl." His arm stiffened around her shoulders when Carter walked back into the room.

"Uncle Rex, you've met my friend, Carter," Bailey said.

"Not really. I never asked his name," Rex said. "Why is he still here?"

"He drove back with me from Las Vegas."

"Why?"

"To help me drive my new car back. Didn't you see it out front?" Bailey asked.

"Your mom said you went down there with a friend of yours. Why couldn't *she* help you drive home?" Rex was giving Carter the wild eye now. One eye staring up at Carter's hair and one on the lettuce that Olivia was chopping.

"Liza flew back. Don't you want to come see my new car?" Bailey pulled on Rex's arm. Better to get his mind on something other than how to get rid of Carter.

Rex went along stiff-legged, and Carter followed right along behind them, unfazed by Rex's wild eye. Bailey was impressed. But not surprised. After all, he was a super duper security man who lived among Las Vegas hit men and Mafia types, and she wouldn't have expected anything less. To him, Rex was a pussycat.

Rex's eyes gleamed as he looked over Bailey's car. He walked a full circle around it twice and stroked it admiringly.

"I thought you won a *new* car," Fiona said. She stood with her hands propped on top of her bony hips and looked the T-Bird over from trunk to hood. "They made these cars back in the fifties. I know 'cause your Uncle Rex bought one right off the showroom floor. Beautiful car it was. Just like this one. Only his was black like the night. So black you couldn't see it in the dark unless you had the head lamps on. Made it easy for us to get friendly right out in front of my parents' house. Wouldn't surprise me if that's why Rex bought it."

"Take Fiona back in the house," Rex told Olivia. "If she gives you any trouble, give her one of them pills

Bailey's been offering. Can't be any worse than those ill-nesses she comes down with playing that game."

Bailey knew he didn't mean it. Rex loved his wife dearly.

Olivia ushered Fiona back up the steps and Fiona yelled over her shoulder. "You been cheated. That ain't no new car. I know 'cause your Uncle Rex bought one. I was a young thing then . . ."

The door closed and Bailey could hear her aunt's ranting all the way up the stairs.

"It's a beaut," Rex said. He looked up at the blue, cloudless sky. "Let's take off the top and go for a spin. I wanna see the look on Fred Wilson's face when he sees me drive this past his house."

Bailey grimaced. She wasn't so sure she wanted her uncle driving her new car. His wild eye had been caused by an injury some years back that had left him with im-paired eyesight, and a few years after that he'd been forced to give up his driver's license because he couldn't pass the reading test when it came time for renewal. That didn't deter him from driving around town, though, and luckily Coupeville's law enforcement didn't give him too much trouble, so long as he didn't stray far. He even bought himself a new compact SUV, saying "I'll show them who they can tell to drive."

"What about the top? It won't fit in the trunk," Bailey said.

Rex nodded toward his RAV4. "I'll put it on top and bring it over to your place later."

Bailey looked up into the sky. The weather was clear. But for how long? This *was* Washington, where the tem-perature could go from feverish to frigid at a moment's notice. "I don't know, Uncle Rex. What's the forecast?"

Rex waved a dismissive hand. "Don't worry about the weather. That's why they equip these cars with a hard top."

While they contemplated the weather, a yellow Mustang

convertible drove by with its top down. That was all the encouragement Rex needed. He gave Bailey a raised eyebrow and she sighed in resignation.

Bailey and Carter watched as he got in and looked around for a way to release the hardtop. After a minute, he climbed out and stood back, scratching his head.

"Seems like things have changed some since they first came out with these cars."

Bailey slid Carter a nervous look. As was becoming the norm, he read her thoughts and went into action, reaching inside the glove box for the owner's manual. He handed it to Bailey and she quickly flipped to the section on how to go about removing the top. When she was satisfied that she could properly supervise her car's top removal, she had Rex go to one side of the car and Carter, the other. Together, they lifted the eighty-pound top up and over the front of the T-Bird and placed it up on the top rack of Rex's RAV4.

Now for the birth of the soft top. How hard could that be? Bailey quickly located the small button on the dash that had a picture of a convertible car on it.

"I'll let you do the honors, Uncle Rex," Bailey said sweetly. His good eye gleamed and his face stretched into a big smile.

He slid into the driver's seat and pushed the button. Nothing happened. He pushed the button again and held it a few seconds. Bailey grimaced at the whirring sound it made. Rex went to press the button again, but Bailey stopped him.

"Wait," she said. "Maybe I should read some more of the manual."

"Let me try once more," Rex said. He pushed the button and held it until the whirring turned into a full-out buzz.

"Please stop, Uncle Rex," Bailey said. "I really think I should read the manual." She looked up at the blue sky again. "It's a nice day. Let's just leave it down for now. If Carter and I can't figure it out, I'll take it down to Coupeville Auto Repair and have Mark or Brian figure out what's wrong."

"That'll cost you. Let me take a look at it. Could be it's just stuck," Rex said. He began poking around the back where the mechanism for the folding canvas top was located.

"No, Uncle Rex, really. It's under warranty. It won't cost me a thing. And it specifically says in here that only licensed mechanics can work on the car or the warranty is void." Bailey pointed at the owner's handbook. She didn't want to hurt her uncle's feelings, but he didn't have the best track record when it came to fixing stuff around the house. He was what one might call mechanically challenged, and chances were about fifty-fifty that her windshield wipers would end up controlling her headlights if she let him "take a look."

"Dinner's ready," Olivia called from the doorway. She had a dish-towel in her hand and was wiping a piece of silverware.

"Let's go eat. We can worry about this later," Bailey said. Rex stuffed his hands in his pockets and backed off and she took his arm, steering him toward the house. She wanted to make sure he wasn't tempted to make a detour back out to her car.

Olivia had set the table with her best dishes, and had even lit the centerpiece candles.

Bailey had Carter sit on her right, with her aunt directly across from them. Uncle Rex sat at one end and the chair at the other end was left empty, as always, in honor of her dad. Bailey thought her dad must've been quite a man to still have his seat saved after all these years. She couldn't remember his face, but she did remember that he smelled real good, like a spring day. She'd snuggle up into his lap and tuck her head close to his neck and fall asleep with that smell. She realized later that the scent was from the clothes softener her mom used. Snuggle. She smiled.

Olivia came out of the kitchen with a big salad and set it down before Carter, and then she went back out to the kitchen for the meat loaf and potatoes. Bailey hadn't thought she was all that hungry after having lunch at the Knead & Feed, but the smell of her mother's cooking had her stomach grumbling impatiently for that first bite.

Olivia sat next to Fiona, and Rex said a quick prayer of thanks.

"Amen, and just in time," Fiona said. "A woman my age has got to keep up her strength. Did you get me some of those little chocolate Viactiv chews when you were out?" Fiona asked Rex.

"I picked some up for you, Fiona," Olivia said. She got up from the table and returned with a box of Viactiv mint chocolate chews.

Bailey started to object. Giving her aunt free rein to eat those things like candy was not a good idea. Her mom put up a hand, stopping her.

"It won't hurt for her to supplement her diet with calcium chews at her age, even though we all know she just wants an excuse to eat chocolate," Olivia whispered.

Fiona opened the box and pulled out an oblong piece of chocolate. Bailey had seen Viactiv chews and this was clearly not one of them. In fact, they looked suspiciously like the candies sold by Macy's. Bailey leaned in and took a closer look. The wrapper said "Frango."

Fiona popped the piece of chocolate into her mouth and held her lips together in bliss. She was none the wiser. She couldn't see close enough to even see the food on her fork, let alone the small print on a candy wrapper. A few minutes later she popped in another. Bailey and Olivia smiled at each other, and Bailey thought her mother was a very clever woman.

Dinner went surprisingly well. Aunt Fiona managed to get through the entire dinner without claiming to have been poisoned, and her mother did her best not to stare in awe at Carter.

Bailey felt herself begin to relax. It seemed she was home free. Uncle Rex even seemed to soften toward Carter during the meal.

"When are you two gonna have children?" Rex asked.

Boy, had he softened.

Bailey looked her uncle square between both eyes, right at the bridge of his nose, which was easier than trying to figure out which eye was the good one and having to shift her gaze from eye to eye. Right now his wild eye stared at the picture above her head and the other gazed straight ahead at her.

"Children?" Bailey felt every ounce of blood in her body rush to her face. "I, um, geez, Uncle Rex, Carter and I just met." She felt a bead of sweat trickle down her back, and she wondered if she'd remembered to put on deodorant that morning. She looked over at Carter. His lip curled devilishly. *Great.*

"He's a punk," Aunt Fiona said. "They'll have punk kids on drugs."

"Lord." Olivia got up and started to clear the table.

"Anyone want to play a game?" Aunt Fiona asked.

"NO," everyone shouted at once and Bailey heard her mom swear under her breath that she was going to disown her nephew Freddie.

Freddie's intentions were good. He'd wanted to be a Boy Scout for about five minutes and had asked for Worst-Case Scenario for his birthday, thinking it would teach him all kinds of cool things that the other boys didn't know. They'd all been suffering for it ever since. Each of them had made several attempts at getting rid of it, but

Fiona kept a close eye on the game, even taking it to her room at night when she went to bed. She accused them of conspiring to keep her in the dark about her medical conditions.

Uncle Rex excused himself from the table, saying he was exhausted from his walk and needed to go up to bed. He grabbed Fiona's hand and told her he had something to show her. He wore a cheesy grin on his face as he led her away. Everyone but Fiona knew that exhaustion had little to do with his wanting to turn in so early.

Bailey washed the dishes while Carter dried, and Olivia just sat at the table and ogled him. After the last glass had been dried and put away, Bailey thought it'd be nice to put her mom out of her misery. They needed some rest after their long day, anyway.

Olivia walked them out to the porch and the three of them paused to look up at the stars. A warm breeze swirled about them with the faint scent of salt air. It was a perfect night for a romantic interlude and Bailey had ideas about her and Carter sitting on her deck, listening to the water's rush to shore. She wasn't the only one with ideas. Olivia kissed Bailey's cheek and then she stepped over to Carter and planted a big lip lock on him. Bailey counted to ten. If her mom didn't come up for air soon, she might be forced to intervene.

Olivia finally stepped back, touched her fingers to her lips, and whispered, "Sweet Jesus."

Carter grinned. The kiss hadn't fazed him. Of course, why would it? Women threw their underwear at him for a song. Bailey smoothed her tongue over her lips. She had some underwear she might be able to spare.

But not before they talked. Not only did she need to tell him the truth about her not being a virgin, but there were a lot of important things to consider in a budding relationship. They had a lot to learn about each other. Was he a toothpaste tube squeezer, or did he roll it up neatly from the end? Did he like to go out and party every chance he got, or did he enjoy spending a quiet evening at home? Would he object to sharing every inch of his house with two big dogs? Maybe she was just stalling for time, but she really did need to know a little more before making the big jump.

Bailey remembered her aunt telling her about yawning being an unspoken signal between married couples that one of them wasn't in the mood. From what Bailey could tell, that ploy had never worked with Rex, but Carter wasn't Rex. Not even close. Bailey figured it couldn't hurt to give it a try. She yawned all the way home and was more than a little dismayed that it worked like a charm.

Carter didn't even object to sleeping in the guest room, which was actually the dogs' play room. It housed about a hundred squeaking, croaking, crackling toys in all shapes and sizes and colors, and they were scattered over every inch of the floor. Tucker and Maggie May usually slept in her room and didn't climb on the guest bed, but just in case, Bailey put on clean sheets and blankets.

After a quick goodnight, Carter disappeared behind the guest room door and that was the last she saw of him. Bailey told herself it was fatigue. She went across the hall to her own room, and although she too was tired, as soon as her head hit the pillow, she was wide awake. Carter's kisses were still fresh in her memory and, now with him just a short twenty feet away . . .

Chapter Eighteen

By morning, Coupeville was enshrouded in clouds and Bailey knew she had to get the T-Bird over to the shop, and soon, or she'd have a very wet car. She dialed the shop and Mark Jefferson picked up on the second ring.

"Peaches," he said into her ear, his voice deep and seductive.

Not seductive enough to fool her a second time.

Even so, he was one of Bailey's best friends, he and his brother, Brian. The same age and grade in school, they'd made it a point to get to know her from the day she'd arrived in Coupeville, and their early friendship was quite possibly the only thing that had made moving to Coupeville from Seattle at the age of fifteen bearable.

It'd been traumatic, leaving behind the city and all her friends, especially Liza, but Mark and Brian had made life, to say the least, interesting. To be sure, the twins had spent considerable time thinking of new ways to get themselves into trouble, and they did their best to help engage her in their adventures every chance that presented itself. High school be damned.

Looking back now at some of the things she did with the twins made Bailey shake her head. Although truancy and running wild over every inch of the island seemed like nothing more than a simple adventure compared to the trouble kids were getting into today, it was trouble nonetheless.

Bailey had even experienced being a jailbird. She'd spent half a day in the town's jail cell with the twins, but the real highlight of that day was that the three of them had smoked pot while they were waiting for their parents to come and claim them.

Lucky for her mom, that was pretty much the worst of it from Bailey. She shuddered to think where she'd be if she'd fallen victim to the same kind of trouble that three of her friends had, getting pregnant before finishing their last year of high school.

Even though she'd stopped running around the island, skipping school, Bailey still felt guilty whenever she thought about all the things she'd done. Her mom had her hands full with Aunt Fiona, even back then, and she could have used some help.

And although Bailey and Mark *had* remained good friends, she preferred to keep her past adventures with him a secret from Carter. Probably it wasn't a good idea for a man to have certain images in his mind of his future wife. If Mark and Brian had any sense—and Bailey wasn't so sure they did—they'd keep their lips zipped about the past.

A girl could dream.

For sure, boredom bred trouble, but the heavy breathing in her ear was just one more reason she needed to hightail it out of Coupeville. Mark didn't give up easily.

"Don't call me Peaches," Bailey said to Mark. She thought she heard a chuckle on the other end. At the very least, he was grinning.

"Welcome home. I hear you won big in Vegas. In more ways than one," Mark said.

"That's why I'm calling. My car's got a problem with its soft top. Can you fit me in?"

Silence on the other end. Now she was sure he was grinning.

"Mark?"

"Peaches."

Bailey did an eye roll. "Geez."

"Name the place."

She considered scolding him, but he'd only soak up the attention and try to take it further. "Your shop. Now," she said.

"*Peaches.*"

Bailey thought she heard some slurping noises. "No. Not Peaches. And I'm only coming over to get my car looked at."

She hung up and held her head in both hands.

"Something wrong?" Carter asked behind her.

Bailey turned and was faced with one gorgeous man and two equally gorgeous dogs. The three of them were getting along famously. She immediately forgot about Mark, and her face spread into a smile. She hadn't seen her dogs all morning and last night they chose to spend the night with her guest. Lucky dogs. She didn't know if she should feel guilty for making them share their room, or if she should be jealous that they preferred Carter's company.

Bailey went to the refrigerator and took out a package of deli meat, which she split between Tucker and Maggie just in case they were considering changing ownership.

"If we hurry, we can get my car over to the shop before the sky opens," she said. She washed dog spit off her fingers and dried her hands on a paper towel.

Carter didn't look excited about the morning's plans. "I could take a look at it first. See if it's something simple."

"That's sweet of you, but like I told my Uncle Rex, I really think I should have a licensed mechanic work on it."

Carter pulled her into his arms before she could say another word. Her lips parted and he wasted no time in planting his over them. He kissed her hard, driving his tongue into her mouth and she forgot all about the car. He had a bunch of her hair in his fist and his other hand roamed over her back and down to the swell of her hips. She whimpered.

Maybe the car could wait. A little rain never hurt anything.

"How about some breakfast?" Bailey said on a breath. She might be horny, but she hadn't forgotten how to be a good host.

Carter kissed her again.

Okay, forget breakfast. Maybe they needed to lie back down for a while.

"You really want to eat right now?" Carter asked. His voice was husky and deep and his lips were moving against her cheek as he spoke.

Bailey's chest rose and fell with her heartbeat. She nodded and then slowly shook her head. "Maybe," she said, her voice a tiny squeak. "Diced ham. And eggs?"

"How about you? And you?"

Carter still had his fingers tangled in her hair. He gave it a gentle, yet demanding, tug. The kind of tug that made a girl feel like a woman. Bailey felt herself slipping. God help her.

She tried to fill her mind with other things. Like cooking. *And Carter's hands.* Her Aunt Fiona's obsession with that blasted game. *And Carter's lips.* How she had to take her car over to the auto shop. *And how she would convince Carter they belonged together*—even if it killed her.

Carter kept up his onslaught of seduction by kissing all the way down to the base of her throat, then he continued up the other side and nibbled on her ear. By the time he'd kissed her full circle, Bailey's knees were Jell-O. It was going to take something more than willpower to turn back now.

Bailey glanced over at Tucker and Maggie May. Maggie May was lying on her back with all four paws in the air and Tucker was humping his pillow bed. A large dog humping a stuffed bed was just what she needed to get back on track.

"*Tucker,*" Bailey scolded the large yellow dog. "Stop it. That's disgusting."

Carter looked over at Tucker and laughed. He released Bailey. "Okay, you win. Let's have breakfast. But don't think I'll forget my place. We'll continue this later."

Gulp.

Carter went to take a shower, and Bailey went to work in the kitchen. She did her best, but she'd suddenly forgotten how to cook. By the time Carter returned, though, she'd managed to blacken some toast, turn some eggs into brown crusted crumbly bits, and create two large disks of charred ham. Daydreaming had a way of taking one's mind off what one was doing.

Carter walked up behind her, smelling so good even the dogs raised their noses into the air for a whiff. Bailey didn't need to raise her nose into the air to smell him. He was pressed tight against her back. And he was bare chested.

His skin was damp and oh, how she loved the scent of Dove soap. It would be so easy to turn, pour herself into his arms, beg him to take her right there on the kitchen floor . . .

Ding, ding, ding, the chime on the coffee pot sounded, and Bailey sighed. Carter backed off and sat down at the table. Bailey resisted the urge to yank him back as he walked away, and instead, she poured them each a cup of coffee. She slid a plate full of burnt offerings over in front of him, along with some fresh crabmeat to go on top of his scrambled eggs.

Bailey watched Carter eat. The burnt ham cracked between his teeth and he didn't even seem to notice. His eyes never left her face. A drop of grease rested on his bottom lip and she wanted to lick it off. She licked her own lips instead. Carter began to play footsie with her under the table, moving his foot in small circles all the way up her leg. She let out a small gasp as he reached the top. He was true to his promise. He'd warned her he wouldn't forget where he was, and he hadn't.

The sky rumbled, and Bailey turned to look out her sliding glass door. "My car," she said, standing up.

"Perhaps we should find some indoor activity to keep ourselves occupied," Carter said, waggling his eyebrows.

She'd seen that waggle before. She knew exactly what activity it went with.

The sky split and small white pellets began to strike the kitchen window. Hail.

"My *car!*" Bailey ran to the hallway and got a blanket out of the closet. By the time she opened the door, everything was covered in white. And it didn't matter. Aunt Fiona was standing on her front porch and Uncle Rex had just finished spreading a tarp over the top of the T-Bird.

Bailey adjusted her clothes. "Auntie! Uncle Rex!" She pulled them inside and three eyes gazed up at her hair. The fourth, Rex's wild eye, looked up at the ceiling. Bailey gave her hair a quick pat, a useless gesture after Carter's mauling.

"We didn't mean to interrupt anything. She insisted we come over and talk to you about the concert." Uncle Rex jutted his thumb at Fiona.

Bailey's eyebrows shot up. "Concert?"

"With Elvis. He's still here, isn't he?" Fiona leaned to one side and looked around Bailey into the living room.

"I'm still here," Carter said. He walked up behind Bailey and stood close enough for her to feel the heat from his body. It was hailing outside, but it felt like summer.

"What concert?" Carter asked.

"We told all our friends about your comeback, just like in '68," Fiona said. "Mavis at the parlor said she'd do her part and hand out a flyer to everyone that comes in."

"Flyer?" Bailey had a sinking feeling. If word got out that *Elvis* was in town, every woman in Coupeville would turn into a raving maniac, especially since her mom had most of them convinced he'd been in hiding for all these years.

Uncle Rex handed Bailey a piece of blue paper. It had an announcement on the front. *Elvis has made his long awaited return! Come and hear him perform all your favorites in one unforgettable night. Ten dollars per person or eighteen dollars per couple.*

"We would have charged more, but being as most of us are on Social Security, we wanted to make it afford-able," Aunt Fiona said.

"Where did you get this?" Bailey turned the paper over in her hand.

"Don't bother thanking me. I was happy to get them made," Fiona said proudly.

"I bet," Bailey murmured. She turned to Carter. "I'm so sorry. I had no idea . . ."

Carter waved a dismissive hand. "Don't apologize." He gave Fiona a smile and Uncle Rex put an arm around her, staking his claim. "I'd be happy to sing for your family and friends."

"You would?" Bailey's heart thumped hard in her chest and all the lust she'd felt up to that point turned into love. He'd seen how weird her family was and here he still was, right there next to her, agreeing to put on a show for a town full of old people who couldn't even tell that he wasn't the real Elvis. Bailey wrapped her arms around Carter's neck and kissed him. Tonight just might be his lucky night.

"Maybe he's not a punk after all," Fiona said.

Rex cleared his throat and gave his wife a little frown. "We'll be going now. I need to get Fiona home."

Bailey stifled a giggle. Uncle Rex was jealous. And it was sweet. She glanced up at Carter. Maybe one day they'd be old and in love the same as her aunt and uncle.

She and Carter said their good-byes to Uncle Rex and Aunt Fiona and Bailey noticed that a clear blue spot had pushed its way through the clouds.

Saved by the sun? But who had been saved, she or Carter?

When they arrived at the auto shop, a dozen women from her Aunt Fiona's garden club were gathered out front. Most likely the work of her aunt. As soon as they were parked, the women rushed over for a closer look at Bailey's new car and especially *Elvis*. Bailey tried explaining that Carter was only a tribute artist, but they wouldn't hear of such nonsense and she gave up. Old people had dreams, too, after all.

Gretchen Carlyle straightened her wig as she stood in line waiting for Carter to sign a piece of paper she'd dug out from the bottom of her purse. "He's even better looking in person," she said, clicking her uppers. "And younger than I imagined."

"I intend to get me one of those silk scarves he gives away," Mary Appleton said. "I won't even wash the sweat out of it."

"Not before me," Lea Townsend said, shouldering her way through the crowd. "Do you think he'll like my dress?" She smoothed her hands over her backside, which was held taut by a superstrength girdle.

Lea's dress was a leopard print and, for the most part, she still had it going on. Of all the senior women in town, Lea was the cream of the crop and she wasn't afraid to flaunt what she still had. Bailey could only hope to have as much going on when she reached *her* golden years.

Bailey was surprised to see Lea pushing a baby carriage. Spry as Lea was, as far as Bailey knew, she was no longer able to bear children. It had to be a new grandchild. Bailey stepped over to take a peek, ready to "ooh" and "ahh" over a cute little bundle of pink, or blue, but as soon as she looked inside the carriage, she nearly fell backward. It was either the furriest baby she'd ever seen or the child had a severe hormone problem. It was neither. It was Lea's dog, Missy, a cute little Yorkshire terrier, and she was dressed in an outfit cut from the same material as Lea's dress.

Bailey loved her dogs, but she wasn't about to dress them up and push them around like babies. Still, she whispered to Lea that she thought Carter would love her dress, as well as her dog's. What good could it do to dash an old woman's dreams?

Carter was on his fifth autograph and it looked like it might be a while before he finished, so Bailey left him on his own. She went inside the shop. It was better to get Mark straightened out before he and Carter met anyway.

Brian Jefferson was at the front desk, which gave Bailey a glimmer of hope that Mark might be at lunch or maybe even had gone home early.

"Glad to see you came back," Brian said, his lips spreading to a wide grin. "Congratulations on winning that car. When you gonna take me for a ride?"

"Um," Bailey said, biting down on her lip. "Soon. I promise."

"I heard you brought someone home with you. I'm hoping it's Liza." Brian looked around Bailey and saw Carter and his mouth turned down. "That's not Liza."

Poor Liza. She'd made the mistake of giving Brian a kiss for his birthday a couple years back and he'd been lusting after her ever since. And poor Brian. He didn't seem to realize that it was his brother, Mark, that Liza had her sights set on.

Bailey shook her head. "Nope, that's not Liza."

Brian stared hard for half a minute and then he stepped around to the front of the counter. "What the hell's going on out there?"

Bailey turned around. The crowd had doubled in size and one corner of the lot was overflowing with women waving their hands in the air like they were at some kind of revival meeting. *Dear God,* she prayed, *don't let any of them fall and break a hip.*

"That's Carter Davis," she said, doing her best to sound nonchalant, but her voice was twinged with pride. "He's, uh, a friend. I brought him home from Las Vegas with me. He's kinda a star."

"Movie?"

"No."

"TV?"

"Nope."

Brian gave her a puzzled look and she could see his brain searching for another option. He stepped closer to the window for a better look. After a long pause, he turned and gave her a smarmy grin. *"Porn."*

Bailey's mouth dropped open and she gave him a good shove. "Brian Jefferson, what kind of girl do you think I am?"

Brian slid her a look. "I know what kind of girl you are, Peaches."

"What?" She gave him another shove.

He stumbled back and caught himself. "Geez. Just kidding. You're all pure and innocent and—"

"Okay, stop. Now you've gone from one extreme to the other. We'll let it rest at that. All I want is for you and your oversexed brother to keep rule number one in mind when you meet my friend."

Brian raised a questioning eyebrow.

"No kissing and telling." Bailey pushed a finger into his chest. "Got it?"

"Aye, aye, Captain."

The door opened and Carter squeezed inside, pulling the door shut after himself. He was breathing hard and it reminded Bailey of, well, herself, whenever he kissed her.

"Older women can be mighty powerful," he said. He

kept one hand on the door handle, holding it so that it couldn't be opened.

One by one, the women stopped trying to get in and Lea gave Carter one last lingering look. She blew him a kiss and he responded with a crooked grin that probably had her girdle on the verge of splitting.

Bailey grabbed his arm. "Don't encourage her," she said. "She's old enough to be your mother. Maybe even your grandmother."

Not that she was jealous of Lea Townsend. And anyway, Carter didn't seem like the type who'd get turned on by running his fingers through neck wattle—as little of it that Lea had. She'd heard of younger guys getting their thrills with older women, but she'd just never actually witnessed it. And she didn't care to.

After Bailey introduced Brian to Carter, Brian scribbled something resembling her name at the top of a repair form.

"Shall I add *his* name?" Brian asked Bailey.

"Now why would you do that?"

Brian gave her another smarmy grin. "What happens in Vegas stays in Vegas, Peaches."

Bailey narrowed her eyes and Brian took a step back.

"So what seems to be the problem?" he asked, changing his tone to one that was purely professional.

Bailey didn't care if he gave an Academy Award–winning act, she was never going to feel at ease with either one of the twins in the same room as Carter.

"Yeah, what seems to be the problem, Peaches?"

Bailey felt all her blood drain into her toes. A tall man with boyish good looks and dirty blond hair stood in the doorway, rubbing a rag over his grease-blackened hands. Mark Jefferson. He puckered his lips at Bailey and she gave him a look that could rival a bolt of lightning.

Carter gave her a curious look and the corners of his mouthed twitched up a notch. "Peaches?"

The blood surged upward out of Bailey's toes and went directly into her face. She had two choices: either explain or completely ignore the reference. She chose middle ground. "Did I, um, forget to mention that Mark and Brian are old friends from school?"

"*Good* friends," Mark said smugly and Bailey willed daggers to shoot from her eyes and put Mark Jefferson out of *her* misery.

"Not that good," Brian countered. He stepped away from his brother.

Bailey gave him a "thank-you" smile. Clearly it was a good time to get on with the reason for her visit. "I can't get the soft top to come up on my new car. I push the button, but all it does is make a funny buzzing sound."

"Let's go take a look," Mark said. He grabbed a couple of car interior protection shields and went out to the car. He put one shield on the seat and the other on the floor before getting in.

Bailey half expected the top to do a Murphy's Law kind of thing and raise when Mark pushed the button. She felt slightly relieved when it was just as she'd said. A lot of whirring and buzzing, but no action.

"It doesn't seem to be working properly," Mark said.

Bailey did a mental eye roll and she felt Carter doing the same.

"Maybe we should take it back to your place and I'll take a look at it," he offered.

Bailey glanced over at the corner of the parking lot. Five cars were queued up for work, the newest a mid-nineties American made. Carter looked too and his expression said he wasn't impressed.

"I don't think these guys have the kind of training it takes to work on newer cars," he whispered in her ear.

He had a point. Most of the folks in town with newer cars took them over to Oak Harbor to the dealer where they'd purchased them. Probably for a couple of reasons:

they were under warranty and also it gave them a reason to go into a larger town where they could do some real shopping. Well she didn't have time to go to Oak Harbor and when it came to cars, she trusted the twins. Sort of. Although why she couldn't say. Neither of them had ever gone to any kind of mechanic's school. Their training consisted of working on their own cars throughout high school, with additional experience picked up at their after school jobs working for the man who had run this very same shop before he'd died.

On the other hand, Carter might not be a trained mechanic—so far as she knew—but he was smart and good looking and it made her breathe hard to think about him bent over the hood of her car, maybe even with his shirt off.

"Let's go," she said.

"Wait just a minute." Mark grabbed her wrist, smudging it with a greasy black film. "At least give us a chance." He leaned close enough for her to feel his breath on her cheek. "If I don't have your car back to you by the end of the week, you can make me your love slave."

Bailey choked and glanced nervously at Carter. "As much as I appreciate the offer, I'll pass on that," she snapped at Mark in a low voice.

Two women had walked up and had their faces pressed close to the window, intent at getting a look at *Elvis*. One had a piece of paper in her hand, and the other, an old 33 rpm record album that had the King's image on its front. Carter pushed open the door and signed his autograph and the women giggled like young schoolgirls. Just as he started to close the door, a few more appeared and Carter slipped outside to do some more signing. Better to get it done now than to have them all gather later on her front lawn.

Bailey had the feeling that, from now on, it was going to be hard finding time alone with Coupeville's visiting celebrity. And if he attempted to work on her car while it was sitting in her driveway, he'd only garner more attention, which, in turn, meant that he'd probably never get it fixed. She shrugged. "I guess I don't really need my car this week."

"Is he your new boyfriend?" Mark asked, nodding at Carter.

"Maybe."

"Looks like your type."

Carter's dark hair was combed so that it feathered back perfectly. He'd trimmed his sideburns that morning, but they were still reminiscent of the King. She didn't care what Mark thought so long as he got it through his head there'd be no more drinking peach schnapps and swinging from Madrona trees with this girl. Carter was the only man she wanted to swing with from now on.

"He is definitely my type."

Mark gave Carter a long appraising look. "Let me know if he gets outta hand. Me and Brian'll take him down to the waterfront, smash his hands with barnacle rocks."

Bailey grimaced. "I appreciate your concern, but that won't be necessary. You have until the end of the week to fix my top."

Mark and Brian both smiled a greasy smile as she walked out the door.

Chapter Nineteen

Carter was none too happy about Bailey's decision to leave the T-Bird with the twins, but she figured it'd be easy to make him forget all about the car. She was a woman, after all.

The twins offered her a loaner car, and seemed proud to be stepping up their customer service to compete with the car dealers in Oak Harbor. The problem was the loaner was in worse shape than anything that might be brought in for repairs. It listed to one side and the trunk was held shut with a bungee cord.

"It don't look very good, but it sure runs great," Brian said, his chest puffed out like a rooster about to crow. "I fixed it myself. One of our customers left it here to have us rebuild the carburetor. We told him it would take a couple of weeks, but it's been two months and he hasn't come back."

Bailey knew the man they were speaking of. He'd come into the Medical Center with chest pains and had never left. "I'm sure you did a fine job, but I think we'll walk. It's only a few blocks and the exercise will do me good."

As they approached Front Street, Bailey's stomach growled in response to the whiteboard at the top of the wood staircase that displayed the Knead & Feed's lunch menu. Shrimp bisque soup, salad, turkey sandwich, and homemade pie, the same as it was every weekend. The same as it had been every weekend for all the years she'd lived in Coupeville. She supposed the menu was for the benefit of visitors who'd come to expect their favorites when in town.

"I like a woman who's not afraid to eat," Carter said when their food was placed before them.

Bailey chewed a mouthful of turkey sandwich slowly, eyeing him. She'd heard about guys like him. Guys who claimed they liked hearty eaters, but then complained about the extra two hundred pounds hanging around the house.

She took another bite and felt her flesh begin to expand. She could take the remaining half of her sandwich home, say she wanted it for her dogs, but the temptation to sneak and eat it herself would be too great. She'd lie awake later that night, stomach grumbling, mouth watering, until she just couldn't stand it anymore. Then she'd tiptoe out to the kitchen, and just as she opened her mouth to take that first delectable bite, light would flood the room and there he'd be. Carter. Leaning up against the doorjamb, giving her that crooked grin, dressed only from the waist down.

"I'm stuffed," Bailey said, pushing away her plate. Her stomach grumbled its protest. Carter reached across the table and Bailey watched in horror as he took a big bite of her sandwich. He pulled her bowl over in front of him and scooped a big spoonful of creamy tomato soup and shrimp into his mouth. It was enough to make her cry.

Three gulls soared outside the open window, screaming for a tidbit, but Carter wasn't sharing. And when he finished off her food, he had the nerve to order pie.

Bailey suffered in silence while he ate, doing her best to keep from drooling.

Finally, he was finished. Almost. He got up to pay,

leaving behind a small corner of pie on his plate. Bailey quickly shoved a fruit-filled bite into her mouth. She chewed a couple times and swallowed, then dabbed her mouth to erase the evidence.

Carter got his change and walked back over to her. He grinned, looking down at her, and then leaned in for a kiss. His tongue lingered on her lips in a most pleasing way, and Bailey soon figured out that he wasn't just kissing her, he was licking her. Cleaning up "evidence," to be more exact.

Evidently her dabbing hadn't been thorough enough.

She decided right then and there that pie was the one thing she'd always be sure to have in the house.

Bailey caught some of the other patrons watching them. When Carter removed his lips from hers, the place was silent. She smiled up at him and took his offered hand. She could see the headlines now in the local paper. *Elvis Gets His Licks In With Local Girl.*

She didn't care. If she was to be the object of local scandal, she couldn't think of any other man she'd rather share the honors with than Carter. She stood, holding her head high, and smiled at the whisperers as she and Carter passed by them on their way out the door.

Back at her cottage, Bailey got another good tongue cleaning. This time it was Maggie May doing the licking. Tucker made his usual minimal effort of lifting his head and wagging the tip of his tail. Exhausted from the exertion, he quickly let his head sink back to the floor. Snoring immediately ensued.

The phone rang and Bailey answered it, while Maggie moved on to her next tongue washing victim.

"I heard you were sucking face all over town," Fiona said.

"That's impossible. I haven't *been* all over town." Bailey propped the phone between her ear and shoulder and slipped off her sweater.

"Gertie down at the Knead & Feed said she saw you."

"Gertie? She wasn't even there."

"I know. But Claire was, and she told Grace and Grace called Gertie. They said he *licked* your face."

Bailey reached up and traced the path Carter's tongue had taken across her lips. "It was a dab of marionberry pie," she started to explain. "Anyway, who cares? And why is that news?"

"It's not good for business," Fiona said. "If the gals think Elvis is taken, there's likely to be a boycott. They might not come to his concert."

Of course. The concert. "Sorry, Auntie. I guess I just lost my head."

"Well, he is quite fetching if I do say so. If I was a younger woman, I might be willing to let him lick my face, too. You be sure to tell him that."

Bailey assured her she'd pass it on and that she'd try and keep things casual when she and Carter were out where his adoring public could see them.

"By the way, we might have to move up the date for the concert. My pee was discolored this morning. I may have hepatitis. Your mother's taking me to the doctor in an hour."

Bailey felt momentary alarm, until she remembered who she was talking to. "Are your skin and eyes yellow?" she asked. She heard the phone drop and then a patter of feet. A minute later, her aunt came back on.

"My eyes are blue, and my skin is leaning toward red. Forgot to put on sunscreen this morning before I went out to work in the garden," Fiona said.

"I'm sure you're fine."

"Maybe it's the Bubonic Plague. All those foreigners coming into our country. They bring all kinds of things over in their suitcases."

"That's unlikely, Auntie. Is Mom there?"

"She's out in the garden."

"Well, I think if you had the Bubonic Plague, she would not be working in her garden."

"Life goes on," Fiona said.

"I think probably you just need to drink more water. How many glasses have you had today?"

"Does Whidbey's liquor count?"

Bailey glanced over her shoulder. Carter was on the sofa with his head resting back and his eyes were closed. Tucker was draped crossways over his lap and they were both making light snoring sounds. Maggie May was on the floor next to the sofa, splayed out with her legs open wide. Her eyes were open, but she was snoring, too.

"Tell you what, I'll come by for a minute and take your temperature. I'll also bring you a six-pack of Evian, which I expect you to drink."

"Does it mix well with Whidbey's?"

"Everything mixes well with Whidbey's, Auntie."

Bailey scribbled a note telling Carter she'd gone over to her mom's house and that she'd be back in about an hour. She grabbed the Evian from the refrigerator and tiptoed over to the door, shutting it with barely a click. Old man Winston peered at her through a gap in his front curtains and she waved and continued to tiptoe down the drive until she was sure her dogs wouldn't pick up on her departure.

Ten minutes later, Bailey was in her mother's kitchen, watching her stuff daffodils into a green glass vase.

"Where is it?" Bailey asked.

Olivia looked at her with raised eyebrows.

"That blasted game. Where is it?" Bailey opened the pantry door and looked inside. She walked into the living room and gave it a quick scan. No yellow box in sight. She went back to the kitchen and stuffed tight fists onto her hips.

"I think Fiona took it with her upstairs. She and Gretchen Carlyle and Lea Townsend have some crazy idea about going camping. Your aunt thought it might be good to read up on wilderness survival skills." Olivia laughed and shook her head.

"Camping? Auntie? Does Uncle Rex know about this?"

"He's out buying her some grizzly spray."

Bailey rolled her eyes. "That ought to be some camp-out. Do you know she just called me and said she thinks she might have the Bubonic Plague?"

Olivia joined Bailey in the eye roll. "Lord."

Bailey went up to check on her aunt, just in case, and found her in her room, studying a handful of yellow cards. Bailey snatched them away and stuffed them into her back pocket. She intended to put them in the garbage disposal as soon as she got home.

"That's okay. I've already got them memorized. Wouldn't do me no good to have to go sorting through cards while I'm being chased by a bear now would it?"

Bailey put a hand to her aunt's forehead. "Why do you want to go camping, Auntie? Uncle Rex could put up a tent right out back."

Fiona snorted. "When did you ever hear of waking up to the sound of screaming seagulls in the middle of the forest?"

It was no use. Bailey didn't know why she was worried anyway. Chances were her aunt would read about some dreadful disease on one of those cards and she'd decide sleeping in the forest wasn't worth dying for. "As long as I'm here, I'll take your temperature."

She went to her mother's room and opened her lingerie drawer, where Olivia kept the thermometer hidden from Fiona.

Bailey shoved aside a stack of folded underwear and she uncovered not only the thermometer, but also a picture. She pulled it out. A man and a woman smiled up at her. The photo had been taken in dim light and it was well-worn from being handled, but Bailey immediately recognized the woman as her mother. At first she thought the man must be her father, but the longer she stared, the more she was convinced otherwise. He wasn't her father. Not even close, but he *was* familiar.

Bailey walked over to the window to get a better look. *Elvis! Elvis?* Having a meal with her mother? *Mom.* Bailey put a hand to her mouth, stifling a delighted giggle. While it was no secret Olivia Ventura was in love with Elvis Presley, she'd never let on that she'd actually *known* the man. Let alone known him well enough for them to share a meal.

"A woman could die waiting for medical treatment in this house," Fiona called from the bedroom.

Bailey was careful to place the photo back right where she'd found it. She pushed her mom's underwear back in place covering it like it was some saucy secret. She and her mom definitely needed to talk.

As soon as Bailey confirmed her aunt's temperature was normal, Fiona perked up. She tucked a handful of game cards under her pillow and followed Bailey downstairs.

Olivia was finished with her flower arranging, and had moved on to looking for recipes in her latest issue of *Cooking Light.*

"Did you show her the new flyer for the competition?" Fiona asked.

"Competition?" Bailey grimaced, not sure she really wanted to know.

"I'll get it. Wait right here." Fiona tossed her hands into the air and scuttled out of the kitchen. She returned a minute later with an 8 x 10 sheet of hot pink paper and shoved it into Bailey's hand. "We'll need to get some copies made, so we can paper the town with them."

Bailey glanced at the flyer and blinked hard. It wasn't the same flyer her aunt and uncle had brought over earlier. "I thought you just wanted to have a private show with a few friends and family?"

"Fiona thinks it'd be fun to have some kind of prize for

whoever can pick out the real Elvis. Of course, I could pick out the real Elvis with my eyes closed." Olivia's eyelids dipped shut. "All I'd need to do is touch him. His hair, his lips . . . feel his cheek against mine . . ."

"Mom," Bailey said with a groan. One more word out of her mother's mouth and she'd cover her ears.

"I'm just saying . . ."

"We all *know.* We don't need to hear you *say* it." Bailey thought about the picture she found in her mom's dresser drawer. Too much information.

"So what do you think?" Fiona asked.

Bailey took another look at the flyer. A one hundred dollar prize would be given to the person who could pick out the real Elvis. She sighed. "What do you win if you predict that no one will be able to pick him out? He's—"

Olivia's hands flew to cover her ears. "Hush. I don't want to hear such nonsense. Don't say another word!" she shouted, blocking out Bailey's voice. "I'll have you know—"

Bailey cringed. Now she'd done it. Why, oh why couldn't she just keep her mouth shut? She'd rather have a bowling ball dropped on her foot than listen one more time about how it had never really been proven that Elvis died when they say he did, that he's not really buried where they say he is, and that too many people have seen him for it to be a mistake. Lord, *please,* turn back the time just two minutes and she'd bite her tongue to be spared from hearing another Elvis lecture.

Olivia took a deep breath, but she didn't continue. Not with the lecture anyway. Instead, her voice trembled and she sat down, like explaining it once more would wear her out.

"Well," Olivia said, "I won't waste my breath. You know where I stand on the subject."

Bailey mentally knocked herself in the head. She was a mean daughter. Why should she care if her mother wanted to believe that Elvis Presley was still alive? Who did it hurt? No one. Who was she to force her opinion on her mother? Bailey thought of the picture she'd found. Her mother wasn't hanging on to a simple fantasy. Elvis had been her dream. He'd been the man to light the stars in her mom's eyes, and those stars were still burning bright.

She was a mean, mean daughter.

"I'm sorry, Mom. I don't know what came over me. Of course Elvis is out there somewhere, and he's just waiting to come back to all of us," Bailey said, feeling genuinely sorry for making her mother feel bad. "But for Carter's sake, I hope he stays out there just a little while longer."

Olivia gave her a hard look.

"Just for a week. If Elvis were to show up now, what would happen to Aunt Fiona's show?" Scooting over close to her mother's side, Bailey gave her a little nudge. "Just how well did you know Elvis?"

Olivia's hand shot up to her hair. She shook her head. "I'm sure I don't know what you're talking about—"

"Come *on*. Daddy's gone. I'm your daughter. You don't have to keep any secrets from me."

Olivia gave her a blank-faced stare.

"I saw the picture."

"Oh."

"So tell me, tell me . . . how did the two of you meet? Did you wait for Elvis to come out the back of some building after one of his concerts?" Bailey clasped her hands together and looked up at the ceiling all dreamy-eyed. "Did you and the King have a secret love rendezvous?"

Olivia brushed a shaky hand over her hair and Bailey saw a blush color her cheeks.

"Oh. My. God. Don't tell me . . . I'm Elvis Presley's love child!"

"Heavens *no!* Don't say such a thing. I was always faithful to your dad. Physically, anyway. A woman can't help the things that go on inside her mind." Her blush deepened. "Let's just say, yes, I was fortunate enough to actually meet Elvis after one of his concerts—never mind how—and we had a connection . . . of sorts." And then it was her turn to get all dreamy-eyed. "Elvis was the sweetest, the most gentle, kindest man I'd ever met."

"I'll just bet," Bailey said, amusement riding the corners of her mouth.

"A true gentleman, so pure of heart, so sexy—"

"Okay. I get it. He was a regular prince," Bailey said.

"A King."

"Right." Bailey stood corrected. Obviously, she'd have to wait until her mom and Aunt Fiona had indulged in a little after-dinner sip if she wanted to drag any juicy details about Elvis out of her mom.

Bailey picked up the flyer and continued reading. In small print, at the bottom of the page, it described the *second place prize as a ride in the red Thunderbird convertible that Coupeville's own Bailey Ventura won in Las Vegas.*

"If it's not raining," Bailey grumbled.

"Raining?"

Bailey shrugged. "My new car is in the shop. I can't get the soft top to come up. Brian and Mark are taking a look at it as we speak."

"Those two? Lord." Olivia shook her head and closed her eyes. "Thank you Jesus for not giving either one of them boys the talent to sing like Elvis."

Bailey looked up and gave thanks, too.

The sofa was vacant when Bailey returned home. She paused inside the door for signs of life, like the slapping of Maggie May's tail against the furniture, but all was quiet. Until she heard Carter's voice. He was out on her one-person, two-dog deck talking on his cell phone. Although his voice wasn't raised, she could see the muscles tense in his jaw, and the hair on the nape of her neck prickled to attention. He was back at that place. The dark side. She half-expected dark clouds to swoop in and blacken the sky.

Carter's voice growled deep and Bailey suddenly had a

vision of heads bobbing up from the surface of the Nevada desert, like a scene from the movie *What Dreams May Come.*

His gun was lying on her kitchen counter, and the clip was lying next to it. Her mouth went dry. Murder and mayhem didn't exist in Coupeville. Not in her world. Las Vegas wasn't Coupeville, though, and that was Carter's world. And she'd brought his world here to hers.

It's simply business, she told herself. Nevada business. A man in Carter's line of work needed to have a tough exterior or he wouldn't last. She knew that. She didn't understand it, but she knew it was so. She also knew she shouldn't eavesdrop on a conversation that could lead to multiple forms of torture. He'd made that clear.

She walked away, went to her room to give Carter some privacy, and lay down on her bed. She tucked her white down comforter around her like a cocoon. Now she felt better. Being with a man like Carter might prove challenging if she had to get up each morning and wonder whether she'd be spending the day with security guy, or *Elvis.* Bailey sighed. A little of each would please her very much, if only it didn't have to include guns and violence.

"Where the hell are you?" Twinkie yelled into Carter's ear. "Frank has been after me for two days, saying you took that fat little man's diamond."

Carter rubbed a hand over his face. "I thought we agreed you'd take some time off—"

"Some of us have to work for a living. We can't sing and dance our way through life."

"Yeah, a lot of good it's done me. Now, what did Zoopa say? Exactly."

Twinkie sighed into the phone. "He says the Azuri went missing after the night of his party and that you're his prime suspect." She laughed nervously. "He isn't happy, Carter. You know what happens when Frank isn't happy. He takes it out on everyone around him." She sighed again. "God, Carter, tell me you didn't have anything to do with this."

"I didn't." Carter grimaced at his lie. "All right, maybe I know something."

"Shit, Carter. You trying to get me killed?" Twinkie's voice hit shriek level.

"Calm down. Pack a bag. I'll come and get you."

"And then what? You'll take me to your place again? Well, guess what? Frank and his boys know where you live."

"Just pack your bag. I'll be there." Carter flipped his phone shut and he worked the muscles in his jaw. His vacation was over.

Bailey heard her sliding door ease open and then close and she anticipated Carter's knock at her bedroom door.

"Trouble back home?" Bailey asked when he opened her door.

Carter sat on the edge of the bed and put a hand in her hair, pulling her up to him. His mouth was turned up, but his eyes didn't crinkle at the corners. "Nothing for you to worry about, honey."

Then how come she could feel sweat forming on her back? Bailey looked into Carter's eyes and saw fire burning in them.

"Liar," she said quietly.

Carter grinned. He sang a couple bars of "Suspicious Minds."

Okay, maybe she wouldn't worry. When a man like Carter sang, it was hard to think about anything bad. He stopped singing and tipped up her chin. His kiss was long and hard, and she felt herself begin to shake. Carter's anger seemed to be on constant simmer, and she didn't know what might happen after the kiss, but she sure wanted to find out.

"Okay, I forgive you for being a liar."

He moved onto the bed, stretching out next to her, one leg pinning her in place—not that she intended to move even one inch—molding his body to hers. He began to sing "I Can't Help Falling In Love." Bailey's pulse raced. She hadn't gotten around to telling Carter the truth about her bedroom experience, yet, but somehow she didn't think it was going to matter.

Maggie May had ideas, too. She didn't want to be left out of the fun. She jumped up onto the bed, and nosed her way between them, snorting and rolling around on her back. By the time she was finished, the fire had gone out of Carter's eyes and he was laughing. Maggie May gazed up at them with big brown puppy eyes.

The thumping in Bailey's chest slowed. She considered shoving the dog out of the room and closing the door, but her babies hadn't been out since that morning and it would kinda spoil the moment if she and Carter got up and found a special surprise on the carpet.

"I should take them out for a short walk," she said.

At mention of the word "walk," Maggie May became still like a statue and Tucker bounded into the room like an antelope. Ears up, tail doing a weak impersonation of a wag, he was ready, too.

"Want to go with us?" Bailey asked Carter, but he declined, saying he had a few more calls to make.

Bailey reluctantly left him behind. She walked up Madrona Way for a while and let the dogs relieve themselves about eighty times, and when she returned, old man Winston was peering out his front window. As always, she gave him a friendly smile and a wave that prompted him to step outside to retrieve his daily paper.

"Good afternoon, Mr. Winston," Bailey said. She looked up into the gray sky. "Lovely day, don't you think?" At least it wasn't still hailing.

Mr. Winston muttered something, then went back inside. Probably he'd wished her a good day.

She walked in her front door and called out to Carter. He didn't answer. She looked out back. He wasn't out there either, but a few minutes later he came through the door with two bags of groceries.

"I tried to catch up to you, but you'd disappeared, so I went to the store and picked up a few things for tonight's dinner." Carter put the bags on the table and began unpacking them.

Steaks for grilling, potatoes for baking, and the makings for a salad. Great. She was finally ready for sex and he was ready to fill his belly.

"And lastly," Carter said, reaching into the final bag. He pulled out a bottle of wine and two candles.

Things were looking up.

Carter pulled up the covers over Bailey's chest with a gentle tug. She wore a relaxed smile and he brushed the back of his hand over her cheek affectionately before he left the room. Maggie May's tail whacked the floor a couple of times as he passed by, but Bailey remained still. Lucky for him, she was a lightweight drinker. She'd sleep till morning.

He slipped down the hall and caught his image in the mirror on the way out. Dressed in black, he looked like a cross between the King and a cat burglar. The only body part he might have to worry about showing in the dark were his teeth.

The walk to the auto shop was uneventful. No neon lights, no music, no slot machines dinging through open doorways. The night air was crisp and it felt good ruffling through his hair, but it didn't do much to clear his head.

Bailey's sleeping face haunted him. He'd looked back at her before he'd left the room and she'd looked like an angel bathed in moonlight, so trusting, so completely in love with him. And she'd made it clear that it wasn't just the King who had her heart all wrapped up with a tidy bow. Of course, he'd thought Irene was an angel, too, the night they'd stood at the altar and said their vows. That opinion had quickly changed when another impersonator had come along and sang in her ear.

Carter shook his ex from his thoughts, but the pain of what she'd done would remain with him for a very long time. Admittedly, meeting and getting to know Bailey had dulled that pain, and his feelings for her were growing stronger each day, but he didn't see how it could work with him being an Elvis tribute artist and her being a small town girl. It was better to leave before things got out of hand. Before both of them got hurt.

He had to go back to his life and leave Bailey to hers. If she found out that she'd unknowingly helped him screw Zoopa over by bringing him and the Azuri diamond to Coupeville, that would more than likely end any ideas of romance she might have. But she'd also feel used, and no way did he want that. Better for her if she didn't know the truth.

Carter blew out a big breath. He was a bastard, but at least he could be proud of himself for not taking advantage of Bailey while she was under the influence.

The shop was dark, just as he'd expected. Cover of darkness was even better than wearing all black, so he was doubly protected. He circled the shop around to the back and found an entry that couldn't be seen from the street. It took him about a minute to open the door and he told himself he'd have to brush up on his B&E skills. A lot could happen in one minute. People could happen by, cops could arrive with lights flashing . . . well, maybe not in Coupeville.

The T-Bird sat in the middle bay. Carter flashed a light on the top assembly. It hadn't been touched. The twins had probably parked the car inside to discourage errant teens from having some good old-fashioned fun. Damn kids.

Carter took a leisurely look around the shop. He could be there all night without being bothered, even turn on the overhead lights, but that was an unnecessary chance to take and he wasn't warm on the idea of spending the night as a guest of Coupeville's finest. Even though he could probably pick that lock, too.

A few minutes was all he needed anyway. Just long enough to retrieve the black bag from the gear assembly. Carter stuck a hand inside, but it didn't get far. Space was tight. He pulled it back, took off his jacket and tried again. His finger tips barely brushed over something soft. He shined the flashlight inside and saw the bag. He jammed his arm back inside, reaching as far as he could, grimacing as he felt the gear assembly bite into flesh. He gripped the material between two fingers, but the bag was stuck and he couldn't hold it tight enough to pull it free.

"Damn," he grumbled, pulling out his arm. A small jagged line on his forearm oozed blood and he wiped it away with his other sleeve. It continued to bleed, but he'd live. He'd had worse.

He shined the flashlight around the shop again, looking for anything he might use to extract the small bag. Tires were piled high on a rack along one wall, batteries were stacked into a pyramid shape in one corner, and dozens of belts in various sizes were hung on the wall in another corner. Carter was impressed. The twins hadn't struck him as being that organized.

He shined the light up into one corner and stared for about two seconds, before turning it off.

Shit.

Come morning, the twins were going to have some interesting viewing. Carter quickly headed for the same door he'd come in, but he paused long enough to face the camera and give it a crooked grin.

Chapter Twenty

"Dude," Brian Jefferson said to his brother. "Look at this."

Mark looked at the monitor and nodded. "That's Peaches's new squeeze."

"What'dya think he's up to? He didn't seem too enthusiastic about us lookin' after Bailey's car."

"I'm not too enthusiastic about him lookin' after Bailey," Mark said.

Brian nodded. "Maybe he was going to steal it." He squinted at the screen.

"Seems like he's lookin' for somethin'."

The twins watched in silence for a moment.

"You think Bailey's gonna marry him?" Brian asked his brother.

They looked at each other.

"Guess if she does, that means we can't call her Peaches anymore," Brian said.

"Guess not."

Bailey squinted her eyes open and looked around. Carter wasn't in bed with her. Had they had sex? A sinking feeling came over her. Had he realized she'd lied and been so disgusted with her that he'd taken the first plane back to Vegas?

Bailey reached a hand up to her chest. She still had on her T-shirt, but her jeans were lying on the floor, next to the bed. She peeked under the covers. Her panties were still on. *Whew.*

She frowned and thought hard about the previous night. The last thing she remembered was Carter pouring her a third glass of wine. And then they did some kissing, and then—nothing? It was like her brain was a computer that had been infected with some kind of virus and her hard drive had been all but erased.

She lay still. Maybe if she just laid there for a minute and didn't think too hard, it'd all come back. Bailey closed her eyes. Air blew softly through the heat vent, Tucker's breath came in a steady rhythm, her clock buzzed faintly.

She licked her lips. She glanced over at her nightstand. If it'd been a normal night, she'd have put a glass of water within reach before going to bed. But nothing about the previous night was normal.

She slipped out of bed, went and got herself a drink of water, then tiptoed across the hall and peeked in the spare room. Maggie May was belly up on the floor. Her tail swished back and forth when she saw Bailey.

"Hey, girl," Bailey cooed a motherly greeting to Maggie and rubbed her chest. "Where'd you hide that man?" Maggie swished her tail some more, but she didn't have an answer. Tucker came and sat next to Bailey, nudging her hand away from Maggie. He wanted equal time. Bailey stroked his head lovingly.

It wasn't the morning Bailey had been hoping for, but the day was young. Things could pick up. She had a thought. Maybe Carter was in the kitchen brewing coffee and cooking her a delicious breakfast. She inhaled deeply. All she smelled was dog. Her babies were due for their weekly bath.

She went out to the kitchen. It was clean. The dinner dishes had been washed and put away, and there was a bouquet of fresh-cut flowers on the kitchen table. Bailey leaned in to smell them. They weren't breakfast, but they did make her smile. She made herself a cup of instant coffee, and then took it and her phone out to the deck. The morning air was brisk. Penn Cove was cloaked in a foggy mist that obliterated everything except a twinkle of light from a boat that was about five hundred feet out on the water. A single gull cried out from somewhere in the fog, and small waves gently slapped the rocks below her cottage.

Bailey filled her lungs with a cleansing breath of salt air. She settled onto a damp deck chair and called her mom to see if Carter had been kidnapped by anyone in that household.

"My God, you haven't lost him, have you? You didn't have a fight, did you?"

Bailey felt three new lines being etched into her forehead.

"No, Mom. We didn't have a fight." At least she didn't think so. Some of the details from the previous night were clear—everything, in fact, before her third glass of wine. Of the clear parts, fighting would not be the appropriate term for what had happened between her and Carter. Just thinking about it made her body temperature rise. He sure seemed like he'd been having a good time. So where was he?

"You don't think he's gone back to Las Vegas, do you?" Olivia asked, panic riding the edges of her voice.

Bailey fingered the string tie on her sweatpants. The flowers were a good sign, but trying to remember all the details made her brain begin to swell. "I don't know, Mom," she said. "Where's Aunt Fiona? Maybe she's heard from him."

Her mother paused and was quiet for a moment.

"She's still asleep. I can hear her snoring. And I'm not going to wake her. She's exhausted from making lists of symptoms and things to watch out for when she goes on that cruise with her friends. Fair warning . . . I'm killing your cousin next time I see him."

There were times when Bailey had also thought that killing cousin Freddie would be enjoyable. Why couldn't he have given Aunt Fiona *The Game of Life*? Although that might not be such a good idea either. She'd land on a space telling her to add a girl *and* a boy to her little plastic car, and she'd think she was pregnant.

"I thought Auntie was going camping."

"Lyme disease. Ticks," Olivia said.

Of course. Bailey made her mom promise to call if Carter showed, and just as she hung up, the front door opened.

Thank you, God. Bailey gave a quick glance heavenward. She crossed the room and grabbed Carter by his collar. "I thought you'd gotten your fill of my crazy family and had hightailed it back to Vegas." She pulled him to her and kissed him. "Promise me you won't ever leave me here with them."

"Honey, I'll always be right here," Carter said. He touched a finger to her chest, then slipped his hands around her waist and raised her up onto her toes and kissed her.

Bailey's head swam and her thighs burned with desperate need. Carter had beaten a path to her soul and she was ready to dive into any pool he wanted. Even Frank Zoopa's.

"You do things to a man, baby," he said.

She knew that. She'd felt it plenty of times. Bailey reached up to his chest and played with the dark hairs that peeked over the top button of his shirt.

"Sorry about last night," she said. "I didn't mean to get drunk." She gave him a coy smile and shrugged. "You are partly to blame, though."

Carter raised an eyebrow.

"You're the one who kept filling my glass."

Carter smiled. "I didn't have my gun to your head." He grabbed her by both arms and pushed them to her back, holding her tight against him. "Be glad I'm a gentleman. When you fell off the couch, I carried you to your bed. I also undressed you."

Bailey swallowed. Heat filled her cheeks as he continued to talk low into her ear.

"And then I let you sleep. But, don't you worry. I didn't see anything I haven't seen before."

His lips brushed over hers like a feather, and Bailey felt her nipples harden. If he continued touching her that way, kissing her, breathing those wonderfully seductive words into her ear, she couldn't be held responsible for her actions. "I guess that's true," she managed with a quiet squeak. "So we didn't . . ."

Carter shook his head. "No, honey. It wouldn't be right for a man to make love to a woman under those circumstances."

His voice was all sultry and Elvislike. Bailey gazed into his face and sighed. How could she *not* fall in love with this man? Surely he could see what she felt for him. And if he couldn't, she'd show him. He wouldn't need any mind-reading powers to understand.

Bailey reached both arms around his neck and their lips met. She dipped her tongue into his mouth and he held her tight, like he'd never let her go. Finally, he scooped her into his arms and carried her down the hall to the bedroom. Her heart knocked against her chest so hard it hurt. It was meant to be, and who was she to mess with fate?

Carter's eyes locked onto hers, as he lay her on the bed, and he didn't miss a beat when he slipped her shirt off over her head. Nothing was going to break this magic moment.

And then the phone rang.

Bailey tried ignoring it, but by the fifth ring, the shrill *trilling* sound was ruining everything. She reached for the noisy little mood wrecker, but Carter caught her hand.

"Ignore it," he whispered, his voice all deep and husky. He cupped her breast gently, kissed the swell above her bra.

Another ring.

"It could be the garage," Bailey said.

"That damn car's not going anywhere."

Carter ran his tongue down to the soft mound of her belly and she moaned her pleasure.

Ring.

Bailey bit into her lip. It was torture. For her, anyway. Carter continued as though he couldn't even hear it, but it was like a pesky gnat that wouldn't go away and she couldn't concentrate with all that noise. This was their first time. First times were supposed to be perfect.

Bailey's heart thumped all the way into her throat. *Concentrate*, she told herself. *Maybe it'll go away.*

Ring.

Maybe it won't. Bailey stretched her hand over to the nightstand and felt around until she found the receiver.

"Hello?" she answered, her voice in a soft pant.

"Peaches?" Mark Jefferson said into her ear.

Something hard pressed against Bailey's side. This time it wasn't Carter's gun. "Uh, huh," she squeaked.

"Are you all right?" Mark asked.

"Mm-hm," she fairly hummed as Carter's tongue continued to do its work. "Oh, yeah."

"You don't sound all right. That friend of yours didn't hurt you, did he? 'Cause if he did, me and Brian, we'll take care of him for you."

Bailey did an eye roll. "What the hell do you want, Mark?"

Mark was quiet for a moment and Bailey envisioned

him pulling the phone away from his ear and staring at it. She sighed. She didn't want Carter to be put off or have the idea she wasn't fully engaged in the activity they were about to embark upon, but with one man talking in her ear and another one kissing her and licking her in such delicious places, she simply could not focus.

Something had to give.

Bailey made a quick decision that she hoped would satisfy both men. She put her mouth over Carter's and let her lips linger there for a lengthy moment, then she gave him a gentle shove back and held up one finger.

"I'm here, Mark. What's up?"

"Uh," he started and then paused as though he'd forgotten his reason for calling. "Your car is fixed."

"Great. I'll come pick it up later."

"Don't you want to know what was wrong with it?"

Carter reached around behind Bailey and unhooked her bra. She sucked in some air.

"Don't worry, it's nothing bad. I don't think."

Carter removed his own shirt and Bailey moaned softly when he pressed his nakedness against her.

"So you're coming?"

God, she hoped so. "I'll be there," she said, nearly breathless. "Later."

"In case you're interested, something was stuck in the top's hinge assembly."

She was at the brink of hyperventilation, her brain was starved for oxygen, there was only one thing she was interested in right then. She didn't care if the entire friggin' Space Needle was stuck in her car's hinge assembly.

Unfortunately, Carter did. All the talking and ringing had finally taken its toll on his patience and he rolled away from her.

Bailey sat up and gathered the sheet around her chest. "For God's sake, just tell me," she told Mark. "I'm in the middle of something here."

"Maybe you should ask Sideburns," Mark said. "See you when you get here."

Sideburns? She glanced over her shoulder at Carter. What the hell was Mark talking about? "Wait, wait . . ." she said. No way was that mood wrecker hanging up now.

Bailey flung a leg over Carter to stop him from getting up. He lay back against a mountain of pillows and groaned.

"Why don't you just make it easy for both of us and tell me?"

"See you when you get here, Peaches."

The phone clicked in her ear, and Bailey sat there waiting for the steam to stop coming out her ears. Finally, she turned and faced Carter. "That was the shop."

"I gathered that, honey." He slid her leg off him and got up. He took a swipe at his hair and it was perfect again.

Damn Mark. Damn, damn, damn him. He'd done this on purpose. He didn't want her giving to Carter what he'd been trying to get from her since the first time she'd given it. Well, she was going to give him something, all right.

"I think I'll just run over and get it." Bailey got up and pulled her shirt back on. "The less time Mark and Brian have my car, the better the chances I'll get it back in working order," she said.

"I could have told you that," Carter agreed.

Bailey slipped on some sandals. She didn't want to waste one minute tying shoelaces. The sooner she got her car back, the sooner she could get back to Carter and his hands.

"Want me to go with you?" Carter asked.

She wanted him by her side every moment of every day, but she had a few things to straighten out with Mark. "I need to talk to the Jefferson boys alone." Plus Carter might stop her from killing Mark. The only way that Jefferson boy's life might be spared is if she could convince him that *Peaches* no longer existed and that she was in love with another man.

She gathered her hair up and pulled a ponytail holder around it. Carter made no attempt to remove it.

He gave her half a smile and said, "See you when you get back."

Carter watched Bailey walk down the street, ponytail swinging from side to side in concert with the sway of her hips. "Damn," he muttered, feeling like he'd just been gut punched. Leaving that gal was going to be hard, like having a red-hot poker run through him.

The past week had been good, one of the best in his life. Lunch at the Knead & Feed, dinner with Bailey's family, sitting on her tiny deck watching the sun forge its way through the gray mist. He'd been at peace from his very first day there in Coupeville. It was how life was supposed to be. Normal. And he had a strong feeling it was his for the taking, if he chose to stay.

Carter shook his head slowly. Maybe someday he'd be ready, but not now. Tranquil skies didn't fit into his world just yet. He and Vegas weren't finished. His eyes hadn't tired of all those neon lights and he wasn't ready to give up singing.

He ran a hand through his hair, liking the way it felt. Since leaving Vegas he'd stopped using all that gunk to keep it in place. Bailey seemed to like it, too. She'd spent considerable time with her hands in his hair over the past couple of days.

It'd been a good time, but like all vacations, a person had to eventually go home.

Packing took but a few minutes, seeing as he'd only brought enough clothes to last for a couple of days.

After making sure he'd collected everything, Carter took one last look around Bailey's room. His eye caught a picture that sat on one corner of her dresser, and right now, one of her nylon stockings hung over the top, half covering it. He smiled. That was Bailey. Sweet, impossible, and not the tidiest woman he'd ever known. But, what the hell, he was a neat freak and, together, maybe they could do each other some good. Anything was possible.

That was a sucker bet, though. She lived over here in this little Mayberry R.F.D. town, and he lived in big bad Las Vegas. She was a small town girl who was convinced she wanted out, but a city like Las Vegas would only swallow her up.

Carter shook his head. Jesus, if he kept thinking about a life with her, it'd drive him crazy. He might even convince himself that it could work. *That* was crazy.

Carter picked up the silk stocking, rubbed it between his fingers, releasing Bailey's scent into the air. Giorgio. It was the only fragrance she wore. He swallowed hard and allowed the stocking to slip from his fingers. He picked up the picture and studied the faces of Bailey, her mom, and her aunt. They made up one of the wackiest group of women he'd ever had the pleasure of knowing, and he felt genuinely bad about leaving before the show. Fiona would be disappointed, would probably hate him.

He shrugged tightly. Stuff happened. Business was business.

And, as soon as Bailey came through that door, he was taking the Azuri diamond from her and heading back to Vegas. That was business, too.

Chapter Twenty-one

"Okay. I'm here. What was wrong with my car's top?" Bailey asked Mark in a huff.

"Did you ask Sideburns?" Mark inquired.

Bailey waved a hand. "He has nothing to do with it. I'm asking *you*."

"I think he might have a lot to do with it. He paid us a visit last night," Mark said.

Brian shrugged. "Could be he was just checking up on your car."

Mark gave Brian a look and he shut up.

"What are you talking about? Carter was with me. All. Night. Long." Bailey gave Mark a smug grin.

"You sure about that, Peaches?" he asked.

"Stop calling me that. And, yes, I'm sure."

"We got this tape here that says different. What'll you give me if you're wrong?"

Mark's eyes gleamed wickedly and Bailey had a feeling this was one bet she had no chance of winning. She'd seen that gleam before. Once.

"Plug it in," she said.

Mark did as he was told and the three of them stared at the screen. Bailey watched in fascination as Carter entered through the shop's back door and then used a flashlight to look into the T-Bird's top assembly. She didn't take her eyes off the screen until after Carter looked up, realized he was busted, and smiled for the camera on his way out.

"Okay." Bailey held up her hands. "Enough." Obviously, sometime during the night, while she was out of commission, Carter had sneaked out of the cottage.

She shook her head in slow frustration. Had he planned on getting her drunk so she'd pass out? Had she never even had to worry about him finding out about her not being a virgin? Bailey frowned and pressed her lips together to keep the lower one from trembling.

"I'm sure he has a logical explanation. Probably he was checking up on your work," she said in Carter's defense, though she didn't know why.

Mark gave her a look that said *That's bullshit*.

"I gotta go," Bailey said.

"Don't you want this?" Mark held out a small black bag.

Bailey raised a curious eyebrow. She'd seen little black bags like that before—in movies—and they usually contained things that either got people into trouble or made them very happy. "What's that?" she asked.

"Your problem. It's what we fished out of the top assembly. It's probably also what your boyfriend was looking for."

Mark opened it and Bailey peeked inside. Her breath caught in her throat and she stumbled back a step. Mark grabbed her arm to steady her. She snatched her arm and the bag away from him.

"Thanks," she said. The little black bag did indeed spell trouble—in five letters. Zoopa. Her stomach churned. "This belongs to Carter. He misplaced it during our drive home. I'll see to it that he gets it."

Both Mark and Brian looked at her and said, "That's bullshit."

"What? You don't believe me?"

Mark touched the side of Bailey's cheek, rubbing it gently. "Peaches," he said softly. "Do you have something you want to tell us?"

"Yeah. When's the date?" Brian asked. "Seeing as Sideburns doesn't have any friends in town, I'll volunteer to be his best man."

Bailey ran out of the shop, hopped in her car, and raced home.

Carter's cell phone rang just as he zipped his bag shut.

"Twinkie tells me you'll be back in town soon," Zoopa said.

"What the hell do you want?"

"Is that any way to treat a man you've robbed?"

Carter's jaw muscles tensed and he felt it all the way down his back. "Is Twinkie there with you? Let me talk to her."

"When our business is done."

"Our business *is* done. Put her on."

"Relax. She's working her little tush off and then when she gets done here, she's going over to the MGM and she's going to work her little tush off over there. God, I like the sound of that word. It even sounds soft and round. Tus-s-sh-h-h."

Carter's lip curled in disgust. "If you care about her, why don't you do her a favor and cut her loose."

"You know how love is . . . It makes you stupid. Don't let love make you stupid, Carter. Love and business don't mix."

Carter ran a hand over his face. Didn't he know it. Too bad he couldn't take his own advice. Even though he wouldn't call his relationship with Bailey business, she was smack dab in the middle of his.

"Love has nothing to do with me being here. Now let me talk to Twinkie."

There was a lengthy pause and finally Twinkie came on. She did her best to sound like everything was fine, but Carter heard the tremble in her voice and he knew Zoopa was taking his anger out on everyone around him.

"Hey, Carter, don't worry 'bout me. I'm fine," Twinkie said.

Carter could almost see her fake smile. Guilt bit at him like a hungry dog. "I'm on my way, honey."

"Frank tells me you left town with some cute thing," Twinkie said, and then she lowered her voice. "Don't let this rat bastard mess up a good thing for you, Carter."

"No one's messing anything up for me, sweetheart. You hang in there and I'll see you tonight. Remember, I love you."

Bailey stopped short just before she reached her front door. Her bedroom window was open and Carter was in there talking to someone. She stepped over closer. She didn't hear any other voices. He must be on the phone conducting some important *business*. Ha! She'd show him business. She pressed the hard object in her pocket into the palm of her hand, and suddenly realized, she was carrying around something worth more than the house she lived in.

She stepped away from the window, started to go inside, but then she heard Carter say something else, something disturbing. *Sweetheart? I love you?* Bailey squeezed the lump of expensive glass. She had half a mind to chuck it through the window, right at his lying lips. Instead, she sagged back against the house.

It was Twinkie, she was sure of it. And of course he loved her. A man didn't get as angry as Bailey had seen Carter unless he was in love. But how could he love Twinkie when it was *her* he'd caressed, *her* he'd been kissing? Was she being foolish in thinking that he might really care for her? Maybe she didn't qualify to become a member of Mensa, but she would've bet her new car that Carter's kisses had been the real deal.

Or had they? He did, after all, spend half his time acting like someone else. She thought about him up on stage singing to an auditorium full of screaming women. He had them all fooled.

Bailey took a deep breath and steeled herself. As much as it hurt, she wasn't about to let a man she'd fallen in love with stand in her bedroom and call another woman "Sweetheart" and whisper words of love in her ear.

She frowned. And another thing . . . If Carter and Twinkie were so close, and if she was so important to him, why was he here in Coupeville with *her*?

A tear formed in one eye and Bailey reached into her pocket for a Kleenex. Instead, she pulled out the little black bag. *Of course.* The diamond. Bailey's head fell back against the house. It plunked hard on the siding. A moment later, Carter stuck his head out and spoke to her.

"What are you doing out here?" he asked.

Bailey rolled her eyes skyward and stared up into his face. Ignoring the thorns on her rosebush, she snapped a couple roses off and put them to her nose. "I thought I'd pick some for the house," she said, forcing a smile to her lips. She even managed to coerce the corners of her eyes into a crinkle. "I'll be right in."

As soon as Carter drew his head back inside, Bailey shoved the little bag down the front of her sweater. She didn't have as much cleavage as Miss Bountiful, but it was at least enough to conceal a small package.

She went into the house and tossed the roses into a small vase without making any attempt at arranging them or even adding water.

As far as she was concerned, Carter had one last chance. He was a smart man. He knew she'd just been to the shop, seen the tape, gotten the diamond. Now it was up to him to say something, anything, that would make all the crazy things she was thinking disappear.

Carter came down the hall. He didn't say a word at first, just walked up to her and gave her a friendly kiss. *Friendly,* not passionate. Bailey's female antennae went up. Something was brewing behind his calm facade. How dare he turn this around!

"We need to talk," he said.

"Huh?" Bailey swallowed. *Way to stand up to him,* she silently scolded herself.

"I think maybe you have something of mine."

"Huh?" At the moment, it was the only word her mouth was capable of forming.

Carter slowly circled around behind her, and she felt like a wounded animal out in the desert, just waiting to be pounced upon. He stepped close and she nearly stopped breathing. "Don't make me ask you again," he said, his voice low and husky.

Bailey swallowed. Well, if he was going to put it like that . . .

He placed his hands on her waist and Bailey felt the hairs on her arms creep up. She couldn't see his face, but she was willing to bet his eyes had that hungry animal look in them.

Maggie must've heard some heavy breathing, because she suddenly decided she wanted in on the action. She wiggled up to them and stuck her head between Bailey's legs.

Bailey patted Maggie's head, and muttered something about what a good girl she was. Maggie wiggled around them full circle a couple of times and then went and laid back down with a groan.

Bailey stood straight and tried to gather her wits. The man was a thief, and what if—a chilling thought entered her mind—what if he'd done worse? What if he'd done things like she'd only seen in those horror flicks?

What then? Call 911? Promise not to say anything to anyone—ever?

Carter's mouth was on her neck now, and Bailey felt her head tilt involuntarily to one side to allow him better access. God help her, but it was impossible to think straight with his lips on her.

His lips weren't his only weapon. He also had great hands, which he now began to move up and down her back in a movement so smooth it was like he was spreading soft butter. Against her better judgment, Bailey allowed herself to relax into him.

Carter turned her around and she completely forgot about the diamond as he moved his hands slowly down, down, down . . . until he crouched and lifted her sweater to give her stomach a dozen gentle kisses. His hands were on her thighs, where they lingered just long enough to make her moan. Then he stood and moved them tenderly all the way up the sides of her waist.

Bailey sighed. This was exactly what she needed. She could even forgive him calling another woman "Sweetheart."

Carter moved his hands slowly from her waist, up to her breasts, and Bailey held her breath in anticipation of his next move. He continued up. His fingers were on the back of her neck now, and he was working them into her hair. It was unnerving, exhilarating. Methodical.

Methodical?

She was panting like a dog deprived of water and here he was, not even breathing hard. His exploring hands weren't getting the same charge out of feeling her up as she was getting from being felt up. What was this? A mercy feel? Suddenly she knew . . .

He was frigging searching her!

Bailey leaped back, shoving hard off Carter. "What the hell are you doing?"

Carter looked straight into her eyes and said, "This is business, Bailey. Where's the diamond?"

Bailey crossed her arms and did her best to look indignant. "You can go conduct your *business* on some other unsuspecting female. I don't know what you're talking about."

"I think you do," Carter said. His gaze held hers with a look of determination. The same kind of look she imagined his eyes might have when he made love to a woman.

God help her. She still wanted to see that look.

Carter grabbed her by both arms and pulled her to him. He waited about two seconds before plunging his lips into hers with a kiss that sent her over the edge of reason.

Lord, take me now and I'll die a happy woman. Light-headed and unable—mostly unwilling—to continue fighting, Bailey participated until Carter was finished.

His lips moved smoothly over hers and a charge of electricity zipped down her spine, along her thighs, and all the way down to her toes, and he continued kissing her until a hard plunk sounded at their feet.

They both looked down and Bailey drew in a sharp breath.

"That's what those two men were looking for when they stopped us, isn't it?" she accused. She kept staring down at the black bag. "That's the diamond that man was screaming about at your buddy Frank Zoopa's party."

She looked up at Carter. He was frowning. Probably he had to kill her now, although after a kiss like the one he'd just given her, she was feeling cautiously optimistic.

"Frank Zoopa is not my buddy. But, yes, it's the Azuri diamond, and you need to stay out of this."

Carter reached down and picked up the small bag containing the diamond. He brushed some lint off it and then tucked it into his pocket like it was nothing more than a dime he'd found on the sidewalk.

"Let's talk," he said. He grabbed her arm and led her down the hall, toward her bedroom.

Bailey planted both feet firmly. If she was going to be killed, she'd rather it not be where people might assume it was a crime of passion. She looked to Tucker for support. He yawned.

"Let's talk here," she said, grabbing the bathroom doorjamb as they went by.

"I need to get my bag," Carter said. He let go of her arm, and gave her a warm smile. "You don't have anything to fear from me, honey." He took her hand and kissed the back of it.

Bailey reluctantly followed him, although she didn't know why. What was left to talk about? He'd taken his precious stolen diamond back and he'd packed his bag. Now he was leaving. The end.

Probably he intended to go back to Vegas and fence the Azuri rock, or maybe he'd have it made into a baseball-sized ring for his beloved Twinkie. Whatever his plans were, she didn't want to know.

She sat on the edge of her bed and watched while he put the black bag into the side pocket of his bag. Then he sat next to her. Bailey swallowed a lump of hurt in her throat. "Really, you don't need to explain anything. I understand. Or maybe I don't, but it doesn't matter." She shook her head and stood, wanting to leave before the tears came.

Carter pulled her back down next to him.

"Sit. And listen." Amusement rode the corners of his eyes and his mouth twitched like he was trying to keep from doing the crooked grin thing.

Now that she was reasonably sure he wasn't going to cut out her tongue or do something equally as painful, Bailey thought that if he knew what was good for him, he'd fill his mind with something really awful to keep that grin at bay.

"You're jealous," he said. "You overheard me on the phone."

Bailey considered denying it, but what good would that do? It was true.

"It's very becoming on you." Carter put a hand to the back of her head and snapped her hair band. He tangled her hair around his fingers.

A smart woman would slap his face, tell him to go to hell. Sometimes she wasn't very smart. Like right now. She was weak and in love and ready to have him tangle more than her hair between his fingers. Damn him and his special security-guy powers.

He pressed his mouth to hers lightly and every thought in her head disappeared, including the bad thoughts she'd been having about Miss Bountiful. She was ready to take up where they'd left off, before the phone had interrupted them with all of this nasty stolen diamond business.

Carter touched her cheek gently. "I want to explain something," he said.

He slid a hand down her back. His eyes were full of tenderness, but Bailey was sure his next words were going to be something like, "It's been fun. Good-bye." Explanations. Excuses. She didn't want to hear them.

"Do you really have to?" she asked on a sigh.

Carter nodded. "There's something you need to know."

"Will it cause my heart to ache?"

"No, honey."

His hand was warm on her back and it made her feel safe and scared all at the same time. Maybe she could forgive him being a jewel thief.

"Twinkie is my sister," he said.

Bailey's heart pumped wildly. "Sister?" she said with hesitation, giving him a doubtful look.

"Now for the bad news."

Uh, oh. There's always bad news.

"I've got to go back to Las Vegas. Right now."

Bailey put both hands to Carter's chest and she shoved him backward against the headboard. The wood cracked, but it held. "Liar. You said it didn't involve a heartache."

Carter put his arms around her. He kissed the top of her head. "Baby, you didn't really think I would just come home with you and never go back home, did you?"

Bailey looked into his blue eyes. They were like the sea, and she'd taken the plunge, fallen head over heels in love, and now she was drowning. *Yes, absolutely, I thought you'd fall in love with me and want to make me your bride.* "Of course I didn't expect you'd just give up your life and stay here with me."

It was just as Liza had said. Carter was an exotic animal that couldn't be tamed. He was the kind of man who needed thrills, like a lion needed his daily kill. He'd never last in a place like Coupeville. It was too boring, and too far removed from his element.

He was a jewel thief, after all. And a security expert, and an Elvis tribute artist, and no telling what other faces he had hidden behind that easy smile. A liar perhaps. Like Twinkie being his sister.

"What about the show? My aunt will be so disappointed."

Carter shook his head slowly.

"But we haven't . . ." Bailey smoothed a hand over her bed. "I haven't . . ."

Carter lifted her hand to his mouth. "It wasn't meant to be, honey."

Yes, yes it was. It was meant to be. Take me now, she wanted to scream. Couldn't he see that she was ready, willing, and more than able? And not only that, but she'd lied too. They made the perfect pair. She wasn't a virgin. But as badly as she wanted to say those words, a painful lump clogged her throat and choked her into silence.

A long moment passed. Neither of them spoke. Carter stroked her hair and she couldn't even feel her heart beating anymore. It was broken and she'd already died.

Carter stood, and Bailey felt her heart go *thud.* Okay, maybe she wasn't dead yet. But soon.

Maggie stared up at them with big sad eyes, like she sensed Carter's leaving.

"Perhaps you could take Tucker and Maggie May out for a potty break? It'll give you a chance to say good-bye to them, too."

Carter took the dogs out and Bailey lay back on her bed. She rubbed her hand smoothly over the comforter. If they could have made love just once, she'd at least have that memory. As it was, she'd have nothing. Not even a picture of the two of them together.

In a couple days, Carter would shove her to the back of his mind and his memory of her would become dimmer with each passing day. If only *she'd* given him something to remember *her.* Then maybe there'd still be a slight chance he'd return.

Bailey had an idea. She rushed over to the window, took a quick peek out, and saw Carter and her dogs halfway up the street. Tucker was relieving himself on a bush.

She turned to her dresser and dug in her panty drawer until she found a black thong with a red lace heart cutout on one side. It seemed pretty *memorable,* although it might have been more so if she'd had the chance to personally model it for him.

Too late for that.

Bailey sprayed a light mist of Giorgio over the thong; then she struggled with the zipper on Carter's bag. It was stuck. She gave it a hard yank and the entire bag tipped over onto the floor, its contents scattering about. She scrambled to retrieve everything and put it back all neat and tidy. Her idea of tidy might not be Carter's idea of tidy, but it'd do, unless he'd intended to keep his clean things away from the dirty things. If it wasn't good enough, he could sort everything out when he got home.

"Get a whiff of this, loverboy," she said, and she tucked the thong into Carter's bag, just under one of his black shirts.

Bailey smiled smugly. Carter would get home, empty his bag, probably utter a few obscenities at her for making a mess of his things, but then he'd find her thong, and he'd think about her. And he'd smile—she hoped.

She started to zip the bag, but paused. What exactly did a man like Carter bring with him on a trip anyway? She thought she knew him, but she didn't. Not really. He was a puzzle that she hadn't quite been able to fit together.

Bailey ran her fingers along the inside of the bag and stopped when she felt something hard. She pushed aside some clothes and there it was. His gun. She didn't know anything about guns, but this one looked big and bad enough that if a man like Carter had it pointed at you, you'd know he meant serious business.

Bailey shuddered and covered it back up.

She slid her fingers over a side compartment that was covered with a flap of leather. It bulged bigger than the gun. She reached inside and a thread of excitement ran through her as she stared at a packet of one hundred dollar bills. Bailey touched them and quickly drew back her fingers as though she'd been burned. Carrying around that much money wasn't normal. She was tempted to flip through the stack, like she'd seen men do in the movies, but she'd never held that much money in her hands and she wasn't sure she wanted to take a chance on getting addicted to the feel.

Probably if she kept looking, she'd find all kinds of secret weapons and things, things that might scare her, maybe even excite her. She shook her head. Could be she was already crazy for wanting a man like Carter. She didn't need to find even more evidence of his question-able activities.

With her curiosity satisfied, she picked up Carter's black shirt and pressed her nose to it. Geez, but she was going to miss the color black.

Her front door clicked open and she quickly zipped the bag closed. She met Carter and her babies out in the living room and received a warm greeting from all three.

Carter headed straight for her room and she fol-lowed. He grabbed his bag, but paused, his fingers grasping the zipper.

No! It's too soon. She didn't want him to find her thong until he was home. She didn't want pity sex. Bailey stepped close to him. "You made me believe you cared for me. How could you leave?" she asked. She was look-ing up at him and wearing her most sorrowful look, which she'd mastered by watching Tucker and Maggie May. "You were even going to make love to me."

"I do care for you and, of course, I was going to make love to you. You offered, I was going to oblige." His hand was still on the bag's zipper.

"Oblige?" Bailey turned and grabbed a brand-new bottle of Giorgio. Fifty dollars a bottle and she didn't care. She threw it at Carter with full force. It missed him and hit the wall and a powerful flowery scent exploded into the room, showering both Carter and his bag.

Carter looked down at his shirt. "Damn," he said. He looked at her and his eyes were full of fire. He stepped toward her.

Bailey wasn't sure whether she should be afraid or ex-cited, but she quickly grabbed another bottle, this one only half full. She drew back her arm, but Carter was quick. He lunged at her and wrestled her to the bed, shoving her loaded arm above her head. After a minute of rolling around, Bailey paused to catch her breath, and that's when Carter pulled the dirtiest trick ever. He kissed her. A mind-blowing, give-it-to-me-now kiss.

Lord, Jesus, help me be strong, she prayed. It might be what she'd wanted for days, but not now, not if he was just going to leave her lying there with a broken heart. She began struggling to free herself, but it was useless. Carter moved his body over on top of hers, pinning her in place, and then he held his mouth to hers. With each passing second, her struggle became less of a quest for freedom and more of a combined effort at passion. She made one final weak attempt to free herself, but Carter's security-guy powers were turned up full throttle, and she was helpless.

She could no longer keep her feelings secret.

"I love you," she whispered, looking straight into his eyes.

Carter's body stiffened and he stared at her for a long minute, before rolling off to one side.

"Did you hear me?" she asked quietly.

"Ah, honey, you don't know what you're saying. You're just overcome with hormones or something."

Unbelievable. The first guy she'd ever uttered those words to and he was blaming it on hormones. Oh, he'd see hormones. Crazy woman hormones.

Carter must've seen that look in a woman's eyes before, because he jumped up off the bed, grabbed his bag and headed for the door, pausing to blow her a kiss before leaving. Bailey grabbed the half-empty bottle of Giorgio and heaved it, but he was already gone.

Chapter Twenty-two

Carter's first stop when he got back to Las Vegas was his house on Lake Mead. He was a bit surprised to see it was still standing. Though he supposed if it hadn't been, he'd have heard something about it by now. As it was, everything checked out fine. It even smelled good—like something appetizing had recently been prepared in his kitchen. The aroma of Indian spices met him as he walked through the door, and when he went into the kitchen, he found a note on the counter from a woman he'd known for half his life. Nikki Amsterdam. Tall, dark, and more woman than most men could handle. Even him. She had a gleam in her eye whenever he saw her and he knew that gleam was meant for him. Lucky him.

Nikki's note said she'd had a craving for something spicy, so she'd stopped by and cooked herself up a little dinner, hoping he'd make an appearance. Spicy food, spicy woman—he was beginning to sweat just thinking about it. Maybe another time, Nikki. Or not, now that Bailey Ventura had made her entrance into his life.

Carter chuckled thinking about their last few minutes together, rolling around on her bed. He'd been sorely tempted to take her then, and perhaps he should have.

Sometimes it didn't pay to be a nice guy, though it wasn't often he got accused of that.

Although she'd claimed she was a virgin, she'd shown more passion and desire than any woman he'd ever known. His cute brunette was no more a virgin than he was—well, maybe a little—but it was so obvious she wanted him. She may have been saying "no," but her eyes had eaten him up, ripped off all his clothes the instant she'd met him, and yet she'd continued to hold back. She'd wanted something, but she wasn't willing to compromise herself for a moment's pleasure. He liked that. Restraint. That was something he himself could use more of.

He shook his head. He knew it was unfair to judge every woman he met by his ex-wife's actions, and hell, if he was being honest, he'd have to admit that he found it refreshing to come across a woman who wanted to take things slow. Still, it'd given him cause to stop and think seriously about whether or not he wanted to pursue a relationship with a woman who would lie straight to his face.

Carter went to his bedroom and tossed his bag on the bed. He did a quick clothes change, and then pulled his gun from the bag. He felt around some for the Azuri diamond but came up with nothing. He ran his fingers along the bottom of the side pocket and into each corner. Nothing there, except the bundle of cash he kept for just-in-case situations. He didn't remember putting the diamond in the pocket, but hell, the way he and Bailey had said their good-byes, he couldn't remember much else but the feel of her soft body beneath his as she struggled to get free. It made him hard thinking about it.

Carter unzipped the side pocket and stretched it open to look inside. Cautious anger rippled through him as he pulled out every article of clothing. Where the hell was it?

His eye caught something unfamiliar, something that didn't belong. He picked it up. A silky black piece of fabric with a red heart cutout on one side.

Carter crushed the thong in his fist, releasing the scent of Giorgio into the air. He ran a hand through his hair and inhaled deeply. It was as if Bailey were right there in the room with him.

What had she been thinking? As if he even had to ask. But she'd given away a perfectly good thong for nothing. No way was he ever going to forget her, even though at that very moment what he really felt like doing was strangling her.

If by some chance they did get back together, he intended to make some ground rules very clear. He was in charge and she was going to listen. Yeah, that'd be the day.

Carter picked up the bag and emptied the rest of its contents onto the bed. A spare cell phone, a couple of red silk scarves, and a shaving kit, but no little black bag. No diamond.

Damn woman.

Bailey pushed the vacuum over the carpet with minimal effort. What did she care if she picked up every dog hair? She didn't care if the sun was shining, and she sure didn't care if she never heard another Elvis song. Carter was gone, and she only had herself to blame. She'd wanted everything to be perfect, and he'd tried to be patient, but it was probably just too much to ask of an adult alpha male like him. That kind of man had needs.

But what about *her* needs? Why did men think their needs were all that mattered? Bailey gave the vacuum a hard shove against the side of her bed. The vacuum responded with a whine, and then she smelled something burning. Rubber, or dog hair, or God knew what. She quickly stomped the "off" button and the whine stopped. She flipped over the vacuum.

A giddy sensation flittered through her chest when she saw what was causing the problem. It was a small black lump of material and she had a pretty good idea what was inside it.

The giddiness turned into cautious delight. Carter would think she'd done this on purpose. He'd think she'd taken the diamond so that he'd have to return to Coupeville, which come to think of it wouldn't have been such a bad plan, had she thought of it.

Bailey freed the bag from the vacuum roller. She emptied the diamond out onto her palm. Just to examine it for damage, of course. It sparkled like the brightest of stars on the clearest of nights. No wonder so many people were after it. It had to be worth . . . a lot.

Bailey suddenly felt sick. People? After it? Some of them not so nice? If they got a clue she might have it, they'd invade her peaceful little town like locusts in the spring of '72. They'd come to her cottage, go through all the likely places, her kitchen cabinets, her dresser drawers . . . Her mouth went dry as she remembered how Zoopa's men had stopped her and Carter in the desert, how the bald guy had fingered through her panties. She wasn't about to give him the satisfaction of finding the Azuri diamond, while he got his kicks doing that again. She'd put the diamond somewhere safe, just until Carter returned for it.

Maybe she'd even make him beg a little.

Bailey went to the guest room and looked around. A stuffed turtle lay in the middle of the floor. It had a hole in its belly that was filled with fuzzy little green balls that her dogs enjoyed pulling out. She picked it up. "Move over, you've got company," she told the green balls.

The phone rang and she tossed the turtle up on top of the dresser on the way back to her room.

"How're things going with Mr. Hunk O' Love?" Liza asked.

"He's gone," Bailey told her. She curled into a ball on her bed, and pulled the covers up over her. "He left yesterday and I still haven't heard from him."

"Oh," Liza said plainly.

Bailey yanked the covers a little higher. "What do you mean, 'Oh'?"

"I mean, oh. Sorry, girlie, but I'm not surprised. And you shouldn't be either."

Bailey's legs shot out straight and she sat up. *"Why?"*

"Did you show him a good time?"

"I took him to the Knead & Feed, we walked the waterfront, we had some nice moments alone."

"Yeah, but did you show him a *good* time?"

"*I* had a good time." Bailey pulled her knees to her chest.

"See, therein lies the problem. A woman's interpretation of a good time is not the same as it is for a man. Going along with a woman, doing all the things she thinks are fun and romantic is no more exciting for a man than going to the fabric store. He doesn't want to go in, but he knows if he doesn't he's not going to get dressed."

Bailey's face scrunched up as she tried to untangle that thought. "Whatever," she said. "Besides, that's not why he left."

"Honey, that's why they always leave."

"Not this time. I'll explain everything if you'll just please come and console me." Liza didn't respond right away and Bailey knew she was going to have to up the ante. "I have it on good authority that your presence here would be very much appreciated," she said. She sensed Liza perking up.

"Would that good authority be that gorgeous Jefferson boy?"

"Uh, huh," Bailey said. She chewed her lip. It *was* one of the Jefferson twins, just not the one Liza was hoping for.

"I'll check the ferry schedule," Liza said and hung up.

Bailey was still curled up in bed when Liza arrived. She'd gotten up a few times, once to get a snack, once to use the bathroom, but that was all she'd had energy for, that and reminiscing about her last moments with Carter.

"What, no men?" Liza said when she opened Bailey's bedroom door.

"There may never be a man in this house again."

Liza turned and started back down the hall.

"Where're you going?" Panic rode Bailey's voice.

"Home. You promised me Mark Jefferson."

"I never said I'd have him waiting here in my bedroom for you when you arrived."

"You implied."

Bailey buried her face in her pillow. When the air ran out, she looked up all teary-eyed and blurted out. "My boyfriend's a criminal. Probably part of some Las Vegas Mafia gang."

"Wow," Liza said. "Okay, I forgive you for not having Mark Jefferson waiting here naked." She sat and slipped an arm around Bailey. "Well, at least it's a step in the right direction. He's gone from security guy to Las Vegas Mafia man."

Bailey slid her a teary look.

"Okay, tell me all about it. The sooner you get it off your chest, the sooner we can move on."

"Move on?"

"To Mark Jefferson."

Bailey did an eye roll. She rocked back and pulled her knees to her chest. "Carter is a jewel thief."

"Jewels? Wow, things *are* looking up."

"This is *serious*. He could be on the verge of setting up permanent residence in the Nevada desert."

"I thought he already lived there."

"He might have new living quarters. Like under a ton of sand." Bailey sniffed into a Kleenex. "I almost gave myself to him. I thought we'd make beautiful children. Dark hair, olive skin. Not sure about the color of the eyes. His are blue, mine are brown. Brown is generally dominant."

Liza joined her in considering the eye color. "I think you're right. They'd be brown. Anyway, back to Carter being a jewel thief. How Thomas Crown of him."

"That was art."

"Honey, jewels *are* art. Tell me more."

"We took the hardtop off the T-Bird, the soft top was stuck in the down position, so I took it over to the auto shop to have Mark and Brian find the problem." Liza's eyes began to get that dreamy look at the mention of Mark's name and Bailey snapped her fingers in front of Liza's face to regain her attention.

"As I was saying, I became intoxicated and passed out."

"You mean you got drunk? I'm liking this security guy better and better."

"It was an accident."

"Sure," Liza said. "God, you don't think he fondled things while you were incoherent, do you?"

Bailey's chin lifted. "Carter's a perfect gentleman. He's just a . . . a . . . ." Bailey didn't know what Carter was. "What do you call a man who sings like an angel, packs a Glock, and has a fetish for jewels?"

"Elvis," they both said at once.

Bailey huffed. "How could I ever be at peace with him? I'd always be wondering if he'd get caught and end up in prison. Or, maybe, I'd get a phone call from the morgue saying he's been found dead with some Mafia guy's calling card stuffed in his shirt pocket."

Liza gave her a consolatory back rub.

"He might be back," Bailey said after a minute. "I might have something he wants."

Liza gave her a doubtful look.

Bailey felt the blood drain from her face. "You think he's gonna get killed?"

"No. God, no. It's just that he's back in Vegas, land of

a million half-naked women, and if you didn't show him a good time . . ."

Bailey gave her a smug smile. "I have a feeling that won't matter." She jumped up and Liza followed. She grabbed the stuffed turtle and handed it to Liza. "This is what was making the top of my car stick."

Liza took the bag and looked inside. Her eyes fluttered and rolled back in her head. She sat on the edge of the bed. "Holy crap. I think I just had an orgasm. Did Carter give this to you?"

Bailey shook her head. "He accidentally left it behind." She shrugged. "It kinda fell out of his bag." She took the black bag from Liza and stuffed it back inside the turtle.

"Sure, okay. Now let's go celebrate." Liza jumped up and slapped her hands together. "Let's go see that delicious Mark Jefferson."

"That's it? That's all you have to say about it?"

"Well, honey, it's not like he's a murderer."

"Murder and jewel thievery go hand in hand. Such as in, if you're a thief and you steal a diamond from another thief, then you might get murdered." Bailey unwadded her tissue and blew her nose into it.

Liza sat back down. "Okay, straighten me out. Are you upset because he's a jewel thief, or is it the thought of him getting murdered that's got you worried?"

Bailey considered Liza's question. She finally answered, "Both. But I'm also hurt. I think he may have used me and my car just so he could get that diamond out of Las Vegas." Bailey pouted. Oh, how she missed Carter's thieving hands. So warm and strong, they did things to her that a woman could only dream about.

"That bastard! I say we go and let the Jefferson twins console us."

"*Us?* Why do *you* need consoling?"

"Whatever hurts you, hurts me," Liza said.

Liza's loyalty was overwhelming.

The Jefferson twins were a poor replacement for Carter, and Bailey was in no mood to see them, but she'd promised Liza and if she didn't come through, it'd be weeks, maybe months, before Liza would come back for another visit.

Liza paced while she put on a little mascara and pulled her hair up into a ponytail. If Carter was here, he'd have her hair band snapped in two seconds flat. Bailey's heart thudded heavily. Maybe going out on a foursome with her friends was exactly what she needed to help her forget that she'd just had her heart stomped on by a jewel thief.

"You know Frank's not going to let this go." Twinkie stood in the middle of her hotel bedroom.

Carter almost laughed. She had her hands stuffed on her hips and her chin tilted upward, and damned if she didn't remind him of Bailey.

"And if you were supposed to be getting that diamond back for Mr. Azuri, why doesn't *he* have it?"

"Long story. Let me worry about that," Carter told her. "Get some stuff together and pack light." He shoved a travel bag over in front of her.

"Pack? I'm not going anywhere," Twinkie said. She sat down in a huff.

"You are, and don't argue. I'm keeping you with me until this mess gets cleared up."

"Excuse me, but why am I being punished for a mess you made? What about work?"

Carter stood in front of her, arms folded across his chest. "You think spending time with me is punishment?"

Twinkie was quiet as she pondered his question.

He didn't really care what her answer was. He grabbed

a black sweater from her closet and tossed it into the bag to get her started. "Get busy," he said.

"It's 105 degrees out. I don't need a sweater."

"You might."

"All right—stop. Where the hell are we going that I'll need a sweater?" Twinkie pumped a foot nervously.

She was stalling. Carter knew it and she knew he knew it.

"You need a little vacation. A little rest somewhere quiet. A small town where bad things only happen once in a millennium."

"Ha! That place doesn't exist," Twinkie said.

"It does in Washington state. I'm thinking we'll spend a little time there. Two, three weeks. Hell, maybe we'll move there."

Twinkie stared at him for a long moment. Then she did a little twirly thing with one finger on the side of her head. "And, I'm thinkin' maybe you've gone plum loco."

Carter didn't laugh, partly because he agreed with her. But until he could get the Azuri diamond back from Bailey, no one he cared for was safe. "Pack. Don't make me say it again."

Twinkie opened her mouth to say something, but Carter gave her a hard glare, a warning, just like he used to give her when they were young and she was about to rat on him.

"Shit, Carter. I hate this." Twinkie stomped over to her dresser and took out a handful of colorful undergarments.

A red lace thong fell to the floor and Carter avoided looking at it. He didn't care to know what kind of panties his sister wore.

"I might even hate you after this," she said.

"That I can take. What I can't take is having anything bad happen to you. Now hurry up."

Twinkie continued grabbing things and tossing them

into the bag, all the while mumbling obscenities about how unfair it all was that she couldn't have a normal brother who did normal things. One last look around and she zipped up the bag. "There," she said, facing Carter with a frown. "You happy?"

"Almost." Carter took her arm with one hand, her bag with the other, then they headed out of the hotel and across the street. He'd figured it would be safer to park off-site.

He was wrong. As soon as they crossed Las Vegas Boulevard, and approached his car, two of Zoopa's men appeared out the front of a small souvenir T-shirt shop.

Chapter Twenty-three

Carter and Twinkie were invited, acceptance not up for discussion, on a long drive to a place that Carter didn't like the looks of. It was a big block of a building that looked like it had been constructed with the sole purpose in mind of housing people who were brought there against their will.

Carter and Twinkie were pulled from the car and then shoved along through a couple of doors. The doors closed behind them and they were shoved once more into some hard wooden chairs.

A minute later, Zoopa appeared.

He propped a foot up on the side of Carter's chair and leaned toward him until Carter could smell stale cigar smoke on his breath. "You know what happens to jewel thieves here in Vegas?" he said. A vein bulged in his neck and, in the dim light, he looked a bit like he was starved for oxygen.

"You should know," Carter said. "How's the construction coming on your new casino?"

Zoopa shoved off on his foot and Carter's chair tipped, almost going over sideways. A backhand to Carter's face almost toppled the chair again. He spit blood and

Twinkie started crying. She jumped up and ran over to Zoopa, dissolving at his feet.

"Frank, no. Leave him alone. He doesn't know anything about that diamond."

"He's never listened to you. He's not gonna start now," Carter said to Twinkie. He spit some more blood onto the concrete floor. He could've easily taken Zoopa down right there, but it wouldn't do him or Twinkie any good. Zoopa's men would just rush in and save his sorry ass.

Keeping his focus on Carter, Zoopa shook Twinkie from his leg. "Maybe I have you wrong, Davis. Maybe you're just like the rest of us and all you need is a little incentive to mind your own business. How does a percentage of the house take sound?"

Carter laughed. "And be tied to you for the rest of my life?" He shook his head. "Not gonna happen. Besides, if I wanted, I could get rid of the Azuri diamond and have enough to live on very comfortably for a very long time. I don't need your lousy percentage."

Carter moved his jaw around. It was beginning to stiffen from Zoopa's blow and he suspected significant bruising would be showing by the time he got in front of a mirror. Good thing the competition was over. "Don't you have a casino to build? Time is money. Isn't that what you're always saying?"

Zoopa sneered. He crouched in front of Carter. "There's a lot of things I could do to get that diamond back. Might be it'll come to that, but I ain't gonna hurt your sister. She can't help it she's got an Elvis wannabe thief for a brother." He paused, grinding his teeth. "I *will* get that diamond back. One way or another."

It was the "another" that concerned Carter. In fact, there was a long list of "anothers" that would give him cause to worry. Not least of which was any kind of threat to Bailey or her family. Zoopa had only seen her with him once, but he knew who she was and Carter was sure Zoopa's men had reported that they'd left town together.

Bailey was home now, away from this mess. But, God knew how big this mess might get with her having taken the diamond. He couldn't be angry with her, only himself. She was a woman in love and women in love didn't exactly function on good sense. He should have trusted her enough to explain the situation, or better yet, he should have given the diamond to Azuri, as planned, and then let the Metro police take over where Zoopa was concerned. Then he could have gone back to Coupeville to finish his business with Bailey. That's the way it *should* have worked out; no telling how things would go now.

The only thing he did know was that he was right in leaving Bailey. With any luck, Zoopa would see her as just another woman who couldn't tame him. Carter swallowed hard. And that would be a lie.

"I'm gonna leave for a while, take care of some business." Zoopa spread his arms wide. "Try to look at this as an opportunity." Frank pulled Twinkie to him and kissed her. "Talk to your brother," he said in a low grumble.

As soon as Zoopa was out the door, Twinkie wiped his kiss from her mouth. Then she glared at Carter. "Do you see what you've done?"

As far as Carter could see the only thing he was guilty of was taking drastic measures to get Twinkie out from under Zoopa's control. Okay, so she wasn't happy right now, but if they lived through this, she had at least seen a side of Zoopa that might make her consider other options.

"What *I've* done? Wow." Carter shook his head. Her denial was mindboggling.

Twinkie started to say something more, but Carter held up his hand. He heard a car's engine start up. With any luck, Zoopa was a passenger.

Carter took a long slow breath. He hadn't noticed it before, but the smell of fried food was in the air. Bacon, eggs, good greasy comfort food. From the look on Twinkie's face, she needed some comforting. Maybe even something stronger to calm the murderous look in her eyes. There was another smell, too. Waffles. It reminded him of the pastry smell from the Knead & Feed, and he was pissed at Bailey all over again for having the nerve to go through his things and steal from him. A thong, no matter how stirring, was not a fair exchange for a million dollar diamond. She was going to have to do better than that. He grinned at the possibilities.

Carter went over to the door and gave it a quick check. Of course it was locked. Not that it'd do any good even if it hadn't been. At the very least, a couple of Zoopa's men would have been left behind to make sure he and Twinkie behaved themselves. And the SOBs were out there right now cooking up a feast.

Carter scanned the dim room. The only light was what filtered through a grimy window up near the ceiling, too high up for them to reach. Other than the chairs they'd been sitting on, and the smell of food filling their breathing space, the only items in the room were several boxes of varying sizes stacked over in one corner. Carter tried jiggling one of the larger ones. It didn't budge. The label on the outside of the box said "Pears." Gallon cans. He looked at the other boxes. Sauces, vegetables, more fruit. He and Twinkie were locked in some kind of food storage room. He could think of worse places to be.

"You sure know how to show a girl a good time," Twinkie said with plenty of sarcasm. "Hmm, that must be why you can't keep a woman."

Carter slid her a sideways look. She was mad. She'd get over it. He attempted to pick up a couple of the larger boxes. Heavy.

"Tell me this Azuri diamond thing is all just a big misunderstanding." It was more a plea than a request.

Carter ignored her and she grabbed him by the arm. *"Tell* me."

"Can't do that." He walked to the other side of the mountain of boxes and lifted a couple of the smaller ones. Still heavy, but manageable.

"Are you crazy?" Twinkie's voice went up a pitch. She put a hand to her forehead and pinched her eyes shut. "We're gonna get killed. You know that, don't you?"

"That would seem so."

"Great." She slapped a thigh. "I'm glad you're so calm about this." She began pacing, four steps up, four steps back. "I was doing just fine, things were going well, and you had to go and pull a stunt like this."

Carter carried one of the smaller boxes over and shoved it against the wall below the window. Had the blond dye finally seeped into his sister's brain? "You were doing fine? Things were going well? You're involved with a criminal, for crissakes."

"I think the Metro police might be of the opinion that you're a criminal, too. Jewel thief."

"Touché." Carter moved another box. "But, let's get something straight. I didn't steal that diamond. Frank did. I simply retrieved it for Mr. Azuri."

"And how convenient for us that you forgot to give it to him." Twinkie shook her head. "Like I said, you're going to get us both killed."

"No, cupcake. I'm going to save your ass from a life of hell with a man who cares about only one thing. Money." He grabbed hold of one of the large boxes and strained to pick it up. "Give me a hand here," he said.

"O-o-o-h, don't put this on me," Twinkie said. She folded her arms across her chest and stood against the wall.

Carter let go of the box and looked at her. She had her chin up and had entered her stubborn mode. With her like this, he wasn't going to get any cooperation.

Time to make a power play. He took three steps toward her. She stood her ground.

"You're going to get your skinny butt over there and help me move these boxes. We're going to build a way up and out of here." Carter pointed up to the small window. "If you don't, I'm going to put you over my knee and paddle your behind, just like Mom used to do whenever you got too big for your britches."

Twinkie frowned, began nervously tapping her foot. After a moment of pondering Carter's threat, she moved toward the stack of boxes.

A cup of sweat and two broken fingernails later, Twinkie had helped Carter move enough boxes to form a makeshift staircase.

Carter stepped back and surveyed the situation. While impressive, it wasn't quite high enough for either of them to comfortably reach the window. He figured he could give Twinkie a boost and then he could jump, grab the ledge, and pull himself up—maybe. At the very least, she'd be free.

"There you go," he said, waving a hand at the stack.

Twinkie stared up at the window. "You're kidding?" She started to cross her arms again, until Carter gave her a warning look.

"It's our only escape route," he said. "Look, it's only eight boxes high. Anyone can climb eight boxes—even you."

Twinkie glanced up again and then put a hand on one of the boxes. She gave it a good shove and the entire stack jiggled like it was going to topple. She shook her head. "I don't think so."

"Don't think. Just go." Carter grabbed her by the arm and pushed her toward the boxes. "Your involvement with Zoopa is over. You're going to take your butt out that window first and I'll be right behind you."

Reluctantly, Twinkie climbed. She managed the first

three boxes with no trouble, but when she tried to get up on the fourth, it jiggled precariously, and she paused. Carter prodded her on, smiling at her angry mutterings. This was no time to soften. No telling how much time they had before Zoopa or his men made another appearance. He'd ease up on her later, apologize for being such a bastard brother.

Finally, Twinkie made it to the last box, but she was still two feet down from the window.

"Now what?" she said, turning carefully to look down at Carter.

Carter didn't waste any time worrying about the precarious nature of the stack. "Now this, cupcake." He climbed up next to her, grabbed her around her legs with both arms, and boosted her up onto his shoulders. Luckily, she only weighed about as much as her cat, Romeo.

Twinkie slipped her small frame through the window with ease. Then it was Carter's turn. He was able to get up to the window, but getting through it was another story. He carried a hundred pounds more than his sister—all muscle—and unfortunately, muscle didn't compress and squish around the same as flab did. Getting his solid mass through the small opening was much like shoving a square block of wood through a round hole. He imagined himself an overstuffed Santa trying to make his way down a small chimney. Not a fun place to be and the fire was bound to be just as hot if he got stuck. Finally, with a lot of grunting and swearing, he managed to get his bulk through with only minor wounds.

Scrapes ran up his chest, making him look as though he'd tangled with an overzealous woman. He grinned. A woman like Bailey perhaps.

"Okay, now what?" Twinkie said when he dropped to the roof beside her. An ocean of dirt and sand and plants that had no business growing in a place as hot as hell lay before them. No cars, no other buildings, but most importantly, no cars in sight. They'd been left alone. Zoopa's men must've finished their meal.

The desert sun soon made Carter forget about food. And it was probably for the best. He didn't need anything to contribute to the thirst that was sure to hit while he was out walking in the desert heat. At least ninety-five degrees and climbing, their skin would soon feel like it was on fire. He looked at his watch. In another hour or two, it'd reach a hundred and ten. But if he knew his sister, long before that, she'd be complaining about how parched she was, and how she was going to need a complete facial to reverse the aging effects on her skin.

His own mouth began to go dry just thinking about their lack of available water. Lucky for his sister, him not being a normal kind of brother would probably be the very thing that would save her hide. He looked around. They were surrounded by brown hills. Mountains really, but they were so far in the distance that they only looked like hills. Carter took stock of the resident cacti. They'd be good for at least an occasional wetting of the mouth. Their only other hope was for a curious tourist to happen by, but the road that lay before them didn't look well traveled enough for that to be much more than a dream. Odds were this day would not have a happy ending.

"Let's go," Carter said to Twinkie. He hung from the roof and let go, falling ten feet into sand and dirt. It rose in a billowy cloud around him. When it cleared, he looked up to see Twinkie standing above him, hands on hips, looking disgusted.

"You don't think I'm going to drop down into that filth, do you?"

"I'll catch you."

Twinkie looked down for a long minute. She didn't budge. "I don't know."

"Jump, then."

Twinkie crossed her arms and shook her head. "There's no way. I'll break my legs."

"Look, bird legs, I'll catch you. Jump. And make it soon." Twinkie took another minute and when she looked down again, Carter gave her his meanest brotherly glare. She closed her eyes and made the plunge. It was good that he'd bullied her somewhat when they were kids. Made for easier control over her now.

Carter caught her just like he promised, only she wasn't eight years old anymore, and from ten feet up, she weighed a bit more than her cat. They both fell hard onto cement-like ground, and Carter made some guttural sounds as he lay there in the dry dirt.

Twinkie got to her feet and dusted herself off. She looked down at Carter and smiled.

"Thanks. I can get up myself," Carter said with a groan. He got up, holding a hand to his back, and walked around the perimeter of the small stucco building. Although there were no cars out front, it was entirely possible one of Zoopa's men could still be lurking inside. The front door was closed and Carter paused in front of it. No sounds. He stuck his head inside. The smell of bacon slammed into him and his stomach growled angrily. Carter took a quick look around the grill. Zoopa's boys had eaten everything.

Carter led the way and Twinkie followed, plodding along behind him like a child who had better things to do. Just as he'd figured, she started to complain almost immediately. A few minutes more and she stopped walking. She struck a pose with her hands on her hips.

"I can't walk anymore. I need water. My body can't take these conditions."

Carter said a quick prayer that a stray tourist would come along and save him from having to strangle her. He ran a hand through his sweat-dampened hair, and took a look around.

"Okay, cupcake," he said. He fished a knife from a pocket in the waistband of his pants and walked over to a cactus. Twinkie watched in amazement as he proceeded to coerce the desert plant into spilling forth some of its precious broth.

"You're a bit of a sneaky fellow, aren't you?" she said.

"Boy Scouts," Carter responded, holding the cactus out to her.

Twinkie's lips squished into distaste. "You must have sunstroke. I'm thirsty. *Real* thirsty. I'm going to need more than a drizzle from one of those stinky plants."

"Suit yourself," Carter said. He sucked some liquid into his mouth, and then rubbed a small amount over the gritty layer of dirt on the back of his neck. Twinkie turned up her nose in disgust. That was okay. Another ten minutes, she'd be begging to suck on the end of a cactus.

A flurry of dirt rose in the distance, and Carter watched as a car turned in their direction. Either Zoopa was back, or this was the day one of his wishes was about to be granted.

As the vehicle got closer, he saw that it was a minivan, probably a rental. A grin stretched across his face. "Looks like today might be your lucky day, baby sister." Carter said.

Twinkie immediately began hopping up and down, waving her hands high in the air, but Carter stood quiet, choosing to reserve his excitement until he'd made a positive i.d. on the vehicle's occupants. Another minute and they could be back to square one.

Carter squinted, watching the vehicle approach, the muscles tense in his back.

Half a minute passed, and a dark blue minivan stopped fifteen feet back from where they stood. A window opened and a woman with red hair and a face covered in freckles stuck out her head. She looked sheepish as she said, "We're kinda lost."

Another window opened and two kids who looked just like the woman, only with more freckles, stuck out their heads. "Yeah, and our dad is swearing at the map," one of them said.

Carter blew out a relieved breath and smiled. "Maps can be frustrating."

A man got out of the driver's side and walked around to Carter and Twinkie. He pulled a bandanna from his pocket and wiped sweat from his face and neck. "It's hotter'n a son of a bitch out here. How the hell can you be out here in this?"

Carter gave Twinkie a look. Her eyes were ringed with black mascara and sweat dripped off the end of her nose. "It is getting a bit warm," he said. "I think I can probably help you with that map if you'll give us a ride into town."

Chapter Twenty-four

Mark and Brian picked up Bailey and Liza promptly at six P.M. Mark's eyes gleamed, somewhere between scary and seductive, and to Bailey's dismay, they were focused right on her. It seemed he had his own ideas about who his date would be for the evening. Too bad. Bailey had taken that trip and she wasn't interested in going back.

"Peaches," Mark said.

"Mark." Bailey gave him a polite nod and smile. Liza shamelessly puffed out her size C—verging on D—cups, and she stepped around Bailey to give Mark a welcome hug.

"Hey, Bailey," Brian said. His lips stretched into a smarmy grin. "Hey, Liza. Good to see you," he said, giving her a moment's glance before returning his gaze to Bailey.

Great. Bailey did a silent groan. She'd have both twins' full attention for the next several hours, when all she really wanted was to crawl back in bed and wait to see what God had in store for her next.

After a few minutes of small talk and flirtatious behavior between Liza and the twins, they all piled into Mark's '67 Plymouth Barracuda—a fitting car for Mark. Probably even for Carter.

Mark steered Bailey into the front seat by opening the door and then shoving her inside. Once they were all buckled up, he pointed the beast north, toward Oak Harbor.

Oak Harbor was the closest big town, and it was where everyone of legal drinking age went when they wanted to get crazy on the weekend. Not the kind of crazy you could find in Seattle, perhaps, but nevertheless crazy enough to satisfy certain needs, especially if you compared it to Coupeville's Big Weekend Bingo Bash. Oak Harbor had bars for cowboys and cowgirls, bars for wannabe hip-hoppers, and movie theaters and bowling alleys for the tamer set.

Bailey shifted uncomfortably in her seat as they traveled to their destination. She felt a sharp sensation in the back of her head, no doubt coming from the laser beam Liza had focused on her. Crimonies, it wasn't her fault Mark had chosen the seating arrangement. What was Liza worried about anyway? A couple of hours, and several strong drinks later, and it wouldn't matter. She and Liza would have switched places, and the twins wouldn't be the wiser.

She and Liza had the moves down perfectly. First they'd visit the ladies' room and, upon returning, they'd change chairs. Bailey would feign a sprained ankle when it came time to dance and Mark would be forced to take Liza out on the dance floor. After that, Liza was on her own. She'd have to work her magic to hold his interest, which at that point, would amount to just keeping him on his feet.

As designated driver, Bailey would have to drive them all home—which might be just as scary as having Mark drive while under the influence.

Their plan to switch partners worked beautifully, thanks to Jack Daniels. Mark and Liza spent most of the evening out on the dance floor and Brian was content to keep Bailey and her "sprained" ankle company at the table.

Swapping partners had been the safe choice. Mark was what most women would call a lean mean sex machine. Literally. And being as Bailey was at such a vulnerable point right now, it probably wasn't wise to take any chances by leaving the door to opportunity open. Although for that to happen, she'd have to do some serious kissing up to Jack D., too. And right now, the only kissing up she wanted to do was with Carter.

Bailey closed her eyes and imagined what it would be like waking up next to him. He'd be gazing lovingly at her, and all the bad things would be a distant memory. No Azuri diamond, no Frank Zoopa, no Twinkie Martinson. Just Carter's lips, his hands, his . . .

"You okay?" Brian asked. He looked down at her glass. "You've only had a few sips of your drink, but you're kinda wobblin', just like Mark does when he's about to fall over."

Bailey looked over at the crowded dance floor. Liza and Mark were dancing to a Kenny Chesney tune that had their bodies pressed together so tight they were breathing as one. Mark probably would be wobbling, but Liza had a good hold on him and he didn't look like he'd hit the floor anytime soon.

"I'm fine," Bailey said on a sigh.

The night wore on, the drinks rolled in, and not long after the clock struck eleven, Brian's hands did some rolling of their own, right over to Bailey's thigh. She brushed them away, and Brian gave her a can't-blame-me-for-trying shrug.

Maybe then he couldn't blame her if she gave him a good jab to the groin.

Carter needed a place where he could shower and get cleaned up before heading back to Washington. Someplace where Zoopa wouldn't come looking for him.

Nikki Amsterdam, casino host extraordinaire, immediately came to mind. He called her and thanked her for stopping by to cook him dinner and then he reminded her that she owed him a favor.

Nikki was only too happy to pay her debt to Carter. She wasn't thrilled about Twinkie being part of the deal, but right now, he and his sister were a package, and Nikki was going to have to suck it up.

Nikki gave Carter and Twinkie the use of a suite, one that had an adjoining room so Twinkie could make herself scarce should Carter desire some amenities of a more personal nature. Tempting, but he wasn't about to give his sister any opportunity to run off and get them both into more trouble. And not only that, but Bailey was the only gal he wanted to put his arms around right now.

Nikki fingered Carter's collar for a moment and then rested her hands on his chest. "I stopped by to see you the other night," she said, sounding like she was about to purr.

"My loss." Carter felt a stirring in his loins, but he ignored it. Those stirrings were on reserve for his brunette.

Twinkie made a gagging sound and disappeared into the bathroom.

"We need to get on a flight as soon as possible. Do you think you can help us with that, too?" Carter asked Nikki.

"Carter, honey, you're leaving town? For how long?" she asked.

"Not long." He gave the tip of Nikki's nose a friendly kiss. "I'll be back before you miss me."

"I already miss you," she said. "How about you and I have some time alone before you go. It seems a shame to waste that other room."

Twinkie shut the bathroom door, louder than was necessary.

Nikki's eyes sparked with fire, and Carter's mouth twitched into a grin. He'd never been able to figure out why Nikki and Twinkie had such a hate-on for each other, but he supposed it was just one of those woman things that only an idiot of a man would get in the middle of.

Nikki drew herself closer to Carter. He could feel her breath on his cheek, smell the perfume she'd put on that morning. Nature was fighting to take over. She was an enticing woman, to be sure, but until he figured out what was going to happen with Bailey—if anything—the raven-haired casino host was off-limits.

"Maybe another time," Carter whispered gently into her ear. He didn't see any reason to upset the cart just then, not when he needed a favor, and there'd be plenty of time for them to talk later, when he returned.

Nikki pouted, acknowledging her defeat, but she wasn't finished torturing Carter. She raised high on her toes and kissed him, rolling her tongue over his lips and then dipping it deep into his mouth. Carter groaned. Even on a bad day, that's all it would've normally taken to change his mind, but when he closed his eyes, Bailey's face was looking right back at him.

Carter put his hands on Nikki's waist and gently pushed her away. "That flight?"

Nikki shrugged. "Anything for you, baby. You know that." And she left the room.

Twinkie came out of the bathroom. *"Anything for you, baby,"* she mimicked.

"What can I say? Women love me."

Twinkie tugged on one of Carter's sideburns. "Maybe it's just Elvis that Nikki loves."

Carter shook a leg and settled into a karate pose. He cleared his throat and curled his lip into a sneer. "Thank you. Thank you very much."

Daylight. Bailey sucked the dryness from her mouth and squinted at the bathroom door. She heard the shower running and smiled. And then she remembered, it wasn't Carter in her bathroom. It was Liza, her friend, the woman who'd convinced her to go out for an evening of "fun" with the Jefferson twins. She moaned and rolled over. The only fun she'd had was the moment they'd dropped her and Liza back off at her little cottage, where she could still smell Carter's aftershave on her pillow.

A few minutes later, Liza skipped into the room, looking as fresh as morning rain. In fact, she was still dripping wet. She'd barely dried herself off. And covering herself had obviously been too much of an effort.

Bailey moaned again and closed her eyes. Being faced with Liza's perky breasts was a tad too depressing so early in the day. "You're dripping all over the carpet."

"Dripping and alive." Liza twirled around.

Great. Liza was alive and kicking, all refreshed after downing at least half a dozen drinks the previous night, and Bailey was feeling half dead after only two. A clear sign she was entering the next phase of her life. Soon, she'd be sitting on the front porch with her mom and aunt after their evening meal, and the three of them would be sipping their nightly flutes of Chambord to aid in their digestion.

"Wasn't last night great? I tell you that Mark Jefferson can really use his—"

"Stop," Bailey said, holding up a hand. "Let's not go there." She raised herself up on her arms. "Going out last night was a bust. I feel even worse than before."

"Worse? As in guilty?" Liza finished towel drying her hair and tossed the towel onto the floor.

Bailey's eyebrows shot up. The act of thinking forced the fog in her brain to lift. It took a minute to replay the previous night, but she was 99 percent sure she had no reason to feel guilty.

So much for having a good time.

"Why should I feel guilty?"

"Having so much fun with the Jefferson twins, while your precious jewel thief is back in Vegas pining away for you. When the cat's away . . ."

"If only that were true."

"Yeah, you're right. He's probably already serenading some other unsuspecting fan."

A sharp bolt of pain shot through Bailey's chest and she sat up. *He wouldn't dare!* She jumped out of bed and grabbed a blue robe off the back of her door. "I'm taking a shower to wash away the memory of last night, and then you and I will spend the day doing something fun."

"Uh, Mark and I are spending the day together."

Bailey stopped and studied Liza. Liza used to be so sensible. "Are you on some kind of medication?" she asked.

Liza shrugged. "You don't want him."

The phone rang, saving Bailey from having to give her friend a good talking to. It was her mom.

"Your aunt is sick," Olivia said.

Bailey did an eye roll. "Let me guess. She's got the first stages of Lyme disease."

"That very well might be. She's really sick."

Bailey was suddenly flushed with guilt for the eye roll.

"Could be the potato salad. You know how mayonnaise can spoil. I suppose she could have the flu, but she did have a flu shot this year. My Lord, do you think she could've gotten some parasite from digging around in the dirt?"

"Parasite?" Bailey wondered if her aunt's hypochondria was beginning to rub off on her mom.

"She's been planting annuals. I'm not sure she was wearing any garden gloves."

Bailey could almost see the lines wrinkling her mom's forehead. "Where's Auntie now?"

"Upstairs. I wanted to take her over to the emergency

room," Olivia said, and then she lowered her voice, "but, your Uncle Rex says since we've got an almost doctor in the family, we might as well call you."

Now Bailey was really fueled with guilt. "Please God, let Auntie be okay," she mumbled, looking up at the ceiling.

"Are we praying now? Oh, sweet Jesus."

Bailey knew her mother's eyes were fixed on her own ceiling. "No, Mom. We're not praying. I was just talking to myself. Tell Auntie I'll be right over." So much for fun.

"Don't forget to bring your little black bag. It'll look more official."

"Uh, I'm not sure I know where it is."

After a long pause, her mom finally said, "Improvise," and she clicked off.

Bailey chewed her lip and tried to remember the last time she'd seen her doctor's bag. She opened the hall closet and found an old makeup case. It was only half the size of a doctor's bag, but her mother *had* said to improvise. Bailey shrugged and pulled it out.

"Oh," Liza said, with a scowl, and took a step back. "That's nasty. What are you going to do with that dust-covered thing?"

"Do you think it'll pass for a doctor's bag?"

"Who do you have to fool?"

"Uncle Rex, my aunt . . ."

"Honey, Rex only has one eye that'll be lookin' and the only thing your aunt will see are all the dust mites crawling around on it." Liza fluffed her blond hair and sprayed hair spray on it until it could withstand an October windstorm.

Bailey left the cottage, wishing Liza good luck with Mark. Probably Mark was the one who really needed the luck. Liza was petite, but she was a force.

When Bailey got to her mom's house, it was quiet, only the ticking of the grandfather clock and some unidentifiable background hum. She didn't know if her aunt was sleeping, or if she'd had a miraculous recovery and she and her mom had left to do some shopping. She climbed the stairs to Fiona's room, wondering with each step what kind of imagined illness it would be this time.

Fiona's face was moonlight pale, and Bailey rushed over to her side. "How're you feeling, Auntie?"

Fiona attempted a smile, but the corners of her mouth barely lifted. "It won't be long now. Stay close," the old woman said in a whisper. "Where's your mother?"

"I'm right here," Olivia said over Bailey's shoulder. She went around to the other side of the bed and sat, taking one of Fiona's hands in hers.

"Rex, where's Rex?" Fiona asked.

"I called him over at the Hall. He's on his way."

Bailey put a hand to Fiona's forehead. It felt neither cold nor warm. "Where does it hurt?"

"There's no pain. Not anymore. I'm at death's door." Fiona let out a groan.

"Okay, where *did* it hurt?" Bailey asked.

"My bowels." Fiona pointed to the upper right quadrant of her abdomen. "Got gas something awful. It's embarrassing. I musta got up twenty times last night to go downstairs to the bathroom. Couldn't let your Uncle Rex hear me makin' all them sounds. You'll do well to remember that. A lady never admits to doing any of that business."

Bailey bit her lip, stifling a smile. She'd heard all about how to be a lady her entire life. Ladies don't burp, have gas, go number two. Heck, a lady doesn't even blow her nose unless it's behind a closed bathroom door. "I'll remember, Auntie."

"Could be that Legionnaire's disease that's going around." Fiona sputtered and coughed dryly.

"It sounds more like gallstones. Are you nauseated at all?" Bailey rested the back of her hand against her aunt's forehead once more. "You don't feel warm, but I think I'll take your temperature, anyway." She went into the adjoining bathroom and returned a minute later, empty handed. "I couldn't find it." She looked from her aunt to her mother. Olivia shrugged.

"Imagine that," Fiona mumbled. "Where's Elvis?" She gave another dry cough and made a weak attempt to lift her head and look about the room. As though exhausted from the effort, she quickly let her head fall back onto her pillow. "If I don't make it, tell him I'm sorry about the competition."

Bailey's heart skipped at the mention of Carter. And then she got angry. How dare he leave, just when her aunt might really be sick? She considered making up some little white lie about his whereabouts, rather than disappoint her aunt, but why prolong the agony? Bailey did a mental sigh. "I have something to tell you, Auntie . . . Mom. It's about me and Elvis, uh, Carter. We sort of—"

Fiona coughed dryly until she was gasping for air. Finally, she caught her breath. "I wouldn't mind seeing that young man once more before I go," she said, squeezing Bailey's hand. "It'd do this old woman's heart good. Maybe even get my blood flowing so's I could make it to the competition."

The way her aunt lay there, all washed out and still, Bailey was willing to do anything, say anything, just to make her feel better. If Fiona was truly sick . . . if she lost her aunt, and didn't even try to grant her a last wish . . . it was just too painful to imagine. Bailey felt her heart thud.

"Mom, can I see you out in the hall?" Bailey said.

On their way out of the room, Fiona called after them, "Don't be long. I don't want to be alone when it happens. Death is a lonely place . . ."

Bailey shut the bedroom door with a quiet click and she turned to her mother. "I think Auntie might really be sick this time."

Olivia put a hand to her chest and rolled her eyes up to the ceiling.

"I think we should call her doctor," Bailey said.

"But she wants *you* for her doctor."

"Okay, here's the thing . . . I'm not even in medical school anymore. Auntie needs a real doctor. I'm going to call Doc Russo." Bailey started down the stairs.

"What kind of crazy talk is that? You don't need to call that old coot. You made the Dean's List three semesters in a row. That means you're plenty qualified to figure out what's wrong with Fiona."

"Um, yeah, I'm calling Doc Russo."

Olivia gasped. "No."

Bailey stopped and eased her mom down to the steps to sit. God, don't let her have two patients to deal with. She waited for her mother's breathing to slow, and for her eyes to become more focused, then she went on to explain one more time that she wasn't going to be a doctor, that all she really wanted was to open her own bakery.

"That's just a phase," Olivia said, patting Bailey's knee.

"No. It's not. I've been working at the Knead & Feed," Bailey told her.

"But how? How could you be working there?" Olivia shook her head. "What if somebody tells your Uncle Rex?"

Bailey looked sheepish. "That's not likely. I kinda bribed all of Auntie's friends, made them promise not to say anything if I gave them discounts on homemade marionberry pie when I open my own place."

Olivia stared at Bailey for a long moment like she was trying to figure out who this person was pretending to be her daughter. "Your uncle promised your dad he'd see to it that you get an education. This will give him a hernia."

"I think you mean aneurism. And that's precisely why

I haven't told him yet," she said with a sigh. "I thought it'd be better to wait until my plans were more concrete."

"Secrets. Lies." Olivia put her head in her hands and muttered something about not knowing how this could happen in her family. She got up from the stairs slowly, like she'd aged twenty years, and went back into Fiona's room.

Chapter Twenty-five

With Bailey safely downstairs calling Doc Russo, Olivia slipped back into Fiona's room. Fiona cautiously opened one eye and peered over at her, then she pulled a Worst-Case Scenario card out from under the covers and read it. *"Gallstones.* What the heck are they teaching our Bailey in school anyway? Can't she tell I've got Legionnaire's disease?" She held out the card for Olivia to read.

"Well, that's something we'll have to talk about. Anyway, you got the dry cough right, but your alleged bowel pain seems to better fit gallstones." Olivia crossed her arms over her chest. "Now explain to me what's going on and why I just had to lie to my daughter."

"It's for her own good. Some of the girls were over to the Fish Shack yesterday. They told me they saw Elvis heading south."

Olivia waved a dismissive hand. "That doesn't mean anything. Elvis wouldn't run out on my girl. He could've been going . . ." Olivia paused, trying to think what lay south.

Fiona pulled her lips into a thin line. "Lea Townsend called this morning. She was over to that wild cowboy joint last night in Oak Harbor. That Lea can still draw the looks, can't she?" Fiona cupped a hand around her mouth and lowered her voice. "I hear she wears one of those derriere lifter girdle thingies."

Olivia threw up her hands. "What does that have to do with Bailey and Elvis?"

"Lea says she saw Bailey and that friend of hers from Seattle, and they were out with those Jefferson boys."

Olivia gasped. She put a hand over her mouth and lowered herself to the edge of the bed.

"That Brian Jefferson, he's not such a bad boy," Fiona went on. "But, Mark, that one's got something wild in his pants. You always hear about twins . . . one good, the other touched with evil," Fiona said, shaking her head and making a clucking sound.

Olivia raised both eyebrows.

"Word is Mark Jefferson has entered the competition," Fiona continued, "and with Elvis gone, the girls down at the parlor are bettin' he'll win. He can't sing a lick, but he's got some moves . . . you know what that could mean."

Olivia looked to the ceiling and put a hand to her chest. "Lord, take me now. Put me out of my misery, if you plan on making Mark Jefferson my grandchildren's papa."

The door opened and Bailey came back in. "All right, Doc Russo says he'll be right over." Fiona slid lower under the covers. "Auntie, are you feeling worse?"

"She's delirious, I think," Olivia said, sliding Fiona a look. She checked her watch. "Where's your Uncle Rex? I called him an hour ago and he said he'd be right home. He wouldn't want to miss your passing, now would he, Fiona?"

Rex burst into the room. "Fiona, darling, Papa's home." Fiona peered at him over the top of the covers. "What's wrong with her?" he asked Bailey. "Where's your doctor's bag? Your stethoscope?"

"We called Doc Russo over at the clinic. He'll be here shortly," Olivia said.

"We don't need that old has-been," Rex said with a

snort. "We got us a doctor right here." He put an arm around Bailey's shoulders and gave her a good squeeze. "Isn't that right, girl?"

"Um . . ." Bailey chewed her lip, looking over at her mother.

"We thought Fiona might need a more experienced member of the medical profession," Olivia said.

"Yes, we'll go downstairs and wait for him," Bailey said. She grabbed her mother's arm and they left Rex alone with Fiona.

A half hour later, Doc Russo arrived. He apologized for taking so long, said that he had to stop off and check one of his patients who'd been suffering from chest pains for the past couple of days. "She thinks she saw Elvis right here in town recently. Got herself so worked up, I had to give her something to calm her down."

Bailey made no mention of how he might be getting more calls like that. She took him up to Fiona's room, and Fiona immediately suggested everyone wait downstairs while Doc Russo examined her.

"I may be at death's door, but I still have my pride. It's going to be a while before I let any of you wipe my bottom."

Olivia, Bailey, and Rex filed out of the room and Fiona waited to hear their footsteps going down the stairs. She threw back the covers, swung her legs over the side of the bed and began pacing the room and fanning herself. She was wearing a Playtex girdle, a white eighteen-hour bra, and a pair of fuzzy purple socks that had seen better days.

"It's about time. A couple more minutes and I really woulda needed a doctor. It was getting darn hot under there."

Doctor Russo's eyebrows shot up.

"What's wrong? It been a while since you saw a woman in her Skivvies?"

"Now, Fiona, why don't you lie back down? Let me take your temperature." Doc Russo took her arm and tried to steer her back to the bed.

"Get your hands off me, you old coot," Fiona said, shrugging off his hand. "Bailey already put her hand on my forehead. I'm fine." She ducked into the bathroom to take a look at her face. It was still pale from the cake flour she'd patted on, but it was beginning to crack. She made a mental note to use less the next time she wanted to look sickly.

"If you're fine, why am I here?" Doc Russo asked.

"Here's the deal . . ." Fiona said. She stuffed her hands on her hip bones. "You keep my condition to yourself and I'll give you front row tickets to the upcoming Elvis competition."

Doc Russo looked confused. "Elvis? Oh no, not you, too. Fiona, why don't you lie down? Let me take your temperature." He held up a glass thermometer.

Fiona grabbed the thermometer from him and snapped it in half. "Get with the program, Doc, these things are outdated. They use them other things now. You stick it in your ear and *wham,* you're either sick or you're not." She tossed the broken thermometer into the wastebasket and continued fanning herself.

Doc Russo's mouth hung open.

"Dammit, man, you drive a hard bargain. Since my niece's happiness rides on this, I'll have the concession stand throw in some gummi bears."

Doc Russo looked thoughtful.

"Now listen closely. Elvis has left the building and we've got to get him back here."

Fiona explained the situation with *Elvis,* about how with him being such a respectful young man, that he'd at least come back to say his farewells if he knew she was ill. "He just can't help that his hips move around so loose and free." She got a faraway look in her eyes and took a moment to reminisce. "Rex's hips moved like that once upon a time. Damn near killed me . . . So what do you say? You in?"

Doc Russo reluctantly agreed to go along with Fiona's plan, but only on the condition that she get regular health checkups and maybe a psych evaluation, too. He put on his serious face and ushered Bailey, Olivia, and Rex back into the room. He cleared his throat before speaking.

"As you know, any of us could go at any time. God works in strange ways. We just don't know . . ." he said, shaking his head.

Olivia looked at the ceiling and moved her lips and Uncle Rex rushed to Fiona's side. He grabbed both her hands and smothered them with kisses.

Fiona coughed and slid a look at Doc Russo and he continued. "Uh, she conveyed to me that there's a certain young man she'd like to see before she goes."

Olivia sputtered.

Bailey raised a hand. "That would be my friend from Las Vegas. But, he's gone home."

Doc Russo shook his head slowly and lowered his gaze to the floor. "Do your best."

When Bailey got home, she found Maggie May perched on the back of the sofa with a small towel stuffed in her mouth. Tucker lay coma-like on the cool kitchen linoleum. He raised his head briefly and flopped his tail three times before returning to quiet slumber.

"Hello to you, too." Bailey gave each dog a welcome pat. "What'd you guys do with Auntie Liza?" Maggie May cocked her head and looked around the room. Bailey heard animal sounds coming from down the hall and the image that popped into her head made her think perhaps it might be time to strip the bed and put on clean sheets.

The guest bedroom door swung open and Liza bounded out, her curves barely covered by a large white bath towel. Mark Jefferson was close behind and he, too, had more skin showing than Bailey cared to see. They both stopped when they saw Bailey.

Mark grinned and his pupils dilated. *"Peaches."*

"Mark just finished giving me a massage and we were on our way to wash off the oil. Men who work with their hands really do know what they're doing," Liza said, giving Bailey a wink.

It was definitely time to change the sheets.

"How's your aunt?" Liza asked.

Bailey sighed. "I'm not sure. Could be gallstones. She thinks she's on her way out. She wants me to bring Carter to see her before she goes."

"Did you tell her if she *goes*, she'll be able to see the real Elvis?"

"First off, I don't want to think about her really *going.* And, second, I didn't think it was the time to bring up the subject of the King being dearly departed. My mother doesn't need the extra stress and I didn't need to hear her rantings about how he's in the witness protection program, waiting to make his comeback." Bailey looked at the ceiling. "Damn it, Elvis. If you're not up there serenading angels, I sure wish you'd make an appearance so we could all collect on our bets and get on with our lives."

The doorbell rang and Bailey fought her way to the front door through a roadblock of barking dogs and wagging tails.

"Carter," Bailey said, sucking in some air. Her heart skittered and she said a silent prayer. *Please, God, don't let this be just a dream. Or, if it is, don't let me wake up until he kisses me.*

"Hello, honey," Carter said.

The dream was smiling, but the smile didn't reach his eyes and Bailey felt like she'd been blasted with cold air.

"Hi, Bailey." Twinkie leaned around from behind Carter and gave Bailey a little wave.

Maggie May chomped on her towel and tried to push her way through Bailey's legs to greet Carter, and Tucker took one look at Twinkie, then backed around behind the door and proceeded to growl.

"Hey, girl," Carter said. He crouched and grabbed Maggie and she did a somersault, then came to rest on her back with all four paws in the air. He rubbed her belly for a moment, then stood and took a step forward, toward Bailey.

Liza stepped into the room, giving Carter an eyeful of her towel-clad body. "Well, hello," she said.

Mark stood behind her with a scowl on his face.

It was a man thing.

Carter gave Liza a polite nod and then his attention went back to Bailey. Huge bonus points for resisting staring at Liza's half-naked body. After all, during their first encounter, he'd stared at Bailey in all her glory for what seemed like an hour, before he'd finally tossed her a towel to cover her goodies.

Liza'd had enough of them ogling each other, and she trotted into the bathroom with Mark on her heels.

"You remember Twinkie?" Carter said. "My sister."

Bailey drew in a huge breath of air that filled her lungs. *Sister?* So he hadn't lied? Twinkie with the three B's really was his sister? Bailey felt a giddy smile forming.

"Sorry if I'm intruding. It wasn't my idea," Twinkie said. "Carter thought I needed a vacation."

"Glad to see me?" Carter asked Bailey in an even voice.

"Very much," Bailey said, and she meant it.

"We have something to talk about, don't we?" he said. His voice was quiet and firm. It gave her goose bumps.

Suddenly, Bailey wasn't so sure she was glad to see him.

Was he just here to get the diamond? Rip out her heart and light it on fire? Take it back with him and bury it in the desert? No. Talk could wait. She had something more important to do than discuss the Azuri diamond with him.

"I was just on my way out. My Aunt Fiona is sick and—"

"Honey, your aunt is always sick. She can wait."

Bailey's eyes welled with tears and she threw in a couple of sniffles, too. That did the trick. Carter touched her arm and his forehead wrinkled with concern.

"She's really sick?" he asked.

Bailey nodded. "Really." She shrugged. "Or maybe she's just getting really good at faking it."

"Anything I can do to help?"

Yeah. Hold me. Let me get lost in your arms. As usual, Carter had his security powers turned on, and he did as told. He pulled her to him gently, and then he kissed her. Not with the wild abandon she might have hoped for, after not seeing him for two full days, but enough to remind her they did indeed have unfinished business. She relaxed into him and kissed him back, until Twinkie cleared her throat.

"Don't think this means we don't have some talking to do later," Carter whispered against Bailey's hair. He gave her one good squeeze, then released her.

Bailey's emotions teetered between anger and unwavering love. She knew darn well the reason he'd come back was the Azuri diamond. Yet here he was, willing to put "business" aside until he found out what was wrong with her aunt.

"I'm surprised you came back," she said. "You were in such a hurry to leave."

A grin played at the corners of Carter's mouth. "C'mon. You didn't think I'd just walk away from you, did you?" He pulled her close again. "By the way, I forgive you. But that's something else we'll talk about later," he said. "Tell me about your aunt?"

Bailey spread her arms. "Honestly, I don't know anymore. I went over to see her, expecting it to be the same as always, but this time, it was different. She actually looked . . . sick." Bailey wrinkled her nose in distaste. "Pale, all chalky looking. I'm really worried."

"Anything I can do?"

Bailey nodded hesitantly. "If you will. Auntie wants to see you before she goes."

"Goes?"

Bailey glanced up. "To the big upstairs. Oh, and she says she's sorry about the competition. Not that you'll be here for it." Bailey looked into Carter's blue eyes. She wanted to hear him say that he realized they belonged together and that he couldn't live without her, but it was probably more likely that he'd say something like, "Give me back my diamond, I've got a plane to catch."

"You, baby. I came back for you."

There they were. The seven little words she wanted to hear. So why didn't she feel any better?

Bailey looked hard at Carter and then at Twinkie. Not much family resemblance between them. Her female antennae raised an inch. "I have a question," she said. "When you came home with me, was it all about the diamond?"

Carter nudged Twinkie and nodded in the direction of the back deck. Twinkie gave a little huff, but she ambled out to the deck like an obedient child. Maggie May followed behind her with the towel still hanging from her mouth.

Bailey waited for Carter's answer. If he said the right words, she just might give him back his blasted jewel, and maybe she'd even still let him make love to her.

"When we left Las Vegas, yes, it was all about the diamond. But, after the first hundred miles, you became just as much a part of the equation. I know it hurt you when I had to leave, but I had good reasons, and they were reasons you don't need to know. I'm back now. Do you want to argue, or do you want to dance?"

"Are you planning to still be in my aunt's show?"

Carter nodded once. "I'm a man of my word. I wouldn't want to disappoint Fiona. Or you." Carter brushed Bailey's cheek with the back of his hand. "I couldn't get you off my mind." He grabbed a handful of her hair and pulled her to him.

Carter's lips touched hers, and every bit of anger Bailey had been feeling over the last couple of days dissolved. His mouth was warm and sweet and all she wanted was to take his hand and lead him to her bedroom, so they could continue where they'd left off before he went back to Vegas. Unfortunately, with a houseful of guests, privacy was scarce.

"I really think we should go over and see your aunt, tell her that I'm back and the show is on," Carter said.

Bailey sighed. "If only it was that easy." She shook her head. "I'm not sure what's wrong with my aunt, but I think she really could be sick this time."

"Serious?"

Bailey shrugged. "Depends on who you ask. Gallstones."

Carter flinched. "Ouch."

"Yeah. But she'll be happy to see you. I almost told her you'd dumped me, but she was in so much pain and so sure her time was limited . . ." Bailey shrugged. "Guess I didn't have the heart to tell her you were a jewel thief and that you were only here to collect your bounty."

Carter put a finger under her chin. "There's more than one kind of bounty."

Just then, the doorbell rang. Bailey turned to open the door, but Carter grabbed her by the arm and gave her a gentle push toward the hallway. She didn't need any explanation. Some kind of primitive female intuition made all the hair on her body that hadn't been shaved or waxed stand on end. Her pulse was running at full throttle. Not the same as when Carter performed his magic on her, but more like the way it would when a sensible person realized it was time to run for their life.

Twinkie poked her head in the door and he gave her a head gesture. She seemed to know exactly what he wanted, because she stepped into the hallway with Bailey.

When they were both tucked safely behind her "bullet proof" wall, Bailey whispered, "Are we going to die?"

Twinkie put a finger to her hot pink lips and they waited while Carter opened the door.

"*Fiona*," Carter said, swinging the door open wide.

Fiona? Bailey's mouth hung open. *Her* Aunt Fiona?

"What a pleasure to see you again," Carter said. "And so good to see you up and about. Bailey told me you weren't feeling well."

Bailey stepped out from the hallway. She stuffed her hands on her hips and glared at her aunt. Fiona was dressed smartly in a floral print dress that rustled when she walked along with a hat that looked like a large corsage. This was no woman close to death. "What's going on here?" Bailey said. Carter stifled a smile, but she could see it hiding behind the curl in his lip.

"I was in the neighborhood and thought I'd check out the rumor. Lea called, said there was an Elvis sighting over on Highway 20. She said he had some show girl with him." Fiona leaned to look around Carter. Twinkie gave her a little wave.

"Why aren't you home in bed?" Bailey asked. Then she felt a sudden chill sweep up her spine. She turned to Carter. "Do you think she's delirious?" Bailey made a move to put her hand to her aunt's forehead. Fiona batted it away.

"Never mind me. We've got some planning to do." Fiona moved over to the kitchen table and spread out some brightly colored sheets of paper. Bailey picked up a lime green one and began reading. The more she read, the further her mouth hung open. She glanced over at Carter and mouthed an apology.

"Seeing as how it's an official competition, me and your mom had new flyers printed up. We couldn't decide which one was best, so pick whichever you like and I'll get some copies made," Fiona told them.

Bailey looked at the flyers. There were three to choose from, each with their own color. Lime green, hot pink, and sunshine yellow. The pink ones showed Carter signing autographs outside the auto repair shop, the green ones had Carter licking marionberry pie off Bailey's face, and yellow showed Carter and some woman leaving a Las Vegas hotel. Bailey picked it up and studied it. The woman was Twinkie and they were in front of the Bellagio. At the bottom it said, *Vegas Comes to Coupeville*.

"How did you get these pictures?" Bailey asked her aunt. Fiona waved a hand. "I got connections."

Bailey stared at her aunt and tried to imagine what kind of connections a seventy-five-year-old woman living in some obscure little town in Washington state could possibly have. None, she decided. But trying to comprehend how her aunt really could have gotten the pictures was even harder, and she accepted her aunt's explanation.

"Mayor Evans has even agreed to donate five hundred dollars to the prize pot," Fiona said. She looked all pleased with herself. "Gretchen Carlyle over at the salon is donating an entire year of her haircutting expertise to the winner." She gave Carter an appraising look. "I don't know that I'd let her touch a hair on your head, though. She's got cataracts and might cut off something you want to keep."

"I thought you were *sick*," Bailey said.

"One of them game cards might've given me some wrong information. Turns out, all I had was gas from eating your mom's homemade chili." She patted her stomach. "A roll of Tums and I'm a new woman. So which flyer do you like?"

Chapter Twenty-six

In the best interest of the competition, everyone decided on the flyer that showed Twinkie and Carter leaving the Bellagio. Fiona went to make copies and came back an hour later with enough flyers to wallpaper the entire town. She decided it would be best if they worked in teams, and she chose Carter as her partner. That left Bailey with Twinkie, which was okay with Bailey. It'd give her a chance to get to know the woman who she hoped would one day become her sister-in-law.

The two teams spread out and in a few hours the town was abuzz with talk of Coupeville's show of the year, starring *the man* himself. Bailey wondered if that constituted false advertising.

When they finished putting up all the flyers, the four of them met back at Bailey's cottage. Fiona had a healthy glow about her, which Bailey suspected was as a result of spending time with Carter. Carter was the kind of man whose presence could invigorate a woman on her deathbed.

His return was a good thing for all of them. Fiona had found something to occupy her time, besides some evil illness waiting to make its move on her, and Bailey's heart was no longer on the verge of breaking.

"By the way, your mom wants all of you to come over for dinner tonight," Fiona said as she was leaving.

And Olivia had a reason to cook big family meals.

Bailey immediately thought of at least ten reasons why they couldn't make it, the least of which was that she wanted to spend some quality time with Carter that evening. With the competition only a few days away, she wanted to make the most of what little time they had remaining together. It might very well be her last chance to convince him that she was as much the woman for him as he was the man for her.

Fiona must've seen the excuses forming, because she quickly interjected, "I accepted the invitation on your behalf. And bring the show girl. Her presence should liven things up."

Bailey could think of something much more exciting than lively dinner conversation, but evidently Carter liked the idea of another home-cooked meal.

"We'll be there," he said.

She was outvoted.

It'd been a long day for Carter and Twinkie, flying in from Las Vegas and then canvassing the town to hang flyers, and probably it was going to be a long evening. Bailey's mother, no doubt, would do everything in her power to keep Carter in her presence for as long as possible.

Twinkie took a shower, and Carter took the dogs out while Bailey straightened the guest room, put clean sheets on the bed—for Twinkie, she hoped. Carter had, after all, deposited his bag in *her* room.

While he showered, Bailey found Twinkie out on the deck, staring out over Penn Cove. Strands of blond hair whisked about her face with the breeze coming off the water. She didn't have on sunglasses, and that's when Bailey finally saw some family resemblance. She and Carter both had "kind" eyes, with just a touch of past hurt.

Bailey watched Twinkie a moment. She seemed lost in thought.

Bailey slid open the glass door and stepped out onto the deck. "Warm today, huh?" she said. Weather was always a good conversation opener, but she was an idiot. Twinkie had just come from heat that could melt mascara in thirty seconds flat, to a place where it wasn't unusual to still wear a winter coat in June.

Twinkie glanced over at her and smiled gently. "Chilly to me, but I like it." She inhaled deeply. "And I like how it smells here. It's fresh, clean. Relaxing." She continued to stare out over Penn Cove. A gust of cold wind washed over the deck and she wrapped her arms about herself.

Bailey was more than used to the Pacific Northwest's weather, and she barely felt the chill. "I could get you a sweater," she offered.

Twinkie shook her head. "I'm fine."

Okay, they'd talked about the weather. Now what? The only thing they had in common was Carter. And, after all, he was Bailey's favorite subject. "It must seem silly Carter getting so much attention from all the townfolk."

Twinkie laughed gently. "It's always been that way. I've spent a good portion of my life hearing people 'ooh' and 'ahh' over my brother's singing talent." She was quiet for a minute, and then she turned to Bailey. "Carter seems more relaxed here. I think you play a big part in that."

Bailey felt her heart swell. Sisterly approval was a good thing.

"Just don't ever lie to him," Twinkie continued. "Not ever. If you can just remember that one thing, you'll stand a good chance of hanging onto him. If you care to."

Bailey's swollen heart deflated instantly, and she felt the word *liar* raise up in big red letters across her forehead. Perhaps she should have had surgery to restore her virginity while Carter was gone. She gave Twinkie a weak smile.

Five o'clock rolled around and Bailey still hadn't managed to gain any enthusiasm about going to dinner at her mother's. The only good thing was that she wouldn't have to worry about things between her and Carter moving forward sexually. That gave her a few good hours to come up with an acceptable excuse for lying to him.

Olivia's face beamed when everyone sat down at the table. She'd prepared honey-baked ham, au gratin potatoes, and a green salad with homemade blue cheese dressing. She'd also gone over to the Knead & Feed and picked up a marionberry pie, so they could enjoy a low-fat dessert.

"Everyone knows berries are low-cal," she said. "And the crust is so thin, it doesn't even count."

Right.

Twinkie had a better way to prevent caloric intake. "Just say no" was her motto. While everyone else piled food high onto their plates, she took one slice of ham, a small spoonful of potatoes, and plenty of salad with dressing on the side for dipping.

"Sure wish your dad could be here," Uncle Rex said. Olivia and Fiona nodded in agreement. "He'd be so proud of you . . . almost through your second year of school . . ."

All eyes turned to Bailey.

"School?" Carter said.

"We're going to have us a doctor in the family soon," Rex said. He spooned a mouthful of potatoes into his mouth.

"School?" Carter repeated.

Bailey felt her breath catch in her chest. With any luck it was a prelude to cardiac arrest. Now wasn't the time to reveal that she'd quit med school to practice baking pies.

She coughed and gave her mom a pleading look. Her mom was already looking flustered.

"How about we do this again tomorrow night?" Olivia said.

"Sure," Bailey said.

Rex looked from Bailey to Olivia. "Something going on?"

"No," Bailey answered quickly.

"Why do you two look so green around the gills?" Fiona asked. She licked blue cheese dressing from her bottom lip and then looked down at her plate. "Maybe it's something in the salad. Hard to get everything off that lettuce." She stared down at hers and pushed it away.

"The salad's fine, Fiona." Olivia pushed it back.

"Something's up," Rex said. His good eye narrowed, while the other looked up at the light fixture. "Can we expect some kind of announcement from you and Elvis?"

"No," Bailey said. "There is no announcement. Of any kind." She gave her mom a now-see-what-you've-done look.

"It'd be embarrassing to be the last to know," Fiona said. She shoved a mouthful of lettuce into her mouth. "I got word today that Mark Jefferson has entered the competition. He could give you a run for your money," she told Carter.

"Not hardly," Bailey said with a nervous laugh. "Mark is tone deaf."

"Sometimes a person's so busy looking at the pretty package, they don't see what's inside," Rex said.

"Course I guess she already knows what's inside," Fiona said.

"Sweet Jesus," Olivia muttered, and she forked a mouthful of potatoes into her mouth.

Bailey's face filled with heat. She knew how she was going to spend the rest of the evening . . . coming up

with the perfect excuse why they couldn't all get together the following night.

"Lucky for you," Fiona said to Carter, "my niece
dropped that Mark Jefferson like a hot potato when she
found out he couldn't sing like Elvis."

"Now, Fiona, a man doesn't care to hear about a girl's
past," Olivia said.

Bailey slid lower in her chair, and the only thing that
prevented her from sliding all the way under the table was
that every inch of space was already occupied by Tucker
and Maggie May. They were on errant crumb watch.

Carter focused his gaze on Bailey. "You and one of the
Jeffersons?"

"*One?* My niece has gone out with one or the other of
them on and off since high school. That Mark . . . he can't
sing, but he can move. If I were ten years younger . . ."
Fiona glanced over at Rex, whose mouth was stuffed with
ham. He had one eye on his plate and one on the salad
bowl at the end of the table. "I'd let him audition for me."

"Those boys were just toys. She's got the real thing
right here," Olivia said, nodding at Carter.

"Yeah, thanks, Mom . . . Auntie," Bailey said. "I'm sure
Carter isn't interested. And by the way, I only went out
with Mark. Brian and I have never gone out. The two of
you just can't tell the difference between them."

"What about the other night at the cowboy joint? I
heard Brian and you were getting all cozy while Liza and
Mark were out on the dance floor," Fiona said.

Bailey's mouth fell open. "How could you possibly
know about that?" she asked. For someone who rarely
left the house, her aunt sure knew a lot and it was beginning to scare her. "Never mind. Carter and I have to
leave now." Bailey got up.

"What about dessert? It's some of that delicious marionberry pie from over at the Knead & Feed," Fiona said.

Carter pulled Bailey back down.

Bailey groaned. With marionberry pie on the line, it was going to take drastic measures to get Carter out of his chair now. Ever since he'd licked it off her lips, he'd claimed marionberry was his favorite. The only thing she could think to do to get him to leave was entice him with something she knew he wanted more. She reached over to his lap and softly stroked his upper thigh. Carter sat up straighter and slid her a grin.

"We've even got vanilla ice cream," Fiona added.

"We'll stay," Carter said. He gently pushed Bailey's hand off his leg.

Great. He wanted marionberry pie more than he wanted to roll around her bed with her.

Everyone had a large slice of pie, except for Twinkie, who settled for just a bite. At least with everyone's mouth full, the conversation had come to a full halt, but finally, Rex shoved back from the table, rubbing his full belly.

"We got a spare room up there," he said, pointing at the ceiling, and looking straight at Carter with his good eye.

"Twinkie won't mind staying here," Carter said quickly. He gave his sister a smile, and she returned it with a death look and mouthed "I hate you" to him. "Bailey and I have business to discuss," he explained.

"Oh my." Olivia put a hand to her chest and started clearing the dishes.

"'Oh my' is right," Fiona said. "We're going to be the envy of the neighborhood, having a real live show girl stay with us. We could use something to liven this house up."

Stuffed with food and stories that Bailey would rather keep a secret, they set off on foot back to her cottage. Twinkie had to pick up her things and Bailey told her she could drive the T-Bird back to her mom's. Twinkie's anger dissipated somewhat at the offer.

Tucker and Maggie May frolicked alongside them down the street, stopping every thirty seconds or thirty feet, whichever came first, to leave their calling card. It took no more than ten minutes to get back to the cottage, but it was long enough. Bailey was ready for some private time.

So, too, was Carter. As soon as Twinkie had gathered her things and was gone, he grabbed Bailey and kissed her until she trembled. Then she held her breath waiting for his next move. Maybe he'd lift her into his arms, carry her to the bedroom. Or, maybe he'd whisper huskily into her ear how he'd missed her and that he couldn't live without her.

"Give it back, Bailey," he said. Huskily.

"What?" Bailey pushed away from him. He'd just kissed her like they were about to hit the sheets and now here he was telling her to give it back. That damned diamond. She'd been so caught up in his return that she'd completely forgotten about it. Why couldn't he?

Bailey studied his face. First he'd chosen marionberry pie over her, and now a piece of expensive glass . . . and he hadn't even bothered to ask whether she'd taken it or not. He'd simply assumed.

She shook her head in disappointment. "I'll get it for you." She left him standing there—surprised, actually, that he didn't follow her—and she heard him mumble as she went down the hall, something about it being "just business." Maybe it was as the book said, "he just wasn't that into her." It was pretty clear their relationship was not as important to him as it was to her.

Bailey walked into the guest room, and her panic button was pushed when she didn't see the turtle on top of the dresser. Panic morphed into nausea when she looked around and saw a dozen little white tufts of stuffing scattered about the floor. Her heart raced as she picked them up. She could already see Carter's face. It was filled with anger and doubt. He'd think she planned the whole thing.

Bailey looked under the bed, in the closet, in the

nightstand drawer. All she found were a couple of the turtle's little green eggs that were still intact, but there was no sign of the little black bag that held the Azuri diamond.

Maggie May wiggled into the room, all wide-eyed and innocent, but as soon as she saw the green egg in Bailey's hand, her ears dropped and she sat crookedly, avoiding Bailey's stare.

"Oh, no," Bailey whispered with a groan, but Maggie's guilty face said, "Yes."

Keep your cool, she told herself. *Carter will understand. After all, it's not lost. It's just been misplaced. Slightly. People misplace things all the time.* She swallowed. Not things that were worth . . . a lot.

Bailey heard herself whimper. She looked up at the ceiling, said a little prayer, and went out to face Carter.

"Um, I might have some bad news," she said, avoiding the cold hard look in his eyes. And then she saw something that restored hope. More white tufts, sticking out from under the edge of the sofa. She looked closer and saw that it was only another turtle egg. It'd been scrambled.

"Like I was saying . . . I might have bad news," she said to Carter, swallowing dryly. "You see . . . the thing is I had to hide your diamond." Just as she'd imagined, he gave her a suspicious look, which only made her feel like she had to defend herself. "Well, I couldn't very well leave something that valuable lying around in plain sight. I mean, what if someone broke in here and took it?"

"Get to the point, Bailey." Carter wasn't smiling. He wasn't even doing the crooked grin thing.

"Uh . . ." She shrugged. "I think it might be a little while before I can give you back the diamond."

Maggie May sat down next to Carter and burped. He looked at the turtle in Bailey's hand and then at the tufts of stuffing on the floor.

"You mean . . . ?"

Bailey nodded. "Maybe. But don't worry. It'll just take a little while. That little dog can poo. Sometimes she's been known to poo three or four times in one day."

Carter's face screwed up.

"Look at it this way," she said. "At least we know it's safe. We just need to keep an eye on her."

Carter went into the kitchen and Bailey followed him. He scooped two cups of dog food out of a forty-pound bag and dumped it into Maggie's food dish.

"What are you doing? I've already fed her," Bailey said.

"I'm helping things along."

Bailey looked down at Maggie, and Maggie seemed to be in total agreement with Carter's plan. She was sitting in perfect form, waiting for him to set down her food dish. She devoured every last crunchie in less than a minute.

Afterwards, Carter took her outside to do her business, but he wasn't smiling when he came back in. He sank into the sofa, and turned on the TV.

"Now what?" Bailey asked.

"We wait."

Waiting sounded good to Bailey. When people had to wait, they usually got bored and had to find something to do to pass their time. She glanced at Maggie and gave her a silent "thank you."

While Bailey sat there on the sofa next to Carter, planning and plotting what they might do to keep themselves occupied, Carter came up with his own plan of how they'd pass the time. He plugged in Elvis's *Kid Galahad,* claiming that watching the King would help to get him in the right frame of mind for the competition.

From what Bailey could tell, Carter was *always* in the right frame of mind when it came to performing like Elvis. He had everything down to perfection—the singing, the moves, the kissing . . . *Whew!* She was getting overheated just thinking about it.

Even though she'd seen *Kid Galahad* more than a dozen times, she sat quietly next to Carter and, together, they watched Elvis do his thing. Kissing, fighting, kissing some more. It was enough to warm the entire cottage. Even so, every now and then, Bailey took the opportunity to snuggle closer to Carter, until finally, she couldn't get any closer. If she was a real lucky girl, he'd eventually take a hint from Elvis and do his own share of kissing.

But he didn't. He just kept right on watching and punishing her for what he *thought* she'd done. It was too much. The leading lady in the film was getting what she wanted. Why couldn't she?

Bailey sighed. She didn't care about seeing no stinking happy ending. She'd seen it. It was her turn to be kissed, and maybe even fondled. And to hell with her lie about being a virgin. Carter might hate lying, but some insignificant little lie about her being a virgin wasn't going to make one bit of difference in another hour.

And if her lie *did* bother him, perhaps she'd use the abducted-by-aliens-and-used-for-sex-experiments explanation. Bailey almost laughed at the thought. That tactic might work with the Jefferson twins, but Carter was at a different level of intelligence.

Kid Galahad played on, and Elvis started singing some happy song about getting lucky, and it must've made Carter start thinking about his own luck, because he turned and brought his mouth to Bailey's. Then he cupped a hand gently over one of her breasts.

Bailey swallowed. Her heart beat fast and furious as she realized they were both going to get lucky.

Thank you, Elvis.

Carter's mouth moved from Bailey's lips, down onto her throat. He reached up under her shirt, and placed a warm hand over her bare flesh. Desire flared through every inch of her body, and it was just as she'd imagined.

Perfect. Almost. Until Twinkie's warning about not ever lying to Carter forced its way into her head.

Damn.

Soon he'd know, and if what Twinkie had said was true, that would be the end. That stupid little fib could very well ruin what might be the romance of the century. Bailey put a hand to Carter's chest and she gently pushed him away.

Her lips were dry and she licked them before she spoke. "There might be something you should know."

Carter's hands were on her back, moving slowly up toward her bra fastener. They stopped moving mid-back. "Might?"

"Is. There *is* something."

"Would this be more bad news?" Carter's eyebrows raised.

Bailey opened her mouth to speak, but she hadn't quite thought the explanation through. After a long pause, Carter finally brushed back the hair from her face and cupped her chin in his hand.

"Baby, you don't have to worry. I'm not about to do anything you don't want. You just tell me to stop if it gets to be too much."

Carter gave her his much-practiced slightly crooked grin and, Lord help her, she was in far too deep to be able to stop him from doing anything he wanted to do. In fact, in another minute, *he* might have to stop *her.*

The little voice belonging to her conscious continued nagging in the back of her mind, but Bailey's sexual energy was running amok, and she told the little voice to "stick it." The nagging voice disappeared into the drumming beat of her heart.

Carter tightened his arms around her and he spent a good five minutes kissing her into submission, which was pointless, considering she'd been ready to submit ever since he'd shown up on her doorstep. "Get on with it," she wanted to scream. She was running out of patience. And willpower.

"This is no time to be a gentleman," she whispered into his ear. "Undress me."

Carter paused to look into her eyes, and then without a word, he scooped her into his arms and carried her to the bedroom. His own clothes fell from his body into a heap on the floor, and then he started removing Bailey's. Her shirt went flying, her panties soared and landed on her dresser, their flesh mingled into one burning mass of passion.

It was all so easy. And so very very right.

For a tiny second, Bailey struggled with whether or not she should stop him, tell him the truth, but that would only spoil the mood, and besides whenever she opened her mouth, all that came out were gasps and moans.

Carter's lips moved from her stomach to her chest, and he paused to take each of her pink nipples into his mouth. She applauded his effort at taking things slow, but her body had been quivering with anticipation for a while now, and she couldn't wait a moment longer for the sweet promise of release.

Bailey grabbed Carter's head and she looked straight into his eyes. "I want to feel you in me—now."

Carter moved, sliding his body over on top of hers. She was ready. Moist and filled with something beyond desire, she opened her legs to receive him.

"You sure about this?" he asked huskily.

Bailey nodded and he groaned, entering her slowly. She felt him tremble with restraint, and she knew what he was doing. He was making sure she was comfortable her first time. Screw comfort, she wanted passion.

Bailey took a deep breath, dug her fingers into his back, and pulled him to her. She raised her hips to meet his as he pushed himself into her and she pulled even harder, forcing him deeper inside.

"Oh, God," they moaned together.

Bailey gasped. She may not have been a virgin, but it'd been a lifetime since she'd felt anything like this. She was starving for all that Carter was giving, and she lifted her body to meet each of his thrusts. They'd both held out so long that it didn't take them long to reach the crest of the wave, and together they rode it, until finally, they were both swept over the top.

In one final moan, Bailey lay gasping for breath and Carter groaned his approval. After a minute of hushed kisses and love murmurs, he began to stroke her hair. She glanced over to see him smiling.

His eyes were closed. He looked content. So was she.

Then there it was, right there on her pillow, sticking out its tongue at her. That nagging little voice.

Bailey sighed. Had Carter been able to tell? She watched him rest. He remained quiet, but she knew he wasn't sleeping, because he was still stroking her hair. She wanted to ask him what he was thinking, but she'd read somewhere that dumb girlie questions were the one thing that men most hated after sex.

She came up with a dozen things a man like Carter might be thinking at a time like this. *His job . . . the Azuri diamond . . . like hell this woman was a virgin . . .*

Bailey bit her lip. He'd probably slept with enough women to know when he was with a virgin just by kissing her.

She lay there another five minutes. Still, he didn't say a word. If he did suspect her virginity was in question, he obviously wasn't going to say. Of course, he wouldn't. If Carter was anything, he was a true gentleman. That much she knew.

She also knew that having this between them would

always gnaw at her. And that could only mean trouble for their budding romance.

Bailey watched Carter's face for another minute. His eyes remained closed, but he smiled in response to her stare. She narrowed her eyes and silently mouthed "I love you." His smile grew. Oh, God. How the heck would she ever be able to hide anything from this man? She'd never be able to buy a new outfit and keep it in her closet for a month, only to bring it out and claim it was just some old thing. What was she getting herself into?

Carter opened his eyes and turned on his side facing her. "What're you doing over there?"

"Watching you."

He did the crooked grin thing and kissed her nose. "I can think of something more fun than watching me." Another kiss, this time on her lips, then her cheek and . . .

Bailey squirmed away. He'd just had his fire extinguished. Maybe he'd be more receptive to explanations. "Wait," she said. "I really need to tell you something."

"I know," he said, and he kissed her again.

"You know?"

"Mmm, hmm. And it doesn't matter that you haven't really told me until now."

"It doesn't?"

"I've known for a long time."

"You have?"

"A man can tell these things."

Bailey let out a sigh. Almost laughed. She'd been torturing herself all this time, and now here he already knew the truth and he didn't even care.

"Mmm, hmm. A man knows when a woman is in love with him."

Bailey's mouth hung open for a beat. "But—"

Carter put a finger to her lips, and then he leaned in for a kiss.

Chapter Twenty-seven

Carter lay grinning in the dark. Bailey, a virgin? Not if he was any kind of judge. And she hadn't denied loving him either.

He closed his eyes with that thought on his mind and her in his arms. When he opened them again, daylight was peeking through the pale blue curtains that hung soft and flowing in the morning breeze. The window had been left open all night and he could hear the day beginning. Birds twittering, a bell clanging somewhere out on the water, kids playing. A world different from the noisy bustle of Las Vegas mornings on the Strip.

Carter glanced down at Bailey's sleeping face. Smooth and worry free, still unmarred by life. If he took her away from here, that could change.

He blew out a resigned breath. This was her way of life. For a gal like her, going to Vegas for a few days of fun was one thing, but to move there and try to make a life for herself would be nothing short of culture shock. And maybe a shock she'd never get over. She'd had a hard enough time just being at Zoopa's party, having to mingle with people who were like aliens to her. No, she was far too innocent for that kind of life. She'd been stressed over him finding out she wasn't a virgin, for crissakes, as if that would turn him away. He'd known one, but that was so many years ago, he didn't think they existed anymore, beyond the age of sixteen.

Carter held Bailey a little tighter. He brushed his lips across her forehead and she stirred, snuggling closer to him. Her body was warm and perfect and God knew he wanted her again, but if they made a habit out of this, it'd only be that much harder for both of them when he had to leave.

He glanced at the clock. Six A.M. He didn't have anywhere in particular he had to be, but he was so used to rising early that he couldn't sleep any longer. If he was back in Vegas, he'd have a full day ahead of him, taking care of guest complaints . . . making sure guests were having a good time—but not too good . . . rescuing beautiful women from defective shower stalls . . . It was a tough job and he was just the man to do it. Still, it was nice to have a few days off. Maybe if he just shut his eyes . . .

Ten minutes later, he'd only grown more restless. He gently slid his arm out from under Bailey, and started to get up.

"Where are you going?" Bailey asked, her voice heavy with sleep.

"Not far," Carter said. He slipped on his pants and closed the bedroom door after himself.

Tucker had stayed behind without raising his head, but Maggie May followed after him. Good. He needed to keep a close eye on her. Right now, she was the most valuable dog in the state. Maybe the country.

Carter filled her food dish with two cups of Ultra, and then added another scoop for added incentive. She sat waiting, thanking him with big brown eyes. "Here you go, girl," he said, setting the dish before her.

Maggie stuffed her head into her metal dish and didn't lift it until the bowl was licked clean. She looked back up at him, her eyes pleading for more.

"Sorry. As much as I'd like to fill your dish again, your mommy will have my hide if she gets up and finds you've gained five pounds since she last saw you."

Maggie wiggled her chunky body through Carter's legs and he gave her a good back scratch. With all the food she'd eaten in the last twelve hours, no doubt she was ready to do some business. Carter slipped on her collar and leash and took her out for a short stroll.

After fifteen minutes and no luck, Carter and Maggie returned to the cottage. In a final attempt to coerce the happy dog's system into action, Carter tossed her a weight management biscuit.

He was only slightly disappointed that Maggie was being stubborn. Getting the diamond back only meant his time in Coupeville was done. And so, too, was his time with Bailey. It was inevitable, he knew, and he wanted it to be as easy as possible for both of them, so he'd already decided that if he got the diamond back before the show, he'd slip out as soon as he finished his last song, just as Elvis always had. If Maggie remained uncooperative, he'd have to stick around a while longer, maybe another night. But either way, his business in Coupeville would soon be over.

Carter went to the sliding glass door. Penn Cove Bay lay before him, shrouded with a fine mist that was thick like fog. Beautiful, gloomy Pacific Northwest. Local weatherman Rich Marriott had forecast sunbreaks by the end of the day, but by the looks of things right now, it had a long way to go. Washington state was like a lovely woman whose face was only occasionally lit by a smile. Maybe that was it. Maybe Bailey was tired of the gloom. Although if she moved to Las Vegas, she'd only be trading one kind of gloom for another.

Carter squinted into the sky. Was he ready to love again? Would Bailey really leave here? Her home? If he took a chance on her and it turned out all she really needed was a long vacation, he'd be in for a bigger heartache than before, when he'd taken a chance on a spirited redhead.

Carter rubbed the back of his neck. He was still limping from that one.

Bailey waited several minutes before deciding to go look for Carter. She'd hoped he was only getting up to take Maggie out, and that he'd come back to bed, but half an hour had ticked off and he was still a no show.

She found him out on her deck, just standing there staring out over the water—what little of it was visible through the heavy sky. She padded softly over to the door, came up behind him, threaded her arms around his waist. He jumped and she giggled. Him being ever the big bad security guy, it was probably the one and only time that she'd ever get away with sneaking up on him. She snuggled close to his back, feeling safe and warm and satisfied.

She stood on her toes and whispered into his ear, "I waited for you, but you didn't come back, so I thought I might find you out here making me breakfast. Only I don't smell any bacon frying or coffee brewing. What gives?"

Carter turned around and she thought she saw something heavy in his eyes. He held her body snug against his.

"Honey, there's more to me than my ability to maneuver in the kitchen," he said lightly.

Maybe what she'd seen in his eyes was just concern about the show. Although she couldn't see why. He'd had much stiffer competition than he'd ever find in Coupeville. Without a doubt, Carter was the sure winner.

"Want to see more of my abilities?" he asked.

Bailey bit her bottom lip. "I think I might've seen some of those last night. Are there more?"

"Much more." Carter pressed his mouth to hers, and her toes curled into ten tight little balls of flesh.

She giggled and almost lost her balance. "I'm not used to being seduced before I have my morning coffee."

"Get used to it, baby. I do some of my best work in the early morning hours."

"Jesus, are you two still at it?" Liza's voice crackled behind them and they both turned.

Liza was a sight. And not a bad one. She had on pink fluffy slippers and pink baby doll pajamas. Her blond hair stuck up at a sharp angle on one side and from the black smudges beneath both eyes, Bailey surmised she hadn't taken the time to wash off her makeup before hitting the sack. Still, she was glowing.

"I thought you were spending the night with Mark," Bailey said.

"I guess that means neither one of you slept in the guest room," Liza said in return, giving Bailey a way-to-go smile. She stretched her arms toward the ceiling, lifting her tiny nightie to dangerous heights, which gave Bailey and Carter a good view of her mile-long legs.

Bailey suddenly felt self-conscious in her plain, white terry robe. Sure, it was fluffy and white and had a cute little Tweety Bird with ruffled head feathers embroidered over one breast, but it wasn't sexy and little and really really sheer.

Liza Blair could very well be one of the wonders of the world and Bailey admired her guts at being able to show herself barefaced and sleepy eyed to the world, and especially a man, but she just wished Carter wasn't that man.

"Did somebody say something about breakfast?" Liza stuck her nose in the air and sniffed the same as Tucker and Maggie May did when they smelled just about anything.

"Sure, I'll fix you some coffee, bacon, and some of my special scrambled eggs," Carter said.

"Ooh, an offer a girl can hardly refuse," Liza said all

throaty. She fluttered her eyelashes at him in a most feminine seductive way.

Bailey considered getting jealous, but her green hue quickly faded when Mark Jefferson walked into the kitchen.

"Peaches. Elvis," he said, and headed straight out to the deck for a smoke.

Bailey did an eye roll. Probably one day Carter would be asking her about the name Peaches. Would that be cause for one more lie? She pulled a spatula out of a drawer and a fry pan out of a cupboard and handed them to Carter. "Kitchen's all yours."

She and Liza left Carter in the kitchen to do his thing and a few minutes later, the smell of frying bacon made its way all the way to the bathroom. Liza offered to let Bailey use some of her eye lotion and Bailey took her up on it without asking why. She already knew why, but she didn't need to hear it. But, hey, she had a good excuse for the dark circles and lines. She'd had a rough night. The most spectacularly rough night of her life.

Liza's magic potion did a great job of plumping some of the lines that were beginning to feather around Bailey's eyes, but it'd take a lot more than lotion to achieve half the sexiness that Liza had even upon awakening.

"Breakfast is about ready," Carter said from the doorway. He watched Bailey finish with the blow dryer and then pull her hair into a ponytail.

"You're quick," she said. She turned from the mirror and he put his hand around to the back of her head, pulling free the band that held her hair. It tumbled in lazy curls about her shoulders.

"I like you wild," he said. And then he kissed her.

"Jesus, the bacon's gonna burn," Liza said. She brushed past Bailey.

Bailey felt like her furnace had been turned up to ninety. Maybe she was sick. No. She shoved that thought out of her head. She'd been around her aunt far too long. Maybe she wasn't sick or hungry. Maybe she just needed to feel the weight of Carter's body on hers once more.

Carter must've had his super spy guy powers going because he pulled her close and began to nuzzle her hair. She relaxed into his arms, but quickly reminded herself that Liza was just in the next room and Mark was . . .

"Peaches," Mark said behind her.

Bailey rested a hand on Carter's chest. "We've got things to do, places to go—" She gave Mark a look. "People to avoid."

Mark gave her a wide smile and moved on to the guest room.

Carter's teeth grazed Bailey's earlobe. "Ah, honey, I'm doing exactly what I want to do, and I'm already where I want to be."

A whimper escaped Bailey's lips. *What about the people to avoid?* She swallowed and closed her eyes and tried to think of something that would turn off her desire button. The only thing she could think of was the sight of Tucker humping his bed. She giggled and Carter backed up a step.

"Sorry," she said. "I just thought of something funny." She grabbed him by the arm and steered him toward the kitchen. "Let's eat."

Over the next couple of days, it seemed everyone in town was getting ready for the big event. Bailey wasn't even aware her aunt knew how to turn on a computer, let alone actually use one, but Fiona had gotten word out over the Internet somehow, and they were getting responses from as far away as Sedro Woolley. Aunt Fiona never ceased to amaze her.

As the number of potential entrants grew, Bailey became concerned that Coupeville might be overrun with every man, woman, and child who thought they could hold a note, and she suggested to her aunt that she might want to limit the number of people allowed to compete. A town full of Elvis clones might have had some appeal a few weeks ago, but as far as she was concerned, her search for the perfect man was officially over.

The day before the competition, a couple of the local entrants stopped by Bailey's cottage to see if Carter would mind sharing some tips about things like lip curling and leg shakin'. He taught them what he could and then he sent them on their way.

That same evening, while he was practicing singing, a group of women—ages eight to eighty—gathered outside the cottage to listen and maybe get a glimpse of Carter. It soon became clear to Bailey that it wasn't just her mother who was still enchanted by Elvis Presley. The King's magic was never going to die, and she was never going to get a moment alone with Carter until the competition was over.

Carter was attentive to his fans and even more attentive to Bailey, but she still wondered what their future held. She'd told him she loved him, but he hadn't reciprocated, and Bailey feared that as soon as the event was over, he'd leave her behind to pick up the pieces of her broken heart.

While her home may have been somewhat of a madhouse, with fans stopping by at all hours, the other Ventura household was running smoothly. Aunt Fiona hadn't been "sick" for days and Twinkie had settled right in. She seemed to thrive on all the attention she was getting from the men townfolk, which surprised Bailey, considering all the attention she got working the floor at the MGM. Of course, the men in Coupeville enjoyed her company and were happy with just a smile. They didn't expect any kind of free handout.

Now that Carter was sleeping in her bed, Bailey told Twinkie she could come back to the cottage and use the guest room, but Twinkie insisted she was having far too much fun spending time with Fiona. Every afternoon, she and Fiona would dance around the house, doing some show girl dance moves that made Olivia fear Fiona would suffer a broken hip. Olivia didn't complain, though. She was glad to have Fiona distracted from that darn game and having her think she was dying every other day. The way Twinkie and Fiona got along, you'd think they were mother and daughter.

Finally, show day arrived. Carter had eased himself out of bed, no doubt to allow Bailey a couple more hours of sleep, but she was wide awake and eager for the day to begin; not so eager for it to end. She heard Carter singing a soft tune in the shower and she snuggled her face into her pillow. "I Can't Help Falling In Love" rang painfully in her ears and a tear gathered in one eye. He hadn't pledged his love. He was leaving.

The tear slid down the side of her face and onto her pillow. They'd already shared so much—watching old movies, making love, him rescuing her from that shower—it seemed as though they'd known each other for years. How could he leave after all that? Bailey turned her face into her pillow and cried. His departure would leave her with a wound so great she might not recover.

Bailey heard Carter turn off the shower, and she quickly wiped away all evidence that she'd been crying. She lay still and kept her eyes closed.

A minute later, Carter came out of the bathroom smelling of lavender and fresh dampness. His image, all wet and glistening from head to toe, sent a warm flush through Bailey and she ached to have him touch her. She wanted nothing more than to reach out and pull him back into her bed, but that would only make it harder to get through the day. She continued to feign sleep.

She heard his feet pad across the soft carpet and pause next to her bed. A moment later, his lips brushed across her cheek. Bailey's heart pounded. If he didn't leave soon her willpower would disintegrate. She forced her breathing into a steady flowing rhythm, although she didn't know why. Probably he was reading her mind before she could even think.

Finally, he left.

She didn't get up right away. Instead, she lay there quietly and tried to imagine how life with a man like Carter might be. The past week had been great, but it was only a glimpse, a mere shadow, of how day-to-day life with him might look. Based on the chemistry they shared, she could well imagine their lives would include plenty of TLC, but there would also be trying times.

He'd get up early for his security guy job, she'd get up and go to her bake shop to create some delectable goodies, and then they'd meet later for lunch or a little afternoon delight. In the evening, they'd have a romantic dinner with candlelight and soft music and then he might have to leave to do a quick show. All the women in the audience would offer themselves to him and he'd touch their hair or their cheeks and they'd scream and hyperventilate . . . maybe even grope him. Then he'd come home and nibble leftover cookie dough from her hair and they'd start to kiss . . . and then the door would burst open! Frank Zoopa would be standing there with two big gorilla-looking guys. "Where's my diamond?" he'd demand.

Bailey sprang upright, her pulse racing. She looked about her room, and sank back against her pillows with a sigh. She heard sounds in the kitchen and soon after got a whiff of strong coffee.

Liza had come back for the big event, just as she'd promised, though Bailey suspected a big part of her reason for returning could be blamed on Mark Jefferson. Probably he could be blamed for the rosy glow that filled Liza's cheeks, too. Liza was so deep in love or lust or whatever that she couldn't even hear how awful Mark's voice was.

Love. It was a funny thing. It had a way of closing one's eyes to the truth, even when it stared you straight in the face.

Bailey wondered if her eyes had been closed by love. Could be, but they were happily closed, and she had no intention of ever opening them.

She and Liza shared some girl talk over coffee, and then they both squeezed out onto Bailey's one-person deck and whiled away the afternoon. An hour before showtime, Liza disappeared into the guest room, and came out twenty minutes later looking like a supermodel. Bailey looked down at her bouncy little skirt and tank top and then immediately went back to her room to change. This was her last chance to work her magic on Carter, so she had better make it good and show him what he'd be missing.

Ten minutes later, Bailey reappeared wearing something darker, sexier, and much shorter: a black dress, with sequins that clung to her curves and draped seductively at the mound of her breasts. When she moved, the sequins caught the light and sent shimmery prisms of color bouncing off the walls. Not bad, until she stood next to glamour puss Liza.

Bailey glanced around her cottage before she and Liza headed out. This is where it'd happened. She may have already been falling in love with Carter before she and Carter had arrived in Coupeville, but this was where it had all happened. She felt strangely euphoric, and deeply apprehensive. How would the night end? She sighed and looked at her watch. In a few hours, she wouldn't need to wonder. Carter would either ask her to go back to Vegas with him or he'd give her one last kiss and tell her "good-bye."

Bailey took a deep breath and sighed. It would do her no good to think the worst. If she had nothing more to come home to than heartbreak hotel, then she was at least going to spend their last evening together pretending they still had forever.

Chapter Twenty-eight

Carter spent the day making sure everything concerning the show was in order. Bailey didn't know it, but he'd made a few calls and called in some favors and tonight's show was going to be a big surprise for everybody. Uncle Rex was in on the whole thing, but he'd told Carter they'd better keep quiet about it, or Fiona would be down at the salon spilling to everyone.

When Carter was comfortable that things were running smoothly, he grabbed a cup of coffee and sat down to take a load off his tired feet. His thoughts immediately turned to Bailey and her odd behavior that morning. He chalked it all up to love. Love and nerves. Girls did all kinds of weird or goofy things when they were in love. But being in love didn't explain why Bailey had pretended to be asleep when he left the house that morning. He shook his head. No sense in worrying about it. Being a man meant he'd never really understand women, anyway. Another good reason to think twice before pledging his troth to another. Lame excuse, and he knew it. Hell, he could come up with a hundred reasons for staying single, and they'd all be just as lame. Except maybe for his number one reason: Irene. After that fair redhead had doled out her punishment, he never thought he'd see the day when his guard would be lowered and he'd let love take him for another ride.

Carter swallowed hard and fought to wipe Irene's image from his mind. Just thinking about taking a chance on that kind of pain again made him wince. He took in a heavy breath and blew it back out. He hadn't had to worry about it until now, but if any woman was worth taking a chance on, it was Bailey. The only question was, how quickly would Bailey tire of the adventure and want to come back home?

The auditorium was in a frenzy. Good thing they'd decided to move the event from the Hall to the high school. The Hall was good for events, like small wedding receptions and such, but tonight's event had grown in magnitude, until they'd had to turn people away. In all her years of living in Coupeville, Bailey had never seen such a turnout for any event. Even the annual crafts fair during a bout of good weather couldn't compete. Her Uncle Rex had cut the number of entrants down to twelve men and one woman. Thirteen total and that only added to Bailey's discomfort—thirteen being unlucky and all—but the auditorium held 412, which added up to seven, so that evened things out.

She sat in the front row, with Twinkie and Liza on her right, and she saved three seats on her left for her mom, Aunt Fiona, and Rex. After only a minute, Liza began fidgeting in her seat. Finally, she got up and headed toward the stage. Bailey caught her arm. "You won't find any slot machines back there."

Liza did an eye roll. "Can a girl go pee?"

"Bathroom's thataway." Bailey jutted her thumb over her shoulder.

"I'm taking the scenic route."

Bailey let her go. Probably Liza wanted to give

Coupeville's man most likely to father children out of wedlock some final words of encouragement. At least he was no longer trying to fill his hands and mind with *her.* For the moment.

It was a good thing they'd arrived early, because in only ten minutes most every seat in the place was filled. A wave of cool air brushed across the back of Bailey's neck and she looked over her shoulder. Lea Townsend and Mary Appleton were sitting right behind her and every time a dark-haired man in a jumpsuit crossed the stage, they fanned themselves with their programs.

The contestants milled about in attire from various stages of Elvis's career and the local women were watching them like they were going to swoop in for the kill at any moment. Some of the entrants stretched, some were warming up their vocal cords—although from what Bailey could hear, it'd take a lot more than just a quick warm-up to help some of the voices.

Bailey caught a glimpse of Carter backstage. He was sitting quietly by himself. He'd gone for the black leather look, and she was glad. If this was to be her last night with him, she couldn't think of any other image she'd rather have than him in black—and leather. She closed her eyes and could almost smell his scent, fresh morning shower soap, with a touch of cow hide. It gave her ideas about taking him home right then, so they could relive the events of last night. Bailey sighed.

An Elvis in a white jumpsuit walked by and Bailey did a double take. *Steve Sogura?* It couldn't be. She squinted up at the stage. Steve looked her way and gave her a crooked grin. Two other impersonators, also wearing jumpsuits, walked past. Daryl Bachman? Quent Flagg? What the heck was going on? What had been in her afternoon tea?

She glanced over at Carter, still sitting by himself in a chair at the back of the stage. He looked up and smiled in her direction. Her heart jumped. *He'd* done this. For her. Or, maybe for her aunt. No matter. He was an angel among men, and he'd just told her in his own way that he loved her.

Aunt Fiona and Olivia arrived and took two of the vacant seats to the left of Bailey, but Uncle Rex remained backstage to coordinate. Bailey suspected her aunt liked that arrangement. She could ogle the contestants without Rex giving her the wild eye.

Five minutes before show time Liza returned to her seat and she immediately pulled out a tube of lipstick and a small mirror from her handbag.

"You applied about ten coats before we left the house. What happened?" Bailey asked.

"Kissed off," Liza said. She puckered into the mirror and smeared a fresh layer of color over her full lips. She checked her hair as best she could in the compact mirror and then tucked it away and folded her hands in her lap, looking somewhat like an obedient child sitting in a church pew.

Bailey chuckled to herself. *That'd be the day.*

"I wouldn't mind having my lipstick kissed off," Fiona said. "Only I don't wear lipstick anymore since it started running into the lines around my lips. Makes me look like I cut myself shaving."

At exactly eight P.M., Mr. Riley from Riley & Forester Accounting came out and stood center stage. He fumbled for a moment with several sheets of paper, then began his introduction of the evening's program. Bailey looked ahead in her own program and saw that Quent Flagg was first up.

As soon as Mr. Riley finished the introduction, Quent sprinted onto the stage. He was young, energetic, a serious contender in the big competitions. He had on a royal blue jumpsuit, which he filled out nicely in all the right places, and before he even sang one note of "Follow That Dream," the screaming started and a pair of panties sailed overhead, landing on the stage at his feet. As he moved about the stage, the blue gemstones on his even darker blue jumpsuit glittered crisp and clear like stars in a wintry night sky. Great song choice, since watching him was like a dream.

"Damn," Liza said, "I think I could very well follow *that* dream." She fluttered long eyelashes when Quent approached the edge of the stage. He tossed out a blue silk scarf and Liza grabbed it like a frog snatching a mosquito from mid-air. She held it tightly in her fist lest anyone should have any ideas about trying to relieve her of her prize.

The crowd went wild, the screams rising in such volume that Bailey couldn't be sure where one song ended and the next began. Quent eased into "Are You Lonesome Tonight?" and Fiona leaned over and shouted in Bailey's ear, "I might be lonesome tonight if I thought he'd do something about it."

By the time Quent finished the song, women were weeping. As he took a bow, they begged for more.

Coupeville's own Max Cooper, resident pharmacist, was up next. Max was scheduled to sing only one song, "It's Now or Never," and it was a good thing. The ladies weren't quite as enamored with him as they had been with Quent. Especially Fiona.

"Make it never," she shouted at the stage. "Old coot, can't even get the labels right on my prescription bottles."

Bailey grinned, feeling slightly guilty. Poor Max. Per her instructions, he'd been filling Fiona's bottle with sugar pills, and he was always so nervous about it that his hands shook terribly while he affixed the labels.

"He's doing the best he can," Bailey said, giving Fiona a nudge. Her aunt was right about Max's voice, though. If he'd been performing at the *Gong Show*, he'd have already been yanked from the stage.

Fiona booed through her hand and Bailey slid deeper into her seat. She held her program up in front of her face, but that only seemed to spur Fiona on. She stood and shouted through her rolled-up program for him to take a fall, anything to get him offstage.

Olivia pulled Fiona back down into her seat. "Now you sit there and behave yourself. Don't make me take you home."

That seemed to do the trick. No way did Aunt Fiona want to miss the show. She tucked her hands under her legs and watched the remainder of Max's performance with her lips pulled into a tight grimace.

"I'm going to run to the bathroom," Liza said to Bailey. "When is your man up?"

Bailey gave her a why-didn't-you-go-before look. "He's two away, after Daryl Bachman and Mark. If you can hold it and go after Daryl, you'll probably save your hearing. Besides, you don't want to miss Daryl. He puts on quite a performance."

Liza waved a hand and got up. "Honey, they're all Elvis to me. Besides, I'll be back before he finishes his first song."

All Elvis? Hardly, Bailey silently scoffed. Maybe other so-called fans couldn't tell them apart, but that's where she and they differed. She was confident that if she sat through ten performances with her eyes closed, she'd be able to name each artist.

A wig flew overhead onto the stage and Bailey looked back to see Maxine Cooper, Max's wife, gazing lovingly up at her husband. Bailey surmised that she, too, was afflicted by the love virus—deafened instead of blinded—even though they'd been married for over thirty years.

At the end of his performance, Max ripped off his Elvis wig and sideburns and used one of his silk scarves to mop his forehead. He tossed it out to the audience and everyone in its path leaned aside so Maxine could get it. She held it to her bosom and mouthed "I love you" to her husband.

Bailey sighed . . . to find love like that.

Max Cooper bowed and left the stage, amidst plenty of clapping and only one or two boos, but all in all he seemed pretty satisfied with his performance.

Daryl Bachman was next, and he swept onto the stage without pause, before the auditorium had quieted from the previous performance. He had on a white jumpsuit, with plenty of multi-colored gemstones, and a cape was attached to his back that made him look like he was about to take off in flight. To show it off, he strutted around for a full minute, and when he'd given everyone a good look, he whipped it off and tossed it to someone over at the side of the stage.

"Shoppin' Around" was Daryl's first song, a short, lively tune that most of the audience wasn't familiar with. Bailey smiled. She knew the song. It'd been recorded for Elvis's movie *GI Blues*, but unfortunately had never been used.

Even though the audience didn't know the song, they didn't waste any time adding to the growing pile of lingerie.

In just under three minutes, Daryl did a smooth change of course and went softly into "Separate Ways." Bailey heard a sniffling sound to her left and she looked over at her mother. A tear slid down Olivia's cheek, and Bailey slipped an arm around her shoulder.

Poor woman. Much of Elvis's music, especially his ballads, had that effect on her and she just couldn't help getting emotional.

"It just shows how honest a singer he is," Olivia said. "My family could take some lessons on that particular subject."

Bailey agreed—on both counts. When Elvis sang, he sang with all his heart and soul as if his words really meant something, and yes, it was about time she was honest with her Uncle Rex about quitting school.

Daryl ended the sadness and his set with "Burning Love." He gyrated, perspired, and swiveled his hips about the stage until women were ripping at their hair and nearly frothing at the mouth. If he didn't stop singing soon, Bailey thought she might have to put her CPR skills to use.

Liza returned just in time to see Daryl's grand finish. "You didn't tell me this guy was so flexible . . . or young . . . or good-looking. I'd have made sure I didn't miss one note out of that perfect mouth," she said, practically purring her approval.

"There are only two things you need to know about Daryl Bachman," Bailey shouted between screams. "He's married and it's happily."

Liza's lips pooched into a pout.

"Besides," Bailey said, "you've got your own Elvis wannabe—Mark."

Liza gave Bailey a you've-got-to-be-kidding look. "Mark may be cute and, heaven knows, he's got some moves, but we both know what's going to happen when he gets up on that stage."

"Booing and gnashing of teeth?" Bailey said.

Liza nodded.

Daryl left the stage, and Mark rushed out in front of the cheering audience like a pro. He even did a pretty good job of gyrating from one side of the stage to the other. Then he opened his mouth. Five notes later, the screaming stopped, and everyone stared. Probably in disbelief.

Bailey looked down at her program. He was supposed to be singing "Stuck on You," but the only thing he seemed to be stuck on was how to sing in tune. Even so, the townfolk gave him some polite applause when he finished, but Bailey suspected it was simply because he was one of only two men in town who could fix their cars.

Perhaps he could be a dancer if he ever decided he didn't want to be a grease monkey anymore.

Finally, it was Carter's turn to do his thing. Bailey's heart raced in anticipation. A minute went by, then two, then the audience began stomping their feet and chanting. *Elvis, Elvis, Elvis.*

Bailey looked two seats down at Twinkie. Twinkie's fingers were interlaced and her legs were crossed and she was pumping one foot in short little jerks. Her forehead was creased and Bailey suddenly got that something-isn't-quite-right feeling.

This is silly, Bailey thought. They weren't in Las Vegas, land of hit men and thieves, after all. She tried shaking the feeling of doom away.

Another minute ticked off, and Bailey's own foot started pumping.

The audience kept stomping their feet and the chanting grew louder. Some of the audience members were claiming fraud. They'd come to see Elvis, and they weren't leaving until he showed. Bailey's heart swelled with pride. All these *Elvises* and the only one they wanted was Carter.

Another minute ticked by and that nasty little uneasy feeling took hold again. She finally glanced over at Liza.

Liza shrugged. "I saw him out front talking to some man when I went to the bathroom. Looked like a football player of some sort. Wide receiver if I had to guess. I didn't eavesdrop, but now that I think about it, I probably should've. Neither of them looked very happy."

The bottom of Bailey's stomach dropped out. A thread of something related to fear skittered up her back. *Football player? Wide receiver?* A man fitting that description had recently run his callused fingers up her legs.

My God, she thought, *big city crime has come to Coupeville.* And she'd brought it. Bailey had a fleeting vision of being buried in the Las Vegas desert and she gave silent thanks that there wasn't any sand to speak of on the beaches in Coupeville. Oh, she'd wanted some adventure in her life, all right, but murder and mayhem weren't exactly what she'd had in mind.

Bailey whipped her head around. The auditorium's double doors were closed. "I'll be right back—I hope," she told Liza. She got up. "If I'm not back in my seat in two minutes, call the Whidbey Island Air Force."

Bailey was halfway up the aisle when Twinkie caught up with her. Bailey paused. How much did little sister know? "I'm just going to take a look out front," she told Twinkie.

Twinkie put a hand on Bailey's arm. "I know these men," she said sullenly.

Gulp.

Bailey wasn't sure what two skinny women could do against a man built like a gorilla, but she wasn't about to leave Carter out there alone if he needed help. She swallowed her fear and, together, she and Twinkie pushed through the double doors.

The doors swung closed behind them, and Bailey's ears rang with relief. They felt like they were plugged with cotton from all the screaming and stomping and yelling. She had no idea old people could make such a racket.

She and Twinkie walked through the outer lobby area, where Liza had said she'd seen Carter. No Carter, no gorilla. But the good thing was, there were also no signs of violence. Bailey stopped outside the men's bathroom door and listened. A toilet flushed and moments later an elderly man emerged.

"Good show, huh?" he said.

Bailey smiled and nodded.

"Let's look outside," Twinkie said.

Outside certainly seemed like the next logical place to look, but Bailey suddenly felt like she had to throw up. Then she remembered Carter's lips on her cheek that morning, and it gave her strength. This was no time to desert her man. She stood taller and took a deep breath. "Okay, let's go," she told Twinkie, pushing open the heavy wooden door.

Chapter Twenty-nine

Carter was over at the far side of the parking lot standing under a flickering pole lamp. The bad news was Liza was right: Carter was talking to a big angry-looking man.

There was no good news.

But there was badder news: the big angry-looking man had friends. Two of them. One of whom was the guy she'd almost had an involuntary intimate encounter with, in the middle of the desert. The other one was Frank Zoopa.

Twinkie crouched behind an older model Ford pickup truck and Bailey followed her lead, figuring she had more experience in these types of situations, her being a bona fide Las Vegas resident and all. With over a ton of protective metal shielding her, Bailey felt bravery rear its head and she peeked around the truck's slightly bent chrome bumper.

The light continued to flicker above the men, giving an eerie strobe effect to their faces. Zoopa had his finger in Carter's chest, jabbing at it vigorously. He wasn't nearly as tall as his two friends, but he was twice as intimidating.

Power was a scary thing.

"Where's my diamond?" Zoopa asked Carter. Even with the light strobing, Bailey could see a pulsating vein in the side of his neck.

Carter sneered and it wasn't the same sneer he used on Bailey when he wanted to make her heart flip. It was the kind that makes a man want to shove another man's teeth down his throat.

Bailey got a sick feeling in her gut. This was no time for Carter to be macho. Couldn't he see he was outnumbered? Not that he'd care.

"You hard of hearing? I told you, *Mr. Azuri's* diamond is back in Vegas," Carter answered Zoopa.

Zoopa raised his right arm and Bailey squinted in helpless horror as she watched him bring back his fist and unload it against Carter's face. She and Twinkie both sucked in a lungful of air, but Twinkie quickly put a finger to her lips, and Bailey pinched off a scream.

Carter spit out some blood and Bailey turned her head. When she dared look again, Zoopa had his fist raised for another strike. *Just tell him!* she wanted to shout. *Tell him for God's sake!* She hung her head, squeezing her eyes shut.

Twinkie placed a reassuring hand on her shoulder. "Carter can handle himself. He'll be okay," she whispered.

The men were huddled together and if one didn't know better, one might think it was a group of men out for a night without their women. Only that would be strange in Coupeville, seeing as there was nowhere to go for a night out.

A clicking sound echoed through the air, forcing another gasp from Bailey. She'd heard sounds like that before. Once on TV, while watching *Third Watch*, and then another time, when Carter checked his gun, while they were being stalked on their way home from Vegas.

She glanced over at Twinkie for some more reassurance. Fat chance. Even Twinkie's face had that aghast alarmed look. Her eyes had nearly doubled in size.

Queasiness took hold of Bailey's stomach and she tipped back onto the gravel. She froze where she sat, holding her breath. Twinkie looked at her and then they both looked over at the group of men. Carter made no indication he'd heard anything, but Zoopa's goons were staring in their direction.

Shit!

Bailey's heart thumped so hard she thought it might bruise the inside of her chest. If the night continued like this, both she *and* Carter might need CPR before it was over. How had this happened? She was just Bailey Ventura, small town girl with big city dreams. This had to be a bad joke. She took a quick glance around the parking lot, half expecting someone to pop over and tell her to smile at a bush, tell her she'd just been "punked."

No such luck.

Zoopa made a motion with his head and one of the goons walked toward the truck. Bailey shuddered as fear snaked a path down her back. Time was up. She had no choice but to confront the men who were beating up on her man.

"It's Now or Never" screamed inside her head as she counted. At three, she took a deep breath, and then popped up from behind the truck.

"I seem to have misplaced one of my earrings." She hiccuped once and pretended to search the ground. She took a couple of steps toward the men, adding a slight tilt to her walk for added effect.

"Get the fuck outta here," one of the men said—the one who'd come close to fondling her. His eyes showed no recognition when he looked at her. Well, it had been awfully dark out there in the middle of the desert.

"Huh?" she said, hiccuping again. She pretended to steady herself on the hood of the truck. "I'll have you know I belong here."

"This is private business. Go back inside."

Bailey leaned to one side and squinted at the man. Then she squinted at the others. "What kinda business?

Can a girl join in? I've been known to be a helpful kinda gal at times."

"Drunken bitch. We don't need no help. Go back inside."

The man stepped toward Bailey and she moved over in front of the truck. Twinkie shuffled in the gravel behind her, going around to the other side of the truck. The goon closed in and grabbed Bailey's arm. He turned her roughly toward the building, but she pulled her arm free and glanced over her shoulder at the others.

"Hey, you," she said, looking at Carter. "Why aren't you inside? I think it's your turn to perform? You got stage fright or somethin'?" She hiccuped loudly and put a hand over her stomach. "I don't feel so good," she said, staring straight into Carter's eyes. "Would you be so good as to help me to the bathroom?" She flung out an arm and pointed toward the door. "It's right in there."

"He's not going anywhere," Frank said to her. He made a head gesture and the goon took hold of her arm again, squeezing her flesh in his fingers like it was soft butter.

Bailey winced. If she *had* been drunk, the pain being inflicted on her right then would be enough to sober her right up. Yesiree. She frowned, looking down at her arm. "That hurts, y'know."

Carter made a move to come to her aid, but Zoopa's other man halted him with a gut punch. Bailey heard a whoosh of air being expelled from Carter's lungs. Now she really *did* feel sick. No doubt about it, she and Twinkie were no match for these guys. They needed help.

"Fine. I think I'll just go back inside now." Bailey turned toward the door. "I can find the toilet myself."

"Wait," Zoopa shouted to her.

She stopped and waited.

Frank walked over to her and his squinty little eyes squinted up even more as he examined her face. "I've seen you somewhere. Yes, I do believe we've met."

Bailey shook her head. "No, sir. I don't think so."

Frank studied her a moment longer before his mouth spread into a wide grin. "Little lady, you've arrived just in time." He took one of her hands in his and kissed the back of it. "It's nice to see you again, *Ms. Ventura*."

Bailey made a mental note to disinfect her hand as soon as she got home. She stepped back and her leg hit the truck's bumper. Trapped. "Sorry to say I can't say the same, *Mr.* Zoopa," Bailey said. She could almost smell the evil on him, and she was suddenly thankful that they were far from the deep desert sand. Coupeville did have plenty of water, though, and it was plenty deep and she supposed that for these men, a watery grave for their enemies would probably suffice.

"She's got no part in this," Carter spoke up. He shrugged away from Zoopa's men, and this time they let him go to Bailey.

With Carter's warm body next to hers, Bailey felt safer. A teensy bit. She still had plenty of sweat running down her back, though.

"Your boyfriend's got two things of mine, and I want 'em back."

Bailey hitched her chin. She was ready to admit nothing and deny everything, if that's what it would take to protect Carter.

"You're out of your league, little lady," Zoopa said. He chuckled and looked at Carter. "Doesn't she know she's out of her league?" His eyes narrowed. "Two things: my diamond and your sister. You say the diamond's back in Vegas. We can deal with that. Now where's Twinkie?"

"Right here," Twinkie said. She stepped out from behind the truck. "I'm done with this boring little shit hole. Watching the waves roll in and out . . . smelling this putrid salt air. Let's go home, Frank." She made her way over to them and stood beside Zoopa, greeting him with a light kiss on the cheek.

"Was your brother telling the truth? Is the diamond back in Vegas?"

Twinkie smiled. "It is. I convinced Carter it would be in his best interest to return it to you. He only came back here for *her*," Twinkie said, nodding disdainfully in Bailey's direction. "She doesn't know anything. Carter made me come with him. He seems to think he can tell me what to do just because he's my brother." She glared at Carter. "I'm tired of you bullying me."

"Let's get the show on the road," a voice shouted from across the parking lot.

Everyone turned.

Bailey sucked in some air. *Great*. Her Aunt Fiona stood in the doorway of the auditorium, and her mom was with her, peering over her shoulder.

With the door open, she could hear "Suspicious Minds" winding down inside. Bailey recognized the singer as Johnny Thompson. Johnny was last on the program. They'd skipped over Carter.

"They're gonna put the show on hold for a few minutes. We told 'em we'd go and find you two. We don't have enough seats left for your friends, though," Fiona said.

Bailey knew if she didn't do something to get the situation resolved so that Carter could get up on that stage, her mother and aunt, and probably a whole lot of townfolk, would soon be joining them in the parking lot. That might not be such a bad idea. Frank Zoopa probably wasn't in the mood to fight the entire town, but that might force him into taking his business elsewhere—and Carter with him.

Bailey chewed her lip. "We'll be right there," she said, waving to her aunt. "Just meeting a couple of Carter's friends from Las Vegas."

"Make it quick. I've got friends in there that have paid good money to see Elvis."

Fiona and Olivia ducked back inside and Bailey

turned to Zoopa. "At least let Carter finish the show. If you're worried about him running off, have your bullies watch the doors. There are two side ones and a back." Carter gave her a look and she gave herself a scolding. *Way to help the bad guys, Bailey.*

Zoopa grinned. "I always enjoy a good show."

As it turned out, the bad guys didn't need any help. They walked right inside like they belonged there and one of them even took the empty seat next to Twinkie. Mr. Winston wasn't going to like that. He'd vacated his seat, probably to go use the bathroom.

A minute later, Mr. Winston did indeed return, and Zoopa's goon gave him a "get lost" look. Old man Winston returned the goon's look with a scowl and he retreated back up the aisle. Bailey prayed he'd gone out to his car to get a shotgun.

"Last to be performing tonight is a man some of us have already had the pleasure of getting to know over these past couple of weeks," the MC said. "And if she's smart, our own Bailey Ventura will manage to convince him to stick around so we can get to know him even better."

"Here, here," a handful of women shouted from the audience.

The MC continued. "Maybe we'll even have some baby Elvises running around town one day." He gave Bailey a thumbs-up.

Bailey choked on her own spit and slid low in her seat, while her aunt and her mother clapped their hands with determined vigor. The entire audience cheered and Bailey slid lower, until her knees were almost touching the floor.

She could see Carter through the gap in the curtain preparing for his performance. He was warming up, and hadn't seemed to hear. He shook both arms loosely at his sides and then he started on his legs, ending with a couple of karate moves. He paused just before coming out, and looked in her direction with a devilish grin.

Bailey felt a rosy glow fill her cheeks. Maybe he *had* heard what the MC said.

In theory, marrying a man like Carter was exactly what she'd been hoping for—wanting—all her life. Problem was, she had a few stipulations when considering a man for marriage material. First, he couldn't be a jewel thief or a bank robber or some such sort. Second, his odds of staying alive to see their children grow to adulthood had to be greater than fifty-fifty. Things weren't looking so good for Carter in either area.

Carter entered the stage in a brisk walk. He'd put on enough makeup to cover any bruising on his face, and he looked straight at Bailey and mouthed the words "I love you." The crowd continued to cheer, but the cadence of Bailey's heart was like a bass drum—strong and steady—and the cheers from the audience faded into the background. Maybe her stipulations for a husband weren't that important after all.

Carter stood silent, waiting for a long minute, until the audience fell into a hush. Only the sound of Bailey's heart and a few coughs and sniffles remained, and then the auditorium was filled with the purest, sweetest voice she'd ever heard come out of any Elvis tribute artist. "Wonder of You" had every woman in the place holding her breath, and their hands to their hearts.

Bailey's mouth went dry. Carter didn't look away from her the entire song and, when he finished, everyone in the auditorium was looking at her, too. *Please, God. Let the earth open up and swallow Frank Zoopa,* she prayed. Carter had stolen her heart, soul, and every other body part, and she wasn't ready to take them back.

The music kicked into high gear and, in seconds, Carter had the house rockin' to "Viva Las Vegas." From there he gyrated his way into "Burning Love" for a hot and heavy finish that included some heavy sweating from him, and a lot of panting from the female portion of the audience.

The room swayed, women screamed, and Bailey felt like she was the luckiest girl in the world. She ducked as an object sailed over her head and landed on the stage. Black panties. Big enough for a woman twice her size.

Bailey looked over her shoulder. Gretchen Carlyle, Mary Appleton, and Lea Townsend were all in various stages of undress. *Zing* went Lea's leopard print bra.

Caught up in the heat of the moment, Bailey considered ripping something of her own off, to add to the growing heap on stage, but she quickly reconsidered when Fiona stood up and rolled back her arm. A second later, a pair of bright red panties flew from Fiona's fist. Bailey grabbed the back of her dress and pulled her down into her seat.

"Don't worry, dear. They weren't mine," Fiona said.

Bailey raised an eyebrow.

"They're yours. You left them at the house a while back, after doing your laundry." Fiona peered at Bailey over the top of her glasses. "I expect your guy will know where they came from."

Bailey felt her face grow hot, and she was glad the auditorium lights were down low. She placed a hand over her forehead and tried to make herself invisible. This wasn't exactly the image she wanted Twinkie to have of her family. Or Carter either, for that matter, although it was a little late for both. Carter had seen enough to know just about anything could happen with the Ventura clan, and Twinkie, well, she'd spent the night at her mom's house. No further explanation necessary.

Still, for some reason, Bailey had wanted to hang on to her idea of what she thought a family should be. And then it hit her, her family was special. So what if her mom was crazy in love with the ghost of Elvis Presley; she was brave for sticking to her own ideas about whether or not he was still alive. And Fiona . . . she provided all of them with much needed laughter. Then there was Uncle Rex, the one who kept all of them looking straight ahead, even though he himself couldn't physically do that.

Bailey sat up straight in her seat. She had no reason to be embarrassed. Her family was perfect, and Twinkie and Carter would make a nice addition to her world. That is, if they got out of this ordeal alive.

She took a quick glance over to the seat on her right.

Twinkie was gone.

And so was the goon.

Bailey turned and scanned the crowd. Heads were bobbing, arms were waving, it was a regular rave, but there was no sign of Twinkie or even any of Zoopa's men guarding the door. She turned back to the stage.

Carter was gone now, too.

And so were her red lace panties.

Bailey smiled for a brief second—Carter really did know her—and then she was filled with cold fear.

Although she'd believed, albeit briefly, that Carter had used her to get the diamond out of town, she was now convinced he cared deeply for her—maybe even loved her. That being the case, he wouldn't just disappear, not without pulling her into his arms and kissing the breath out of her. Not without telling her he'd be back.

The hair on her arms stood so stiff it hurt. She didn't have to wonder where Zoopa and his men had taken Carter. Her mind raced with thoughts that were mostly gruesome. This was not going to end well for one side of the party, and though Carter's side was outnumbered, she was confident he had more tricks up his sleeve than the dark side, and that all would turn out well. Maybe.

Bailey rubbed her arms, pushing the little hairs back into place. If only there was something she could do to help, but if she called the police, it might cause Carter even more trouble. He had stolen a diamond, after all.

She sighed helplessly. The only thing she could do was

trust that Carter really was the super security guy she'd always believed him to be.

"You coulda taken a minute to say good-bye to your honey," Zoopa told Carter. "I'm not entirely heartless." He chuckled raspily.

"Tell that to my family," Carter said. He leaned against the rail of the Whidbey ferry and stared out over a sheet of black that was Puget Sound. The night was cold and the air damp, but through his anger, Carter barely felt the wind biting into his skin. The first time he'd breathed Washington air, he was surprised at its clean, refreshing smell, just the opposite of Vegas's stagnant, heat-cooked air. But, right now, with Zoopa standing on one side of him, and his hired hands on the other, Washington's air was rancid, unfit for breathing.

"Your sister's in this mess 'cause you brought her into it." Frank flicked his cigarette into the ferry's wake and its orange glow was snuffed out before it hit the glassy rippling water.

Chapter Thirty

It was two A.M. by the time Carter and Twinkie arrived back in Vegas with their escorts. They walked through an employee entrance at the side of the casino and the stench of cigarette smoke hit them like a blast of summer heat. Carter had almost forgotten how bad it was to be surrounded by that smell. Even with a state-of-the-art ventilation system that poured in a continuous supply of fresh air, it permeated the atmosphere. In just a few minutes, he'd need a shower to get the stink out. That's one thing he could add to his list of things he wouldn't miss if he ever left Vegas.

The Oasis was alive with activity. Slot bells were ringing, a table of card players were shouting with excitement over a win, and the voices of hundreds of people melded together to create a steady roar of noise. A couple more hours and things would wind down to a dull buzz. Even die-hard gamblers had to get a little sleep.

Sleep. That was something he probably wouldn't be getting tonight. Odds were, Bailey wasn't sleeping either. Carter imagined her lying in bed waiting to hear from him, wondering where he was, what was going on, if she'd ever see him again.

Stan Truman, pit boss and good friend, waved at

Carter as the group moved through the casino. Zoopa fell in close to Carter's side and Carter felt something hard jab into his rib cage. It'd be easy enough to give Stan a signal, but the outcome couldn't be guaranteed. Zoopa plastered a phony grin on his face and he, too, gave Stan a wave.

They reached the elevators and waited. "Do you really think we need to take an entire party up to my office?" Carter asked, smiling big for the surveillance camera located directly above them.

Zoopa's frozen smile was beginning to make him look somewhat like a wax dummy. Carter supposed it was the most smiling Frank had done in over a year.

"Fine," Frank said, holding his smile. He patted one of his men's back. "Rikko, you and the boys take Twinkie and wait at the house."

Twinkie gave Carter a pleading look. His muscles involuntarily contracted and Zoopa's gun jammed into his ribs again. "I'll be seeing you soon," he said to her.

She pretended like she couldn't care less.

One of Frank's men held Twinkie's arm in a firm grip as they walked away, and Carter decided, before the night was over, he was going to rip the guy's hand off and stuff it down his throat. And he wasn't thinking too kindly toward Zoopa either.

"Before this night's over, one of us is going to be dead," Carter said through grinding teeth.

Zoopa chuckled. "Or wish he was."

Carter's office was cold. The air-conditioning had obviously been repaired while he was away. He went around behind his desk and Zoopa sat opposite him in the leather guest chair.

Zoopa was quiet. Carter knew what he was waiting for and it wasn't an offer of coffee.

He pulled open the middle desk drawer. A .38 Smith & Wesson that he kept strictly for emergencies was right where he'd left it. He reached inside the drawer, palm up, and slid his fingers along the top until he felt two smooth nubs. He pushed the one on the left and a barely audible click was heard coming from each corner of his office. The cameras were off. Zoopa continued to wait. Carter pushed the other button. A faint hum was heard and then reinforced steel panels lowered over the windows. Zack Gray, out in the control room, glanced over at the motion, but his face registered no concern. It wasn't unusual for Carter to hold private meetings in his office. With security so tight throughout all areas of the resort, his office was often the only place clients and others could come for some privacy. The one place that could be completely shut off from prying eyes. A blessing and a hazard.

Carter closed the desk drawer most of the way, leaving it open just enough, although he didn't intend to do anything foolish that would put Twinkie at risk—unless he had no choice.

"Glad to see you've finally found yourself a woman," Zoopa said. "Christ, it's been long enough."

"There're women all over this place," Carter said. He jabbed a pen into the front of a notepad.

"Yeah." Frank chuckled dryly. "That's why you were out in that godforsaken town. What the hell was the name of that place? Whoville? Corpseville? Mayberry fuckin' R.F.D.?"

Carter ground his teeth together. He hated that Zoopa had referred to Bailey's home in the same vein as he had. "I needed a vacation."

"Vacation?" Frank huffed out some air. "You live in the best vacation spot in the world. You and I both know you were there 'cause you've gone sweet on that little lady."

"She's got nothing to do with our business."

"You know, I believe you. 'Cause I don't think she's like us. She lives over there," Frank said, waving a hand, "in that part of the world where bad things don't happen to good people." He leaned forward, close enough for Carter to smell the stink of stale tobacco on his breath. "She sure as hell doesn't fit into this kinda life."

"Then it's a good thing I've left her and her world behind, huh?" Carter felt sick just saying the words. His arms already ached to hold Bailey again.

Frank nodded once. "Okay. Enough of the sweet talk. Where's my diamond?"

"Funny you keep referring to the Azuri diamond as yours. I don't think Mr. Azuri would agree."

Zoopa held out his arms. "What? You don't think I won it all legal? On the up and up?" He shrugged. "Mr. Azuri is a sore loser."

"He says the game was rigged."

Zoopa laughed, but a vein in his neck bulged. "You and I both know I wouldn't be in this business for long if my games were dishonest. The Gaming Commission would be on me like a horny man on a prostitute."

Carter figured in Zoopa's case, it'd be more like flies on shit.

Zoopa stood. He leaned across Carter's desk and his suit jacket hung open just enough to give Carter an eyeful of his Bulldog .38.

"Relax, Frank. You'll blow your carotid."

"I've given you about as much leniency as you're gonna get. The only reason you're still breathing is because of your sister."

"And she's precisely the point." Carter held his ground. "Twinkie deserves better than what you've got to offer. I want you out of her life."

"Look, you little weasel. That bitch sister of yours is lucky to even have a job, all coked up and no party to go to." Frank gave a guttural laugh. "If I hadn't taken pity on her, she'd have her picture on one of them cards those low-lifes give out down there on the Strip."

Carter was over the top of his desk with his hands

around Zoopa's throat and had him pushed up against the wall in the time it took for the man to take his next breath. After a long minute of trying to decide if Zoopa was worth killing, Carter relaxed his grip. Odds were if he and Zoopa didn't show up at a certain prescribed time, Twinkie would be in for more trouble than he could get her out of.

Zoopa grinned. "Wise decision. Like I said, Azuri's a sore loser, and a piss-poor poker player. Now, what do you say you open that big black box behind that big beautiful painting and give me my big expensive diamond?"

Carter sat down. He held out his hands. "It's not in there." Zoopa's face turned bright red. Carter suspected if it got much redder, he'd need to dial 911.

"You'll be suckin' sand before the night is over, my friend," Zoopa said. He rubbed his neck where Carter had nearly squeezed the life out of him.

"Tell me, does it get you all excited to hurt women and animals?" Carter reached a hand into his pocket and pulled out the little black bag that held the Azuri diamond. He tossed it across his desk.

As it turned out, Maggie hadn't swallowed the diamond. It had just gotten shoved under the corner of Bailey's sofa, and he'd found it when the dog begged him to retrieve a crunchy for her that had gotten lost under it. He hadn't told Bailey, because he hadn't wanted her to worry that he was going to leave right away. He should have.

Frank opened the bag, pulled out the Azuri diamond, and then reached into his own pocket and pulled out a jeweler's loupe. "Pardon me for not trusting you," he said to Carter, putting the tool up to his eye. Once he was completely satisfied that he indeed had possession of the Azuri diamond, he relaxed against the back of the leather chair.

"A man can't be too cautious nowadays. Lots of thieves

out there." He rubbed his neck again. The mark from Carter's hand was still bright red. "Now. About your sister . . . Whaddya say we go get her?"

Bailey opened her eyes to a dark room—weather dark. Penn Cove was socked in with heavy fog for the third straight day, and would probably remain that way for the better part of the day—or forever. *Great*. A gray day to accompany her gray mood. Probably it was the kind of day that made an unstable person want to end it all. She sighed. No man was worth that kind of sacrifice.

Except maybe Carter.

Bailey closed her eyes against the dark and she immediately saw Carter's face. He'd ended the competition with "Burning Love," and, indeed, by the time he finished, most all the women in the audience were burning up. Maybe not with love, but certainly with passion. Her included—on both counts. Another sigh. She rolled over and watched her curtains flutter in the wake of the heat vent.

After that got boring, she propped herself up on her elbows and looked over at the gold-colored statue sitting atop her dresser. It was supposed to be Elvis doing one of his karate moves, but the likeness missed its mark and, instead, it looked like Carrot Top having a good hair day.

No matter. Carter had won, which was no big surprise what with all the local talent, but, he'd also beaten his buddies, Daryl Bachman, Quent Flagg, and Johnny Thompson. Carter would be proud.

If only he knew.

If only he'd call.

But why should she be surprised? She'd known he'd probably leave right after the show, but he could at least call and let her know that he and Twinkie were all right.

Worry lines etched her forehead. And then she sat up

straight. What if they weren't? What if they needed help? She got out of bed and began pacing. After a few minutes her head started throbbing. She couldn't just sit around and wait. Either way, she had to find out.

First she dialed Carter's cell phone.

No answer.

Then she dialed the other number he'd given her.

"Oasis," a woman answered.

"Yes, I'm calling for Carter Davis," Bailey said.

"Mr. Davis is still on vacation," the woman said.

Still on vacation? If that were so, he'd be there with her. Oh, God. He *did* need help.

Bailey dialed the Las Vegas police. An official-sounding female voice answered.

"I want to report a kidnapping or, uh, some kind of crime."

"Location?"

"Coupeville, Washington."

Long pause.

"Washington state, ma'am?"

"Yes. That's where I live."

"Is that where the crime occurred?"

Bailey bit her lip and thought for a moment. "I'm not sure."

"Ma'am, prank calls are not tolerated—"

"I can assure you, this is no prank call. My boyfriend has been abducted. Maybe."

"Maybe?"

"Yes. I'm 80 percent sure of it."

Another long pause.

"Okay, where did this abduction take place?"

"Coupeville. Or, maybe Las Vegas," Bailey said. She squished her face together at how ridiculous she must sound.

"Ma'am?"

"Yes?"

"I'm hanging up now. If you want to call back with some more concrete information, please feel free."

Click.

Bailey pulled the phone from her ear and stared at it. How dare they hang up on her! On an emergency call! She shook her head. Well, they hadn't heard the last from her. She pushed redial.

"Las Vegas Emergency Services. Location, please."

Bailey opened her mouth to say "Coupeville," but caught herself. She wasn't about to waste any more precious time going through that again. She cleared her throat and disguised her voice before speaking, just in case it was the same operator who'd just hung up on her.

"I'd like to speak with someone upstairs, please." Bailey squeezed her eyes shut. *Stupid, stupid, stupid.* She did a mental head bang against the wall. "The captain, please."

"Captain?"

"Yes, um, the captain of the detectives—please."

Two rings later, another line picked up.

"Detective Forester. Can I help you?"

"My boyfriend may have been kidnapped." Bailey gushed out the entire story about her winning the car, Carter coming with her to Coupeville, the night of the Elvis competition. Finally, after she was satisfied she'd explained things thoroughly, she took a big breath.

"Does your name happen to be Bailey Ventura?"

Bailey pulled the phone away from her ear and gave it a good look. She picked up the phone base and looked under it. Nothing suspicious looking there. In one swift motion, she swung her head down and took a peek under her bed. Nope. No super spies hiding there. Boy, she'd hugely mistaken the powers of the police. And, most likely, her very own security guy.

Bailey's gaze circled around the room in search of anything that could pass for a tiny camera. *Gasp.* She was naked, except for her teeny weeny panties. They were new, and she'd worn them in hopes that Carter would come back late and remove them. She grabbed the sheet off her bed and pulled it to her chest, even though whoever was surveilling her had probably already gotten a full frontal view.

She put the phone back to her ear. "Who are you?" she asked.

"Las Vegas Police, ma'am. Is this Bailey Ventura?"

Bailey winced. What else did they know? Her mind raced back to her previous year's tax return. Maybe she should have claimed that fifty dollar prize for winning first place in the marionberry pie contest.

"This is she," Bailey whispered. She continued looking about the room.

"Are you calling about Carter Davis?"

Bailey drew in a sharp breath. Then her heart thudded hard, like it would come to a complete stop.

"Yes," she said, her voice a raspy squeak. *Oh, God, Carter is dead. Dead. He had your name and phone number on a piece of paper in his wallet and they found it and that's how they know who you are.*

Bailey went numb. Tears filled her eyes. A couple of big ones splashed onto her lap. *Why?* Oh, why hadn't she called the police last night when Carter first went missing? She'd rather have him in jail for being a jewel thief, than dead, with no hope for them to ever have a life together.

She tried to breathe, but it was useless, the pain was too intense. All she wanted right then was for the earth to open and swallow her whole. More tears slid down her cheeks and dropped from her chin. *Carter Davis, how I loved you.* Bailey wiped her eyes, and sniffled into her Kleenex.

"Ma'am?"

Her response was more sniffles.

"Are you all right, ma'am?"

All right? Was this guy kidding? "Yes, sir, I'm fi— Can you tell me what happened?"

"We're still not sure about all the details, but it's clear there was an explosion of some sort . . . out in the desert."

All the air left Bailey and she slid in a heap to the floor.

"Ma'am?"

"*Stop.* No more. I don't want to hear anymore." She was quiet for a minute and the detective on the other end waited. Finally, she managed in a raspy whisper, "What about Twinkie?"

"Twinkie?" A pause. "Oh, you mean Miss Martinson. Yes, she's fine."

Carter's sister was fine. That was good news, but Bailey was in so much pain she couldn't talk anymore. It wouldn't do her any good to get the gory details anyway. She didn't need to know how his end had come. It'd only give her nightmares.

"I've got to go," Bailey squeaked out. She dropped the phone next to her on the bed, and lay back down, pulling the sheets up to her chin and wrapping them around herself. "If only . . . if only," she lamented. Two miserable hours passed and she finally drifted into a restless sleep.

When she woke up, she thought of Twinkie. It was only right of her to call and offer her some comforting words.

"I'm so sorry," Bailey managed to push past the lump in her throat. Pain sliced through her, but she took some deep breaths and gained control of her voice. The last thing Twinkie needed was for her to break down, so that she'd feel like she had to offer *her* comfort. One of them had to be strong and Bailey knew it had to be her.

"I have something I think you might want," she told Twinkie.

Twinkie sniffled on the other end, and Bailey felt like her heart would split in two. Damn Frank Zoopa. Damn Las Vegas. Damn her for being so crazy in love.

"It's a trophy," Bailey said. "A silly little thing, really. Carter won the competition. It was a unanimous vote.

Everybody loved him." Bailey's voice cracked. It was only a matter of seconds before she broke down and started wailing in full force.

Twinkie sniffed into the phone. "Tell everybody thanks," she said, and then she laughed softly. "It's his first win, you know. He's come in second many times, and third, and fourth."

Bailey squeezed her eyes shut. "Then whoever the judges were, they didn't see what I saw."

"No. I don't suppose they did."

Bailey swallowed hard and sucked in a painful breath. Her chest was heavy. It burned like it was full of embers. Any more pain and her entire throat would constrict and she would no longer breathe. The silk scarf Carter had given her lay in the middle of her bed. She picked it up and put it to her nose, breathing in his scent. Somehow, she had to push all her pain deep inside where it couldn't be seen.

"When you're up to it, I'd like to come and bring the trophy to you."

"You keep it. My brother loved you. He'd want you to have it." Twinkie paused and Bailey heard more sniffling. "Stay in touch, please," she finally said and clicked off.

Tears burst from Bailey's eyes and spilled over her cheeks. Carter had loved her. It's what she'd been waiting to hear. But now, it hurt to even think the words. She cried so hard that Tucker and Maggie May came into the room and rested their heads on the side of the bed, looking up at her with big eyes. They seemed to be asking if there was something they could do to help. There wasn't, of course, because nothing would ever help.

"She practically hung up on me," Detective Forester said. Carter stepped aside and let the detective into his hotel suite.

"Who?"

"Your little honey from out there in the sticks. I did as you asked. To her, you're officially dead. Both she and Twinkie think your body is scattered around the desert . . . no hope of an open casket funeral."

"Let's keep it that way," Carter said with a grumble.

Detective Forester shook his head. "That's cold. That's the one thing my wife says is her worst fear."

"You don't have a wife."

"That's right. But I used to, so let that be a lesson to you." Forester shook a finger at Carter.

Carter walked over to the large tinted window that overlooked the Strip. He could feel the heat beaming strong through the protective shield that was supposed to serve two purposes: keep out the heat, and keep stray bullets from hitting their mark.

"As long as she—along with everybody else—thinks I've gone to the great beyond, I won't have to worry about Zoopa going after her. She'll be safe this way. It's up to you guys how long she suffers."

Forester started to open his mouth in protest, but Carter held up a hand. "We're not going to have this conversation again. We had an agreement. I give up all the information I have on Zoopa. You guys go get him."

The detective flipped a pencil and it hit Carter directly in the chest. "You're a cold son of a bitch."

"Yeah, so I've heard," Carter said. "With all the evidence I've helped you gather, Frank Zoopa won't be opening, or running, any casinos for a good long time. Now get back to work. You're wasting taxpayers' money."

Forester huffed. "At least let your sister know. She's been driving us all crazy, wondering why we're all acting like you didn't exist."

Carter didn't respond one way or the other. He heard his friend turn to leave, and he didn't miss seeing the

hand sign reflected in the window that Forester gave him
behind his back as he went out the door.

Yeah, he was cold. And probably Bailey would think
so, too, if she knew he was still breathing. But a relationship, of any kind, just wasn't in the cards until things
there were wrapped up. It was better this way, at least
until Zoopa was way out of the picture.

Carter thought about Twinkie and the look on her
face when Zoopa's men forced her into the back of
Zoopa's SUV. If he had thought she was in any danger,
he'd have already rode in on his white horse and rescued her by now. Still, the look of helplessness on her
face as she watched him from the back window would
haunt him for a good long time, or at least until he
could put her mind at ease.

Carter rubbed a hand over his tired eyes. Twinkie
knew better than anybody what was at stake. If he
couldn't trust her . . . The hell with it. He tucked his gun
in his shoulder holster and put the DO NOT DISTURB sign
on his door as he left.

Chapter Thirty-one

Twinkie had her back to Carter when he walked in the door. She was sitting over by the window, staring off into space.

"Just leave a couple of fresh towels," she said without looking to see who had come in.

"No little bars of soap?" Carter asked her.

Twinkie spun around. First there was surprise, then a wide grin, and then her eyes lit up brighter than the neon lights on the Strip.

"*Carter.*" She ran to him and he gathered her into his arms. After she hugged him for a good long minute, she pushed him away and looked him over real good. As soon as she seemed satisfied it was really him standing there in front of her, and that he was all in one piece, she punched him hard in the chest. "You son of a bitch! Where the hell have you been?"

Carter grinned. He expected to be called worse before this was over. "It's a long story, Sis." He explained how Frank's men had taken him back to their favorite shack in the desert and how they'd tried to blow him into a million tiny bits, but they'd made the mistake of not sticking around until the job was finished. Again.

"Stupid criminals," Twinkie said.

"Yeah, stupid criminals." Carter ruffled Twinkie's hair and planted a big kiss on her forehead just like their mother used to do when they were kids.

"What now?" she asked.

"Now we wait. And you don't say anything to anybody about seeing me." He stood to leave and was halfway out the door when Twinkie gasped.

"Oh, God," she said. *"Bailey.* I just got off the phone with her. She's dying over you. Although I don't know why. You're really not worth the trouble."

"Thanks."

"You've got to call her." Twinkie grabbed the phone and held it out to him. Carter stared at it and she shook it at him. "Now. *Right* now."

"I'm afraid I can't do that," Carter said, and he did some more explaining. When he finished, he gave her a grin. "Forester says you've been driving them crazy."

"Hmmf. It'll be the last time. I don't care how long you're gone."

"Yes, you do. Now do you think you can keep that pretty mouth of yours shut? or am I going to have to put a gag on you?"

Twinkie stuffed her hands on her hips. "You could try."

Carter laughed. "It'll only be for another couple of days. Even *you* should be able to keep a secret that long."

A week went by before Bailey heard from Twinkie. And when she did, it was only to talk about details for a service of some kind. Just as well. Bailey didn't know if she could handle any details about what had happened to Carter, especially since they were sketchy. No remains had been found, but there was plenty of evidence to suggest he'd met a most brutal end. And with no body, there'd been no need for a speedy service.

Twinkie had told her she wanted to put together

something special—a show of some sort—that would fully honor her brother's memory. Bailey had to admit it was a fitting good-bye, but the thought of sitting through an evening of other tribute artists performing songs that were Carter's favorites was enough to make her want to crawl into bed and curl into the fetal position for at least a year. Bailey knew that time was a great healer, but it was going to take more than a week or two for her heart to be whole again. If ever. And she doubted she'd be able to listen to any Elvis music for a very long time.

Unfortunately, Twinkie was certain that's what Carter would have wanted, and Bailey didn't have any choice but to agree.

The service was to be held the following week at the Imperial Showroom, and it was open to all of Carter's friends and fans. At least five hundred were expected to attend, including Bailey, Olivia, Aunt Fiona, and Liza. Rex had agreed to stay behind and take care of Bailey's babies. At least then she wouldn't have to worry that Tucker wouldn't eat. And with any luck he wouldn't just sit mournfully at the window waiting for her return.

The morning of their flight, Bailey packed a small bag and she and Tucker and Maggie May set out for her mom's house. It was a nice walk in the early morning sun, but Bailey felt like she was on a death march. Her eyes teared up as she took slow steps and Tucker seemed to sense the heaviness of the situation. Instead of doing his usual running around, he walked alongside her, looking up at her with soulful eyes. Bailey reached down and patted his head. "He loved you, too," she said, her voice cracking.

Ever since Carter had left, both dogs had gone to the guest room each morning and sniffed around for him. She'd only yesterday tried to explain to them that Carter wouldn't be coming back. She didn't think they understood.

The drive to the airport was a blur and the flight to Las Vegas could've taken two hours or five minutes. Bailey was unaware of anything but the all-encompassing hollowness that seemed to grow deeper with each mile, the closer she got to her destination. Fiona held her hand for most of the flight and her mother sat on the other side of the aisle with Liza. Having the love of her family and her best friend was what she needed to get through this, and it gave her great comfort just knowing they were there.

The Oasis had offered them rooms, and when they arrived, two men and the casino host she'd been assigned when she won the car met them at the front desk. They took her and her family up to the eleventh floor and put them into two adjoining rooms. They could've stuck Bailey in a closet for all she cared.

The ceremony was scheduled for later that evening and she didn't have any idea how she'd make herself presentable. Any eye makeup would be smeared down her face not long after she put it on and, really, why even bother? Who cared how she looked?

"Look at it this way," Fiona said. "With all Carter's impersonator friends, you might meet another one while you're here."

Olivia rolled her eyes. "Lord, Fiona, Bailey's heart is broken, her spirit is crushed, her soul is bruised—"

"I'm going to take a nap," Bailey said. *Forever.* She gave Liza a pleading look.

Liza took the cue and she herded Olivia and Fiona to the adjoining room. "I'll check on you in a little while," she said and quietly shut the door behind her.

Bailey wished for a quick death. Honest to God, if her mother had loved the real Elvis half as much as she loved Carter, she didn't know how her mother had ever survived his passing. Of course—head slap—how could she forget? Her mother *hadn't* survived his passing. According to her, that tragic event was still to come.

She crawled onto the bed and lay there in the darkened room. All she had energy for was what she was doing right that very minute: being alone in the dark, crying, and sleeping for the rest of her life.

Three hours later, she felt a hand on her shoulder.

"Time to make yourself beautiful," Liza said. "I've put all your stuff on the bathroom counter. I've even already stuffed the complimentary shampoo and soaps into your overnight case."

Bailey managed a smile. "Do I really have to go to this thing? Couldn't you just go on my behalf?"

Liza gave Bailey a sympathetic look. "Sorry, hon, it doesn't work that way. Besides, everybody is expecting to see you there. They all know how much Carter loved you."

Tears spilled from Bailey's eyes.

"Nope. Don't do that. Save those for later." Liza handed her a tissue.

Liza was right. Tonight was about Carter. She had the rest of her life to cry. She sat up and ran a hand through her hair. No ponytail tonight. She'd wear her hair down, just the way Carter liked it. She thought about all the times he'd given her ponytail a playful tug. And how if he didn't want it up, he'd simply snap the band that held it and let it fall. Up, down, it made no difference to her. Another tear sneaked out and she swiped it away. It was time to be strong. Like Jackie Kennedy or Nancy Reagan. They'd both loved and lost the loves of their life and now it was her turn. Bailey lifted her chin and coerced her lips into a hint of a smile.

They arrived at the showroom at seven sharp. Bailey'd had to swallow her pain and think about other things several times over the last hour to keep the tears from flowing, but as soon as she walked into the large room, it really hit her. The pain of what she'd lost felt like it was swallowing her. Her throat felt like it was constricting. She couldn't breathe.

Liza took her arm and helped her along, steering her to her seat and handing her a water bottle. "Drink," she said softly.

Bailey took a few small sips and it helped. If she removed herself from the situation and pretended she was just an observer, the pain dissolved temporarily.

Twinkie was waiting when they got there. She'd saved seats for Bailey and her family, plus a couple extra, just in case. She greeted Bailey with a thin smile and a kiss on both cheeks.

"This is going to be good. I might like living here myself one day," Fiona said.

Bailey looked at her. *One day?* Her aunt was seventy-five years old. It was now or never.

"You couldn't live here," Olivia said to Fiona. "Who'd take care of you when you get Typhoid Fever or Legionnaire's disease?"

Fiona slid Olivia a look. "In case you haven't noticed, I've been symptom-free for a while now."

"That's only because I gave that game back to cousin Freddie. God help him if he dares bring it back."

"He won't," Bailey said. Fiona and Olivia looked at her. "I paid him to keep it."

"Well, I never—" Fiona started.

"And another thing, Auntie. I'm not becoming a doctor. In case *you* haven't noticed, I haven't been in school for months. I've been working over at the Knead & Feed and I like it." Bailey put her hand over her mouth. She hadn't meant to just blurt it out like that. Stress. It made a person do crazy things.

Fiona smiled smugly. "I know it. Everyone in town knows it. The only one who doesn't know yet is your Uncle Rex." She clasped her hands in her lap and looked straight ahead.

Great. Bailey sighed. She not only had to survive saying good-bye to the love of her life, but now she had to go home and face her uncle before someone else informed him that she was going against the promise he'd made her dad. She shook her head. *Mother Earth, could you please just open and swallow me?* If it was true that bad luck came in threes, she couldn't wait to see what was coming next.

After several minutes, a man dressed in a red jumpsuit came out from behind the curtain and solemnly walked over to the microphone, but Bailey didn't even care which tribute artist he was and she just stared into her lap. She heard him clear his throat before he spoke.

"As all of you know, this is a very special night. We're here to honor one of our own, a man who it seems was perhaps hated as much as he was loved. All of us here loved him—partly because he never beat us in any of the competitions, even though he was better . . ." The tribute artist paused and a solemn quiet filled the theater. He cleared his throat once more and then continued. "We've got a bunch of the guys together and you're about to see a show you won't soon forget."

Bailey focused straight ahead on a spot on the long heavy drapes. If she allowed herself to be in the moment, there'd be no stopping the tears. *Hold yourself together,* she told herself over and over.

Finally, the curtain opened and ten men in various Elvis attire stood with their backs to the audience, lined up just as they'd been the night Bailey first saw Carter perform. A lump formed hard and painful in her throat and her heart felt like it would shrivel and die the moment they opened their mouths. This time she couldn't stop the tears—she didn't even try. They flowed down her cheeks.

Each tribute artist took his turn to come center stage to sing a shortened version of a favorite Elvis song, and then he returned to his place in line. With the lights down low, and her tears blurring their images, Bailey wasn't sure who was who until each man came forward. They shook, kicked, swiveled, and sang their hearts out in a tribute to a man they all loved and respected. Bailey was glad she'd come.

After each man had his turn, a hush fell over the showroom, and the audience waited, held captive, for whatever was next to come.

The lights were notched down even more and one by one the singers filed off the end of the stage, until finally, one lone, dark silhouette remained. Just as the others had done, he stood center stage with his back to the audience, and after a long pause, he began to sing, "I Can't Help Falling In Love." His voice, deep and rich, filled the showroom like no other's. Bailey's heart lurched. She swallowed hard and wanted to cover her ears. It was too much. This man sounded so much like Carter she couldn't bear it.

A sliver of pain shot through her. *God help me get through this,* she prayed.

Bailey glanced over at her mom, knowing she, too, would be affected by the performance, but her mother was gone. Bailey swung her head around. She squinted into the audience, but the lights were too low to see much of anything other than dark forms and shadows. Along the sides and at the back, where lights were mounted on the walls, she was able to make out some faces, but her mom wasn't among them. *Breathe,* Bailey told herself. Just because Carter disappeared didn't mean her mom would. She'd probably gone to the bathroom.

As the singer finished, the lights were turned up a notch and Bailey took one more opportunity to look around for her mom. That's when she saw her. Up in the back, in the corner, at a small table. She was sitting there with an older gentleman. His hair was thick and almost white and he looked strangely familiar, but Bailey couldn't imagine where she might have ever seen him. He and her mom were talking, smiling, having a good time like they were old friends. But how? They'd only been in town a few hours. How had her mom already met a man?

Bailey gave her head a little shake and she turned back to the stage. Her breath caught in her throat and she almost choked. The tribute artist was standing at the edge of the stage. And he was looking straight at her. "I Got Lucky" was his next number, but all the words tumbled together, and the only thing Bailey could hear was the beating of her own heart. The lights grew even brighter, until there was no mistaking the man's identity.

"Carter?" she whispered, on a heavy breath.

"Imagine that," Fiona said. "He's not dead, after all. Glory be."

Bailey looked at her aunt. "You *knew*?"

Fiona gave her a smug grin. "I had some inside information."

"And you didn't *tell* me?"

Fiona made a zipping motion across her lips. "I was sworn to secrecy. I didn't want to be next in line to take a dirt nap."

"Sand," Bailey said. "In Las Vegas, it's sand."

Fiona hunched her shoulders. "Sand. Dirt. It's all six feet under and crawling with bugs."

Carter slowed the momentum with "My Way," and, still, he didn't take his eyes off Bailey. If the words to that song were supposed to explain why he'd let her think his body was scattered about the desert in a million pieces, he had a lot more explaining to do. But first, there was something else that was far more important.

Before he could finish the song, or even take a bow, Bailey was out of her seat and halfway up the steps to the stage. She was vaguely aware of thunderous cheering and clapping as she ran over to Carter with her arms open wide and her heart overflowing. Tears fell and she didn't care one bit about her mascara running.

Carter closed his arms around her and he kissed her like they were the only ones in the room. When he finally came up for air, the curtain had closed in front of them. They were alone. He gazed into Bailey's eyes and she gazed back through happy tears.

"Happy to see me?" he asked.

Bailey nodded vigorously. "Delirious. Only, do you think it might be possible for you to find some hobby other than being a jewel thief? It's a big desert and I wouldn't know where to begin digging."

Carter kissed her again and then took her by the hand. "Come with me. There are some things that need clearing up."

Bailey's pulse skittered. *Things? Clear up?* Usually when a man said something needed clearing up, it didn't bode well for the woman.

"I can take it, just tell me," Bailey said. "It's Twinkie, isn't it? She's not really your sister."

Carter looked at her. "That's not it."

"No, don't tell me . . . you'll be doing hard time for stealing that diamond." Bailey shook her head. "I knew it was too good to be true, getting you back only to lose you all over again—"

"Ah, honey," Carter said, going into his Elvis mode. "You're not ever gonna lose me again. There's just one little matter we need to discuss . . ." Carter led her out through the curtain and up the aisle past the audience and everyone cheered their approval once more.

Fiona was standing on her chair to get a better view. "That's my niece and her fiancé," she announced to everyone.

A sinking feeling settled in the pit of Bailey's gut. This was it. The moment of truth. "If this is about my virginity, I can explain." Carter gave her a look and she fluttered her eyelashes, the way she'd seen Liza do a hundred times to charm a man. Charming her way out of that stupid lie might be her only hope. He grinned and continued pulling her along.

When they neared the exit, Bailey glanced over at her mother and her new friend. She took a good, hard look at the man just in case her mother disappeared and she had to i.d. him. This was Las Vegas after all.

Probably the sexiest older man she'd ever laid her eyes on, he met Bailey's gaze with a grin that notched up boyishly on one side, and it caused her heart to leap. She did a double take. Could it really be?

No. She blinked hard. Absolutely not.

Chapter Thirty-two

Bailey accepted Carter's explanation why he had to keep her in the dark about him still being alive, but she'd have much rather gotten some good news, like he was quitting surveillance. Even though Frank Zoopa was out of the picture, Carter would still be out there mingling with guys just like him—or worse. He'd still need to carry a Glock against his chest and a .38 in an undisclosed location somewhere else on his body.

On the upside, Twinkie really was Carter's sister and she'd been wrong about Carter not being able to forgive a little lie. Best of all, Bailey had a man who could lull her to sleep with the sweetest, sexiest voice a man could own.

Carter came to town as often as possible, which wasn't nearly often enough, and though he'd made it clear he was in love with her, she had yet to hear him say, "Come home with me."

It was two weeks before her aunt and uncle's thirty-fifth wedding anniversary and Carter was in town. Maybe tonight would be the night.

He and Bailey went over to the Ventura house for dinner, as usual. They had baby-back ribs, red potatoes, and a salad made with greens that Aunt Fiona had grown herself. Dessert was marionberry pie, of course.

As everyone finished up their pie, Bailey looked around the table and gave silent thanks for the blessing of a great family, and then she got up and left the dining room. She returned a minute later with an envelope in her hand and gave it to her Uncle Rex. He had one eye on the bread plate and one eye on the envelope as he opened it and pulled out two tickets for a nine-day cruise to Hawaii.

"It's that cruise Aunt Fiona's been wanting to take," Bailey said, chewing her lip. She'd told her Uncle Rex about quitting school, and he'd never said a word about it, but she'd sensed a deep disappointment. Her mom had told her that it'd just take some time. What better place to spend that time than in sunny Hawaii.

"I figured that money you've been giving me for school should be used for something much more important."

"I also have a surprise," Carter said.

Bailey heard her mom's and Aunt Fiona's sudden intake of air. Tucker and Maggie May perked their ears in anticipation.

Carter turned to Bailey and took her hand in his. "Will you come home with me? To stay?"

Before Bailey could answer, Fiona jumped up from the table and rushed from the room. A minute later, she returned with a large yellow box. Worst-Case Scenario.

"What? Where did you get that?" Bailey asked.

"I paid cousin Freddy twice what you paid him to give it back to me. If we're going on a cruise, I need to get some medical advice."

Everyone at the table did an eye roll. Tucker groaned and Maggie May rolled over onto her back.

Olivia waved her hands at everyone to shush. "Carter has asked our Bailey a question and I, for one, would like to hear the answer."

"It's 'yes,'" Fiona said, shaking her head. "It was 'yes' the day she brought him home wearing those punk clothes."

"And I already knew that you'd quit school. I may be

half-blind, but I'm not deaf. Word gets around," Uncle Rex said. "Any more pie?"

Bailey's mouth hung open for a moment before it curved into a gentle smile. Her family. Life with them was never boring and even if Carter had never asked her to go away with him, she could think of a lot of things that would be worse than living in Coupeville for the rest of her life.

Fiona spent the next hour trying to convince Bailey to take her to Vegas with her, saying she'd read somewhere that a warmer climate could help relieve pain in the joints. Certainly that was true, and Bailey was apprehensive about leaving her mom to care for her aunt by herself, but her mom said they'd be fine, and that a young couple didn't need an old woman hanging around, getting in their way.

Bailey suspected that Maggie May's pills might occasionally make it into her aunt's water.

To end the evening, Bailey and Carter went down to the waterfront. Bailey took a deep breath of Puget Sound's salt air. She'd miss it, but she'd be back often to check on her aunt and to make sure her mom was managing.

Carter stood behind her with his arms wrapped around her waist. He rested his head against hers. She was in heaven, and she didn't even care that he didn't much look like Elvis anymore. He was her king, she was his queen; that's all that mattered.

After a few minutes, Carter turned Bailey around so that they were face to face. He put his lips to hers, so sweet, so tender, so very Elvis impersonator. His clothes may have changed somewhat, but his kisses were always going to be the same. Electrifying.

Bailey ran her tongue over her lips. "Mmm . . . that was really good. Now how about the other guy giving me one of those?"

Carter leaned close to her ear. "First, how about you tell me why your friends call you Peaches?"

Bailey blinked up at him and fluttered her eyelashes innocently. "Because it's my favorite fruit," she said softly.

Carter grinned. "Right." Then he pressed his lips to hers and made her toes curl into the sand. "And just so we're clear," he said, "I love you."

Epilogue

Bailey walked out of the house in the Calico Ridge development. Carter held back, standing in the doorway, while she continued all the way out to the sidewalk. She understood him stopping in the shaded entryway. He was in full security guy attire, well aware that the next dose of sun was only a day away.

She gazed lovingly at the large, two-story adobe structure, with its vaulted roofline and purple bougainvillaea that sprawled all along one side, like a layer of colorful frosting.

The garden was full of flowers, many different varieties, some she'd never seen before, but she was sure that after a couple of visits, her mom and aunt Fiona would have looked them up in *The Sunset Garden Book*, in order to gather tips on how to keep them thriving. Just as she and Carter had thrived since the whole mess with Zoopa had gotten over with.

Some secrets surrounding that mess remained, but for now Bailey was happy to let them settle into the background. That was then; this was now. She had the perfect man, the perfect house, and soon they'd be living the perfect life here in Vegas.

And what a life that would be—in one word . . .

thrilling. And since the house had been bought and mostly paid for with money that the little man Azuri had given Carter, for recovering his family diamond, their mortgage payments were practically nil.

Oh, the plans she had to fill this house with love, maybe even a couple of kids . . .

Carter must have been reading her mind, because he suddenly got "that look," and swaggered over to her.

"You sure you don't want to forget about catching that plane?" he asked.

Bailey's resolve to keep him at arm's length, until the wedding, was on the verge of melting. It could have been the heat, but more than likely it was that he was looking particularly sultry in his black suit, with his hair grown out a bit longer than usual, for another upcoming Elvis competition. Rich brown strands glistened among the black, bringing out the color of his skin tone and eyes. He was a hard man to resist.

"In case you haven't noticed, the house is already empty. Not much chance we'll be disturbed," he said.

"Carter! You agreed we'd wait until we've said our vows before we do it again."

"It?" Carter stood behind Bailey. Close. His arms wound tightly around her waist. "What is *it?*"

"It. The act. That thing I let you do to me, because I'm weak and I can't resist your charms."

"Are you feeling weak right now?" His mouth moved close to her ear, and he slid a hand up under her blouse. His hand lingered, respectfully, on the bare skin of her back. "Honey, you don't really think you're going to keep me waiting for two months, do you?" His voice was rough, and thick with desire.

With his lips pressed all warm and cozy against her cheek, Bailey let out a long sigh. She turned to face him. "It's actually just a little over a month, but yes, I'm feeling extremely weak—and you know it."

"Then let's go back inside. I'll share something with you that'll give you the strength to last until I see you again."

Fluttering her eyelashes, Bailey traced a finger down his chest. "When you put it that way, how can I resist?" Her fingers locked onto his tie and she pulled him toward her, until his mouth met hers.

When they'd finished giving their new neighbors a show, Carter led her into the house. They'd just made themselves comfortable on the soft carpet when a car rumbled to a stop out front. Bailey poked her head up and peered out.

"Oh, Gawd, it's Uncle Rex and Aunt Fiona." She scrambled to button her blouse and pull her skirt back on.

Carter groaned. He raked a hand through his hair. It fell back into place, perfect, like it had never been touched. "I thought you told them you'd pick them up at the casino later today."

"I did. Maybe Aunt Fiona got tired of playing the slots." Fat chance. It was more likely she'd come down with the Bubonic Plague. Bailey dug in her purse for a hair band, and she pulled her hair up into a tidy ponytail.

Carter promptly snapped it. "Leave it loose."

"Not now," Bailey said, swiping at Carter's hand. She had no idea what a demon she'd create by asking him to wait a month for sex. She found another band, and secured her hair.

Carter grabbed her, held her tightly against him, one hand grasping her ponytail. "Soon as they leave, it's coming out, and you're mine." His eyes were dark pools, verging on dangerous.

Gulp.

The doorbell rang and Bailey let her aunt and uncle inside.

Fiona twirled around to show off her new T-shirt. It had a gold lion embossed on its front, and it hung loosely on her thin frame, almost down to her knees. One size fits all. "I won this over at the MGM. A real good-lookin' guy was handing them out to everyone who got the right combination of sevens at the Dodge Viper carousel."

But Bailey barely heard what her aunt was saying. She was too busy staring at the car that was parked out front in her new driveway.

"What is that?" she asked, knowing full well her mouth was hanging open.

Uncle Rex waved a hand. "Oh, that. I looked all day for a T-Bird, like yours, but this is as close as I could find. It took me a good twenty to finally hit the jackpot."

"*What?* Are you telling me you won a car? *That* car?"

Uncle Rex looked at her with one eye and kept his other eye on the Viper. "It ain't no convertible like yours, but I bet I can give the Coupeville fuzz a good run in this car." He grinned wide and, for the first time ever, both eyes were looking in the same direction, and they were filled with a hint of mischief that Bailey hadn't seen in a very long time.

"I'll just bet you can," Bailey agreed.

"I can even drive us home."

"Home?" Bailey winced at the thought.

"Tell you what," Carter stepped in, "I'll make sure your car gets home; you just make sure my fiancée gets back home, so she can finalize details for the biggest wedding Coupeville has ever seen."

"That's probably the best plan," Fiona said. "Rex, here, he already left the fuzz in his dust on the way over here. He outsmarted them. Took a detour through the desert. I had to direct him around some cacti and sagebrush, but we finally lost 'em."

Bailey said a silent prayer, mostly that her mother wouldn't find out.

Fiona's brow furrowed. "This car could be trouble. I'll have to keep my eye on Lea Townsend. She'll be making a move on my man, soon as we get back to town."

Carter made Rex leave the Viper at the house, while he drove them to the airport. He'd gotten some kind of special security guy pass to go with Bailey to their departure gate and they shared a long kiss before she boarded.

"I'll see you in just one month," he said, his tone more of a warning of things to come. "Don't you be wearing anything to hold your hair up. It won't last." Before he let her go, he hummed one last song softly into her ear—"You Gave Me a Mountain."

It wasn't until Bailey was on the plane and in the air that she thought about what he'd hummed. A moment of uncertainty passed through her, but she shook it off. It was just a song, and a beautiful one at that. And, probably, it was in reference to the fact that he hadn't had a chance to show her exactly how charming he could be before she left.

She sighed. They'd have time enough for that. In a little over a month, she and Carter would be inside Coupeville's First Baptist church, exchanging vows, and then life as she'd always dreamed would begin.

The plane soared, headed straight into a white fluffy cloud, and Bailey glanced upward, mouthing a silent "thank you."